# Tempest of Vengeance

## Tara Fox Hall

Published by
Melange Books, LLC
White Bear Lake, MN 55110
www.melange-books.com

Cover Art by Caroline Andrus

To Lash

\*\*\*

*In Memory of Macavity, who will live on in the pages of this series.*

# Chapter One

I woke still clinging to Devlin, all my strong resolve of the previous night gone like so much thin fog evaporated by the harsh light of dawn.

Danial, my Danial, had been delivered to the front gate of Hayden a drained corpse. Now my always perfect and proper vampire lay unconscious and unresponsive just down the hall, watched over by Devlin's demon, Titus. Danial was just the latest casualty in Devlin's war with Ulysses, the brother of one of his former "turns" who'd died at the end of some vampire hunter's stake. He almost certainly wouldn't be the last.

Last night, after a monster fight with Devlin—and a lot of cutting words neither of us had truly meant—I'd decided to leave Hayden and go back to living with Danial. Sure, this step seemed like just another tawdry chapter in my imperfect, supernaturally-influenced life of trading one handsome superhuman man for another, but at the time, it had seemed like the most rational decision. Theo, my husband by law, had his hands full with keeping our young werecougar son Devon safe from this tempest of vengeance that Ulysses was wreaking on Devlin and all of his allies. There was also the question of his new sex partner, Jenny, a recent werecougar herself via Theo's bite, which he had dispensed to save her from the ravages of late stage cancer. Our resulting "threesome" was its own messy tangle, one I'd have to sort out later. I had enough to worry about right now.

Everything had been going well until this fall, when a moonlight bike ride for Devlin and I had ended in us both being taken prisoner of Ulysses. While I'd been unharmed, Devlin had been tortured terribly, something that still scarred him psychologically if not physically. Lash, Devlin's right hand man— actually weresnake—had arrived in time to save Devlin and wreak his own vengeance, but the cost had been speeding up his own demise, even with eliminating many of Ulysses' men and an older vampire lover of Devlin's— Catherine—who had allied herself with him. I had been the one to step in at the

11th hour to save Lash with my blood, but had paid my own price of temporarily losing my vampirically-enhanced abilities, and possibly accentuating my demon-taint, something I was worried about. According to my doctor, I was human now, probably more human than I'd been in years. I should have been enthused about that, but I wasn't. I'd gotten used to being able to teleport, heal minor injuries with ease, and other cool abilities like seeing in dim light as if it were bright daylight. Who wanted to be human when all it did was make you more vulnerable?

I did feel vulnerable, even here in the arms of my golden-haired god of a vampire who'd sworn on his life to protect me. Everything had gone wrong, like dominos knocking into one another in a huge pattern whose ultimate design I couldn't fathom. Terian, a friend with unrequited feelings for me, had turned from part to full demon, nearly assaulting me, and spending months in magical recovery before recently emerging with a fraction of the power of his old self. Lash was serving a month in prison because of a misunderstanding with human police that had stopped just short of murder. Several of Devlin's employees had been killed and skinned, among them a recent friend, the werewolf housekeeper Robin. My son, Theoron had been beaten and left for dead, escaping only by the thinnest of margins. Now Danial, my Danial, might be lost to me, if he didn't awaken soon from the coma he was in.

Earlier this morning, Devlin had spoken of war, and pledged to not only kill Ulysses, but also to bring Danial back to us. While I knew how much Devlin loved his brother, I wasn't sure he had the power to bring Danial back. A massive "transfusion" of Devlin's blood had saved Danial's life last night. But it hadn't been enough to waken him. Devlin had been badly weakened as a result, so he wouldn't be able to do that again anytime soon. Ulysses, so far, had remained not only out of Devlin's grasp, but also beyond the reach of all the other powerful vampires of the Ruling class.

I had always been an optimist, even in the times of my life when tragedy had struck me down like a pine sapling before a Cat 5 hurricane. However, Devlin's warning that things would get worse before they got better felt like the footsteps of doom for me.

As if sensing my fear, Devlin stirred in my arms, pulling back slightly to look down at me. "I'm glad you're with me," he whispered. "This is not a good morning. But it would be worse if I did not have you here beside me, Sar."

I bit my lip, and swallowed hard. "I'm scared, Dev."

"You'll be safe here," he assured me with a chaste kiss on my brow. He got out of bed, then put on his robe.

"I'm scared for Danial."

Devlin's self-assurance faded before my eyes, as he turned to me with a haunted expression. "He may never wake up," Devlin whispered brokenly. "I don't know if we got to him in time, to save his brain from cell death. His body will heal rapidly, but until he wakes up, I won't know if he's my brother or someone different now."

The bedroom door opened. Titus shifted uncomfortably, his clawed hand remaining on the knob. "I'll be in the nursery nights, if you need me, Devlin," he rumbled. "I've set up a mattress there on the floor. I'll be near Venus. She'll be safe. I just checked and she's still sleeping—"

Venus appeared in the doorway behind Titus, clutching her stuffed cougar, looking afraid, and very alone. "Mom, can I sleep with you and Dad today? I'm having bad dreams. I want to be in here with you guys, not Titus."

We both looked at her, then at each other. Titus shifted his weight, uncomfortable.

"Sure," I said finally, with a lot of false bravado and sternness. "But just for tonight, V. You're a big girl; you're too old to sleep with Mommy and Daddy."

I caught a glimpse of Devlin regarding me from the corner of my eye, a tender look again on his face. Venus came over and climbed into bed, sliding under the covers between us as Titus shut the door. We all snuggled together, Venus in the middle. She was asleep almost instantly. Devlin was still watching me with that affectionate look in his eyes.

"You know, you just looked at me like Danial always does," I said, reaching out to caress his face. "I've seen you wear that expression for Lash, but I've never seen it before for me."

"I never thought I'd hear you say 'Mommy and Daddy' in the same sentence, when it meant you and me," he replied, giving me a radiant smile. "I'm happy to have heard it. Also happy I wore pants to bed last night, because I almost didn't."

We both hugged Venus, and it wasn't long after that I fell back asleep.

When I awoke for the second time, Venus was sleeping on Devlin's chest, and he had his arms around her. I was off to the side, not touching them, but I didn't feel excluded. I took pleasure, watching them both sleeping together, so ethereally beautiful, like a god and a nymph out of a myth.

Venus stirred, and Devlin did as well. He looked down at her, and then started, and I laughed, as I knew he'd expected to see me in his arms. He looked to his left, and then whipped his head right, relaxing when he saw me beside him. Venus had meanwhile settled back to sleep. "There you are." The relief in his words was a living thing. I came closer, and he put his free arm around me, kissing me. "Thank you," he said softly as he drew back, tears in his eyes.

"For what?" I asked curiously, tilting my head as my brow furrowed.

"For making me a father. For forgiving me. For loving me, even when I'm a bastard."

I leaned up and kissed his tears away. "Thank you, Dev."

Now it was his turn to look confused. "For what?"

"For giving me my little girl," I said, caressing Venus's sleeping form. "I love my sons. But I wanted a girl, and it's true that I couldn't have had one more beautiful."

Devlin hugged me to him, and kissed me again. "I wish you could have more children," he said huskily. "I wish we could undo that operation you had. I would love to make another child with you, no matter if it was a boy or girl." There was an abyss of desire in his words.

I trembled in his arms, thinking of how quickly I'd be Oathed by force, if he but knew I was still fertile.

Devlin saw my shaking, and took it for sadness. "Shh," he consoled me. "I just meant I'm very happy, being a father. It's okay, Love."

I knew that hadn't been what he'd meant. And a coldness in my blood remained that his arms around me didn't ease.

* * * *

In the morning, after feeding the dogs, cats, Venus, and myself I called Theo. We hadn't talked since the scene with Devon, and I decided I should make amends. I'd been too hard on him, and as his wife, I should be there for him, especially now, when he'd lost his best friend.

I got Brian, who in a curt and standoffish way told me Theo was still with Jenny, and he had orders not to disturb them. I told him that was fine, but that I'd like Theo to come to Hayden later, or I would teleport there. That I wanted some alone time with my husband, and also to visit both Devon and Elle. They had to all be reeling under the blow of losing Danial.

Brian gruffly said he'd tell Theo, and I hung up, unsure of what my next step should be. I was afraid to get into anything too much at Hayden, as Theo might call at any time, and I didn't trust Dev to tell me if I missed the call. After some brief thought, I decided to work in the basement, doing some filing. I'd mess up the stitches on anything I sewed, with the mood I was in. I would call back later at noon, if Theo hadn't called by then.

Venus's assistance took my mind off things; watching her carefully give me one file at a time a welcome distraction. I made it a point not to let her look inside them even though I doubted she could yet read, not wanting her asking me what "demolition" meant.

We paused for lunch, and I made her a tuna fish sandwich, and some chips. We liked it so much we both had two. Before we had time to clean up,

Serena came to take her from me, and I decided I couldn't wait any longer for Theo to return my call. I notified Dev that I was going to Danial's, and he called first, to make sure Theoron was there. As soon as he confirmed it, I teleported.

My eldest child—now more of a man than boy—T, was waiting for me in the great room when I arrived. I hugged him hard as soon as he was within reach. He looked his normal self, a state I was grateful and relieved to see him in even as it brought back the pain of Danial's current condition.

"I'm sorry, about your father," I said raggedly, as we separated. "Devlin says he may recover, but right now, he is still in a coma-like state. But his heart is beating."

Elle, my werecougar daughter in all ways but biological, came in at that moment, her eyes and face reddened from crying. I hugged her, too, and she began to cry again. I sat with her for a while on the couch, reassuring her that Danial would regain consciousness, trying hard to invest my words with believability. T sat with us too, but he was lost in thought, his forest green eyes serious and also a little determined. "I don't know what to do," he said finally. "Dad did this all alone for a lot of years, with only Theo. But I feel like I'm in way over my head, Mom. There are three meetings tonight, and I have no idea what to say to these clients."

"You are not going, not alone," I said firmly. "Cancel them!"

"Dad would expect me to go," T said stubbornly. "I have to go. But yes, I'm not taking any more appointments. When you answer the e-mails from now on, you can tell everyone we aren't taking cases anymore, not for the next month at least."

How long had it been since I'd done e-mail? A week? Since the night before Lash was arrested? Had it only been a week? It seemed like years. Shit, I would have to work on that later…"I will. But cancel the night meetings, don't go alone!"

"He won't be alone," a strong voice said behind me. "I'll be with him."

I turned to see Terian standing there, looking just as he always had. His cherrywood-colored eyes looked a little hesitant, but he was smiling. I ran to him without a thought and hugged him hard, so hard he let out an "Oof!" Terian hugged me back for a long time, and neither of us said anything.

"I'm sorry, for what I did to you, the things I said," Terian said quietly, his deep voice gentle in my ear. "I can't say I'm sorry enough."

"I forgive you," I said automatically, suppressing a shiver at the memory, even as I quickly stepped back from him.

"It won't happen again," Terian assured me. "I want you to know that, Sarelle."

"Call me Sar, Tears," I said, giving him a smile.

He gave me one back, then turned to T. "We need to leave. The first meeting is at three. Sar, please come and see me, if you would, later in the week? I'll be working nights, but I'll be up by noon."

I nodded, uneasy knowing I'd have to visit his lab. *Maybe I'll ask Titus to go with me.*

As Terian left with Theoron, I turned to Elle. "Where's Devon this morning?"

She gave me an unhappy look. "He's with Jenny and Theo," she said bitterly. "They're outside, playing. They do it every day around this time, and usually every morning, too."

"It's okay," I said tiredly, forcing a smile. "Theo and I talked about this. We're trying to get anyone watching to believe Devon isn't my son, so he'll be safe."

Realization dawned in Elle's eyes. She hugged me. "I didn't know, Mom, I thought—"

"Elle, do you want to come and stay at Hayden with me?" I interrupted. "To be near Danial? I know you think of him as your father. You're welcome to come."

Elle said nothing for a while. "No," she said finally. "I'm okay here. Devon needs me, and so does T."

"I'm very proud of you," I said tearfully. "You are right, they do need you."

I gave her a last hug, then left. I knew I should wait and face Theo and Jenny, but I couldn't do it. What if Devon wouldn't leave them to come spend time with me? I couldn't bear seeing that. It was better to leave well enough alone, since I was popping in unannounced anyway. There was no point ruining the façade of the happy cougar family I was trying so hard to bolster.

The rest of the week passed that same way. I tried to call Theo, and he didn't return my calls. I finally asked Elle to give him a message that Devon be available for me to visit on Friday afternoon. When I arrived, my little cougar son was waiting with Elle, and the three of us spent the afternoon playing games, and watching a movie. Devon was on good behavior, and I was shocked to see he looked even bigger. He had to be at least eighty pounds now for sure.

At dusk, I hugged Elle and he good-bye, and apprehensively went to see Terian at his lab. We exchanged pleasantries for a while, until I couldn't stand it any longer. "Why did you want to see me?"

Terian looked at me, and said nothing.

"Just say it, Terian."

"You know I love you," he said quietly.

I nodded, uncomfortable. "I know it."

"You know I'm marrying Sundown, that she's having my child."

I nodded again. "Congratulations, by the way."

"She's asked you to be her maid of honor," he said in a rush. "Would you step down?"

I got it completely, without his saying the reason he was asking me. That he couldn't marry her with me there as her second, that it was too much, especially after what had happened between us. Everyone in our circle knew his desire for me was the reason he'd succumbed to his demon half, and it would detract from the wedding, if I were up at the altar with him and Sundown.

"Of course," I said quickly. "I'll tell her today."

"Thank you," Terian said, the look on his face indicating he was working up to saying something else. "Sar, I want you to know—"

I left the lab quickly, before he could say anything else to me, heading directly to see Sundown. She was upset that I was bowing out, but she said she'd ask Cia instead. I told her I was sorry, and that I'd still like to attend, if she'd let me. She said fine, to my abject relief. I didn't want to cause any problems between them, not after what they'd both gone through.

We'd had enough problems getting Rip out of Hell two nights after Danial was drained.

Titus, Alerian—aka Leri—, Terian, Devlin, Theoron, and I had all gathered at Titus's house at ten to midnight. I'd imagined the demon abode to be a cozy country cottage, which is what the top part of the house resembled. But the basement was enormous, and obviously used as Titus's and Leri's laboratory/workshop. There were scrolls everywhere, vials, leathers bags, and jars of who knew what on numerous shelves. While the workshop looked a lot like Titus's lab at Devlin's, some of this stuff had to be the witch Leri's magic-making materials, prompting me to stare in wonder. *What kind of sorcery did fairies do?* I'd always heard in legends they could bend reality, and stop time. *Maybe she knows only demon magic?*

"Sar, this is important! Are you paying attention?" Titus said with barely concealed aggravation.

I snapped my mind back to what we were doing. Titus was drawing a plain circle with blood on the concrete floor. "Is that your blood?"

"No. Mostly Theoron's, with a little of Lash's mixed in."

"From the training sessions?" I replied, surprised and sickened.

"I asked Lash if I could draw it magically out of the mats, each time they were done training," Titus said, looking sheepish. "He knew I wouldn't harm T, so he agreed. It's strong magically and it saves me having to use Dev's, or mine and so weaken either of us. I knew Rip was going to need it, sooner or later."

*Why would he know that? Something to ask later.*

"Sarelle, you are the only human here, and Dev, you are the Summoner. I will need some of your blood. Leri will get both samples, if you let her."

We submitted, grimacing, as she took a few drops by knife point. *Where is a pain-relieving spell when you need one?* I didn't voice my thoughts, telling myself I wasn't a wimp.

"Now repeat what I say. We need to open a door to Hell."

The chant was simple, but after I'd said it fifteen times, it was getting old. We did it for a half hour, and suddenly, with a sharp cracking noise of splitting concrete, the center of the circle opened. Heavy choking smoke issued out, and the sound of hoarse screams.

"Sar, get back against the wall and stay there," Titus yelled. "Dev, T, grab him when he comes through! Terian, Leri, help me hold back the rest of them back!"

*Rest of them? Shit!*

Figures covered with smoke and ashes were trying to clamor through the portal, sulfurous smoke and oily greasy fumes still spouting forth, making the air hard to breathe, and difficult to see through. I remained against the wall in a crouch, glad to stay out of the action. T and Dev managed to grab Rip—who'd somehow been right on the other side of the portal—and yank him through, but some other demons weren't letting him go. They had his legs, and were trying to drag him back in with their clawed hands, the sharp snapping sounds of teeth gnashing in frustration. Terian and Leri struck at them with blue fire, and managed to knock them back, though no one seemed to die or burn, even when the fire hit them. Titus had his hands full just keeping the portal functioning, sweat running off him, his eyes burning flames, and his arms outstretched, his taloned hands straining to hold the door open.

Finally, Devlin and T managed to pull Rip free from the other demons holding him. "Close it now!" Devlin shouted.

Titus closed the portal with a quick motion, severing several arms that had been reaching through. Terian and Leri incinerated them with blue fire, and these burnt silently, still twitching violently. Directly after, everyone except me collapsed to the floor, gasping for breath.

The effort had been worthwhile. In their midst, a steaming, smoking Rip was lying on his side sprawled just beyond the closed doorway. Devlin and T let him go, and he climbed to his feet, grinning widely. He seemed none the worse for wear from being in Hell, though he was filthy for sure. "Thanks!" he said with gusto, grinning. "I was sure they weren't going to let me go this time—"

*This time?*

Devlin backhanded him hard with a snarl, knocking the demon to the floor. Rip bared his bloodied teeth in anger, before he swallowed it down. He faced Devlin, and went to one knee. "I apologize for failing you, Master," Rip said very formally. "I am yours to command."

I guessed that solved the question of how Dev acquired his demon servants. I didn't want to know what he had to promise in exchange for their service. But maybe there was nothing, save a few drops of blood, and a ticket out of Hell? I hadn't heard anything spoken tonight about souls.

"Guard us as best you can, and take your orders from Titus, till Lash returns," Devlin instructed harshly. "And know that if you should fail me a second time, and be sent back to Hell again, I'll not spill one drop of blood to get you out. You'll be blacklisted from my employ and from Theoron's as well. And with your reputation, you'll be roasting in Hell a good while before you're free again. No one wants a demon working for them who's careless, or just plain stupid!"

I expected Titus to say something, defend Rip, but his face was neutral, as were Terian's and Leri's, who both stood beside him. T was glaring at Rip, but he said nothing. My mouth had gotten me in enough trouble lately, so I stayed silent, also. But I wondered about Devlin's mention of Rip's reputation, and if Rip was so unreliable, why he's agreed to employ him at all.

"I understand, Master," Rip said quietly, his jaw working in anger. "I'll not fail you again."

Terian teleported T and himself back to Danial's house directly after, and I took Devlin and I back to Hayden. Titus said he and Rip would be along shortly. Devlin and I went upstairs and sat in the Jacuzzi for a while. We were both a little raw from the ordeal, silent and still as we soaked in the steaming water. But when we went in to bed, I couldn't put off the question any longer.

"Where is Diana, Dev?"

Dev's tone when he answered wasn't regretful, as I expected it to be over the fate of Ulysses' innocent sister. His words weren't what I assumed I'd hear, either. "She's in one of the grey rooms, with the door locked, and magically barred. Titus gave her a potion. It will make her sleep until either I kiss her, or I die. When she's awakened either way, the blood I gave her will have worn off—"

"Tell me that's not where the tale of—?"

"Yes, that maiden had the same kind of spell put on her, for much the same reason. She, like Diana, needed to be out of the way for a while. This way she will be."

*Nice way to put it.* "I'm surprised you were so lenient with her, after what Ulysses did to Danial."

9

Devlin said nothing, and then it hit me that he hadn't come to this decision by himself. And it hadn't been anything I had said to him, either. "Venus saw you with her."

Devlin nodded. "Yes. I left you in a rage after our fight in the kitchen, and I went to Diana, to kill her, and to…hurt her first. But Venus saw me opening the door, and she didn't ask me what I was doing, or who was inside, though I'd been careful that she not see Diana." Devlin took a deep ragged breath. "She called out to me, 'Daddy, please don't hurt her.' She was staring at me, tears in her eyes, holding that damn stuffed cougar you bought her—"

"What did you do?"

"Grabbed her up, and headed downstairs, feeling ashamed of myself. I called Titus, told him what I needed him to do, and he said he'd come and do it. He bespelled Diana last night, after I moved her to the other room. But I was still angry, and after he left, I came to you..." Devlin trailed off.

I reached out and grabbed his hand. He looked over at me, his golden eyes a little sad, and squeezed mine. I was glad I'd taken back my words from last night. Maybe I wasn't woman enough to keep his violent nature under control. But Venus seemed already a match for him.

* * * *

It was Saturday morning, the thirteenth of November. I'd not heard from Theo all week, and in spite of spending all of Friday with Devon and Elle, I'd promised them both I'd come for a big breakfast the very next morning, at Elle's request. With all that had happened, I didn't have the heart to refuse her. Especially knowing that Jenny was going to visit Mary for the weekend and would not be at Danial's to possibly run into.

Mary, Danial's retired housekeeper, had waited only a week to make sure her daughter was okay after becoming werecougar before moving out of Danial's estate, and down south. Part of me was glad she was gone now, so Jenny would also be gone for a while. Mary had loved Danial, and I knew Jenny was in part going to break the news to her of Danial's injury. She'd been with him for forty-some years at least, if not longer, and news of his injury was going to hit her hard. Part of me was just glad to know I'd have Theo to myself for a weekend. I'd let things slide with him already for far too long.

I arrived at Danial's at about nine. I felt so odd to be there, and know that if I knocked on Danial's bedroom door, I'd get no answer. Well, I would, but it would be T, not his father. I'd heard from Elle he'd taken over the central bedroom now. It was so strange to think of him there, sleeping on the bed on which he'd been conceived. I shoved the thought aside. *Be grateful he's still alive. If Ulysses had his way, T would be dead.*

I tried not to dwell on that, and went to see Elle. She was asleep in her bed. I woke her by gently shaking her shoulder. "Elle?"

"Sorry," she responded sleepily, looking a little guilty. "I stayed up late watching a movie—"

"It's Saturday, you're supposed to sleep in," I comforted. "Where's your father?"

"Downstairs, I think," she said, giving me a knowing look. "And he's alone."

It was good to have a smart daughter who didn't make her mother ask certain things. "Go back to sleep then," I said, with a smile. "Let Devon sleep in, too. But if you hear him, please—"

"I'll stop him going downstairs," Elle said, giving me a smile. "Don't worry."

I closed the door, then quietly made my way into the basement. Theo had heard me coming, of course, and was waiting for me in bed awake before I reached the bottom of the cellar stairs.

I took it as a good sign that he didn't have a gun in his hand. "Hi."

"Hi," he said coldly. "Why are you here so early?"

"I came to make breakfast," I said, biting my lip. "Do you want some?"

"No," he retorted, and rolled over to face the wall, putting his back to me.

*Great. Be an ass.* I went over to the bed, and sat down. "I'm sorry, for what I said to you that day in the kitchen," I said. "I was upset, and took it out on you."

"You don't give damn for me or for our son—"

"I love him best of my children," I said in the quietest whisper I could manage, not wanting Elle to overhear, or T, if he was indeed sleeping above us, and not with Serena. "And I give a damn about you, too, or I wouldn't be here talking to you when you're being such a jerk."

Theo didn't any anything nasty in retort, but he didn't roll over, either.

I sighed, and deftly slipped off my sweatshirt, jeans, and my underclothes. Then I crawled into bed beside him, though I didn't touch him. "I left messages for you. Did you—?"

"Of course I got them!" Theo growled. "How blunt do I have to be? I didn't want to talk to you, Sar. I didn't want to see you! You had said you didn't want to see me, remember?"

"I'm sorry," I said, reaching out and hugging his body to mine. "It isn't your fault, any of what's happened."

"It's fucking Devlin's fault, all of it," Theo growled. "He's a son of a bitch, and he's brought down this shit storm on us all!"

"It is all his fault."

Theo turned over to face me, surprised. "You aren't going to defend him?"

"How can I?" I said bluntly. "You're saying what I told him a few nights ago, some of it almost word for word. I can't defend the guilty."

Theo stared at me, his blue eyes penetrating and standoffish. "Why didn't you come to me before now?"

"Because Danial told me you were with Jenny every night. And I didn't want to risk coming and interrupting anything."

Theo hugged me to him. "I thought you meant what you said, that you didn't want to see me, maybe not ever again."

"No," I explained, "I was angry, and—"

Theo kissed me suddenly. I shivered a little, feeling his warm body against mine. "I'm safe," he whispered, as he pushed my legs apart gently, but my answer was drowned in his growl of pleasure as he thrust into me. Theo was shaking hard, growling almost continuously, and in a few seconds, he roared out his climax, the warmth of him filling me.

He pushed up from me, shoving back a lock of hair that had fallen over his forehead.

"I'm sorry, I couldn't wait," he said, not looking sorry at all. His face was one big grin.

I rolled my eyes at him. He tickled me. I shrieked, and pleaded with him to stop, which he did, but only when I grabbed hold of his penis, the thickness rapidly firming in my hand.

"Again?"

He gave me a tender look. "Yes, wife. Again."

Theo made love to me a few more times before we lay sated in each other's arms. Every time he came very fast, much faster than usual for him, or what had been usual in the time we'd been together.

"Couldn't wait?" I teased.

"Mating in animal form brings the urge to mate as human, just like the reverse is true," he whispered, his tone hesitant.

He had been unsure how I'd take the explanation, due to the direct reference to sex with Jenny. I wasn't upset. On the contrary, his behavior proved he'd been true to me, that he hadn't been with Jenny, save as animal. "I'm glad you waited for me," I said.

"I love you," he said happily, kissing me. "Of course I waited. I had promised to, besides. It's a—"

Just because I was accepting of his needs didn't mean I wanted details, though. "Want some breakfast?"

"Sure," he said eagerly. "Want me to go wake the kids?"

"No, you can go make us all breakfast—"

That led to another round of tickling, until I yelled out for him to stop again. "I'll go get Devon and Elle," I said, kissing him. "Meet us in the kitchen?"

He nodded. "I'll call T, and let him know where I'll be, and then I'll see you there."

Hearing that made me believe T was indeed with Serena. But it was just as well, because otherwise he would have overheard us, and I still felt funny, thinking of my child, even grown, hearing me having sex. It was hard enough still for me to think of him having sex.

I dropped that line of thinking and slipped on my clothes, and Theo got into some jeans. He kissed me a last time, grinned, and gave me a light slap on my ass as I walked upstairs. I shot him a look to remind him I didn't like it when he did that, and he shot me the look that said he liked doing it, so oh well.

I walked into Elle's room and made the offer of breakfast, giving it even odds that she would fall back asleep after I left. Closing her door, I went down the hall to T's old room, which was now Devon's room. Theo had told me that Devon had been moved in here from the smaller storage room after he began to get so big these last few weeks. It made sense, as T had taken over the upstairs bedroom back then, saying he liked the up in the air feeling of the greatroom's loft. I thought he must have gotten that from Danial. I hated the idea of sleeping so far up off the actual ground.

Devon was in his human bed in lion form, stretched out on top, as he liked to. Briar the black cat was curled up beside him, and she raised her head when I came in the door. But Devon didn't.

I couldn't believe Devon was still sleeping. But he'd probably stayed up last night with Elle. She'd said she'd watched movies late.

"Come on honey, wake up," I said loudly. Briar, always skittish, started, and jumped down, running from the room.

Devon still didn't stir.

"You're as bad as your father," I said, smiling. "Devon, get—"

It was at that moment that I saw he wasn't breathing.

## Chapter Two

My heart seemed to stop, and everything from that point went in slow motion.

I grabbed Devon up in my arms, feeling how cold and stiff my son's body was.

"No! Please God! *No!*"

My next scream deafened me, as I went to my knees, holding the lifeless body of my son. I kept screaming, stopping only to take great draughts of air to give sound to my pain.

"Sar! Sar, what the—?" I felt Theo's hands on me, holding us. As he roared out his rage and agony, I fainted.

When I awoke, I was lying in Danial's bed with Theo. Instantly Devon's death hit me like a ton of bricks. I began screaming again hysterically, and crying. Theo held me, and we cried together for a long time, not saying anything to each other. What was there to say? Our baby was dead. And everything I'd hoped for him to become, and experience, would never happen.

We slept after, holding each other tightly. When I awoke, I felt calmer, the enervation borne of grief that was temporarily exhausted. Theo was sitting beside me. He seemed to have aged considerably, his face lined and grief-ridden.

"Sar, please listen. I have to tell you some things," he said roughly. "First of all, Devon died of natural causes. Terian and Titus examined him for cause of death, as well as Dr. Camlyn. They can't find any reason; Devon was in perfect health! Stephen says that he most likely died of SIDS, that it happens sometimes, there's no cause that's known, that a baby just stops breathing—"

I began crying again, but motioned for him to go on.

"It's important that you know that Ulysses didn't get him. No one hurt him. He just died in his sleep, and he didn't suffer. And as much as we loved him, we have to let him go—"

"He's my baby," I sobbed. "I can't let him go. I won't!"

"We'll see him again, at least you will, in Heaven," Theo said gently. "He

14

never did anything evil or hurtful, so he's there, if there is a Heaven, Sar."

"You're right," I said, wiping at my eyes, grabbing at the comfort in that belief with both hands. "He's there. Suri will watch over him, until you and I get there someday."

Theo hugged me. "I want to put him in Danial's graveyard. I've ordered a rough stone, and I'm going to carve it myself. I've told T that I need a week off, and he said Terian can cover for me—"

"Is that safe?" I said, looking at him in surprise. "You were already shorthanded—"

"T isn't Danial," Theo said harshly. "He wants to make enough money to live, and that's it. We're going to work hard for the next month, and finish the outstanding cases. And then we're only going to take on enough work so the three of us can make a decent living. All of us want to have a life besides work, something Danial never seemed to understand. Terian's got a baby coming, and T wants to have some downtime, too. He's been working sixteen hour days for most of the past six weeks, and at least a few hours on every weekend. And I need to be there for you, and for Elle. We've lost so much. I don't want to lose you too."

I hugged him tightly, and didn't say anything, fresh tears rolling down my cheeks.

* * * *

That very afternoon, we buried Devon. The weather was fitting, as it poured rain and sleet for hours. Terian made a deep grave as he had before for Suri, the whirlwind churning up the half-frozen earth and mud. We placed our son's ashes into the hole, crying anew at the wrongness of that little wrapped bundle down in the cold earth.

"Titus cremated him earlier, under my supervision," Theo murmured to me. "It's safest for Devon."

I didn't know what that meant, and didn't want to ask. Theo had said earlier he didn't want to hear any shit about God, or anything religious, that any God who would take his son from him was a grade A bastard he wanted nothing to do with. I didn't fight him, knowing it would be useless. Instead, Terian spoke some good things about Devon, and so did Cia. Theo and I stood together with Elle, the other foxes, Theoron, Sundown, Brian and Demi behind us, as Tears filled in the hole. There was only a rough stump where the grave was to mark it, though Theo told me again discreetly he'd already ordered the granite, and that it would arrive tomorrow. I nodded absently as he hugged me close, too worn out to speak.

Later, we went back to Danial's, and had a somber gathering in the great room. Everyone gave condolences, and I nodded in return, hugging them back as they hugged me. I got through most of it in a daze, and didn't remember afterward who had even been there, or what they had said to me. All I could think of over and over was that Devon, my baby, was dead. I'd never see him grow up, or smile again, or come to me with a mouse he'd caught, so proud, with his tail in the air like a banner. What hurt me most was that I'd never seen him in human form, only as a lion cub. Now I never would.

Everyone left around four-thirty. I sat for a while, trying to think of what needed doing, trying to make myself move. But even Theo coming to tell me he had to go and pick up Jenny at the airport later that evening didn't get much reaction from me. My only thought was why couldn't he send someone else to get her, and then deciding it didn't matter, anyway.

Terian came in after Theo left to check on security, and took my hand, saying he was very sorry. He also slipped me a vial filled with a little liquid.

I looked at it with revulsion, then at him, not bothering to hide my suspicion.

"It will help you sleep," he said quietly. "Take it, if you need a night's sleep with good dreams. Sleeping pills knock you out, but you don't get to dream, and not dreaming at all can mess you up—"

"I don't want to dream again, not ever again!" I hissed at him. "I don't want any vials, Terian! No more potions! Nothing good ever comes of them!"

"I talked to my father," Terian said, looking earnest, and apologetic. "Titus showed me what happened, Sar. I made that first potion that you took wrong—"

*I hate you, you bastard, for bringing this up now of all times.* "Well, that isn't a big fucking surprise! Didn't your clients ever complain about all the screwing up of spells you always seem to be doing, Tears?"

Terian's eyes flashed red, then they softened as he continued. "It was trying to combine the wings, and the Heart's Truth potion into one. They separated out, when I put them in the vial to give to you, those years ago. And no matter what I did, they wouldn't mix! So I used another ingredient to bind the two spells together, a plant called, appropriately, 'bindweed.' But it didn't just bind the two spells together, it make the one stronger. What you share with Theo is real, Sar, but you were bound together much tighter than normal—"

"Do you have a point in here somewhere?" I said harshly, interrupting him.

"My point is Titus said he'll finally break the last part of the spell tonight," Terian said quietly. "He also said to tell you he was sorry it's taken so long. But he doesn't know how this will affect you both. So please call me, if you need me to teleport you to Hayden. I've put in place some barriers on teleportation in the house that will stop anyone but Titus and me—"

I nodded, but thought to myself there was no way I was calling him. I could teleport myself, thanks very much. I wasn't even happy he knew about the bond being broken. But it had sounded like Titus had needed Tears to show him what he'd done, so Titus could undo it. I couldn't fault him for that.

"—ok?" Terian finished.

"Sure," I agreed absently. "And I'm sorry, for coming down on you. I'm just upset."

Terian left soon after, and I was again alone. For a long time I did nothing but stare into space, marking the passing of each moment like it was a milestone of achievement that I kept existing in this world without Devon. But the more I sat, the more I realized I needed to do something. So I picked up the phone and called Dev. He listened, and said he'd do it. After, I headed to the couch, and took a long nap.

Later that night, when Theo was picking up Jenny at the airport, Devlin, I, and Serena walked slowly through the bitter cold to the cemetery. When we arrived, I laid the mass of white flowers that Devlin had purchased for me on the snowy grave.

White roses. Devon and I had gotten them from Theo when my baby was still growing inside me. Devon was getting them this one last time from me, in remembrance. Then I was never going to have another white rose within my sight again, if I could help it.

"I'm sorry I wasn't there with you today," Dev said softly, hugging me. "I wanted to be, very much. I'm glad you asked me here tonight, so I could pay my respects."

"Theo did it on purpose, held the funeral in the daytime, so you couldn't be there," I said emotionlessly. "Don't feel bad. I needed this anyway, to pray, to take some comfort in my beliefs. I need my faith now more than ever."

Serena made the sign of the cross, and the three of us bowed our heads. We recited the Lord's Prayer, and Devlin recited a poem by a woman by the name of Hitchcock, called "Ascension". I recited one called "If You Go First and I Remain". And finally, Serena said a prayer asking God to watch over Devon, and to be with us all, but especially Venus, in her time of loss.

I felt fresh tears on my face, and looked over at Dev. In all this, I hadn't thought of her, not once. Deep shame flooded me to the core. "How is she, Dev?"

"She's been crying quietly since three a.m. this morning," Devlin said, his expression haggard. "Nothing I did or said would make her stop. Nothing anyone said or did would make her stop."

"Why didn't you call and tell me?"

"Titus said she was fine, there was nothing wrong with her. We didn't understand why until T called, and said Devon was dead."

I swayed, and Devlin steadied me with his hand. "Come home with me now. Please, Sar. Let me take care of you—"

"No," I said reluctantly. "Theo needs me now, like you did back in September. He's lost Danial, and he's lost our son. Elle needs me, too. You need to take care of Venus—"

"Bring Elle to live at Hayden," Devlin urged, hugging me tightly. "Come home tonight with me! Don't stay here! Please, Sar! It isn't just me who is worried. Titus sent his sympathy too, but even he said you shouldn't be here unguarded, with only Theo, T, and Elle! Lash hit the roof when I told him you might stay here tonight. It was all I could do to make him swear he wasn't going to break out of jail to drag you back to Hayden!"

I didn't want to hear about Titus or Lash. I had to be here with the man I called my husband. I'd screwed up enough this whole year, I was not screwing this up, too. "Terian is back, and he's guarding Theoron and me," I said wearily. "He's been staying in the upstairs bed at night, and sleeping days with Sundown, whenever he's not out with either of them at meetings. I'm safe enough. I can teleport if I need to. Danial's home was the only one that wasn't attacked yet, for whatever reason."

Devlin didn't release me. "The roses are partly from Lash, too. He asked me to tell you he was sorry about Devon. He said he liked him a lot, that he would've taught him too, like he taught Theoron, when it was time and if he'd wanted to learn, no matter what Theo said."

I felt a fresh stab of pain, because Devon wasn't ever going to be learning anything again.

And I'd never got to hear him call me "Mommy," or hear him tell me he loved me. I'd thought my tears were used up, but I found a fresh untapped reservoir inside. For a while, I cried, and Devlin held me, Serena hugging me too.

Finally, I let them both go and dried my tears. "You should call Titus, have him teleport you both back," I managed, my tone bone weary. "I need to get back to Theo."

Devlin nodded, and gave me a last chaste kiss on the cheek. "Call me please," he instructed, his golden eyes worried. "Every day you stay here, and every night, Sar. I want to know you're safe. You don't call, and Titus is going to show up wherever you are, to make sure you're okay."

"Okay," I agreed, hugging him.

I walked back to the house after Titus had come to get them. I could've teleported, but I needed the break. I didn't know what to feel, what to think, what to care about. I felt like I'd lost everything that I'd really cared about, so what was safe for me to love anymore? I'd been bereft when I'd met Danial, depressed, but I'd had my pets, I'd had my house, and my memories about Brennan, as well as some good friends, and neighbors.

What did I have now? I'd lost all my close human friends, I'd lost my house, I'd lost my child, and I'd lost Danial to the coma-like sleep he was in. And my parents—my parents still weren't talking to me, after hearing what I'd done with Lash. I still didn't know if Theo had told them, or they'd somehow figured it out on their own. Either way, I'd have to call them now.

Walking improved my spirits, as my usual optimism tried to emerge. I had a home here still, if I wanted one. I had a home at Hayden. I still had Elle, Theoron and Venus. I still had a lot of non-human friends, and Sundown, who was at least partly human for now, even if she might not be after she had her baby. Theo and Dev were healthy, and Danial might still recover. Lash would be getting out of jail in a month or so, and coming back to Hayden. He wasn't dead.

There was still hope.

I entered the house and went directly to Elle's bedroom to check on her. She was asleep in her clothes, wads of tissues around her, her face still red from crying. I covered her up, and threw the tissues away. She didn't awaken as I kissed her forehead, and so I left her there undisturbed.

I called my parents next. My stepfather picked up, and when he heard what I had to tell him, he made my mother pick up. When I told them Devon was dead, my mother started crying, which made me start crying again. I somehow got out that it had been a natural death, if a child's death could be called natural; that no one had hurt him—that he hadn't suffered. There was beginning to be some small measure of comfort from that for me.

"I'm sorry," my stepfather said gruffly. "When is the funeral?"

"We had it earlier today," I said. "I'm sorry no one called you. I can teleport you to his grave if you want to visit him tomorrow. We had him cremated, and Theo's carving a stone—"

"Are you back together?"

I was pretty closed off emotionally, but that comment still seemed odd to me. "Back together?" I said blankly. "What?"

"Do you need us to come and get you?" my stepfather said gently, some of the gruffness gone. "You need family around you now. If Theo and you still aren't talking, if you're not together anymore—"

"We're talking," I said, not wanting to talk about this now at all. "I'm okay. I'll call you if I'm not, promise."

"Listen," Chris said. "Your mom needs me, and she's crying hard, so I'll say this quickly. We're both sorry we haven't talked to you for a while—"

*Only a month or so, Stepfather-Dear.*

"—but we thought you needed to work out things with Theo. Danial called us in late October and told us about your house burning, that you were okay, but you were going into hiding. He said that you wouldn't call us for a while, that there was a dangerous man hunting you and he, and that you wouldn't be visiting us, either, until it was safe."

*How had I missed calling my parents through all of this? Because I had been so preoccupied with my own troubles.* Fresh shame flooded me. "That's true. He's still out there. He's attacked Devlin at least four times, and Danial's been hurt badly. He'll recover, but—"

"What could hurt a vampire? Sunlight? Did someone stake him and miss?"

I began to shake thinking again about Danial, and knew I had to get off the phone before I broke down crying again. "Listen, I have to go. I don't want anyone hurting you, and for all I know this phone is tapped, and I've already said too much. So keep that special gun Theo gave you this summer handy, and your cell phone within reach. Don't let Mom walk the dog by herself in the woods. In fact, don't let her walk out of sight of the house. Buy a treadmill. If you see anything out of the ordinary, anything at all, call Hayden immediately—"

"Danial gave the phone number to us, when he called. He's called here once a week for the last few weeks, telling us how everyone was, so we wouldn't worry about you—"

I felt a fresh rush of feeling for Danial; he'd done his best to protect my parents, to try to make them as safe as he could, while not making them too scared. As usual he'd had taken up the slack for me when I'd been too busy thinking about my own problems with Theo. My eyes welled up thinking of my beloved vampire lying alone at Hayden, unresponsive, with no one to comfort him.

*Focus, Sar. You can go to pieces after you've hung up the phone, but not until then.* "Good. Call if anything strange happens, and we'll bring you to Hayden to stay temporarily. It's safe there. I finished getting furniture, so you'll have a place to sleep. But—"

"No 'buts,' Sarelle," my stepfather stated, his tone gruff again. "We love you, and we'll be here if you need us. We'll call if there's a problem, and evacuate, though you know your mom, and you'd better make sure you lay in a supply of cat food for her twenty cats, because she won't be leaving them or the dog behind—"

"I will," I said, my voice cracking with emotion. "Please be safe. 'Bye."

Totally exhausted, I took a long hot shower, dropping my clothes in a pile on the bathroom floor. After putting on some pajamas and my black velvet robe, I went in to the great room with my novel and a blanket to wait for Theo, knowing I might have an hour's wait in front of me. Before I'd read ten pages, I was fast asleep.

I dreamed of being chased relentlessly through a forest. No matter how fast I ran, I couldn't get away, the hot breaths of my pursuer louder and louder behind me. Just as I turned and screamed, I awoke, gasping and flailing, my heart beating rapidly.

I checked my watch trying to calm myself and got more worried. It was ten to three in the morning! Where were they?

Apprehensive, I changed back into my regular clothes, slipping the small knife Lash had given me onto my belt. If something bad had happened, I didn't want to be lounging in a nightgown; I wanted to be prepared. I sat back down on the couch to wait.

A half hour later, the front door closed with a slam. Theo came sauntering in, reeking so strongly of sex I could smell it as a human. I knew who he'd most likely been with, and that for whatever reason, this time it hadn't just been sex in animal form. I was irritated immediately, because it was obvious he'd done it on purpose. But strangely, my jealousy felt more like an abstract concept than like my real feelings. Some of that was the loss of Devon, but it was almost as if I'd known this was coming, though I couldn't say why I felt that way.

Theo stalked over to me, and gave me a smile that was more arrogance than anything else, as if waiting for me to accuse him. I didn't say a thing, unwilling to give him any satisfaction. The result was surprise and also annoyance. He'd planned to get a rise out of me and I wasn't giving him any reaction.

Even if I wasn't going to scream at him, I wasn't going to stay silent. My name was Sar, after all. "You didn't have to sleep with Jenny to not be with me anymore. You could have just told me to leave, and not come back, and I would have not been here when you got back tonight."

My calm words hung between us for a split second, then Theo's eyes went yellow. "I wanted you to know how it feels," he growled. "For you to be the one who is jealous."

"I'm not," I said casually, surprised myself that I was speaking the truth. *What had happened?*

I stared at Theo, as if seeing him for the first time. My love of the last three and a half years, the man I'd moved Heaven and Earth for, and always put first. The man I'd driven cross-country to find, whose daughter I'd raised, whose child I'd had, whose life I'd sold myself in return for twice over. The man I'd left Danial for, hurt Devlin for, and rejected Lash for, over and over. Sure, he was handsome. Sure, he had a great body. Sure, he'd saved my life, but who hadn't, of my lovers? Why had I thought he was so special? He was a good enough guy, but that was if you weren't the one married to him. When had he ever put me first? Maybe long ago, when we first met, and he first loved me. Why had I chased him so long, tried so hard to be everything he wanted, instead of being myself? I'd almost died, trying to be what he wanted!

"You are so not worth it," I whispered cuttingly.

"I could say the same for you," Theo growled back.

"You don't have to," I retorted, curling my lip. "I'll be leaving now."

"You aren't going anywhere," he growled. "You're my wife, and you go where I tell you. I'll say if you are leaving, or staying."

I looked at him, ready to laugh at how ridiculous he sounded, and saw he was serious.

"You aren't going to go to Devlin again, ever," Theo growled. "You're staying here, with me. And you're going to sleep beside me every night—"

"Jenny's not going to go for that," I sneered, my tone raw sarcasm.

"Sometimes she'll join us," Theo said with a grin that was part eager, part malicious.

I looked at him in shock. Theo had never wanted more than me, had refused when I'd told him to take another lover…*until Titus began to break the bond*. Now, I was betting it was finally broken.

"Why not, Sweetheart? I was in bed with you and Danial before, even if nothing happened. Two women sounds good to me, one on either side of me."

"Getting visions of your own pride now, Theo? Must be a lion thing—"

"It *is* a 'lion thing'," Theo growled provocatively. "Male lions like more than one female lion to mate with usually, Sar. Nineva has three women. Two have already born him children, and the third will give birth in February—"

"That's nice," I said sarcastically, rolling my eyes and getting up. "Count me out."

Theo growled, his eyes still yellow.

"Don't worry," I continued, turning to leave. "There might be no werecougars besides Jenny in the Northeast, but I'm sure you can find someone else to turn if you ask enough women. Then you'll have your very own ménage a trois, or quatre, if you prefer four!"

"I already have someone else to turn right here," Theo purred, his throaty sound of pleasure sending chills down my spine. "You."

I slowly turned to face him. "I don't want to be werecougar."

"I don't care if you want to be or not," Theo said easily. "I want you to be, and you are my mate. You'll do it, because it's what I want!"

"Keep telling yourself that and it still won't happen," I said, and went into Danial's room.

Theo followed me, locking the door behind us. I turned to face him, my eyes spitting sparks. "You think if you lock me in here with you I'm going to listen to your shit?"

"Look, I'm sorry," Theo said in a more placating tone, leaning against the door. "I probably shouldn't have said it like that. It is true though, what I said about Nineva. Most lions have more than one mate, but I don't feel that way. I just wanted you to know how it felt to be the one told that you were going to have to put up with other lovers."

Outraged that he would do such a thing on the very day our son had died, my loud voice became a shout. "Theo, you know without Devlin's protection, I'm sure to be claimed by some other vampire, even someone like Michael—"

"Not if you let me change you tonight," Theo said, a hot current infecting each word. "If you're werecougar, they can't force you to do anything! Danial will leave you alone, that is, if he even recovers—"

"Stop it!"

"And Devlin will too, he'll find some other woman to bed—"

"Like you obviously have?"

Theo looked as if he badly wanted to say something cutting but instead let out a breath. "You've got to understand, my turning her, I did it for you, Sar! I know what to do now! I couldn't risk trying it with you until I knew it would work! But I changed Jenny, and she was almost dead! It will work with you, you're healthy and you're mortal now."

I looked at him with growing fear. He was serious. He was absolutely serious. I tried to teleport, but he reached out and pulled me into his arms, hugging me tight. "No, you don't," he growled. "I told you, you're staying here with me, even if I have to hold on to you all night. And you can't teleport from here anyway. T's worried about someone getting in the house. He had Terian put up a barrier for certain rooms, including the bedrooms and the offices. Go ahead, try it right now!"

I felt a bad feeling of foreboding. I tried it, and nothing happened. *Fuck!*

Theo let me go, and stepped back from me. "See?"

"Devlin would be furious if you—"

"But he couldn't undo it," Theo said triumphantly. "He'd get used to it. He'd have no other choice!"

I didn't say anything, too busy thinking how to get myself out of this situation.

Theo was still trying to convince me. "We can hunt together, and I can love you with everything I am," he purred, that great rumbling sound calming me in spite of the circumstances. "If you're werecougar, I won't have to hold back with you, or worry about hurting you anymore! It could be so perfect, Sar. Maybe we can even have another child."

I felt something cold slither down my spine and clutch my heart. Theo saw the fresh grief and loss in my eyes. "We'll never get Devon back," he said, swallowing hard. "I accept that. But I loved sharing that with you, seeing the two of you together, knowing he was my son, and how much you loved him, that he was part mine and part yours—"

Even as my vision blurred with tears, I saw a problem here, a problem Theo should be seeing, unless he'd found out the truth about me. *I have to know if he knows.* "But I'm fixed, I can't have any more children."

"When you become were, you may heal what Stephen did to you," Theo said with excitement. "I checked, and there have been cases where it's happened to other women when they were turned, Sar. Even if you don't heal your human body, when you change into lion form you'll be able to get pregnant. You could stay in lion form, carry the baby that way—"

I felt a shiver again at his rampant eagerness as relief flooded me that he hadn't found out I had already healed. "No, Theo, I don't want—"

"—with us being both were and the same species, there won't be any danger of the fetus getting too big, and you'll heal fast, too. I'll take care of you, like I did before when you were pregnant."

"Theo, it's not going to work! *I don't want to—*"

"It will," Theo said staunchly. "We can finally be happy together. The way we should have been from the first! When I first changed for you, when you told me how beautiful I was as a lion, I wanted to ask you then to let me change you. We'd just gotten together though, and I didn't have nearly enough control—"

"Theo, you aren't *listening*—"

"But I do now, Sar. I won't hurt you, like I was afraid I might. Aspen told me what to do, that night we saw her in Casper. She told me it would only take a moment's courage, and it would be done—"

I tried another tactic. "Dev will kill you! He treasures the taste of my blood above all else, and it's beginning to change finally—"

"I don't give a fuck what he wants!" Theo roared. "And I'm done sharing you with him!"

Theo squeezed me tighter, and his yellow eyes bored into mine. "You either let me change you here tonight, or I'm leaving you, Sarelle. I'm done with having only part of you, and only being able to share half of myself with you! It's all or nothing. And it's your choice."

"Theo, please, let me go!"

"What's it going to be, Sar? Me, or the two brothers? Well, really now, it's me or Dev! A good life in the sun, with a man who loves you, really loves you, or spending the rest of your life in the darkness with a leech feeding off you every chance he gets—"

"Stop it!"

"You stop it! Stop making excuses! Say yes now, or tell me good-bye. And know that Jenny has already told me if I want her, she's mine—"

"Good! Leave me alone! Go to your whore—"

Theo slapped me lightly, the unexpected blow knocking me off balance. I fell down, but caught myself with my hands before my head hit the floor. I was in too much shock to do anything but look up at him, and put a shaking hand to my mouth. My teeth had cut my lip shallowly and it was bleeding. I lay where I'd fallen for a moment, feeling déjà vu. Theo had never struck me before, never. I hadn't thought he was capable of it. But he'd changed from the man I'd known and trusted, when the spell had been broken. And the man he was now was a man I didn't know. A man I couldn't trust.

"Sar, I'm so sorry," Theo said, starting toward me.

I suddenly realized I had a clear path to the door. Theo did too, and grabbed hold of my hand again.

"Get your God-damned hands off me!" I said, trying to back away on my hands and knees.

"I can't believe I did that," Theo said, tears in his eyes. "Please—"

"Get out! I'm not turning for you, Theo! Not now, not ever!"

"Is that your final answer? You're sure?" His voice was hard now, no longer pleading.

"I'm sure. I'm sorry for you, but—"

"I'm sorry for you!" Theo spat. "You've chosen a monster! You'll be pimped out to his friends to be fucked every way possible!"

"Let me go!"

"But maybe you like that? You seem to love having more than one man in your bed! How many times have you fucked Lash and him together, Sar? Fifty? A hundred?"

"I haven't been with Lash at all—"

Theo heard the truth in my voice and switched tactics, still growling. "You don't ever call Jenny a whore, not in front of me! It's you who is the whore!"

The last bit of my self-restraint abruptly gave way. "You're right. She's not a whore. But you're a bastard, a motherfucker, and an asshole! *Now let me go!*"

Theo let me go, and faced me. "Before you go to your new life in darkness, you might as well have this," he said, and he took off his ring and tossed it to me. It rolled to a stop at my feet.

"It's just as well you aren't going to turn," Theo continued, running his eyes over me appraisingly. "You might have been beautiful once, but you're not anymore, Sar. You have a hard look in your eyes now that never leaves. And you've put on so much weight, living at Hayden. You're just too fat and ugly to be a woman of mine."

I knew it was a cheap shot. I knew Theo probably didn't mean it, that he'd just told me that morning as he made love to me how beautiful I was, how much he loved me. But part of me told myself he did, that this was what he'd thought all along, that Terian's spell had just hidden it. And for some reason, it hurt me more than anything else he could have said. Maybe because in part he was right; I had let myself go a little since I'd had the twins. Maybe it was because I had always been vain. And maybe because it was the path of least resistance, believing him.

But in addition to hurting, his words also made me very, very angry. So angry I forgot about escaping, and decided I had a few things to say to him too. He wasn't getting the last word.

"I want you to know something, before you go," I said, looking up at him with hate. "You owe Lash your life. You're walking around breathing because he saved your ass!"

Theo sneered at me. "What bullshit are you—?"

"That night you challenged Robert, and fought him, Satar and his men, they were there, planning to shoot you as you fought him!"

"You're lying!"

"You never wondered how they suddenly ceased to exist? Why they just seemed to give up trying to kill you? How much of an idiot *are* you?" I laughed maliciously. "Lash killed them. He covered it up, burned the bodies!"

"No!" Theo said looking at me with so much pain and agony, I thought he might be having a heart attack. "That can't be true! You're lying! He would never—"

"I sent him to protect you," I hissed. "He got hurt saving your stupid ass! I went to save him in part because of it—"

"I never asked you to," Theo whispered, belief and horror in his eyes. "Why did you—?"

"I heard you talking to Devon, saying you wouldn't come back! I had to do something! You were going to let yourself be killed over your stupid honor! If you'd have let Terian go with you, I wouldn't have needed Lash's help—"

"What did you give him for his help?" Theo growled in anger, his eyes bleeding back to yellow. "He wouldn't have done it for free. And you couldn't have afforded to pay him money, not what his going rates are."

I narrowed my eyes and looked at him. I'd already said too much. Maybe it was better, saying nothing, because Theo had already come to his own conclusion.

"That afternoon you went to Hayden!" Theo said, his voice rising in volume. "It wasn't to see Serena! It was to see him, to fuck him as payment! That's why you were so calm that night! I thought it was because you believed in me, had faith in me—"

*Stay silent. Let him believe that.* "Theo, I had to save you."

"You didn't do it for me, you did it because you wanted him, just like you wanted him later, just like you lusted after him when you were pregnant, like you want him *now*—!"

"Yes, I want him," I screamed. "I love him!"

Theo's look of revulsion was terrible to see. "Say it's a lie, Sar. Say it now, that you just said that to hurt me, and I'll forgive you."

"It's not a lie! I'm in love with him!"

"He almost killed you and you love him?" he whispered. "What is wrong with you?"

"I wouldn't have died," I spat at him. "He would have turned me, if the demon blood didn't work. He said he would, that he'd done it before. And I told him to do it!"

Theo roared louder than I'd ever heard him, and I realized with fear my mistake. "You'd be snake for him but not cougar for me?" he snarled. "You bitch!"

I tried to jerk free, but he had me too tightly, his fingers digging into my arm painfully. He was changing, his clothes beginning to split as he shifted form.

"You'll never be with him again," Theo growled, his words slurred and rough as his canines elongated. "I'm making sure of that tonight, Wife! Once you're cougar he won't be able to stand the smell of you, no matter what he feels for you! And you won't be able to stand him touching you, for the same reason! But you'll want me for the rest of your life—"

It was now or never.

I said a quick prayer as I slid my hand to my belt, flipping open the blade as I yanked it free. I kneed Theo as hard as I could. He let out a cry, struggling to hold me. I stuck the knife Lash had given me into his arm, and he snarled in pain, flinching back from me, but he still had me with one hand. I bit his wrist as hard as I could, then jerked free. Theo was almost fully shifted into cougar form, but he was not only injured, he was tangled in his clothes. I ran out of the room as soon as I'd unlocked the door, and upstairs to the study, the knife still in my hand.

Before I reached the top step, I heard a throaty purr, and heard clawed feet scrabbling on the stairs as they bounded up them after me. I got into the study just in time to slam the door and lock it, hoping to God Danial hadn't moved the gun he had kept here since the attacks by Manir more than a year ago. Because I was running to a dead end with no way out, if what Theo had told me about teleporting was true. But I'd never have made it out the front door before he was on me. I tried to teleport immediately, and nothing happened. I tried the phone to call Terian, and got only static. An extension had to be off the hook somewhere.

*Shit!*

The office door shuddered under Theo's assault. He roared, and hit it again. Danial, however, had put this door on after the assault by Manir. The reinforced steel and oak creaked, but it held.

I wiped the knife off on my pants and folded it up, clipping it back to my belt loop, thanking God I'd put it on tonight. Unlocked the hidden safe in the wall, I retrieved a gun and bullets from inside, swearing because it was a regular silenced gun, not an explosive bullets gun. At least the rounds were jacketed hollow points. I had just gotten the first bullet into the chamber when I heard a key in the lock.

The door opened, and Theo stood there, nude, his blue eyes determined, a key in his hand. His arm where I cut him was still bleeding. "I'm not healing, Sarelle. You have werepoison on your blade," he growled, advancing slowly. "That's Lash's knife clipped to your belt! I recognize it!"

I trained the gun on him, holding it with both hands so it didn't shake too much.

"That's a regular .38. You shoot me, you'd better hit my heart," Theo growled. "Because you miss, and I'll be on you in a second. This little chase you've led me on is over! Terian isn't here to save you! Danial and Lash aren't here to save you! And Devlin will be too late!"

"You have one chance to leave," I said in a hard voice. "Or I will shoot you, Theo."

Theo looked at me for a few moments, and then he lunged for me with a roar. I fired, pulling the trigger, and Theo was pushed back as the bullet slammed into his torso. He let out a cry of pain and disbelief, looking down at his bleeding chest in shock. He slumped to his knees, and then to the floor.

"You told me to practice, Husband," I said softly, looking down at him. "I have been."

I gave him a wide berth, stepping past him through the door. He'd be healed in a minute or two and I had to get to the great room. I could teleport from there, I hoped.

I thought for a fleeting second about saying good-bye to Elle, but told myself I'd call her tomorrow. For all I knew she'd agree with Theo, and maybe help him turn me. Jenny was here too, somewhere, and who knew what she thought about this. *We could all be werecougars together, one big happy family...!*

I ran downstairs, near hysteria. Trying to teleport from the great room failed. There was the sound of a body moving upstairs, then a groan, and I knew I had no more time. Grabbing my purse from the dining room table, I ran frantically to the front door, and unlocked it, stepping outside. I tried teleporting again, but it still didn't work. With a frustrated cry, I darted across the front lawn, now buried in knee-deep snow and ice, slipping and falling a few times. On reaching the trees at the far side of the lawn, I tried to teleport again and found myself in Hayden's kitchen.

I sank down on the floor, covered with sweat, my clothes wet through, panting hard. I lay there for a long time and just breathed, telling myself I was safe. No one came as the minutes passed, something for which I was very grateful.

Eventually, I stood and slowly made my way to the gold and green room. After showering, I put on one of the guest robes, took my clothes downstairs, and got them washing. I was grateful not to meet anyone, glad it was almost dawn.

Part of me wondered if I should go to Devlin tonight, and tell him what happened. Right now, I wanted no one near me, and no sounds. I wanted to think of nothing for a while, to sleep with no nightmares. But I was sure to, after all that had happened. With a reluctant sigh, I rummaged in my purse, pulling out the vial Terian had given to me, and got into bed.

*Do I trust him enough to take it?*

Terian had given me that potion for sleeping. He said it wouldn't hurt me. Titus would be here, in case I felt odd tomorrow, or had some problem. Screw it. I had to sleep, and without something to make me sleep, I wouldn't. Dev's sleeping pills also weren't an option, as I might have nightmares from which I wouldn't be able to wake. I needed sleep with only good dreams.

Just to be safe, just in case I woke up desiring Theo, I left a voicemail for Titus telling him what I was doing, so he could stop me going to him. Then I swallowed the contents of the vial. It was sweet, like chocolate liquor. Easing myself down on the guest bed, I slipped into dreams.

* * * *

I awoke to find myself in a man's warm arms. *Lash?*

I looked up to greet him happily, even as I snuggled into the heat of him.

But instead of reptilian eyes, cherrywood eyes were looking down into mine.

"Terian?"

"I'm sorry about Theo," he said quietly. "He told me that it's over between you."

*So you thought you'd come and replace him?* "What have you done?" I whispered, recoiling from him. "What is this?"

"Nothing," he said quickly, lifting his hands off me and putting some distance between us. "This is no spell, just a dream, a dream that will fade like any other. You asked me once what my power was, Sar, what faerie magic I had. It's mostly to influence dreams. I didn't know that, when I made that potion for you so many years ago. It wasn't until I told my father what I'd done that he was able to break your bond. It was my fault, because I did the spell wrong, with just one added ingredient. But please don't worry, this one I did right. You won't remember this dream, Sar. But I will. I wanted to dream with you once, even if nothing happened but this, just me holding you."

"Why?"

"Because I love you," he said tenderly, looking down at me. "Because I've loved you for years, and I intend to be faithful to Sundown, when I marry her. And I wanted to be with you like this one time, before I give her my vow."

"Like a last one night stand before your wedding?" *How nice. Ugh.*

"You don't have to do anything with me you don't want to," Terian said simply. "I'm not asking you for anything, Sar. It's enough to be here, dreaming with you. And you could never mean as little to me as any one night stand. Not after all you've done for me."

"You'll hurt her by doing this, even just holding me."

"My body is alone, in a hotel room, states away," Terian said calmly. "Theo called me a half hour ago, and told me what happened between you. He was upset, and he'd been drinking at the Alan's Creek bar with Jenny—"

"I don't care about why he did what he did, or about what he feels now. I—"

"I'm saying there is no one to hear me, if I should say anything in my sleep. Just as I know you are at Hayden, and you are most likely alone, too, somehow, because if Devlin knew what I'm guessing happened between Theo and you, by now I'd have gotten a courtesy call from Titus about how Devlin was sending him to kill Theo. This is just a dream. No binding power, no anything. I made very sure of that, Sar. I've fucked up your life enough over the years with my magic. I'm not going to do it again."

*Yeah, right.* "How do I know that?"

"The spell only gives me access to be able to enter your dream. You are the one who chooses what happens in the dream. With Theo and you, you both chose it, and had equal control. I have no control over what you dream of, none, though I can and will wake you, if you begin to have a nightmare—"

*So that's what he meant about ensuring good dreams.* "I'm sorry," I said, staring up at him. "But nothing is going to happen between us."

"That's fine," Terian said, patting my hand with his. "Fall back asleep again and let me hold you, please," he whispered. "You'll either wake up, or go on to another dream. There are other dreams you can have tonight, Sar. Sleep in this one, and go on to one of them."

I eased back down in the bed, though I kept my distance. I was tempted to ask him if I looked fat, but decided not to. In a few moments I fell asleep.

I awoke in the flame room, but it wasn't the flame room I knew. This room had furnishings, not my sewing supplies. I was in a full size bed, the same one I'd made up in the gold and green room. I was dressed, as I had been before with Terian. And I wasn't alone.

I looked over to see Lash lying sprawled indolently beside me, grinning at me as only he could, dressed in his trademark black. But his weapons were not on his body; they were beside him on the nightstand within easy reach. He opened his mouth to say something, but I grabbed hold of him and pulled him to me and kissed him with all the longing and love I'd been holding back for weeks. He groaned, and his passion for me seemed to match mine. He tightened his arms around me, and began taking off my clothes. I was already trying to strip off his. I made little noises of frustration, as I couldn't seem to get his clothes off as fast as he was removing mine. He pushed me gently back and stripped off his shirt and turtleneck. I ran my hands over his tanned skin, hissing a little myself in eagerness. I reached up and kissed him, and he moaned as he covered my lips with his own. He rolled on top of me, his erection pressing against me. I groaned, and he chuckled roughly, the sound mirth mingled with strong desire.

But I'd had enough foreplay. I'd hungered for him too long, and been through too much shit to wait any longer. I pushed down his jeans and grabbed hold of him, running my hand over the head of his penis in a quick rhythm. He let out a loud cry and his head arched back as he felt me touch him. I moved under him, spreading my legs as he moved into position above me. Then he stopped still, drawing a questioning look from me.

"I love you, Sar," Lash said, his dark eyes full of emotion, as they had been that day in the hotel room. "You're breathtaking, my Love. So breathtaking to behold."

Tears came to my eyes, and I took his face in my hands. "I love you, Lash," I said, looking at him tenderly. There was a sudden look of shock on his face so strong, and his eyes flattened, as if he were trying to conceal his feelings.

"No, don't change, don't hide from me," I said. "I love you. I should have told you months ago, but I had to work out my life. But Theo's leaving me, it's over. And I've wanted you so much for months it's killing me inside."

Lash kissed me, and there seemed a sadness in his kissing that I didn't understand. "Say it for me again," he hissed softly. "Tell me, as we make love, that you love me." Then he very carefully entered me and began to move.

Lash made love to me for a long time, thrusting into me gently, stroking me, kissing me, touching me so tenderly it brought tears to my eyes. And through it all, I told him over and over again that I loved him. And when we finally came, we came together, crying out, clutching each other as if we would never let go. After I lay in his arms, and cuddled him to me.

"I've missed you so much," I murmured, sated completely. "Do you still want to be with me, like you wanted to before?"

"I want you more than anything," Lash hissed. "More than the air I breathe." I ran my hands over his chest and he sighed. "I've longed to feel you like this, to feel you run your hands over me, to tell you I love you—"

I felt a pricking of unease, and looked up at him, into his dark eyes.

"What is it, baby?" he hissed softly, "What's wrong?"

Lash would never say that, not when we were like this. He would have told me I felt good to him. He wouldn't have called me "My Love" either, though Danial or Dev had often. And he would never, ever, call me "baby," though someone else had, someone I knew…

*This isn't Lash!*

I recoiled, and tried to roll my body away, but a warm hand grabbed me gently, and kept me still. It was suddenly Terian who lay beside me, whose body still wore the sweat of our lovemaking.

I began hyperventilating, my surprise switching to white hot rage. He'd deceived me with his magic, so he could have me! *Bastard*! "Are you going to go all demon on me again?" I finally got out, so angry it was hard to speak. "Or are you demon already?"

"No," he said, his eyes sad. "I'm sorry again about what I did to you—"

"Did you just bind me to yourself?" I spat the words at him in fury.

"No," Terian said, his cherrywood eyes tear-filled now. "I promise, no."

I didn't know what to say. I felt betrayed, duped, and disgusted. "How could you do this, add on this betrayal, after everything else you'd already done to me? I trusted you! I thought you were my friend, Terian!"

"Sar, you won't remember this," he said with a trace of sadness. "If you'll remember anything, you'll remember you dreamed of Lash. You weren't supposed to know I was riding your dream with you. It must be your demon blood that revealed my true form to you. Don't begrudge me dreaming with you, please don't, not after all the years I've wanted to—"

"I hate you!" I screeched at him, pulling the covers over my nakedness as I yanked free of him and rose from the bed to run for the door. But the door disappeared, leaving only blank wall in front of me.

"Can't you understand I needed this, to at least try to be with you like this?" Terian said desperately. "I've had this fantasy for years, ever since you and Theo dreamed together! That I would meet you in dreams, and you would want me, love me—"

"But I don't," I said forcefully. "And you can't make me love you!" I stopped with a hitching breath, afraid, because it was easily within his power to make me magically love him.

Terian reached out and grabbed my hand. "I would never do that to you. Never."

*You would do it in a heartbeat, if you thought you could get away with it.*

"I didn't know you loved Lash," he continued. "I took the form of your heart's desire, and I expected to wear Devlin's form, or Danial's maybe. I couldn't see who you perceived me to be. Though I should have guessed, from what happened in September. Why didn't you tell him?"

"That is so none of your business." *Asshole.*

"Tell him," Terian said firmly. "Lash should know, especially now that you can be with him. After everything that's happened, he should know you're in love with him." He got out of bed, suddenly clothed. I looked down to see that I was also, and let the covers drop to the floor. "And it's enough that I shared this with you. Know I love you very much, and that it's meant a lot to me, that you shared this with me, even if you thought it was him loving you."

"If I won't remember any of this, why bother telling me?"

"You won't," he said bitterly. "But I wanted to say it to you, to remember I said it. To remember I had the guts to say it. It was so wonderful to hear you say you loved me, to pretend for just a little that you did, to see what your face looks like when you tell a man you love him, and really mean it with your whole heart. And just for once to pretend that I was that man."

Terian took my hand in his. "Awaken," he whispered.

I woke up, wiping my eyes, which oddly were wet as if I'd been crying. *What time is it?* Why had I woken? *I had a dream. I was doing something...talking to someone...Terian.* But what had we talked about? And Lash was in there someplace too? The dream fragments faded even as I tried to recall details, leaving me with just the vague sensation of happiness.

Turning over, I let it go, relaxing back and enjoying the peace filling me. I fell back asleep, and dreamed no dreams at all.

About noon, I woke up. I lay there for a while, thought about the past horrendous night, and weeks previous to it, and made a plan of action.

# Chapter Three

First, I was going to start exercising every day. I was also going to eat less. When my jeans fit again, I'd slack off.

Second, I was going to spend more time with Elle and Venus.

Third, I was going to find a way to write my parents, and get them letters, since I couldn't call. Titus should be able to teleport them, or maybe there was some other mystical way?

Fourth, I was going to try again to be nicer to Devlin.

Fifth, when Lash came back, I'd tell him if he wanted to be with me, he could be.

And Sixth, I was going to stop doing things because they were best for everyone else. I was going to stop telling myself that it was okay to do something if I didn't want to do something, because someone I loved wanted me to do it, and I wanted them to be happy, and it was better that way. I'd put what mattered to me last for most of the past year, hell, longer than that, since I'd been with Theo. That was over. I needed to put myself first a little more, because I was responsible for my own happiness. If I let myself be pushed around, that was exactly what was going to keep happening. I was finished with that.

That was a good start on a plan. I'd keep going with others, as I thought of them.

Somehow, I'd forgotten to put my watch back on, or lost it in last night's struggle with Theo. *Seventh, get a new watch, or ask Terian to bring me my old one, if Theo hadn't stomped it into pieces of smooshed metal in his anger.* I got up from the guest bed, dressed in last night's clothes, and went looking for the nearest clock, which happened to be in the happily-unoccupied kitchen.

I made a small breakfast of cereal and yogurt, then headed upstairs. I knocked on Devlin's door, and he answered, his sleepy golden eyes becoming shocked.

"Can I come in?" I asked. "I'm tired."

35

"Sure," Devlin said, tilting his head invitingly and offering me his hand. "Come in, Love."

He led me back to bed, and soon had the length of his cool body pressed against mine. Per usual he was naked, and I knew he was wondering why I'd left my clothes on instead of shedding them when I'd gotten into bed with him. "Did you reconsider staying with Theo?" His voice was carefully void of emotion.

I debated what to say. I didn't want Devlin to know what Theo had tried to do. He'd kill Theo for sure, and as much as that had seemed a wonderful idea last night, it wasn't something I was comfortable doing in the light of day, now that I was safe. Theo was Elle's father, and too important to Theoron now for protection. *As much as I hate Theo, I can't just...*

Devlin lost his patience immediately. "Sarelle, what's wrong? Answer me."

"Theo and I are splitting up. He's leaving me for Jenny."

Devlin was silent, but I could feel the pleasure, the utter satisfaction, emanating from him like smoke. He caressed my shoulder, and then kissed it lightly with his soft cool lips. I'm sorry," he said, leaning over and kissing my lips gently. "But I'm happy too, because now you are just mine, Love."

*Why does that seem so familiar? "Love"? Hmm...*

"Will you stay here with me now?" he whispered gently. "Please consider—"

"I'm not sure," I said honestly, leaving my musing. "This changes everything, Dev. I need time."

"Take your time," Devlin replied quickly. "I'm just happy you are here with me."

I knew he knew I didn't have anywhere else to go, just as I did. But I appreciated him not saying it, anyway. Especially as the day progressed and things seemed to go from bad to worse.

T called about noon, as I was having lunch with Venus. "Mom," he said without preamble, "I need to ask you to not come here for a while."

I opened my mouth, but no words came out. T kept talking. "I don't know what happened with Theo and you. He told Terian and me that you'd chosen Devlin over him, but both of us could see there was a lot more to it than that. Terian also told me to leave it alone, that it was between the two of you, and I'm taking his advice. But Theo is going to be staying here in the main house, like he has been these past two weeks, and he said he wants Jenny to stay with him. And the bottom line is that he's my only partner left."

I said nothing. T paused, and seemed to gather his courage. "I need Theo here, and it's true, this is more his home now than it is yours," he said quietly.

"I'm sorry to say it like that, or to tell you that you shouldn't visit, but everyone would be uncomfortable, including you, if you came here to see Elle or me—"

"I assume this is the part where you tell me you'll come and see me instead?"

"I'll be coming to Hayden regularly every week, at least twice or three times to see Serena. I'll bring Elle with me, so she can visit you. Terian can teleport us both. And if you want to spend time with me, if I have any after sleeping and working this month, just ask me, and I'll schedule it—"

He sounded so much like Danial had. Exactly like Danial had. It was eerie.

"Okay," I said tonelessly. "That's good. But what about the filing?"

"Jenny will do it," Theo said "But I really do need you to do that e-mail work for me—"

Shit! I knew there was something I had been forgetting. The thought of familiar work calmed my next words. "I'll spend the rest of the afternoon on it. I'm sorry I haven't—"

"I'm sorry to ask you to," T said quietly. "I know this has been a week from hell, Mom."

I bit my lip hard to keep from crying. "It's okay. Sitting around doing nothing is not going to help me feel any better any sooner. Working will at least help me take my mind off everything."

"I'll be coming for the first time on Wednesday," T said. "It's the seventeenth—"

How could November be passing so slowly? It seemed like months ago that we'd gone to the Hallow's party, and Lash had been free, and Robin and Devon alive, Danial okay…

I shook it off, getting myself under control. *You can handle this. Now do it.*

"I'll see you then," I said. "Please be careful. I love you, T."

"I love you too, Mom."

I hung up the phone and went back to Venus, who was regarding me very carefully, her golden eyes watchful. "Mom, Elle is coming here?" She sounded eager, and also a little scared.

"Yes, this week," I said, kissing her forehead. "Now finish your sandwich. I have to get to work. I'm afraid I'll have to leave you with Serena for a few hours, V."

"Can I help?" she said hopefully.

"Not with this," I said kindly, stroking her hair. "I have to help T with a few things. But later we'll watch a movie, and have popcorn."

"Dad said he had to make some arrangements tonight, that he wouldn't be around. Do you need to help him with that, too?"

"Your dad doesn't need me to help him with that, usually," I said awkwardly, feeling very, very strange to be discussing this with her. "Lash usually helps him instead of me."

"But Lash isn't here. Who will help him, if Lash doesn't?"

My nerves were raw and ragged. But I took a deep breath, and tried to be reassuring. "Your dad is good at what he does. He can handle it himself until Lash is back, which will be very soon. Now eat."

Venus's worried expression lingered, but she finished eating. After leaving her in Serena's care, I went down to the study, and logged onto the computer. There were over five hundred emails in the Solutions, Inc. inbox. I sighed, and got to work, responding to emails without enough information, answering the ones I could, forwarding the more "clean" jobs to Theoron c/o Danial's e-mail, and printing out the ones for Devlin that sounded more like his line of work.

Eight p.m. saw me only into the second hundred, and I'd gotten another fifty during the day. But I had promised myself the time to exercise, and so I shut down the computer, leaving the ten possible jobs for Dev to find on his desk in a printed pile. I met him as I was coming upstairs.

"I need to go now," he said quietly, hugging me. "But don't worry. Titus and Rip are both going with me, and we'll only be gone for an hour."

"Please be careful," I said as I hugged him.

"I will be," he said seriously. "Wait for me to eat?"

I nodded. "I left a stack of jobs on your desk."

"Thank you, I'll read through them later," he replied, as he walked off.

By the time I'd exercised, showered, and dressed, Devlin had returned. "Everything went well," he said quietly, hugging me. "No problems. But I had to meet with Tony and Thane, and they wouldn't come here, not that I really wanted them to anyway. It's done, though, and by the time I have to meet with them again, this should all be over."

"Have you heard anything about Ulysses?"

"Nothing," Devlin said with disquiet, his agitation growing. "Michael and the other Rulers know what happened to Danial, and they are keeping it quiet. It simply cannot get out that a human was able to fell a Ruler, even a newer one. They are livid that Ulysses did what he did to Danial, that he dared to do it! It is good I didn't release Diana, as they would have tortured her even as vampire, even though she told us all she knew, just to make an example of her. Ulysses has no other relatives, Sar, no one else for them to use against him. He has no trail, according to Michael; it is if he never existed! There is no way to get him to move from his lair, to show himself! But the most worrisome is that Lash and I have talked it over, and we can find no angle here! Danial's blood was worth a great deal, and I'm assuming he sold it to the same buyer he had for the werepelts. It would have brought him several million dollars, if not more.

Enough to change his name, and disappear! Which he seems to have done. But this doesn't fit with his revenge schemes! He would not have done all this for money—"

"He wants you to suffer. What else do you have to lose?"

Devlin paused and thought. "You, Venus, my niece and nephew, and Lash," he said finally. "But there is no angle—"

"There must be," I said, sitting down. "Maybe you need to ask yourself what he *thinks* you have to lose besides all of us. Maybe your fortune?"

"I am much too diversified to ever lose it, even a good portion of it, and certainly not enough to feel any pinch," Devlin said casually. "When I say my wealth is vast, Sar, I mean virtually uncountable."

Well, that was good to know. "What about your territory as Ruler of Canada? You can't defend both territories, yours and Danial's—"

"I have spoken to the other Rulers about that," Devlin said seriously. "They have agreed to put Danial's territory and mine together, as it once was five centuries ago. I will rule all of North America, as Perseus rules South America. So that cannot be the reason, Sar! I have gained territory and not lost anything!"

I shrugged my shoulders, and held him close to me, trying to comfort him. I didn't understand Ulysses' plans either. But I had a dark feeling that when both of us finally did, it would be a black day indeed.

* * * *

The next weeks passed quickly.

Most days were the same. I exercised in the mornings, played with Venus, and after lunch, I worked on e-mail. Every other day, I continued with my target practice. I spent only an hour at a time with a gun in my hand, but I knew too well that my recently improved aim had saved my life. I would not be letting that skill slide again anytime soon.

Later, on most nights, Dev, Venus and I watched a movie, or listened to music, or Devlin read us poetry, though Venus preferred by far for him to read her some of the books we had gotten her for her own, such as *Tuesday*, or *Cloudy with a Chance of Meatballs*. I sometimes made us popcorn, though not often, because it made me think of Lash by himself, and I got too melancholy to really enjoy it. But we spent time together as a family, and that was what mattered most.

After putting Venus to bed, Dev and I would usually get in the Jacuzzi for a while to get relaxed, and then go to bed, though sleep was not Devlin's only desire, as it had been for so long. Though he was recovering his stamina very slowly, his body had completely healed. That first week, he made love to me every night for as long as he could, eagerly touching my body as he murmured love poetry softly in his beautiful voice. It was soothing to me, to lose myself in his soft caresses. I enjoyed feeling his strong body against mine, his arms holding me, and his hard flesh encased in mine as he pleasured me. But I could tell even now he was a little afraid that I would leave for some reason, and so I told him finally that I would stay, at least until spring. My home was ashes, and Danial's home was no longer mine. Most everything I cared about was here, save Elle and T. It made the most sense to me, to stay.

Devlin was pleased at my decision, though still wary in those first few days. But after the first week had passed, he contented himself some nights with just holding me, or caressing me gently. I began to fall asleep most nights in his arms, instead of him in mine as it had always been before. And every night I made sure to tell him I loved him, as he lay beside me, looking into my green eyes with his golden ones. We were getting along better than we ever had before, and to say we found happiness in each other would not be a lie.

But there was sadness in spades. The worst was that Danial did not awaken as the days passed, though Devlin gave him human blood by transfusion every week at least twice, as well as a little of his own blood. He no longer looked pale, or wan. He looked as he always had when he was asleep.

"Even if he awakens, Sar, he probably won't be the same," Dev mentioned one morning, as we lay in bed spooning. "He was without a heartbeat for too long. His brain can regenerate, but I'm not sure how long it will take. He also needs older blood, and it will be a while before I can give him any more. But I am doing my best to come up with a plan to restore him to us. Trust me, Love."

I said nothing. There was nothing I could say to make myself feel any better, that the Danial we knew and loved was lost somewhere inside himself, and we couldn't bring him back.

But some things happening were noteworthy, even if they were not happy. On Wednesday, Elle and T came to visit for the first time as he had said he would. Elle was standoffish from the first, but once she saw Venus, and how beautiful my younger daughter was, she became even more withdrawn. I could see she was jealous, but I didn't see how to address it without calling her jealous. It didn't help that Venus was borne of my body, while Elle was not.

So, I got Serena to take Venus for a while, and blew off that afternoon of working, and instead spent it with Elle, walking the dogs on a very long hike with her and Titus. Once she was alone with me, and some time passed, she opened up a little. I could see she missed Danial, and that she was upset, because she'd thought I would be staying with her and Theo. I told her it wasn't her fault that I'd decided to stay with Dev, and told her again she was welcome to stay here, if she chose to. But she refused, saying that even if no one else needed her, Briar did.

"She's missing Dad," she said sadly. "She walks around his door, and cries for him, and also up in the office. And every time T comes out, I can see how upset she is, that he isn't there—"

"Bring her with you and come here to stay," I urged. "Briar can spend time with Danial, and it may do her good to see he is alive."

"No," Elle said. "I can't come and live here. You know Theo would never go for it. He didn't want me to come today. I'm all he has left, Mom."

It was in her voice that the real reason was she couldn't live here with Venus, couldn't see us together every day and think of how I now had a daughter of my own blood.

I felt awful, feeling her hurt. "I'm sorry you're caught in the middle," I stopped walking and hugged her tightly. "You always seem to be caught in the middle, Elle."

"It's okay," Elle said quietly. "And I will bring Briar on Friday, when I come again."

"You know I love you," I said, not letting her go. "You know it was love of you that led to me having Theoron with your dad, and my other children—"

"I know," Elle said, her voice wavering a bit. "T told me, one night we were talking."

We had a good rest of the walk, and when she hugged me good-bye, she almost squeezed the life out of me. But on Friday, T appeared with Briar in her cat carrier, but no Elle.

"Where is Elle?" I demanded.

Theoron shrugged, and handed me Briar. "Theo said it was too dangerous. He said he'd lost one child, he wasn't going to lose another. Elle is under house arrest, practically. She's furious."

Having a new stepmother figure probably wasn't helping. Elle remembered Tasha too well. But there was nothing I could do. Maybe Theo was right, that I was putting her in danger.

Briar was overjoyed to see Danial, and curled up next to him immediately, purring. When T went to leave, Briar refused to be captured, running from room to room to evade us, until finally T agreed to let her stay.

"Work on Theo, please?" I said, as I hugged T good-bye. "I want to see Elle."

"Mom, you know how Theo gets. He said when I tried that Elle wasn't really your daughter anyway—"

*Asshole.*

"—and that you could talk to her on the phone."

I made it a point then to call Elle every day at eight, before I had a late dinner with Venus. For a while that worked, until I began to get no answer when I called. I spoke to T about it on the eighteenth of November, and he said Theo had instructed Elle not to talk to me. I said a few nasty things in retort, and T insisted he would talk to Theo, and try to get him to change his mind. He also said Elle had written me a letter, and he would bring it with him the next time he came. I told him I would leave everything for now, but if he hadn't solved it by December first, I would be showing up in the great room on December second, whether anyone wanted me there or not. T said that was fair, and that he was sorry.

I raged to Dev about it, and he comforted me, but he said there was nothing to be done. He knew as well as I that I had no legal right to Elle, just as Danial didn't. We had never formally adopted her, when Theo was gone those years, and that was coming back to bite us in the ass now.

That wasn't all Theo was up to, of course.

A week after Theo's attempt to change me, on the twenty-first, he sent me a certified letter. Well, actually, his lawyer sent it. I opened it, expecting to have papers to sign, asking for a separation. But I got a surprise. Instead, I found a notice, telling me that on January twentieth, our divorce would be final. And Theo's wedding ring was enclosed, as was my watch.

I read the papers with shock, Devlin reading them too, over my shoulder.

"He must have gone through Danial's files," I stammered. "Danial must have saved those papers we signed, the ones I'd been going to fax to my lawyer back in late January of last year. He must have forged my signature, and bribed someone at the courthouse for this."

"It's good that he did," Devlin affirmed. "The sooner he's divorced from you, the better for you. This way, you will only have to wait another month and a week, or so. According to this, you are already legally separated."

I agreed that was probably best, though I felt a pang of regret. I'd fought so hard for Theo, so hard to stay his wife, to keep us together. I felt a twinge of guilt now that I was giving him up almost without a fight. But I'd never trust him again, and I couldn't be werecougar for him. And that was the end of it.

"You can take my name, Sar, if you wish," Devlin said in a low tone. "Or Danial's, if you prefer it to mine, though 'Dalcon' sounds much more elegant than 'Racklan'—"

I hadn't even thought of that, but realized with a start that I was going to have to think about it. And sooner, rather than later. I didn't want to be 'O'Connor' anymore, anyway. I wanted to be myself. And I already had a name, a good one.

"I'll go back to McGarran, for now," I said firmly. "I don't know why I changed my name in the first place, honestly. I didn't when I married Brennan.

In fact, I swore I never would—"

"Some of it may have been the spell," Devlin whispered. "Titus told me he had broken it, and that there might be a backlash. He had to use the Hellfire, Sar. He said nothing else would break it. That he tried everything else first."

I shivered. *Hellfire; real Hell fire. Cringe.*

"But he asked me to pass on to you that he did take Aran's memories, and Cia's, and Janice's. Aran told only Cia what had happened, according to his memories. So we still don't know who told Terian about what really happened between you and Lash."

I couldn't worry about that now. "Can we go and lie down for a while?" I said, hugging him. "I need to not think."

"I'm sure I can find a way to distract you," Devlin said with a slow enticing smile, taking me by the hand. "Come with me, my dear."

"Wait." I looked down at my finger, at Theo's ring, and the wedding band I'd worn now for a little over a year. I quietly slipped them both off my finger, and put them on the table, near Theo's wedding band. Then I took Devlin's hand again, and led him to our bedroom.

* * * *

I finally got to talk to Titus a week after getting Theo's letter. He gave me a welcoming hug, and then said without preamble, "What happened with Theo?"

"He doesn't love me anymore," I said bluntly, not wanting to discuss it. "He told me he was leaving me for Jenny, and I left. It was over quickly."

I was lying, but what else could I tell him? If I told him what had really happened, he would be livid. I knew what my mother would have done to Theo. My demon father figure would probably do worse, and that was saying something.

"Good," Titus replied, obviously relieved. "I asked Terian to be on call, in case you needed him. I thought there might be…well, never mind. I'm sorry to hear you are splitting up, but glad to hear that it was amicable, or as amicable as such things can be."

I hugged him, then changed the topic to something else. There was no point going over that night ever again.

In the following weeks, I did finally notice a few positive changes.

Elle once again took my phone calls. She'd written me two letters every week, but it was good to hear her voice again, even if I still couldn't see her.

I was losing weight. I could fit into my tight jeans again. Just barely, it was true, but still, I hadn't been able to do that for almost a year. And my jeans that were supposed to be loose were loose. I was very pleased, and kept exercising.

But I had a little chocolate here and there, too. Devlin saw to that, with his Godiva gift baskets, and the occasional chocolate body paint.

I was spending more time with Venus, and things with Dev were still going well, too. We hadn't fought since the night of Diana's deflowering, which was probably some kind of record for us. With work on both of our parts, his stamina was still increasing, just as his sensitivity was decreasing. I was pleased, but hoped it would take a while to return, though I didn't tell him that. I was afraid with his prowess returning, some of his rampant desire would also emerge again. And I was happier with him being only "a few times a week" sort of man now.

I had long ago caught up on the email-work, and was also taking care of some of the return calling for the voicemail system. True to T's word, the caseload had decreased a bit, though not by much. But I could keep up with this level of business, if I worked most weekday mornings. I liked getting a paycheck, even if I went nowhere to spend it, and Devlin insisted on paying for everything I ordered online, like food, pet medications, clothes for Venus, and yes, even the new Vampire Hunter D book that had come out in late November. Some of the steady business of Solutions, Inc. was Theoron being a lot like his father, being unable to pass up interesting work, or work that was lucrative, as most jobs that came in usually were. But most was because Terian wanted his own share of the business now.

T had mentioned on one of his visits that Theo, he, and Tears had discussed making him a partner too, though Theoron said he wanted to wait a few more months to make sure that Terian still wanted the same thing after Sundown had her baby. "But I think he's going to," T finished, a pleased note in his voice. "And I'm happy to have him on board. He's helped so much this fall. We wouldn't have made it, without him."

I was happy for Terian too, but happier still for T. He seemed okay now, like his old self, despite being thrust into his father's role at such an early age. He was an adult now, and looked so like Danial I found it hard to look at him sometimes. He still visited with his father once a week, but he wasn't mourning anymore, and Serena seemed to be happy with his attentions. I didn't know what to feel about that, but decided since they were both happy, it wasn't my business.

Best of all, Titus teleported my parents to Hayden in secret finally to see Venus on December first. My parents didn't believe at first she was my daughter, but my mom was overjoyed to have another granddaughter to spoil. Venus was her normally perfectly charming self. Devlin, too, was on his best behavior, though my mother refused to talk to him, or look at him. But I'd told him to expect that, and he bore it in silence, if with his jaw clenched, and his eyes tinted red.

My mother and I had a side chat about Theo, when I showed her where the ladies room was. And it was there, in my sewing room, she told me that Theo had been by with Elle and Jenny, and that she had seen at once that they had something going on.

"I'm sorry," my mother said, hugging me. "I didn't want to tell you in a letter—"

Anger at Theo flared briefly, then I let it go. "When was this?"

"Three days after the funeral," she said quietly. "They have come every week ever since then with Elle, and sometimes Theoron—"

"You must be the only one besides me who still calls him that."

"That's his name, and I refuse to call him T. Theoron is a beautiful name, a fine name—"

I stifled a laugh. *Like mother like daughter.*

"—anyway, they came to our house for Thanksgiving, too. I haven't said all the things I wanted to say to either of them, because I wanted to see Elle, and you wrote about how you weren't seeing her—"

"Is she all right? How does she look?"

"Sad, a little withdrawn, and a little too old for a teenager," my mom said with authority. "But some of that was the way she was dressed. You know what these young girls wear nowadays, almost nothing. I could see her bra straps."

I nodded, trying to hide my smile.

"But she was in good spirits, despite everything," my mother said, oblivious. "Though she doesn't seem to like Jenny at all."

That made me feel better, and then bad, because I didn't want Elle to be unhappy. Then I realized my mother was saying it in part to make me feel better, and most likely it wasn't as bad as all that. "It's okay, if she likes her," I said, wiping away a tear. "She's cougar, like Elle. And it will be good for her to talk to another female, especially as she'll be going off to find a mate in a few years."

My mother nodded, but she said nothing, her eyes worried as she hugged me.

\* \* \* \*

Finally, on the week before Lash was set to be released, things seem to take a turn for the worse again.

Sundown was attacked in broad daylight, and it was only Terian teleporting her to safety that saved her from being taken. It was obvious she'd been mistaken for me, and that it was Ulysses. It hadn't helped that a pair of werebears had tried for her, and that Terian had said they weren't real bears, but "amateur sorcerers of low standing, and little knowledge," who were wearing the skins they had taken from Devlin's men. With his magic, he had killed them both, and taken the skins, returning them to Titus. I'd wondered if one had been Nick's, but wasn't sure, and didn't know how to ask without seeming insensitive. But one I discovered later was Klara's, the werebear Nick had been seeing on the side. And the inevitable thing happened.

Titus let slip somehow in front of Serena, or within her hearing about Klara, and that she had been the reason Nick had gone to town that day. I could hear her screaming at him in her room later that night, and when he emerged, he slammed out of Hayden in a rage.

I heard her quietly crying in her room, but I didn't go to her. I'd felt guilty all along for saying nothing, but I couldn't bring myself to tell her, especially as it seemed in those past weeks that she was over Nick, and maybe falling for T, though I knew she still saw Nick and the other bears as she had all along. Instead, I finished off the rest of the Godiva basket Devlin had sent me in guilt-induced binge. It wasn't a lot of calories, as I'd let Venus eat a lot of it too, but it was a lot for me to eat after dieting for so long, and it made me a little sick. The chocolate tasted like ashes, not good as it should've, because I felt so bad about not telling her about Nick and Klara, no matter what Dev and my reasoning had told me to do.

I continued target practicing every other day, and made it a habit to practice with not only my .38, but my new explosive bullets gun as well. I hated to waste the time, but I also didn't want to be a bad shot if Ulysses somehow found a way to get to me. And no matter what, I was getting to the point where I needed to get outside for a while. I'd been under house arrest for almost a month now, and even long walks outside with the dogs couldn't cut it. Darkness was also lame again one morning after a long walk, and though I worried about her, it cleared up as before in a few days, and I put it off as a strained muscle.

There was still no change with Danial. I visited him every day for a while, but the stillness of him unnerved me, and I took to reading my book when I sat with him for an hour or so every other day. I tried to talk to him too, but didn't know what to say. And he never responded, or moved. There was only his shallow breathing to show he was alive, and a very, very slow heartbeat.

But perhaps the worst thing was finding out that Ulysses had not sold Danial's blood, as we had suspected. Devlin came home on Wednesday night pale as snow, his eyes traumatized. I hugged him, and asked him what was the matter. He said Ulysses had finally played his hand. He'd showed up at one of Devlin's meetings, but he hadn't been the Ulysses Devlin had previously known. He'd drunk Danial's blood, and was now a vampire himself, and not a young weak vampire, but young powerful vampire.

"This changes things," Devlin said quietly. "While he is not a Ruler, he isn't persona non gratis anymore either. If he gives a pledge to one of the other Rulers, he'll be accepted as a vampire living in their territory. And I won't be able to touch him, at least above the law."

"But won't they want revenge for Danial?"

"They'll get his pledge, wait till he relaxes in a few years, and then drain him dry," Devlin said resolutely. "For the most part, I don't allow any vampire over a few hundred years to live in my territories, Sar. This country is young, so it's not a problem. There are many older Vampires in the Far East, in South America, and in Europe. But Samuel and Perseus are both older than I, almost eight hundred, I think. Michael, he's younger than I am, and I don't know what he does to keep control from slipping out of his hands. But you need to have at least a century on the most powerful you are Ruling, or you lose your edge on them. And then you get dethroned, which usually means you die."

"So what are you going to do?"

"Wait until he challenges me," Devlin said easily. "That is all *I* can do anyway, according to vampire law. And it must be that is what he's after. If he beats me, the others would have to accept him as Ruler. And by vampire law, everything I have would be his to dispense with. My wealth, my blood, my life."

"That's the angle," I whispered.

He nodded, hugging me. "Don't worry," he said in a consoling voice, a devious look in his shining eyes. "I intend to crush the son of a bitch before he learns to run on his new supernatural feet. Lash is going to be out in a few days, and his first order of business will be dealing with Ulysses. He is now subject to the same weaknesses I am: he can no longer move about in the day and he'll need blood and shelter from the sun. We have the two skins back, so that's less resources he has to work with. And he has lost men. He'll also need to rest up for a week at least, if not two to get control of his altered body. So we have a little while to plan."

I was not prepared for what he said next.

"I want you to pick Lash up at the prison, Sar. Teleport close to there. He'll be waiting for you outside, near the doors. After he gets in the car, drive to a park, and give him his weapons. Bring him back here by teleportation after, and say nothing to him."

I looked at him. "Why me?"

"He'll be calmed by you, because you're female," Devlin said quietly. "He might fight one of the men, or Titus, even T. And I can't go in the day, but there is no way I'm leaving him there one more minute than he has to be there.

Call if there are any problems, and don't stop anywhere, to or from." He hugged me close. "But remember, I don't want you to be with him. I doubt he will make any moves on you when you first see him, but I wanted to say it now. Remember, he is with Gina. And you are only to be with me while you are living here under my roof, unless you Oath to me."

"Okay, Dev." What else could I say? I'd counted the days until Lash would be back, but the truth was he'd moved on, after I'd rejected him. And I'd wanted Lash to be with Gina, to have someone of his own. He seemed to be happy with her. I couldn't say I was free now, and why didn't he dump her. That wasn't fair to him or her, much as I might want that. And it was probably what was best for him, not to be involved with me again.

* * * *

I was hesitant as I drove into the parking lot of the police station. But this is where Devlin had said Lash would be waiting for me to pick him up. I was also nervous. It had been almost six weeks since I'd seen Lash, since I'd heard his voice.

*What will he say to me? What will I say to him?*

I looked at the entrance, saw him there, waiting beside the doors, and did a double take to see him smoking a cigarette.

Lash had never smoked to my knowledge. He'd never smelled of cigarette smoke, either.

I watched him, feeling disgruntled. I'd hoped for some kind of big reunion scene, even after Devlin's speech asking me not to touch Lash. How old was I, thinking this was a movie? *Should I call him Trystan, or Lash? And why am I so fucking nervous?*

I pulled up near him, causing Lash to raise his head. He put out his cigarette in the sand receptacle, then tossed the rest of it in the garbage. Then he was sliding into the car beside me, but he didn't look at me. I didn't speak, remembering Dev's instructions. I took him to a local park that was a few streets over, and parked, though I didn't shut off the truck. I handed him his weapons: the whip, then the knife, then the gun. Lash put them on one by one, and then seemed to relax a touch. "Please, drive me home, Sar," he said softly, looking out the window.

I nodded, and drove him back to Hayden. Lash went immediately up to his room, and stayed there for the next hour. Per Devlin's instructions, I'd purchased ten small fish from a supply store earlier that week, and put them live in a large tank of water on the floor of Lash's room. I apologized to them for what was surely going to happen to them, but I told them it would be fast, and there were worse deaths. It wasn't really reassuring to me, but at least

Devlin hadn't asked for rabbits, or mice.

Lash came down later, and paused in the doorway, studying me. After so much time apart from him, it was odd to feel him watching me again.

"What is it?" I asked, looking up at him from my sewing. "Were the fish okay? I wasn't sure what kind you liked best, so I got trout—"

"They were good, Sar," Lash said in a raspy voice. "Thanks for getting them for me. I had to change badly. It was a relief to be snake again."

"How often do you need to change?" It was hard for me to believe I'd known him so long, and never asked him that. But how much did I know about him really? For all we'd talked, he'd rarely talked about himself. I knew a lot about his tastes in movies and books, but not too much else. Killer, assassin, weresnake, part Spanish, had once eaten people, was born back around 1900-something in Florida, had once—well, now twice—been in jail, worked construction in his youth, loved sex/good in bed, and liked to hide his emotions. That about summed it up. Oh, and seemed to still want to get in my pants, maybe.

"I like to do it every week or so," Lash said, looking at me with interest. "I can't do it too much more than that, because I can't guard Dev as well as a snake as I can as human."

I got up and went over to him, touching his arm gently. "Would you like me to make you something to eat? Eggs? Bacon? Pasta?"

Lash reached out for me in a deft movement, pulling me close and embracing me tightly.

"Lash—" I began hesitantly.

"Shh," he hissed. "Don't talk. Let me hold you, and breathe in the scent of you, Sar."

I hugged him to me, going silent. He held me for about ten minutes, breathing deeply, his arms tight around me. But it wasn't a sexual hug. It was a hug of recovering something that he'd been apart from for a long time that he cared for, something that had been lost but was now found.

I realized abruptly why he seemed to look so rough to me. Something was pricking my cheek, where it rested against his face. I looked up in shock to see Lash's lower face was dark with stubble, around his chin, and his upper lip. I gaped at him.

"Has it really been that long since you've seen a man close up?" he said, grinning widely. "I have something else to show you then, little girl."

"Why didn't you have stubble, those days we were together?" I asked, unable to restrain my smile.

"I shaved," Lash said, quietly giving me a faint smile, mirth in his eyes. "Surely you've seen a man shave before?"

"But Theo never had any—"

"I can't say why he didn't," Lash said flatly, his expression turning angry almost immediately. "It might be that he wasn't born were. But it's true that for most weres, no matter which animal, that our human hair grows very slowly, almost like an animal's. I only need to cut my hair every three months or so. It grows only an inch in about that time. It's the only thing that doesn't regenerate on us easily. And my facial hair grows just as slow."

That hadn't been true for Theo. His hair grew as fast as mine did.

"But I've never seen any of the foxes with beards, or anything," I said, disbelief still strong in my voice. "Everyone's always been clean-shaven, always. Frankly, I didn't think weres could grow facial hair for some reason."

Lash seemed to shake himself a little, and his next words were missing an angry tone. "It's true that most weres don't like facial hair," he said thoughtfully. "Vince once said it like this: if you can be covered with fur as an animal, when you are human, you want to feel human. That means smooth, bare skin."

"Why are you suddenly growing a...beard, a guess?" I didn't see sideburns, but maybe they would take longer?

"Just a goatee," Lash said, laughing. "And a short moustache. I'm not going for the mountain man look."

I just looked at him, still trying to get my mind around the concept. This was going to take some getting used to.

"For a change," Lash said, laughing a little at my expression. "Devlin said he was going to do it, too, though he can easily go back and forth, when he renews his body with blood. And it seemed like a good idea, in jail. I didn't want to be too pretty in there."

"It'll take some getting used to," I teased. "But it suits you."

"I'm also tired of looking so young," Lash said, and his face broke into a grin. "God, I'd never have thought I'd hear myself say those words again! But it's true. Some of the clients I met when I first got back from Florida didn't believe I was the 'real' Lash. This might help add a few years onto my face."

It was true that he looked rougher, even with just the 1/3 of an inch of growth on his face. But he was still handsome, and he still looked only about twenty-five, if that.

"Do you not like it?" he said, rubbing his cheek gently on mine. "Am I too scratchy?"

"It looks good on you," I said softly, rubbing him back. "I'm just glad you're back."

"I'm glad to be back," he said, locking his dark eyes on mine. "And glad to see you."

He looked into my eyes, and I knew he was going to kiss me, just as I knew I wasn't going to stop him.

# Chapter Four

We heard a throat clear. Lash and I looked over to see Devlin standing in the doorway.

Devlin moved past me to Lash, gripping his upper arm. "I'm glad you're b—"

Lash reached out and hugged Devlin close to him, much as he had hugged me. Devlin hugged him back hard, so hard that Lash let out a uncomfortable hiss.

Devlin let him go after a minute had passed, and stepped back. "I'm glad to have you back," he said, his voice emotional. "These past few weeks have been hell."

"I'm sorry about Danial." There was real regret in Lash's voice, and a trace of guilt.

Devlin nodded, his golden eyes serious. "So am I. But we all warned him, Lash."

"So we did," Lash said in a cold tone. He didn't look at me, his eyes focused on Devlin.

"We need to talk. Sar, will you excuse us?" Devlin said, his eyes locked on Lash.

"Sure. Lash, I made you some cookies. They're on the counter, help yourself."

Devlin rolled his eyes, but Lash shot me a happy look, and then he shut the door behind them.

Leaving them to work out whatever was going on between them, I went back to my sewing, intending to work for another hour on my quilt. I'd gotten the rows sewed together, and was almost done pinning the whole front onto the batting and back of the quilt. Now for the hard part: sewing each square down to anchor it. It would've been quicker if I'd used batting the sewing machine could sew through, but I wanted this to be both a meaningful gift, and also a warm one. It was simply true that a quilt made with regular batting that a machine could sew wouldn't be very warm, unless I used polar fleece squares. But sewing it by hand one square at a time was going to be a huge undertaking, and I couldn't face the daunting task of beginning that this afternoon. Tomorrow would be soon enough.

I finished up the pinning, and began thinking to myself as I tidied up my sewing room. It was early afternoon. Maybe Lash could be convinced to join me for dinner. I should also go find out where Venus was too, and check on her. I was worried, if I lost track of her for longer than a few hours, even knowing Serena, Rip, or Titus was with her twenty-four-seven, and she wasn't allowed outside at all.

I checked the ballroom first, and sure enough, Serena was there playing with Venus.

"She's winning at 'Dark Tower'," Serena said with a smile, and Venus preened happily. She looked so much like her father I had to laugh. Seeing how happy she was, I was glad I'd helped Theoron go through the toys and books that Elle and he no longer needed back in the late summer. At the time, I'd needed a diversion from my last days of pregnancy. And I'd thought to save them for Devon.

But Devon wouldn't be using any of them now. Devon was dead.

I wiped away my instant tears, and told myself to think about the child I still had alive, who needed me. I went over and sat down beside her. "You want some dinner?" I said, giving her a kiss. "Are you hungry?"

"I'm not stopping now," she said loftily. "I'm winning!"

I cut my eyes to Serena, hiding my smile.

"We ate already," Serena said gently. "T brought us some takeout when he saw me earlier, and he got extra for her. I tried some first, to make sure it was safe for her to eat."

I wasn't sure what to say to that, knowing what she was referring to by saying T had come to see her, so I just gave her a smile, and said thanks. By the looks of the game, Serena would be here another two hours at least. I kissed Venus again, and told Serena that I was going to get some dinner, and to come find me if she needed to take a break.

"I'm okay. Better than okay," Serena said, and there was a note in her voice I wasn't familiar with. *Is she getting over Nick finally, and falling for T?* I didn't want to ask. I just smiled, and went back the way I'd come, past my sewing room. I stopped when I noticed that a light was still on inside, then gave a sigh of self-recrimination. As usual, I'd shut off the overhead light, and forgotten the smaller light by the door. I shut off the light, and closed the door behind me, and walked to the kitchen. But no one was there.

I was a little hungry, but I didn't really want to eat alone. I'd go see if I could find Lash, or even Dev. Dev wouldn't eat with me, but he'd kept me company a lot these last weeks while I ate. And sometimes he'd gotten some more of those spells from Titus so he could join me for a little nibble of whatever I was eating.

I walked upstairs, because I heard faint music. Rip was standing before Lash's door. I looked at him oddly, as it looked like he was guarding it.

"Hi, Sarelle," Rip rumbled.

"Is Lash in there?" I said, and he nodded. Then he moved aside.

I deduced that Lash must be alone, and not with a woman, because otherwise he wouldn't have let me in. I went in, and was enveloped in smoke. And it wasn't cigarette smoke.

Lash was in bed, on top of the covers, lying with a T shirt on, and his jeans, smoking a joint. His weapons were beside the bed, within reach. I looked over at him, but he took no notice of me. He must have been stoned; there was enough smoke here to make my eyes water. Tom Petty's "You Don't Know How It Feels" was playing on a state of the art stereo system. Lash had set it to repeat, and as I came in the song finished, and started again. Lash took another drag, and looked over at me.

"What do you want?" he asked tersely, blowing out a smoke ring.

I wanted to know if he smoked and did drugs regularly, because I was so shocked to see him like this, but I didn't have time to say anything before he read my face.

"The last time I smoked pot was 1969," Lash said, his voice ill-tempered, taking another drag. "I just got out of jail, and my best friend, his lover, and my niece are still being hunted by the maniac who put me there, who is also now a powerful vampire. I am having some downtime tonight to relax, and I don't want to hear any shit about it, Sar."

Well, when he put it like that, what could I say? "Drugs are bad"? I went over and sat next to him on the bed. "I wanted to see if you're hungry, if you wanted to eat dinner with me."

Lash looked over at me, and his expression changed to one of mild affection. "In a little," he said with detachment. "That would be nice. For a while I want to not feel anything, for it to be quiet and peaceful."

I didn't see how it could be quiet with Petty singing loud enough to almost drown out our words, but maybe that was just me.

Lash's bathroom door opened, and I saw Devlin come out with some more joints, about ten. He'd been in there rolling them. To say I couldn't believe it was too weak. He might as well have come out with a tutu on. I gave him an appalled look too, which he took wrongly, of course.

"Sar, I need to smoke a lot to feel even the least effect," Devlin said patiently, putting down the tray. "Now if you would smoke a little, and let me drink your blood, I could feel the effects much easier—"

I rolled my eyes at him, and he grinned. He handed a joint to Lash, and Lash lit it off the end of his. Devlin took a long drag, and lay back beside Lash on the bed, sighing. I wasn't sure what to do, so I sat there, watching them smoke.

"Put on 'It's Good to Be King'," Devlin said absently. "Sar does give a damn, and you know it."

Lash shot a nasty look at him, but he got up, and changed the CD track. Soon, the other song was playing and repeating. I sat there for a moment, and realized I was getting high just sitting there, from all the smoke.

"Want some?" Devlin offered. "We don't do this often, Sar. Like Lash said, every thirty years or so. Or after being held captive somewhere. Neither of us likes being caged."

"Fucking-A," Lash said, taking another hit.

"I can't," I said, looking over at him. "I'll cough. But thanks."

"The age you are, you tried this before, unless you were a narc," Lash said, looking at me searchingly. "Are you going to lie and say you didn't inhale?"

I laughed a little, and got a rush from the smoke I was drawing in. But a lot of that was because of the lack of oxygen in the room, or so I told myself. "I inhaled a little," I said, giving him a smile. "But it never did anything for me, really. I didn't see the point. I get a better rush from allergy decongestant, frankly."

"So you just didn't like it," Lash said, studying me. "Interesting."

"Uninteresting," Devlin said languidly, taking another long drag. "I liked the nineteen-sixties better, when everyone did drugs, and I could enjoy them easily, with so many women offering free love—"

"Now I know why you're so temperamental," I joked. "Too many acid trips."

Devlin laughed, and I knew he had to be a little high, that he wasn't irritated. But who knew how many he'd smoked before I came in?

"You forget how old we are," Lash said absently. "I remember when cigarettes were first introduced. They were the cure all for everything, made you concentrate better, made you relax, made you sexy, made you healthy. Everyone had one in their hand for years, in the movies, everyone—"

"Drugs were thought of the same way, in the early sixties," Devlin said, nostalgia in his voice. "Men have always used them, for religious ceremonies though time. It's only recently that everyone says they are bad."

"It's the use of them when people are driving—" I began carefully.

"Sar, either smoke with us or get out," Lash said, taking another drag.

"You're detracting from my good time."

*Prick.* But it was true they weren't hurting anyone except themselves...

"Come lay by me, Sar," Devlin said gently. "Lash is right, he needs us not to talk, to relax. And I don't want you to leave really, and neither does he."

I debated leaving, but decided I wanted to stay. I wanted company. "Not a word about this to Theoron or Elle," I said, crawling over to lay beside Devlin, who put his arm around me. Neither of them answered me, but I didn't expect them to.

I lay there for a while, none of us saying anything. Then I fell asleep.

When I woke up, nothing had changed. Lash and Devlin were still smoking, but the pile of joints had diminished considerably. I looked at my watch, and saw it was only about seven. I'd only been out for thirty minutes or so. But I was feeling some effects now, from breathing in the smoke.

Devlin finished his joint, and turned to me, pulling me close. "My sweet little queen," he crooned. "Let me have just a little."

I knew I wasn't getting out of this room with all the blood I'd come in with no matter what, so I tilted my head, baring my neck to him. I was thankful for the drug now. It would dull the pain a little.

Devlin sank his fangs into me, and began groaning almost immediately, his body moving against mine. He held me passionately against him, his hands running over my body, caressing me as he swallowed me down. He stopped drinking from me in a few seconds, and in a moment, he had healed me. With a low long moan, he rolled over on his back.

I looked over at him, watching him. Devlin seemed to be utterly happy. He lay there, his lips parted, his eyes closed, sighing over and over, his body moving very slowly, stretching and contracting languorously. I looked over Devlin's form to Lash, locking eyes with him.

"You did him in now," Lash said, smiling widely. "He's feeling ten times the effects I am, getting it through your blood."

The way he said it, I wondered if he wanted some of my blood. But I was still irritated with him over the remark about ruining his good time, and so I didn't offer.

"Good," I said, reaching out to touch Devlin tenderly. "He's been through hell with you and me, and Danial and everything else these last few weeks. He deserves to have a break from the pain of losing so much."

Lash finished his joint, and I was surprised to see it was the next to last one. Either he smoked fast, or I was higher than I thought I was, to have lost time and not realized it. He lit the last one, and took a drag. "I'm surprised you aren't saying he brought it on himself," Lash said, not looking at me. "Or that I did. That I deserved to be in jail, for all the people I'd killed."

I knew his question wasn't offhand, as it appeared. He wanted to know if I judged him for what he did.

"I know you've looked through the files, and seen some of what I've done. Even though there is nothing in there about what was done, I'm sure you can guess what 'demolition' really means—"

"Yes," I said as fast as I could, not wanting to hear any details.

"I have two to do this week," Lash said in a too-casual voice, still not looking at me. "How does it make you feel, knowing that about me?"

"How does it make you feel, doing it?" I said back to him in that same too-casual voice, wishing he'd just cut the bullshit.

"I don't feel one way or the other about it. It's just a job, one I have a lot of skill with," Lash said with a sigh. "This is what I do, Sar, who I am. Who I've been. And who I need to be."

The silence stretched. Was he looking for my approval? What did he want me to say?

"Maybe neither of you should've done some of what you did in your lives," I said finally. "But I care about you both, and knowing what you and he do, and have done in the past doesn't change that. It gives me pain to see Devlin crying over Danial, and to see you like I did, handcuffed, being held against your will behind glass and iron bars."

Lash didn't look at me. "That's why I didn't want you to come back," he said, taking a drag. "But Gina gave me the cookies, and meat dishes you cooked, when she came to see me every day—"

Was this a dig at me, telling me he'd had her every day? I'd ignore it.

"—I wanted to thank you for that," Lash said quietly, his eyes still averted. "It was nice of you. It meant a lot, that you bothered to do it."

"You're welcome."

Lash looked over at me finally, considered something, and offered me the joint.

"No thanks," I said, giving him a smile. "I'm high enough already."

Lash leaned over Devlin and studied me. "You aren't that high," he said flatly, laying back. "But I need it more than you, so I'm glad not to share it."

I thought about telling him to smoke something stronger, to improve his personality, but decided it was not a good idea to push him in his current mood. Devlin was still sighing beside me, and moaning. I decided then and there I'd had enough. I got up very slowly, drawing Lash's attention again. "I'm going to get something to eat. I'm starting to feel dizzy in here. Do you want me to make extra, so there's some for you?"

"Whatever is easiest," Lash said, looking back up at the ceiling. "Don't put yourself out for me. You've done that enough."

I nodded and left. *Wouldn't want to do that, no sir.*

Rip was still outside the door standing guard, and he reached out to steady me a little as I exited. He also shut the door behind me, as I was having trouble gripping the knob. "Sarelle, maybe you should stand here for a bit?" he rumbled, his voice a little concerned.

"I'm going to go shower, and eat something," I managed to reply. "Are you going to be here? Devlin's wasted."

Rip nodded. "I have instructions to watch the door until they both are done, and able to walk."

Devlin, always thinking of everything. Or was that Danial? I couldn't remember. "What's the story with your name?" I said bluntly, looking up at Rip with my squinting, watering eyes.

Rip looked at me and laughed. "Rip is for 'Rest In Peace.' Titus and I were summoned…well, got out of Hell about seven hundred years ago. I was only out for a few days, and got sent back by a Catholic priest who told me I was going to burn in Hell. Like I hadn't been burning for the last three hundred years? Demons can't BE burned, we're already flame temperature naturally—"

*This is interesting.* I tried to concentrate.

"—so, that seemed to set up some kind of pattern. Titus has been out for the last seven hundred years. He's never been sent back to Hell once, not ever. But I've been sent back almost every decade at least. And I hate it, that my little brother's always bailing me out. But I'm glad he does, because Hell sucks. And I'm glad that he's been out this whole time, and not had to go back—"

"What the hell does this have to do with your nickname?" I said bluntly.

Rip looked at me and laughed. "Because when a priest says the banishing spell, or when a demon hunter catches you in a pentagram, or any faith based religion is used to send me back to Hell, the rite always ends with 'Rest in Peace.' And even when it doesn't, these righteous assholes always feel compelled to say it to me, as if they are killing me. I'm a demon, I don't fucking die! And as if anyone ever rests peacefully in Hell who is dead anyway—"

I didn't like where this was heading. I didn't want to think about Hell, as sometimes lately I thought I might end up there. But the thought instantly gave my fogged mine clarity, something I was grateful for. "Thanks for telling me. And for protecting my family."

"I'm sorry I didn't do a better job," Rip said, a single tear slipping down his face to evaporate on his skin before it fell. "Danial's still unconscious."

I put my hand on his arm, and was instantly sweating. "It was his fault too, for insisting on going to his meetings. You gave your earthly body trying to save him. What more could you do?"

"Nothing," Rip admitted. "I did everything I could. But I still wish it hadn't ended as it had."

"Theoron is okay, he's all healed, and running his father's business with Terian and—"

"I'm sorry," Rip interrupted. "I heard about that, too."

"Thanks," I said, and pulled back from him, my hair was plastered to my forehead. Rip had a lot less control over his body temperature than his brother had, or so it seemed. But it would be impolite to mention it.

"Sorry about that," Rip said, eyeing me. "Go have a nice shower in one of the guest rooms. I'll stay here and watch."

The shower did wonders for me, but only increased my hunger. I went downstairs, and fixed a box of pasta, putting in two pounds of hamburger with the sauce. I was just fishing out the noodles to see if they were done when Lash appeared. He came in and peered into the pots.

"Pasta?" he said hopefully. I nodded.

He grabbed two plates, and I doled it out, giving him the larger share as I always had to Theo. Lash covered his with sauce, took his dish into the living room, and didn't return.

I was a little taken aback, but I figured he'd needed some time alone. He'd had to eat with people for every meal for the last month and a half. I'd want to eat alone, too, if I were him.

I ate alone at the kitchen table, reading the latest Vampire Hunter D book. I had agreed to Dev's request to read these books only here in kitchen, and to keep them out of our bedroom. But there was no way I was going to stop reading the series. I enjoyed it way too much.

I finished dinner, hid the book in the lower kitchen cabinet, and went to find Lash. He was watching *A Nightmare on Elm St., Part I*. He saw me as I lingered in the doorway for a few moments, but ignored me. I decided he needed a little space, so I just gathered up his dirty dishes from the dining room table, and went to find Venus. She was just coming back from the ballroom with Serena. Actually, Serena was carrying her, as V was sleeping.

"She won, finally," Serena said tiredly, handing me Venus. "I was just coming to find you. Where's Devlin?"

"Lash got home today," I said softly. "They were spending time together."

Serena nodded. "I have to get to bed," she said happily. "T is stopping by early for breakfast tomorrow."

I was a little worried to see him spending so much time with her. I liked Serena a lot, but T was too young to settle down. I didn't want him hurting her, after she'd just been hurt by Nick, if he wasn't serious about her. Which collectively meant I'd have to talk to him. *Sigh.*

"I'll put her to bed," I said, giving her a forced smile. "Get going."

She gave me a radiant smile, darting off in the direction of her room.

I walked though the living room to get upstairs, but Lash took no notice of me again, or at least appeared not to. I carried Venus upstairs, and took off her clothes, dressing her in her nightgown. Then I tucked her in, making sure the blanket was covering her.

"Have good dreams," I whispered. "You're safe. I love you."

I closed her door, and went into Devlin's bedroom. Devlin was lying on the bed, still smelling of smoke, passed out asleep. I debated trying to get his clothes off, and him into bed, but decided against it. I put a nightgown on myself, folding up the clothes I'd worn only an hour or so to wear again tomorrow. I crawled in bed, and lay down. Even with the napping earlier, I was tired.

I thought as I lay there that some of that was because I felt like I could relax now. Lash was home, and I felt truly safe for the first time in a month and a half, knowing he was here. I fell asleep, and dreamed no dreams.

When I woke up, Devlin was missing, but I heard the shower running, and figured he was in there. He came out as I was getting dressed, and gave me a kiss. "Good afternoon," he said pleasantly.

My gaze shot to the clock. *Shit!* It was nearly two! Venus needed me! I made to bolt for the kitchen, but Dev grabbed hold of me.

"Relax," he said, his golden eyes concerned. "You needed to sleep, so Lash fed your dogs, and Serena fed the cats. She's with Venus, I heard them in the kitchen a little while ago, having lunch."

I took a deep breath, trying to force myself to calm down.

Devlin sat me down on the bed, then sat beside me. "Sar, Lash is going to be a little different for a while, until he gets used to being home again. Don't be surprised if he's distant, or cold, or even angry. He'll be how he was, after some time had passed. Jail fucked him up a little."

*Had something happened to him in prison? Had he had to kill someone inside in self-defense?* "Okay."

"Now come and eat something," Devlin said, helping me to my feet. "Then if you like, I'll help you cut out some more doll clothes for Venus. She told me this morning she wants some 'adventure doll clothes', whatever that means."

"Clothes out of scraps of fur, and fake fur," I explained, laughing a little too exuberantly in my relief to change the topic of conversation. "You're going to cut out doll clothes for me? Don't you have arrangements to make? Lash mentioned his jobs."

Devlin gave me an irritated glance. "They can wait another day. And why not? I can cut out doll clothes as well as you can."

"Sorry, I just didn't think you'd stoop to it," I said without thinking, then saw the anger build in his eyes almost immediately. "I'm sorry," I said quickly. "I just meant that you're the four hundred plus Vampire King of the whole North American continent now, and you're saying you are going to be spending the rest of the day cutting out doll clothes. It's just...surprising."

"I'm a father now also, and that's the more important job to me," Devlin said, still irritated. "I do the other now only to make sure you and Venus are protected. But my child is my first priority, always, and you, as her mother, are right after her. Surely, you, the mother of my only child, know this? Have I not always protected her, and you? Have I ever set anything above you, either of you?"

I looked at him and for a long moment, I couldn't say anything. Then I was bawling, and Devlin was holding me, asking in a worried voice what was wrong, that he was sorry, what had he said, to please stop crying.

"I'm the one who is sorry," I said in a choked voice, holding him tightly. "I always give you too little credit, when you have been perhaps the best father of any I've known."

Devlin looked at me in disbelief. "Danial was better."

"He was not," I said, looking up at him a little sadly. "He never went on any kind of vacation from his job, much as he stayed home to be around when I was pregnant. He always made time for Elle and me, but his job was always equal in importance to him, even after I had Theoron. He would never have blown off a day of meetings to cut out doll clothes. Never." I took a breath, then continued. "I'm not saying I was a better parent than he was. I was there for Elle, but not as much, after we moved in with him—"

"Hush," Devlin said, hugging me. "It doesn't matter."

"It does matter!" I said loudly, putting some distance between us so he'd listen to my words. "It matters that you know I was wrong, that day I said you'd make a bad father. You've made a good one, a very good one, and I'm very glad to have had Venus with you, despite that I didn't want to share that with you at first—"

"Stop," Devlin said emotionally. "You'll have me crying again, and Lash was already giving me shit yesterday, about how men are supposed to be strong, they aren't supposed to be crying all the time."

"Tell him to go fuck himself," I said vehemently, giving him a kiss. "I love you, and it's okay if you cry, especially if you're doing it because of love."

"I am doing it from love," Devlin said affectionately, tenderly kissing my face, my neck, and my shoulders. "I love you. I love how passionate you are, how you feel everything so deeply, just as I do."

Devlin kissed me, and then he was stripping off his towel, and sliding my nightgown off too.

"Shouldn't we be getting downstairs to V—"

"I'm a man too, as well as a father," Dev said seductively. "And it matters that you know how much I love you, how happy I've been with you here with me these past weeks, living at Hayden. And I can think of only one way to best show you the depth of my emotion for you." Devlin brushed me with his fangs, trailing them up my bare shoulder as he kissed me, and I sighed, surrendering to him.

\* \* \* \*

The next week passed slowly. Devlin was as loving as he had been before, but Lash was as cool and distant as he'd been before we'd become friends. He avoided me for the most part, though I still made him extra of my dinner every night, except when I had soup, which he didn't like for some reason. *Maybe they'd given him a lot of soup in prison?*

Sometimes I would watch TV with him, but we didn't talk, and he always stayed on his side of the couch, not touching. I was beginning to think I'd imagined his comments to me when I'd first gotten home, when he'd held me. Why was he being so distant now? I had thought it was the drug at first, that afternoon he'd been cold to me. But though he smoked still, or at least his clothes smelled of the smoke, it was always cigarette smoke he smelled of now, not pot. But there was another reason I thought he might have distanced himself from me: he had a lover of his own again, one that was weresnake like him. For Lash had had a visitor the very next day after the pot-smoking episode.

I had been in the kitchen eating a very late breakfast/very early dinner when I heard the doorbell ring. Curious, I put my book aside, got up, went to the door and looked through the small glass pane. There was a pretty woman on the stoop with dark hair almost to her waist. It had dark pink streaks in it, and there was glitter around her eyes, almost like glitter eye shadow. Her skin was a tanned color, almost the color of Lash's.

I spoke with the door shut, figuring she was likely non-human and could hear me. "Yes?"

"Is Lash here?" she said, offering me a sexy smile.

*Was this Gina? This was one of his lovers, past if not current.* "Stay here, please," I said in a voice that was trying hard to be civil. "I'll go and see."

I thought as I walked upstairs that maybe I should've invited her in. Clearly, the guys knew her at the gate, to have let her in at all. But I was irritated just looking at her. *Screw it. She can wait outside. Who cares that it's ten degrees, and she's likely cold-blooded? Not me.*

I climbed the stairs, and knocked on Lash's door. He opened it, looking at me a little sleepily.

"There's a woman here to see you," I said, trying hard to make my voice and face empty of emotion.

"Who is it?" he asked.

I flushed, remembering I'd been too pissed to ask her name. But it wasn't my job to keep track of his lovers, at least not anymore. "I didn't ask, and she didn't say," I grated out. "If it helps, she has pink hair."

Lash ducked back inside, then returned in his jeans and a shirt, a gun in his hand. He went downstairs, gun still out, and I followed him. I went into the living room, wanting to listen and feeling jealous, and also very stupid to be feeling that way. I'd told him I had to be with Theo. I'd made the right choice at the time; there hadn't been another to make. That didn't make this any easier to endure.

"Lyssa," Lash said, lust and surprise in his tone. "What are you doing here?"

So this was the infamous "Lyssa from PA," Lash's former lover whom Devlin had offered to import when Lash's lover Cin had broken up with him last spring. *Bitch.* I already hated her.

"I was up this way, seeing my sister," she said teasingly. "I thought I'd stop in, as Dev said you'd be back this week, and see if you needed a little loving."

I did a slow burn at Devlin for telling her it was okay to come here, then blushed and was glad no one was there to see me blushing. It was bad enough that Lash had likely smelled the jealousy on me when I'd gone to get him.

"I heard you guys were back in town last February, but I had another thing going then, with a rattler from East Texas," Lyssa said, a little apologetically. "And I knew Cin worked around here, and you were probably with her—"

He was with me, you bitch. *He loves me. Fuck off and die.*

"We broke up," Lash hissed angrily. "She cheated on me, and I told her it was over."

"I'm sorry to hear that, Honey," Lyssa hissed sympathetically. "Anyway, Lynda said she saw you and Dev out one night in the summer riding your bikes, and told me I should get up here, see you. She told me Cin had moved away, down to Tennessee."

Lash didn't reply, at least that I could hear.

"Honey, I got to say, you are looking hot," she hissed. "It's got to be true, the rumors you were dying, and that demon of Dev's, he brought you back with some faerie/vampire potion? Made you young again?"

"It's true," Lash hissed, lust back in his words. "You can see I'm young again."

"I see, but not as much as I'd like to. You busy, honey? You want to come with me now, back to Lyn's house?" Lyssa said seductively. "She's at work now, and we'll have the place to ourselves for hours."

I set my teeth together in fury, determined not to make a sound.

"Sorry, Lys, I can't," Lash said apologetically. "I've got a woman I'm seeing now."

"The blonde?" Lyssa hissed, irritated. "You always said you didn't like blondes, Lash."

I flushed again. I hadn't known that, and it felt odd, to hear her say that with surety and anger in her tone. But what did I know about Lash really? *Next to nothing.*

"The blonde is Dev's Oathed One," Lash replied. "I'm seeing another woman."

"She's not as good as I am, whoever she is!" Lyssa said arrogantly. "She can't feel as good in your coils as I always did—"

"I'm with her," Lash hissed firmly. "And you know me, Lyssa, know I'm only with one woman at a time, and that I expect the same thing back. That's all there is to say."

"I know it." Lyssa's voice was mournful. "Those years we were together, I never doubted you were faithful to me. And you know I was faithful to you—"

"I know you were, but that's past," Lash said almost gently. "It's good to see you again, but nothing more than this is going to happen between us." He paused. "And yes, I like the pink streaks."

"If you change your mind, you know where to find me," Lyssa said brokenly, her tone emotional. "Take care of yourself, Honey."

"You too, Lys," Lash said. There was the sound of the door closing, and his feet walking slowly back upstairs.

I was touched and pleased, to hear from another woman that he was a faithful lover. But I'd believed that about him, when he'd been my lover. It wasn't too much of a stretch now to believe that everything else he'd ever said to me was true.

* * * *

Lash continued to see Gina almost every day, every other day at the least. I only knew as those were the days I either put dinner aside for him, because he said he would be late, or had soup ready instead, depending if I was feeling grumpy or nice. Whichever I did, Lash seemed the same, and treated me the same. He was neither irritated, nor happy. This continued until the following Friday night.

Lash, Dev, and I had gone to the mall, for some food and a movie. I'd thought it quite risky, but Lash assured me we'd be safe enough, between his skills and my teleportation power.

We'd just finished seeing some slasher movie that I couldn't remember the name of, despite having just seen it. I thought it was *Aliens vs. Predator III* or something, but couldn't be sure.

Lash and I were strolling along together, window shopping. Well, I was, and he was keeping me safe. Devlin had gone to feed on a slim brunette he'd seen watching him across the mall, and we both knew he would be awhile, as he would have to take her beyond the security cameras in the mall in order to feed on her. I was a little worried, but Lash assured me again that Devlin would be fine as he had regained his full strength; that Ulysses was vampire now, too, and wouldn't try anything mystical or assassin-like with so many people around, especially as he wanted to beat him in a fair fight to gain everything Devlin possessed. There was too much fear of discovery, now that he, like Dev, had something to hide. I admit it calmed me, even though we still had no sure way to know if that was indeed Ulysses' plan.

"So, what did you think of the movie?" I asked him as we walked, unsure of what to say to him. He'd acted distant again for most of the night.

"It was okay," Lash said with a shrug. "But I would've liked a little more realism in the blood. Slasher films always put too much blood all over, and it's never in the right places."

I tried not to grimace. *You asked for this.*

"I mean, when you cut someone's throat, you want to do it in a way to minimize the blood on you, unless you've been paid extra to decorate the kill scene with it—"

I looked away, feeling queasy, and my eyes rested on two figures walking fast to the exit. I stopped dead in my tracks. *What the hell?*

"Sar, what is it?" Lash said as he stopped in mid-stride, turning to face me. "What's wrong?"

"I thought I just saw Elle," I said in confusion. "But it can't be. Danial would never—"

My eyes grew round with horror. Danial had been unconscious since last month. Theoron had been running Danial's business as best he could, under the tutelage of Theo and Terian. No one had been keeping tabs on Elle, or probably even watching her, except maybe Theo. I'd depended on Danial for so long to guard her and protect her, I hadn't thought…

"Sar!" Lash said urgently, making me jump. "We should go after her. She shouldn't be out here this late at night, alone. Terian and Theo can't be here with her, they're with Theoron tonight having dinner."

*Has he been talking to Brian already, spying again?* "Lash, how could she have gotten here? She doesn't have a driver's license—"

"Sar, get real," Lash said, grabbing my hand, and pulling me with him. "I took a joyride in my first stolen car when I was fourteen, and I never got caught. I looked old enough, and I didn't break any driving regs, so no one pulled me over. I returned it to its owner undamaged, with the keys just as I'd found them. Elle's probably been doing that since she knew she could, that no one was watching her anymore. No one would miss one of the Expeditions for a few hours, maybe not even for a few days."

Shit. Lash was probably right. Why hadn't I pushed Theo to watch Elle? For the simple reason that I'd thought Elle was under house arrest, since she hadn't been allowed to even see me. But I'd been wrong.

Lash went the way Elle had, but he stopped at the next big junction of stores. He closed his eyes, and I saw his fangs lengthen as he changed form enough to access his snake's superior sensory abilities. Lash scented the air with his tongue, flicking it out. Then he turned to the left.

"That way." We had been strolling, but now we were almost jogging.

"Is it her, for sure?" I asked, running alongside him.

"It's her," Lash said darkly. "And she's not alone. The man with her is a werebear, Sar. He's polar bear, not grizzly. The scent is more ice than forest."

I stumbled. Lash grabbed me, pulling me along without breaking stride. "It's Ulysses," I whispered.

Lash turned to me and stopped walking, his eyes flat. "Sar, maybe you should stay here. Go into a store. No one will try anything in a store. There are too many security cameras. I will—"

*Elle needs me. I'm not staying here hiding.* "Do you have an extra gun?" I demanded. "I've been practicing, I can shoot—"

"Sure, in the truck," Lash interrupted. "But not on me. I have my gun on my back, but that's it." I opened my mouth to speak, but he cut me off. "You'll grab Elle, and I'll do the rest. There's likely a group of them outside the mall, and he's leading her to them. Stay behind me and out of sight until they're dead. Got it?"

I nodded.

Lash took off for the exit a hundred yards in front of us, and I raced after him, exiting the mall into the cold and clear night. "There!" he hissed, then he took off at a dead run toward the van on the very edge of parking lot, far from the other cars. Three men were standing around the back of it, as it rocked noticeably on its tires. I bit back a scream of outrage and went after Lash, sticking close to the vehicles so I didn't present myself as a target. I was at least forty feet behind him when he drew his gun, silencer attached, the only record of the shot the flash of the muzzle.

Lash shot two of the three standing there before the third drew a gun and fired back. His gun was also silenced. Lash darted aside at the last second, and the bullet cratered at his feet. He shot back again, and killed the man with a head shot, splattering blood over the van's back in a dark wave.

The van was still rocking, harder now. Lash strode to the back of the van, and then I saw a muzzle flash through the windows, the moment of the van abruptly stopping. A second later, Lash hauled out a badly wounded werebear leaking blood from a cratered chest, and grabbed him by the front of his shirt. He punched him in the face for good measure, and the werebear collapsed to the ground. I walked closer slowly, deathly afraid of what I might find inside that innocent looking blue van.

"Sar, Elle needs you!" Lash shouted angrily. "Get your ass moving and get over here!"

*She's alive.* I shook off my fear, and ran to the open back doors as fast as I could. Lash began dialing his cell phone. The doors were open. Elle lay there, naked, on an inflatable mattress, close to the type I'd been on with Lash in the Everglades. She was unconscious, but her chest rose and fell as she breathed. There was blood on her lip, where she had been punched. And there was blood on her thighs, where she'd likely been forced.

*Oh God...*

For all her talk about wanting to be with a man, Elle had most likely been a virgin. I climbed in beside her, and tried to rouse her.

"Elle?" I said softly, shaking her shoulders. "Elle!"

She blinked her eyes, and looked up at me.

"Mom!" she cried, bursting into tears. I put my arms around her, and hugged her to me. I just held her for a few moments as she sobbed in my arms, biting my lip hard and fighting tears myself. I knew I should be telling her we needed to get her to the doctor, but I kept silent, determined not to rush her. A few minutes wouldn't matter, and she needed this time to feel safe enough to pull herself together.

Devlin's voice called from outside, anxious. A moment later he peered in through the open door, then averted his eyes in anguish. "I'll bring around the Hummer as fast as I can."

I nodded, still hugging Elle.

Lash closed the open door, then stood at the back of the van facing away, his gun still out. Elle saw him, and cried harder, knowing that he'd seen her like this, and knew what had happened to her.

"Here, Elle." I jerked off my jacket, then stripped off my long gray sweater. The long loose garment went to my knees and wrapped about me like a robe, with a tie in front. I helped her put it on, and then put back on my jacket. Elle was thinner and taller than I was, but the sweater still covered all of her, and it was heavy wool. She'd be warm enough. I held her again after she was clothed, and didn't say anything, angry vengeful thoughts flooding my brain.

*Damn it!* I'd done so much to warn her, tried to tell her how quickly control could shift if she was alone with a man! And it was too late now, because no matter what else happened, what those monsters had done to her would never, ever go away. But that didn't mean I wasn't going to burn Ulysses alive for what he'd done to her, him and whomever stood in my way to him.

Devlin pulled up beside us in a few more minutes with the Hummer. I helped Elle into the back seat, where I again held her in my arms. She was subdued, but able to answer my questions, enough so I understood she wasn't in any pain. Devlin got in front, and took the wheel. Lash didn't get in with us, and I surmised as we drove off that he had stayed behind to take care of the bodies, and also to take the last bear back to Hayden, where he could be questioned.

Devlin called Stephen on his cell phone to tell him to meet us at his office, that Elle had been hurt. I thought quickly about teleporting to save travel time, but surmised Stephen needed at least a half hour or more to get there to his office. There was no point beating him there, as we'd just have to wait for him to arrive anyway. I didn't want to involve Titus or Terian to go and get him. I crazily debated telling Stephen to just drink some demon blood already so he wouldn't have to always waste so much time commuting, but decided he might not be receptive to the idea.

Stephen met us at the office, and led Elle and I into Exam Room One. Elle asked me to leave the room immediately, so she could talk to him alone. I nodded, and went back to Devlin, who was in the waiting room. He slipped his arms around me, and I hugged him, though we didn't talk.

Stephen came out a half hour later, shutting the door behind him. "The physical damage is minimal. Elle has healed most of it already. She's sleeping now; I've given her a sedative. But she's going to need counseling for this, Sar."

"Lash said there were four of them. Did they all...?" Devlin said softly.

I couldn't breathe. I'd just assumed we'd been in time to prevent that.

Stephen shook his head. "Just the one. I've given her a morning-after pill, just to be safe. And I've done STD tests, too. She can call tomorrow for the results, I'll rush them through."

I stifled a sob, nodding, as Devlin hugged me tightly. "I need to call Theo. Or go see him. He needs to know—"

"She doesn't want anyone to know about what happened," Stephen said.

"She's adamant about it."

"He's her father, and he needs to know," I said bluntly.

Stephen nodded.

"Can she go home?"

Stephen nodded again.

"Call me tomorrow, and let me know of a good therapist, besides Carol," I said to Steven. "I need one who is a witch at least, if not more powerful." One who knew how to protect her mind, because part of what happened was my fault, for letting Ulysses know Danial and I had a daughter named Elle.

He nodded once more. "Call tomorrow, Sarelle, and I'll give you the name and number."

"Thank you," I said, and turned to Devlin. "Can you carry her?" I asked him. "I'll teleport you, her, and me to Danial's. We can get her settled in bed. I'll tell Theo what happened."

Devlin nodded, and a second later, we three were at Danial's home. I had gambled that Tears hadn't blocked every room from teleportation, just the major ones which staff were allowed in. So I tried to teleport to Devon's old room that was storage space now, and it worked.

We walked to Elle's room, and Devlin and I put her in bed. He turned his back while I put a nightgown on her. Stephen had already allowed her to clean herself up, though I expected she would be taking a long shower when she awakened. I left her a note, telling her to call me if she wanted to talk, and that I would be coming to see her tomorrow, if she wanted to see anyone, that is. I wasn't sure what else to do, so I kissed her sleeping form, and closed the door to her room.

Now for the hard part. "Wait here," I said, looking at Devlin. "I need to talk to Theo."

"I'm coming with you," Devlin said stubbornly. "I don't need to breathe in your scent to know you're really upset by what's happened. And he's probably going to be a jerk when he sees you, like usual—"

"Dev," I said dangerously, and he shut up. But secretly I was thankful of his insisting. I hadn't seen Theo since the night he'd attacked me. I didn't want to be alone with him under any circumstances.

I walked into the great room. No one came out to see who was there, but then, Titus, Rip, Terian and I were the only ones who could teleport in. Terian was most likely at the were compound, if he was home yet, with Sundown. For all I knew Theo was there, too, though I expected he was still sleeping in the main house, in order to guard T and Elle. Great lot of good that had done her, all his bullshit about keeping her from seeing me to keep her safe!

*Stop it, Sar. It's as much your fault as it is his.*

I turned to Devlin. "Who's here?"

He closed his eyes and listened. "T's in Danial's bedroom, sleeping I guess," he said, after a moment. "The upstairs is empty. Jenny and Theo are below us, at least, two weres are there—"

The basement door opened, and Theo stood there, gun in hand, with only his jeans on. He looked as buff as always, and my gaze roamed his skin before I slapped myself mentally, and focused.

He looked at me and Devlin with narrowed eyes. "What are you two skulking around up here for?" he spat, his eyes angry and his tone icy. "Couldn't you have called first, before you barged in?"

"No," I said calmly, trying to be patient. "There's an emergency. Get some clothes on, and come outside with me. I have to speak to you privately—"

"Fuck off," Theo said, glaring at me. "Say whatever it is you need to say, Sarelle, or I'm going back to bed. Jenny's waiting for me."

"Get your fucking clothes on *now*, and go with her!" Devlin growled, his eyes red. "You are going to thank me for insisting later, Theopolis."

Theo caught the note in Dev's voice, and his eyes went a little yellow. He turned without a word, and went back in the basement, closing the door behind him. He appeared a moment later with his shoes on, and a T-shirt. He had just shrugged into a long sleeved cotton shirt when Jenny appeared behind him in her robe. It was like mine had been, a light blue velvet one. She looked a little flushed, too, but I didn't know if that was from being in her bathrobe in front of us or because they had been having sex when we arrived.

I opened my mouth to ask Theo if he couldn't have gotten another color for her, then shut it. It wasn't my business. Not anymore. At least I knew it wasn't my robe. Mine was ashes in the ruins of my house.

"Let's go," Theo growled at me, making me start. "I need to get back to bed." He turned to Jenny and kissed her at length, and then told her to wait for him below.

"I could wait with her," Devlin purred, smiling at Jenny. "Keep her safe for you, Theo."

I saw her expression when she noticed him, that look of instant desire I thought it was likely every woman had when they first saw him. I felt a flash of pride he was mine, and grinned a little, because I knew he'd done this on purpose, to make me feel better.

"Good Evening, Jenny. I'm Devlin, Danial's brother. I'm sure you've heard of me?"

"Jenny, go below *now*," Theo growled, and she turned right around and left without a word. *Just like a good Stepford wife...excuse me, mate, should.*

Theo turned to Devlin. "If I smell you went downstairs, Dalcon, I'll—"

"Save it," Devlin said arrogantly, hugging me gently around the waist from behind. "I've got all the woman I need right here. I don't need to go after one of yours, at least not *anymore.*"

"Jenny's all I need and want," Theo growled, heading toward the mud room. "Get moving, Sarelle, before I reconsider."

Theo walked first out the front door. Devlin drew me back, and put his mouth over my ear, making it look as if he was kissing me. But instead he whispered to me. "Sar, go to the big maple tree on the front lawn. I can see you, and hear you from there if you scream, but I can't hear your spoken words, so no one else should overhear. No one else is around. Scream if you need me, and run toward me. I can make it to you before Theo can, even if he shifts."

"Okay," I whispered gratefully, then turned away from him and followed Theo. He was waiting for me impatiently on the lawn. We walked together to the maple tree, where he turned to me.

"Start talking, and make it fast," he growled. "I haven't got all night."

I didn't know how to say it, so I just said it. "Elle was hurt tonight, Theo."

Theo looked at me in total shock. "She was here all night. I saw her go to her room at six, she said she had a stomachache—"

"She was at the mall by about seven or eight. And she wasn't alone."

"God damn it!" Theo roared.

I slapped him hard. He snarled at me, and I put my hands on his shoulders, and dug in my fingers. "*Lower* your *voice*!" I hissed loudly. "Elle was hurt in a way she doesn't want anyone to know about! Understand?"

Theo looked at me in horror, and then all the fire went out of him. "No, not Elle—"

"She's okay," I interrupted. "Dev and I took her to Stephen, and he took care of her. He'll have results tomorrow on her tests, and she's not pregnant."

"Was it more than one, or…?" Theo asked in a whisper.

I wanted to slap him again harder. What was it with men, that *that* was important? "One," I said coldly.

"I'll have to thank Dev," Theo said morosely. "He saved—"

"You can thank Lash by phone," I said bitingly. "He's at Hayden."

"*He* saved her?" Theo snarled. "That fuck!"

I slapped him again with everything I had, and this time, it was enough to piss him off. "Stop hitting me, you bitch!"

"Your daughter was raped, and you care more that a man you hate saved her than about her," I said hatefully. "If he hadn't been with me when I saw her, and acted as fast as he had, the gang rape they were planning would have happened! Elle might be dead now, not just traumatized!"

Theo closed his eyes and swallowed hard, his jaw working. I gave him a minute to pull it together. "Are they dead?" he asked finally.

"All but one, the one who did the deed. He's at Hayden, I'd assume in the dungeon. Lash is probably questioning him right now."

"Good," Theo growled. "I want to kill him myself." He moved to go.

I forced myself to touch his shoulder, while keeping as far away from him as possible. "She didn't want me to tell you, to have anyone else know. But if it had been you who'd known, I knew you'd tell me. Please watch over her tomorrow. The sedative Stephen gave her should last until noon or so. I left her a note to call me tomorrow, but she may feel too upset. Please, if you think she needs me, call me, and I'll come and talk to her. Agreed?"

Theo pulled me close. "Thank you, Sar."

I was stiff in his arms, remembering him trying to turn me. I'd never been afraid of him before, but I was afraid of him now.

"I'll call you tomorrow. Thank you for telling me, and for insisting we come out here, so no one but me would know. I'm sorry I was so—"

"It's okay," I said, pushing him away, and stepping past him in a fast walk towards Devlin and safety. "But I need to get back."

Theo nodded, following me to the house. Devlin waited, leaning against the front door, watching us. As I came to stand by him, he slipped an arm around me.

"Thank you for insisting," Theo said grudgingly to Devlin. "I'll come tomorrow afternoon or night, to kill that bear."

Devlin nodded. "We'll save him for you."

Theo went past him into the house, and Devlin shut the door behind him. I walked with him to the edge of the trees, and from there, teleported us home to Hayden. Without a word, I let him lead me to his bathroom, where we showered together. I'd held in tears all night, and here I finally let them fall, sobbing loudly. Devlin didn't say anything, just held me under the pulsing flow of water. I was grateful for his silence. There was nothing he could say that was going to make me feel any better about what had happened to Elle.

After I finally calmed down, we got out, and I dressed in one of my nightgowns, the one Devlin liked best, a little slip of black silk that had thin straps, and went to mid-thigh. Sexy though it was, I took comfort from its familiarity, and that wearing it would please him.

Just as we got into bed, there was a knock at the door. Devlin got up to answer it, revealing Lash, still dressed in his clothes from the mall. There was a spattering of blood on the left side of his face, and blood here and there on his clothes.

"He's in a cell, unconscious," Lash hissed, ignoring me. "I think I got everything from him."

"What was the plan?" Dev asked reluctantly. I understood that: I didn't want to hear what had most likely been in store for Elle. But I needed to hear it, too, to remember it, so if Ulysses or his bastards were ever in my sights I wouldn't hesitate to kill them all.

"Ulysses has been watching everyone who leaves and comes to Danial's. Elle's been sneaking out since the week after Danial was drained. She met Violet at first a few days a week, in the daytime, because she was worried that someone would find out, and that she'd get in trouble. But when no one noticed, she stopped meeting only Violet, and began going out at night alone, not just in the daytime. Two weeks ago, she began doing it on weekends too, and sometimes staying out all night. Theo checked on her before she went to bed, but not after that, and she knew all she had to do was say she was going to bed, and she'd be left alone."

"How did the bear know this?" I asked.

Lash cut his eyes to me. "He said he asked her, and she told him. She was proud of herself, that she was so crafty, so smart that she could sneak out and no one knew, or had any idea at all."

I sighed. *The folly of the young.*

"Ulysses saw his opening as soon as she began to appear at the mall alone," Lash continued, his eyes back on Devlin. "He sent an attractive werebear, Jordan, to make friends with Elle. It took a while for him to get close to her, because she was suspicious. But soon they were making out in the movies, and when he didn't pressure her for more, she pushed him for more. He put her off, saying she was too young, that he didn't want to rush her, she was too special, all the standard male bullshit, and that made her bolder."

*Shit.* I'd been there myself, when I was younger.

"She told him she wanted him to…manipulate her. He did. He also taught her how to do oral sex on him, though he said she seemed to know a lot already."

I let out a little gasp, and Lash again cut his eyes to me. "I hurt him bad for a few things he said about her, that among them," he said angrily.

I wanted to thank him, but nodded instead, feeling heartsick.

"Go on," Devlin intoned.

"Tonight, he told her he had a surprise for her, that he'd take her to a hotel, because he had decided he loved her, and he wanted her first time to be special, if she was ready to give herself to him. She said she was ready, and went with him willingly. But the surprise was he had three of his friends waiting, and when he got her to his van he hit her. Hard. He said he'd been instructed to rape her, and he knew if she was out cold, she wouldn't fight him, or his friends, and they'd hurt her less, if she didn't fight them."

It was less horrible, in a way. At least Elle wouldn't have any memories of the act itself.

"She was a virgin, he said," Lash hissed, noticeably distraught. "He admitted he had her a few times, before we got there. But at least we stopped most of what was planned from happening. I'm not going to tell you the details, but suffice to say she was going to be killed, after they'd exhausted themselves, and her body left for Devlin to find."

"Thank you," I said heavily. "I didn't, before. Thank you, Lash, for saving my daughter."

"I wish I could have done more," he hissed back at me, still upset. "If we'd been faster—"

"I'm grateful you were as fast as you were," Devlin interrupted, putting his hand on Lash's shoulder. "So is Theo. He will be here in the afternoon tomorrow, to take his pound of flesh."

Lash nodded. "I'm going to bed," he said tiredly. "I'm beat. Call out, if you need me, and I'll hear you—"

"Don't go. Stay here," Devlin interrupted.

# Chapter Five

My tired eyes shot open in surprise. Lash was also taken aback, studying Devlin as if he was waiting for the vampire to state some kind of condition. Devlin had been holding the edges of the door frame and now he let go of one, and stepped aside. Lash looked past him to me, lying there in Devlin's bed. It was too dark for me to see what he was feeling by his eyes, and even then, he had become a lot better at hiding his emotions, now that his eyes weren't always flat.

Lash stepped in the room. Devlin shut the door behind him, then came back, and got into bed. Lash came to the bottom of the bed and stopped, his face still unreadable.

"What are you waiting for? Go shower and get in here already," Devlin ordered, grief still heavy in his words.

"Dev, why are you saying that this is okay now?" Lash hissed, annoyed.

"Because life is too short," Dev said flatly. "Danial thought he had eternity. That he was going to see Elle and Theoron grow up. He may never get the chance to now. I may have lost him for good. And now my niece has been hurt badly " Devlin paused, swallowed hard and began again. "I've been the cause of a lot of suffering. And I'm not causing any more, not for you or her, not if I can help it."

"You're sure?" Lash hissed in a malicious tone. "Don't offer me this and then change your mind, Dev, like you have before. It's yes or no, tonight and from now on. Because if she wants me, I'm not giving her up because you tell me to, not ever again."

I wanted to say "what about Gina?", but decided to hold my tongue. I was feeling too happy just knowing he wanted me, that he still cared for me as he had months ago.

"I want you here. She wants you here. Stay." Devlin said.

Lash came to the other side of the bed from Devlin, and unfastened his weapons, setting them by the edge of the bed. They he took off his clothes, save his underwear, and put them in a pile. He looked as he had months ago, though maybe a little thinner, his body just as lean and hard as I remembered. An electric charge ran through my body, just from looking at him.

"I'm going to shower," he said softly. "Five minutes."

Five minutes to the dot, Lash was back wearing a new pair of underwear that he'd gotten from Dev's drawer, his hair still wet from the shower.

I felt Lash shaking slightly, as he climbed in beside me. I was trembling myself, the closer I felt him move. He'd wanted and missed me as much as I had him. Slowly he put his arms around me, pulling me to him, the feel of his scales smooth against the small of my back.

Devlin put his arms around my waist, casting a look at Lash over my shoulder. "Are you going to freak out, if I touch you in the night?" Devlin asked, his tone purposefully casual.

I gave him a look that said in sixty years, he had to have shared a woman with Lash, that I knew him too well to think he hadn't.

Devlin shook his head almost imperceptibly. "We've been with women together before, Sar, even slept in the same bed, but we've never done this, because I never trusted a woman to sleep next to me before. Even with Lash in the room, in the same bed."

Lash hugged me tighter, his skin and scales warm against my flesh. I leaned back into him, sighing gently. "Touch me however you want," Lash said to Devlin, all trace of his snake fangs suddenly gone. "I'm not afraid of you, that you're going to make a move on me; I know you too well. You have never liked to bed men. My virtue is safe."

"You reptile, you don't have any virtue left," Devlin muttered.

"Be nice," I whispered softly, kissing Devlin's forehead. "No teasing, not tonight. Please."

"Here," Devlin said, as he reached over on his nightstand and handed me a sleeping pill. I took it without saying anything, knowing I wouldn't be sleeping tonight without it. He hugged me hard, and then moved a little lower to lay his head on my chest, wrapping his arms around my middle again.

I was still upset, but Lash was warm behind me, and Devlin's arms wrapped around me were familiar and comforting. And the pills always worked fast. In a few minutes, I fell asleep.

\* \* \* \*

I awoke in midmorning, the watch on my wrist a reminder of normalcy. At least Theo had returned it, and not stomped it into shards… *Drop it Sar. Forget Theo, you'll just get angry again.*

My position hadn't changed in the night. Devlin was still on my chest, still sleeping, his arms curled around me. Lash was still in back of me, but I felt only one of his hands gently caressing my side. I craned my neck sideways with effort and looked at him.

"Good morning," he said softly, his eyes riveted on me. He was leaning on his elbow, and his other hand was smoothing my hair, where it lay on our pillow.

"Good morning," I said, giving him a welcoming smile. Then it hit me, all of it, Danial, and Elle. Tears flooded my eyes.

Lash moved closer to me in a smooth motion, slipping an arm under my neck, and the other over my upper arm. "Shh," he hissed softly, holding me close. "Danial's not dead, Sar. Dev will figure out a way to make him how he was. And Elle will recover, too, though she'll need your help. She's breathing today because you noticed her last night in a crowded mall, and that's all that matters. She's okay, she's alive, and she'll get through this."

God, I wanted to believe that so much! But so much had gone wrong this fall. I let out a sniffle, trying to get control of myself.

Lash moved his head closer, and kissed my tears away. "You know Dev's a master at subterfuge and strategy. If it can be done, he'll find a way to make Danial okay again. And Ulysses' days are numbered, now I'm out of jail. It shouldn't take me more than a month to find his lair and stake him, if that."

I gave Lash a surprised look, not because he had said that about Devlin, but because he'd used a word like subterfuge.

Lash gave me a grumpy look, narrowing his eyes, because he knew what I was thinking. "I'm more than a good body with killing skills, Sar," he said irritably. "I do read more than weapons magazines, and *Penthouse*. Or did you forget which wereman you were in bed with?"

I felt terrible. I hadn't meant to make him think that. I took one hand off Devlin, and reached back for Lash. "I didn't mean anything by it. I know you read as much as I do. I was just surprised, because you usually don't say—"

He caught my hand easily in his, and then he was pushing it down between us, hissing softly. He slid my hand down his tight abs, and onto his manhood, and I felt him throbbing through his underwear. I reached inside the cloth, and closed my hand around the head of his penis, prompting a sharp hiss. Releasing him, I tugged at the top of his underwear, trying for better access. He slid them off, then pressed himself tight against me, rubbing gently on me with his hard cock as his rough callused hands slid up under my nightgown, gently moving over the bare skin of my back.

"Your skin is so soft," he hissed longingly, running his hands over me. "I never get tired of feeling it under my hands."

It was there in his voice how much he had missed me, how much he had wanted to have me touch him again. I'd wanted to touch and kiss him just as much. Devlin was right. Life was too short to waste any more time. I wasn't going to waste one more second. I reached back again, down between us, and closed my hand around Lash's penis, squeezing gently.

Lash let out a loud hiss, and jerked under my roaming hands. I stroked him skillfully and he moved in my hand, the tip of his cock already slick, "Are you safe?" he whispered, his tone uneven with desire. "Have you been taking what I got for you? Otherwise—"

"Yes," I whispered. "I've been on them for a month." *In case you still wanted me.* "But are you?"

"Yes. Please!" Lash hissed softly. "I give you my word I'm clean. Tell me it's okay, Sar. Please!"

Lash was kissing me very gently on my neck, but his entire body was shaking slightly now with pent up excitement. It was raw need, a lake of it. Lash was acting as if he hadn't been with anyone for weeks…

"You told me you went to Gina," I said in wonder. "That she took care of you. You had conjugal visits, in jail."

"I lied," Lash hissed, cupping my face with his hand. "I only wanted you, Sar. I did go to her, and she did relax me, and ease my tension. But it was through acupuncture, not sex. That's what she did for me on those conjugal visits. And after the tension was gone, she gave me massages, nothing sexual."

"Why would you—?" I began, turning my head to look fully at him. Lash cut off my words with a passionate kiss, his tongue slipping through my parted lips. I lost myself in the sensation of it. We hadn't kissed in so long like this, and I whimpered slightly, feeling his tongue stroking mine.

Lash drew back from me then, his eyes black as hot tar. "It mattered that if you decided to Oath to Dev, that I could tell you I hadn't been with anyone else, that I was safe to be with." He paused. "For all of the things about me you have accepted, I wanted to do this in return, to show you the lengths I was willing to go to for you. It wasn't easy these past months, like it was before you changed me, when I was older. It's been downright hellish. But I told you once that all I was, it was all for you, if you wanted it. I meant that, just as I mean it now."

Tears came to my eyes, remembering our shared time in the Everglades, when I had healed him with my blood, the gift healing not only his dying body but also rejuvenating his youth. "You didn't have to do that for me."

"I did," he hissed softly, kissing my face gently. "I keep my promises, Sar."

*What did he mean? He hadn't made me any promises…*

"Will you let me make love to you?" he hissed insistently. "Please?"

I wanted him, and it was true Dev was a heavy sleeper. Maybe this was doable. "I don't want to wake Dev. He's still sleeping. You'd have to be very quiet."

"I won't make a sound. You know how quiet I can be," Lash hissed eagerly. He carefully aligned my hips with his, still kissing me urgently. I felt him as he stroked me gently with his hand, and when he felt that I was slick for him, he let out an eager hiss as he slowly pushed inside me, fighting to move very, very slowly. Finally, he was all the way inside me, and I felt him take hold of my hips firmly, so he wouldn't jostle Devlin when he began thrusting.

Lash was kissing me feverishly, tremors going through him, and very slowly, he began to move. My lips parted before I could stop myself, and I let out a moan. Lash stopped quickly, putting his hand over my mouth. "You have to be quiet, too," he hissed softly, smiling. "I need both my hands."

"You don't have to be quiet," Devlin murmured.

Lash and I went still as we both looked toward him.

"I might be a heavy sleeper, but I'm not utterly deaf," Devlin said, rolling his eyes at us. "Especially when I hear a woman I'm being held by moan like that."

I gave a relieved smile, though Lash said nothing. He was still inside me, his body shaking.

Devlin sat up, and looked down at the two of us. "Do you mind if I stay, and watch you two, Lash?" he said lustfully. "I know Sar won't mind."

Actually, I did mind a little, but I didn't feel comfortable kicking him out of his own bedroom, not with everything that had happened.

Lash pulled out of me, and sat up, his arms still around me, so I sat up with him. "Dev, you didn't want me to even kiss her, before last night," he hissed possessively "Now you want to watch me have her? Why?"

"I was wrong," Devlin admitted, looking down at the sheets "I was jealous, and I shouldn't have been. I knew how you both felt, and I should have let you be together. But I've never been jealous of you before, Lash, though I know over the years you were often jealous of me."

"Sar, do you mind, if he watches us?" Lash hissed, looking at me carefully. "I don't."

"If you don't, I don't," I said softly, then kissed him.

"Okay," Lash said with a shrug, and then he rolled me over to straddle him. He slid inside me easily, bringing a gasp from me. I slid my hands up his chest, feeling his scales forming beneath my hands, and then he pulled me down with his arms, kissing me passionately, his tongue stroking mine almost frantically as he began to move in me.

I groaned loudly. I'd wanted him again like this so much, for so many months. And he felt so good to me, because I didn't just desire him, I loved him.

I gently pulled his hands off me, and took them in mine. Lash gave me a confused look, and stopped kissing me, and moving in me.

"You know what I like." I brought his hands to my breasts, and Lash gripped them, squeezing hard as his tongue slid beneath my nightgown to tease one breast, then the other. My head fell back as I let out a whimper, my lips parting. Lash released me abruptly, his hands leaving me, and I felt a whisper of cloth, as he lifted the nightgown over my head. I looked to see Devlin tossing it to the side, and then his eyes were all for us again. His eyes were molten, glowing. Seeing us together like this was turning him on.

Lash grabbed my head and brought it down to him again, kissing me roughly, his hips moving rhythmically under mine. I grabbed his hands, sliding them down to my hips. "Move me," I moaned softly, and his eyes went darker still, remembering that night with me, when he'd said those words as he touched me. He was shaking hard now, even as he moved in gentle rhythm, and it suddenly occurred to me that he was trying hard to hold back long enough for me to come first.

But I didn't want him to hold back, not after telling me how much I meant to him. He deserved more. I leaned down close, whispering in his ear. "Come for me, my dark-eyed lover. Don't wait. Sheathe your body in mine the way we've both wanted you to for months."

Lash gripped my hips with his hands, and thrust madly into me, letting out sharp cries of pleasure every time he buried himself in me. I swayed above him, stroking his scales lovingly.

It was over in a few seconds. Lash came moaning loudly, pumping into me, and I arched my back, wanting him as deep inside me as he could get. He clutched me to him, his arms holding me close, as he emptied himself into me, jerking hard. I collapsed on him gasping, and he hugged me to him, kissing me on my face, and my neck.

"I'll be slower with you, in a few minutes," Lash said between breaths, deep satisfaction in his words. "It was because it had been so long for me, Sar, and you felt so good. God!"

"Shh," I said, giving him a soft kiss. "I know. It's okay, Lash."

I felt a gentle caress of fingers down my spine, and knew it was Devlin. Sure enough, his arms enfolded me, as I sat still astride Lash. Devlin turned my head so I faced sideways and he kissed me, his tongue plunging into my mouth, as if he wanted to eat me. I kissed him back the same way, my arousal almost a raging fire in its intensity. His hands tangled in my hair, and I felt his erection as he rubbed himself against my ass.

I froze, a little afraid of what he might ask me to do, because I wasn't going to do it, no matter how much he might want me to. He was much too large of a man for me even to consider it.

Devlin felt me tense, and pulled back slightly from me. "I'll just watch you, for now," he said softly, giving me a smile. "I want to see you come for him, Sar."

I flushed red, and Devlin gave me a sultry look, his smile widening to a grin. He flopped back down beside us, his one arm propping him up on his elbow.

"I'm ready, Sar," Lash said, guiding my upper body down on his. He kissed me roughly again, and I caressed his warm skin with my hands, loving the feel of his body under mine. I cupped his face in my hands, evoking a slight shudder of pleasure from him. He rolled over on top of me quickly, sliding in and out of me, kissing my face, my neck, and my breasts almost feverishly.

I groaned. I'd been close before, just feeling his excitement in having me. It was overwhelming now, to feel his body against mine, stroking me, loving me!

"Say my name for me, Sar," he rasped, burying his face in my neck and sucking on my skin first gently, then harder. "I've waited months to hear you cry it out for me. Say it!"

He bore down, rubbing purposely with each thrust, and I was suddenly there in a sweet burst of pleasure. I climaxed shaking in his arms, moaning his name, "Lash! Yes! Lash! Please!"

Lash uttered a pleased hiss, and began rapidly to drive himself into me hard and fast, and in a few seconds, he came again as well, holding my body to his tightly as he spasmed into me, spurting into me over and over as he let loose a loud undulating scream. This time he didn't let go of me until he'd given me everything he had left. A minute later, I felt him finally begin to shrink inside me, and he pulled out with a soft sigh, giving me a gentle kiss. My heart was pounding, and Lash moved off me to lay by my side, still shaking slightly as he fought to breathe. His hand slid down my arm to clutch my hand, his fingers entwining in mine, unwilling to break contact.

I felt Devlin come up by my other side, and he was breathing hard too, from just watching us. He kissed me deeply, and before I knew it, he was positioning himself on me, aligning his hips with mine.

*Hey!* I opened my eyes fully, as I moved to push him off me, but before I could, Lash's hand released mine, darting out to grip his arm, stopping him.

Devlin gave him a nasty look. "What is the problem?" he said, his voice heavy with lust. "Isn't it enough that you went first?"

"Ask her first," Lash hissed, not letting go, his snake fangs bared, and his eyes flat. "Before you just take her, ask her."

Devlin hissed at him with red eyes, his vampire fangs bared. Lash didn't let go of him or back down.

Devlin's eyes narrowed, then shifted to me. "Do you want me now or not?"

"Yes, of course," I consented. "But first give me a minute to use the bathroom, Dev."

Devlin moved off me, and I went into the bathroom, closing the door. In a few minutes, I came back in and settled down on the bed, beckoning Devlin to me with a smile and a crooked index finger.

Devlin rolled me over to face Lash, and then pulled me back hard against him, thrusting the full length of himself inside my wet center. I let out a sharp cry of pleasure, feeling myself so thoroughly filled. "Kiss her, as I have her," Devlin growled under his breath.

Lash came up in front of me, and began kissing me again, caressing my breasts with his hands, tweaking the nipples. Devlin began stroking me gently with his penis, touching me all over inside as only he could. I moaned and shuddered under their ministrations. Lash kissed me harder, his hands tangling in my hair as his mouth devoured mine. My body was awash in sensation, pure bliss, and I shook in their arms, as they loved me together. Within moments, I was cresting the wave again, crying out my raw fulfillment in piercing screams. Lash drew back to watch me, his hands stroking my face and lips as I sought fervently to kiss his fingers so enticingly beyond my reach.

Dev thrust harder, his face buried in my neck, though he didn't bite me. He shouted my name loudly, and held my hips to his, shuddering over and over. "Sar!"

He softened and withdrew with a sigh and brief touch of his cool lips to my throat, while Lash brought his mouth to mine for one last ravishing kiss.

"That was so good," Devlin groaned, turning me towards him and settling his head again on my chest, in the same position we had started the night. "I love to see you at that last moment before orgasm, Sar." He gave a satisfied sigh, and relaxed against me.

Lash slipped one arm under my neck, and put the other one on my shoulder. "You were just as I remembered," Lash said softly, giving me a kiss on the cheek as he nestled his body in back of mine. "And it was worth it all these months, to wait for you." He kissed the nape of my neck gently. "Get some rest. I'll be right here, keeping you both safe."

I snuggled down between them, and promptly fell back asleep.

* * * *

It was late afternoon when Lash awoke me by moving. "I need to get up, shower, and check on some things before it gets much later," he said, giving me a quick kiss on the cheek. "Duty calls."

I immediately thought about offering to shower with him. "Um, I—?"

"I'll shower later, when I come back," Lash amended, giving me a knowing smile that said he'd guessed at my intended question. "If you'll wait for me?"

"I will," I said warmly, unable to contain my happiness.

Lash gave me another kiss, this one eager. He dressed rapidly, strapped on his weapons, and a moment later, he was out the bedroom door, closing it softly behind him.

"You love him, don't you, Sar? Tell me, if you do."

"Yes, I do," I whispered. But all the intensity of what I felt was there in my soft words.

"Give your Oath to me then," Devlin persuaded. "You don't ever have to be without him again, Sar, if you do. You never have to sleep again without his body beside yours."

I knew when I heard him say that, I was going to do it. I wanted Lash too much not to be in his arms again, to feel him loving me, to be with him, near him. The love I felt for him was so deep I was drowning in it. And there would be no Lash without Devlin as part of the deal. Even if my weresnake lover didn't need Dev's blood right now, he would need it eventually to keep from dying again. Further, Lash would never leave his best friend, even if he didn't need Dev's powerful vampire blood to keep living. Plus I needed Devlin myself, for protection if nothing else. Most importantly, I wasn't leaving Venus again while she was so young, no matter what. Not after what had happened to Devon.

"What Oath do you want? When?"

"I want what you promised me before," Devlin purred with pleasure. "But also that you won't run off with Lash. I want your word you won't marry him, now that Theo and you have separated. I can take it from you tonight, if you like—"

I shook my head. "The divorce isn't final yet, Dev. Don't you think we should wait until it is?"

"Love, Theo's with one of his own kind now," Dev said gently. "You know Theo. I'm betting they are probably already engaged, because I know him, and he's going to want to marry her. To do that, you and he are going to have to get divorced, not just separated. He is not going to reconsider, from what I have heard from Brian. I'd think that you wouldn't want him to anyway, after all that's happened. Or do you want him to be your lover still? Because if you do, you may not be able to have Lash, too."

I sighed. I didn't want Theo to reconsider; I didn't want him anywhere near me, much less in bed with me. But how to explain that, without admitting what he'd done? "You don't understand," I said reluctantly. "I don't want to be with Theo again at all. In fact, you can put a provision in the Oath that I'll never be intimate with him again—"

"I'm not going to do that," Devlin interrupted, hugging me gently. "You may change your mind over the years, Sar."

"I'm not going to change my mind," I whispered. "Not about this."

Devlin moved back from me, and turned my body slightly, so he could look me full in the face. "Did something happen that night you broke up?" he asked searchingly, his eyes tinting red. "You sound almost as if you are afraid of him."

"It wasn't pleasant," I mollified, trying to downplay my true reaction. "He said some awful things to me."

"Time may make you forget," Devlin said patiently. "But I understand your hurt feelings. In any case, I'm asking only that you promise not to marry Lash."

"Just for kicks, what makes you think he would even want to marry me?" I responded. "He's not the marrying kind, I wouldn't think."

"I'm not talking about traditional marriage, Sar. Lash wants you to be his mate. And I don't want there to be jealously, like Theo had. If Lash doesn't have his own separate rights to you, he won't be inclined to fight with me over my rights to you. You saw what he did earlier, when he got between us. I don't mind him reminding me to treat you as you should be treated. I do mind him getting in the way of me having you when and where I want to."

*Ah, Dev, what a charmer you are. Sigh.* "All right."

"I'd want you to Oath to Danial again, too, when you give your promise to me," Dev continued. "Like you, I still have hope that he will recover, and if he does, I want him to be able to be with you, for the both of us to be with you together, like we were before. Lash will not mind that, Sar. He knows I'd ask that of you."

"That's fine. I expected that, Dev."

"And there are a few things more," Devlin went on, eliciting a look of disbelief from me that he still wasn't done.

"No one else," Devlin said possessively. "Not unless I agree for there to be someone else some night with us, besides Lash and Danial and possibly Theo."

"We have enough possible partners in bed with us now, Dev. More than enough, really. And I just told you, I do *not* want to be with—"

"I will give you the unconditional right to refuse any man I might suggest," Devlin said. "You will always have that right, except with me—"

*Not a surprise.* I rolled my eyes.

"—but there are two other men who visit me regularly. I consider them both dear friends. One of them is coming into town in a few weeks. He and I usually share a woman, when he comes to visit. You don't have to be the woman, Love, but I like to do that with him. And if you don't want to be the woman, I would want your permission to still do that, when he visited. It would be here, or in his hotel—"

"I'd rather not," I replied with a grimace. "I'm not a casual sex kind of person. The Lust was an exception."

"You haven't seen him, Sar," Devlin said seductively. "Reserve judgment, if you would, until you do. He wouldn't hurt you. He is a lot like Danial was sexually, both in body and technique, though he has some of my more noticeable...attributes."

*TMI, Dev.* I rolled my eyes, but nodded that I would consider it, though really, I wouldn't. "Anything else?"

"I'd want you to come here to live, with me, permanently. I want you near me, Love, living here with me and V, not miles away. Lash will want that, too."

I blinked at him. "But what about my land? My farm?"

"You love your land like I love mine. I understand that. But your land isn't protected as well as mine, or large enough for all of my men. You should give the land and barn to Theo, let him live there—"

"He wouldn't want to," I said stridently. "I wouldn't want him to, either, not with Jenny."

Devlin was thoughtful and silent for a while, holding me. Finally he spoke. "You know it's not the money," he said, stroking my arm. "We can keep the barn, and the land, but if no one lives there, the barn and land are going to fall into a state of disrepair, like Hayden did when I was gone to Rio." He paused. "Your place is here with us, with the people who love you. This is your home now, Love."

"Let me ask around at Danial's...Theoron's," I quickly corrected. "You're right, that it makes no point to keep my home, if we aren't moving back there. I hate to sell it, but maybe Theoron can come up with some ideas of what to do so I don't have to."

"So you'll do it?" Devlin asked excitedly.

"If I do, you are going to make me some promises, too," I stated flatly.

"I told you I'd always give you my blood, if you needed it," Devlin assured me. "I'll always protect you, and I'll support you, too—"

"I know you will, though the last isn't necessary. But I have some conditions."

"Such as?" Devlin said, his liquid golden eyes expectant.

"No more other women," I said pointedly. "No sharing them with your friends, no—"

"Sar, I told you before, there are some things I like to do that will hurt you."

"If you want rough oral sex with...whomever you went to last time for that, fine. But nothing else. Find something else to do with your friends who visit."

"We like to do that, Sar! We always have!"

"Then save us all some time and heartache, and don't promise yourself to me! I don't have to sleep in your bed, or be your lover, if you miss being with other women that badly. I'll ask Lash if I can bunk with him from now on."

Devlin gave me a terrified look, and pulled me into his arms. "Okay!" he said quickly. "I won't be with anyone but you, save oral sex, and if you give me permission sometimes, for special occasions."

"Dev, it's a fine line you are walking on," I said frostily. "Can you walk that line? Last time it ended badly. And I am not going to give you another chance if you mess up again."

"Yes, I can walk it now," Devlin said seriously. "I'm not going to be the idiot that I was before. I suppose I can think of other ways to entertain guests."

"Are you sure?" I said sharply. "Don't waste my time getting a promise unless you are."

"I'm sure," he said resolutely.

"Then keep your extracurricular activities to Hillary and Tiffany."

His eyes went wide with shock. "How do you know their names? I never—"

"Never mind," I said coolly, enjoying a private thrill of triumph. "Promise you'll keep it to just them. Don't ever do it here, at Hayden. Nowhere here, not even outside on the grounds. If this is going to be my home, if I am going to be Mistress here, I'm going to be the only mistress here. Get my drift?"

"I can do that," Dev said, after a moment.

"I also want you to promise me that you'll let me go to Lash as a snake," I said hesitantly. "To let me be alone with him sometimes, to coil with him, as often as he needs me to do that."

Devlin's eyes went wide again. "You would do that for him?"

I nodded. "He needs it. He explained to me months ago how it is for weres, that they need sex in both forms. He probably won't ask me to do it for him. But I want to try it."

"I don't want you to become weresnake," Devlin said slowly. "It would have to be only temporary, Sar."

"I'll ask Terian for a potion," I explained. "Lash told me once that there was magic that could make me cougar for Theo. There must be one that can make me a snake, too. Tears keeps reminding me he owes me one."

Devlin looked over at me. I'd expected to see jealousy, or perhaps annoyance. But instead, there was intent curiosity. "Have you fantasized about having Lash as a snake?"

"No," I said, feeling more and more trepidations. "But I know he's fantasized about having me that way, and I want to do that with him, for him. Because if I can be with him both ways, I won't have to let him go to someone else for sex in his other form, like I did Theo."

"You'll have to promise to tell me how it is afterwards," Devlin said animatedly. "I never thought about becoming an animal, changing form to have sex as one. I might want to try it with you sometime. Maybe as eagles, or coyotes, or bobcats…there are so many possibilities…"

*Great.* I wasn't sure whether to laugh or throw my hands up in exasperation. I settled for biting my lip and staying quiet. *Maybe he'll forget he suggested it.*

"That is the last thing I'd ask you," Devlin said cautiously. "I would want you to swear you wouldn't become weresnake. Your blood is still not as it was, but I still have hope that in time, it will go back to tasting of summer. When that happens, I want to begin exchanging blood again with you in limited amounts, until you get back to the point where you won't age."

I let out a sigh. Dev's list was long. Lash had been right, that nothing was ever free with my golden-god of a vampire king. But was any of this so bad? I didn't want to die, I was going to be absurdly rich, I had two men that loved me (well, one who for certainly did), and I didn't want to be wereanything, anyway. The only problem was my land, but I'd figure something out with that.

"Lash will be with us, part of what we are, as Theo would never have been," Devlin added. "He's still going to age slowly, Sar, there isn't any stopping it, but with my blood and Titus's magic, he'll last hundreds of years. And he's maybe twenty, twenty-two now in terms of physical age, so he probably won't even need to begin taking the potion again for maybe another fifteen years, depending on when he wants to start taking it, how old he wants to look."

Devlin ran a fang over my bare shoulder, and I shivered in his arms.

"Will you do it?" Devlin whispered seductively in my ear. "Only say 'yes' to me, and you can have him, Love. I see how much you desire him, how much you're in love with him. It's a mirror for what I feel for you. And I give you my word, here and now, that if you but give your promise to me, that so long as we three live, I will do everything in my power to see that no one will ever separate you from him again."

I was quiet, considering his words. There was truth in them, but Dev was also painting me a picture of the best case scenario, because he badly wanted me to say yes. Yet that didn't matter, because I wanted Lash too much to refuse, even though I felt a chill at giving Devlin power over me again. I had faith in Lash, that he would step in on my side if things got even a little out of hand, as he had last night.

"My answer is yes. But give me this week to plan," I said finally. "I would like you to arrange for some special food and wine for us. I also want to be with Lash as a snake one time, probably this Friday, if Terian can get the potion made fast enough. On Saturday night, I'll give you your Oath, with him present. And you will give me yours."

"Wonderful!" Devlin said in rapture, squeezing me tightly. "That is acceptable to me. I will also get you something suitable to wear, for Saturday." Then he stopped. "Sarelle, we cannot do it on Saturday night," he said, his voice annoyed. "Your mother expects you for holiday celebration, doesn't she?"

*My God, how did I forget Christmas? And I do have to be there Christmas Eve. There is no way around it. None.* "Sunday night, then," I amended.

"Sunday it is," Devlin said, his expression pleased, and reached for me.

I got out of bed, eliciting surprise mixed with annoyance from the man I'd just agreed to bind myself to. But when I explained that I had something to do that could not be put off he just nodded, and told me to get going.

\* \* \* \*

I went first to the main house, and knocked at the door. No one answered. I tried my key in the lock, and realized that in the short time I'd been gone, the locks had been changed. Finally, I called via my cell, and got no answer.

Furious that I could not see Elle, I stalked to the werecompound, looking for anyone to give a piece of my mind to. I encountered only Cia, who told me stonily that Elle had Jenny watching over her, and had asked that no one disturb them. Angry that Theo was using this situation as yet another power play between us, yet comforted that Elle was not alone, I asked Cia to please have Elle call me at Hayden later, then headed to Terian's lab.

Asking the half faerie-half demon sorcerer for the shapechanging potion was awkward in the extreme, especially telling him exactly *why* I wanted to be a snake. "This is for sex?" Terian exclaimed, incredulous. "To have sex as a snake with Lash?"

"I can pay if you'd like. Otherwise, I'll go to Titus or one of your competitors," I said bluntly. "You said you owed me one, though, so I came to you to ask."

Terian looked at me, his glowing red eyes bleeding through his tinted contacts, and stayed silent.

"I trust you, though. I'd rather you were the one who made it." That and going to Titus for it would result in a huge fight, because he would know immediately what it was for. I'd never had my stepfather tell me he hated my choice of men; Chris just wasn't like that. But Titus would do that and more. He might even go after Lash with some of his magic. I didn't want Lash hurt, just because we wanted to be together.

"You never asked me for a potion to make you a lioness, so you could be with Theo," Terian said, turning his back on me. "You always said you loved him, Sar, yet you—"

"I'm sorry I came. Forget I asked," I said curtly, and left his lab immediately.

Terian caught up with me as I left the building. "Stop, Sar!" he called, but I kept walking.

Finally, he teleported in front of me, and I ran into him. I tried to go around him, but he grabbed hold of me, and wouldn't let me go. "I'm sorry, Sar. It's not my business to judge you."

"No, it's not. But it's true that I made it your business by asking you. So forget it."

"I'll make it. What kind of snake is Lash?"

"A cottonmouth."

"What type?"

*Type?* "Florida type, I'd guess?"

"All right," Terian said, writing that down on a piece of paper from his pocket. "I'll have it ready for you to pick up Saturday morning. It will take that long to make it."

"How much?" I said with more than a little gratefulness. "I'll pay you for it."

"About five thousand dollars," Terian said softly. "That's the lowest I can go, Sar. I hate to charge you anything, because I told you I owed you. But the ingredients are really expensive. It retails for about thirty grand. I can eat the cost of the demon blood, but I need a few...other things I'm going to have to buy, and that is how much they are going to cost. You'll really be a snake, for about three hours or so. You'll be able to move as one, though I wouldn't recommend eating anything. But I don't think you'll have time to, with Lash."

He'd said that last bit with pointed humor. "That's fine!" I said irritably. "I have some savings. I'll bring you the money—"

"Forget what I said earlier, Sar, about Theo and you," Terian said gently. "Even if I could have made you a cougar, you wouldn't have been were. Theo would have been a lot stronger. Lash won't hurt you as a snake, it's not forceful or anything, having sex as a snake. But Theo would have probably hurt you, having you like that as human."

I flushed, remembering sex with Theo in his lion form.

Terian saw my flush, and went a deep crimson.

I left him immediately and teleported back home to Hayden, because I couldn't say anything, and by then, I was red as a beet myself.

* * * *

I got back just in time to run into Lash as he was walking in the front door of Hayden. "Where were you?" he asked curiously.

"Looking for you," I lied, unwilling for some reason to tell him the truth about the potion, and Terian. "Ready to shower?"

Lash pulled me close to him, and kissed me, groaning. "More than ready. Come on."

Lash and I showered, but I mostly stood there. He wouldn't let me do anything, after I washed my hair. In the time it took me to take care of that, he had completely gotten clean.

He soaped my torso up slowly, caressing my skin in long possessive strokes, and kissing me. Before long, he was pressing me to the shower wall, kissing my mouth over and over so hungrily, as if he were trying to crawl inside me. I ran my fingers over his body, loving the feel of him under my hands.

"Do I feel good to you?" Lash hissed, breaking the kiss.

"You always felt good," I groaned. "Always."

"So did you," he groaned, slipping his hand down to cup my thatch, and push two fingertips inside.

"Feel me," I breathed, taking hold of his hand and pushing his fingers deeper into me. "That's all you, my desire for you."

Lash let out a groan. "Teleport us to one of the guest rooms as soon as we're dry. I want to scream, and to hear you scream, and we do it here, we'll wake Dev for sure. I want you all to myself."

Lash shut off the shower, and we hurriedly dried off. I threw aside the towel and grabbed his hand, teleporting us to the green and gold room. Lash gave me a knowing grin on my choice of rooms, then eased me back on the guest room bed, spreading my legs.

"I love to feel you beneath me," Lash said passionately, as he pushed inside me. "To feel your skin against mine, your heart beating so fast, to hear you scream my name. God, you don't know how often I fantasized about you like this in jail, Sar." He began pumping into me immediately in long, deep strokes as I wrapped my legs around him, my hands on his ass keeping him deep within me as he moved.

We didn't last long. I came first, screaming his name, and he came a second later, screaming mine. I looked up at him, breathing hard atop me, and my mouth opened without even thinking. "I—"

I clamped down on the words before I uttered them, realizing I was afraid to tell him I loved him. I'd never been afraid to say it before in my life, but for some reason, I was now. I felt like I'd been here before with him, like a sense of deja vu, and that the previous time it had not ended well. But that was crazy. I've never been in this room with Lash, though I'd fantasized about it once or twice.

"What?" Lash said, immediately alert, holding my face with his hand. "You what?"

"I...I'm glad to be like this with you again," I stammered, kissing him gently. "I missed you very much. You weren't the only one who had fantasies."

"I missed you, too," he said, grinning widely.

"Do you want to eat lunch?" I offered

"You making it?" he said hopefully.

"I was thinking of soup—"

He grabbed the closest bed pillow and gave me a light whack with it. I laughed, and went to run off, but he grabbed me with a growl, and pulled me back to the bed.

"I'm going to kiss you until you agree to make something else," he teased, hugging me tightly. "No matter how long it takes. I never want to see soup again, ever! Especially not vegetable soup."

"That's not much incentive for agreeing," I laughed.

"Maybe that's the idea. I win, either way," Lash said. He let out a laugh, then kissed me hard, exploring my mouth with his tongue. I reached down for his prick, and felt him hard and ready.

"Answer me a question," I said, pulling back to look in his face, but not releasing him.

"Sure. What?"

"Why can weres go so many times in a row?" I said, stroking his erection with my hand. "Dev said he learned to, with practice, but—"

"But Danial wasn't like that, and neither were the human men you knew before," Lash finished, his tone husky. "But Ol' Theo was, right?"

"Yes," I said, flushing.

"Because we are part animal," Lash answered. "Animals mate for hours sometimes, when it's the right season to rut, depending on the species. A were female needs that from a were male, not just to have that much sex, but in that way, repeatedly. Were females often can't get pregnant from being with human males, though the opposite happens quite easily—"

I grabbed the pillow to hit him again, but Lash stopped me, laughing.

"It's a proven fact! Anyway, that's why we can. But because we are part human, too, we don't have a specific season, like animals do. The result is that weres are very sexual creatures, we think about sex a lot, and we need it a lot, to be content. So, that's why Serena has her job, and also why I'm going to have you again, right now."

Lash rolled me over on my stomach, and slid inside me with one continuous motion, uttering a long low moan of contentment. He slipped his hands under me, squeezing my breasts in his hands. He bit down lightly on my neck, gently sucking, and began moving fast almost at once. In a minute, he was spasming again within me, holding me tightly as he screamed out my name.

"God, Sar, you felt good," he said, kissing me as he withdrew. "Do you want to go again, or have lunch?"

"If I say 'no' now, can I say 'yes' later?"

Lash almost fell off the bed, he laughed so hard. "Yes!" he gasped out finally. "We can be together like this whenever you want. Just tell me, when you're with me, or call me on my phone, if you aren't. I've been leaving it on all the time lately."

"Then lunch," I said happily. "But really, breakfast for lunch. How about bacon, eggs, toast, sausage, *and* pancakes?"

Lash was salivating by the end of my sentence. He handed me a silvery grey terry robe from the back of the bathroom door, and got into one himself. I took it from him, but didn't put it on. Holding it, I remembered I'd bought these for guests, and each guest room had two. I looked at him uneasily.

His eyes shifted to snake in response. "There's no one out there to see us together, or scent us," he said flatly. "I hear no one. I won't say anything, if you prefer I not, though there will be talk if I keep spending my nights in Dev's room."

"It's not that," I said, putting my hand on his arm. "I just don't want to run into Venus. She's old enough to have questions, and you remember Elle, what happened with her…"

I trailed off, because Lash was looking at me skeptically in obvious disbelief.

*Maybe he's right. Why should we be embarrassed, to walk around in our robes? This is my home now, or shortly it's going to be, for good. Everyone has to know where he'd spent last night, and even if they are slow to catch on, Lash is right that it'll be obvious to everyone in a week where he's spending his nights. They'll know he isn't there for sex with Dev. They'll know we're lovers again.*

This wasn't like it had been with The Lust, when I'd had a torrid affair with him. There wasn't any shame on my part. I was going to be with him and Dev, to live here with them. And Danial, if he ever woke up, though every day that possibility seemed less likely.

"You're right," I said decisively, nodding, putting on the robe. "Everyone will smell that we've been together, including her. Maybe it's better to let her see us together when she's younger, so she accepts you and me being together. It's not like Elle, in that V likes you very much."

Lash just looked at me with his cold snake eyes.

*He thinks I'm embarrassed to be seen with him, to have Serena and the others at Hayden know he's my lover again. Does he not get why I was embarrassed the first time, that it was because I was married, and also because I was compelled, that it wasn't been my choice? That that is the reason I'd asked him to keep our being lovers then a secret?*

Maybe he didn't. But it was my choice now, to be with him. He was my choice. The time for secrets was finished. "Come on," I said, kissing him chastely. "I'll make you lunch, Lover."

Surprised, Lash took my hand, walking me to the kitchen. He got out the meat and eggs, and I began cooking the bacon and sausage, glad I'd made a run a few days ago with Titus to restock the fridge. The supplies I'd gotten in November had lasted a while, but nothing lasted forever.

"You joining me?" Lash asked in surprise. "You're making more than you did last time. Or am I remembering wrong?"

"I lost some weight this past month," I disclosed. "I can afford to splurge a little."

"I'm sorry about your son, Devon," Lash said gently. "I'm sorry, too that I haven't said it before now. But I didn't know how to bring it up, and Dev told me how upset you were over it. I didn't want to bring it up out of the blue."

"Thank you," I said, brushing away my sudden tears. "I miss him very much."

Lash put his arms around me, and I leaned back in to him, his closeness easing my sadness. As soon the meat was done, I removed it, stuck it in the oven below on the lowest setting to keep warm, and put a new batch in. As I got ready to turn the meat again, Lash kissed me lightly down my neck. "Once more?" he hissed with ardor.

I put down my spatula, turned around, and stared at him. "Here in the kitchen?"

"Why not?" His voice was easy, but the undercurrent running through it was like a live wire, sparking with energy, desire, and a little rampant naughtiness.

We'd just had sex twice earlier this morning, and a few minutes ago, twice again! What had I gotten myself into, becoming his lover?

"I'll be quick, like last time, if you're embarrassed," Lash assured. "And I'll be quiet, too. I give you my word there's no one here, Sar, except Devlin above us, sleeping, and the one prisoner in his cell in the dungeon. No one will walk in on us."

*Well then, why not?* I turned to him and kissed him. Lash wrapped his arms around me, and slowly lowered me to the floor, kissing me hungrily as he untied my robe and his, and I slipped my hand between us to guide him into me. Lash closed his eyes in pleasure when he felt me wrap my fingers around him, and once I had him in position, I grabbed his ass and pulled him down on me, driving him into me as I groaned. Two minutes later, he was crying out my name again, but much more softly this time.

He helped me up, and brushed the back of my robe off. Good thing I'd picked the dark gray color for the robes, and not white. Dev was going to have to hire a housekeeper. Or maybe I would see to that hiring myself, now that I was going to be something like his wife. The thought was both pleasing and unsettling.

I flipped the bacon and the sausage just in time, and told Lash to mix up the pancake batter. He gave me a blank look.

I cracked up laughing, and he laughed too, even though it was at his expense. I got the ingredients in a bowl, and handed it to him, and he mixed. Then we traded again, and I gave him some bacon and sausage to eat.

"Put in the bagels or toast, please," I said, pouring the pancake batter into the hot frying pans. Lash did it, and then he was easing up behind me again, putting his arms around me.

"You make me so happy, Sar," he said softly, moving my hair with one hand so he could kiss my neck. "I never thought—"

I heard a low growl, and looked up to see Theo and Terian in the doorway.

## Chapter Six

Theo's eyes were yellow, and Terian's were red, as they beheld Lash and me in our robes, him holding me as I made us breakfast. I could smell the scent of sex on myself, and I knew they could both smell it, too, and also probably that it had been only minutes before they arrived.

"I told you we should have driven here, not teleported right in," Terian said, rolling his eyes. He didn't look surprised, likely because I had just asked him for that potion.

Theo seemed unable to take his eyes off Lash and me. I went crimson under his steady gaze and looked down, but Lash just gave them both a wide grinning smile.

"Sorry, we didn't know we had company," Lash hissed gleefully, resting his head on my shoulder, holding me as he looked at them. "As you can see, we weren't expecting any visitors."

I took the opportunity to flip my pancakes, bacon, and sausage, and to thank God they hadn't arrived a few minutes before, to see us making love on the floor.

"I'm here to see your prisoner, Lash," Theo said gruffly. "And to thank you for saving my daughter."

I was surprised Theo was handling this so well, even though I wasn't his anymore. *Or maybe this just makes him believe that I've been lying to him all along about Lash and me.*

"You're welcome, Theo," Lash replied seriously, none of his usual maliciousness in his tone. "I'm just sorry I wasn't quicker. I left the werebear below alive for you, and he's healed, from the meat he's eaten today. But I beat the shit out of him last night, worked him over for two hours, and bit him a few times too, for the hurt he caused Elle."

"Which cell?" Theo's voice was strained.

"He's the only one down there. The other men are already dead."

Theo nodded, and with a last bitter look at Lash and me, he and Terian went down into the basement. I bit my lip, and flipped the pancakes over one final time. *Another minute, at most.*

Lash got the plates without a word, and I loaded them up with food, then turned off the stove. Lash got the toasted bagels, the butter, and a knife. We sat down at the table, and ate together in silence. But this wasn't the comfortable silence we'd shared so many times before. This silence was strained.

I thought a lot as I ate, staring at nothing, not really tasting the food I'd worked hard not to burn. I'd thought so often this fall of using Lash to get back at Theo, of seeing the expression on his face when he found us in bed, or somewhere else naked together, and laughing as I told him I was in love with Lash, that he and I were over. In spite of everything that had happened between Theo and me, it had just hurt me, seeing how hurt he was to know that Lash was my lover again. I'd felt just as bad as I knew I would, knowing I'd hurt him, as bad as I'd felt when Danial had found out Theo and I had gotten married, as bad as I'd felt telling Theo about Devlin and me. Hurting someone you loved always hurt you, too, no matter what else they might have done, or how much they had deserved to be hurt. That was a fact, just as it was a fact that part of me had really loved Theo for years, even if the intensity of that love had just been magic, and I didn't want a life with him now.

*At least I didn't do this purposely.* This wasn't just vengeful sex. Lash meant something to me, even if I couldn't seem to get the words out about how I felt. And for once, Theo hadn't started anything, and neither had Lash, though the latter I thought had probably lost most of his motivation for making nasty remarks now that I was his again.

"I'm sorry you were embarrassed, to have Terian and him see us like this, to have them know we were lovers again," Lash whispered, after a few minutes, breaking into my thoughts. "I should've known something like this would happen, if we did this, to ruin it—"

I looked over at him, and felt worse. He was looking at his plate, not at me. He sounded lost, and very, very upset. I put my hand on his shoulder gently.

"I just wanted—"

"It's okay," I said, leaning over and kissing his warm, scratchy cheek. "I was embarrassed, but not to be with you. I'd have been just as embarrassed to be like this with Dev, and have them walk in, and find us."

Lash didn't say anything, or look up at me. It was obvious he didn't believe me. I didn't believe me, either. I tried to explain it better, hoping I wasn't making things worse.

"I mean to say, I feel bad that Theo found out like he did—that I'm with you now. I remember finding out about him and Jenny after they'd been together, and that was awful."

Lash still didn't say anything, but he closed his eyes as if in pain. "I shouldn't have said anything that morning to you. It wasn't my place—"

*Shit, I'm making it worse.* I got up from my chair, and crouched beside his chair. "I'm glad you told me, or I wouldn't have known until later, Lash. I just meant—"

"Like you felt when you saw Dev and Catherine. I get it, Sar."

"No, you don't," I said loudly, getting up, and putting my arms around him. He was rigid in my embrace. "Catherine didn't mean anything to Dev. Jenny means something to Theo now, even if she didn't when they first had sex. You mean a lot more to me than she does to him. And he knows that, Lash. He knows I wouldn't be with you casually, that—"

*I love you.*

"—you mean a lot to me. He knows this isn't just sex, not for either of us. It's the deepest wound you've ever given him, and I helped you do it. That makes me feel bad, because even though he's an ass, I still care about him."

Lash didn't say anything, or look at me. But he hugged me hesitantly.

"Nothing is ruined," I assured him. "I'm happy to be here with you, Lash. God knows, I've wanted to be with you again like this since we were together in the Everglades."

Lash looked up at me with his snake eyes. But I also saw they were moist, and wondered if he had changed partially to keep tears from falling. I knew better than to say anything about that, or give any sign I'd even noticed.

"Eat your breakfast," I said, giving him a smile. "Or I won't make any more for you, ever. Afterwards, maybe we can finish watching *Fantastic Four*? I've saved it for you and me. I've got to see if Richards was able to build that machine in a few weeks."

Lash leaned over and kissed me, then he grinned. And the grim moment was broken.

＊ ＊ ＊ ＊

The rest of that day passed less eventfully. Lash and I eventually got dressed after breakfast. Devlin roused himself enough to join us, likely more to make sure he got equal time with me instead of any real desire to see the end of the *Fantastic Four*. He'd scented the both of us when we came into the bedroom in our robes, and rolled his eyes, then made some remark to Lash about how he wasn't wasting any time. But Devlin was grinning when he said it, and Lash had grinned back at him, and kissed me, and told him he was damn right.

The three of us had been sitting on the couch watching the end of the movie when the phone rang. Lash got up at once to get it. I shot a questioning look at Dev.

"Gina," Devlin said to me. "Lash had a standing appointment with her daily for about ten minutes ago. I'm sure she's calling to see where he is. He's most likely going to tell her he can go back to seeing her once a week or so for his usual massages."

"Did you know?"

Devlin knew what I meant, and nodded. "I could tell he wasn't getting enough release," he said blatantly. "Not that he was getting none. Gina isn't weresnake though, so I guessed—"

"Why didn't you tell me?"

"Lash obviously didn't want you to know. So what good would it have done to tell you?"

"None, I guess," I admitted. "But I wish I'd have known."

"Would it have made you love—"

"Shut up!" I interrupted sternly.

Devlin's eyes widened. "Ahh!" he said with relish. "I certainly don't want to spill any secrets. Though I'd love to see his face when you tell him."

"Tell me what?" a tired voice said. "You giving him another Oath, Sar?"

I looked over to the doorway, and saw that Theo had finally came back upstairs with Terian. There was more than a little blood on him, and his bloody shoes were in his hand. His eyes were still yellow, as he looked at Devlin and me, but I met his eyes this time, and didn't flinch.

"Yes, she is," Devlin purred, his golden eyes burning with pleasure, as he possessively caressed my shoulder. "Though that's not any of your business anymore, Theo. Why don't you go use one of the guest room showers, before you track blood all over my carpet? And Terian, no more teleporting in without calling first. Is that understood?"

Terian rolled his eyes as he nodded assent. Theo just stared, then said nonchalantly, "Thanks, I will. I want to get back home. If you'll excuse me, Dalcon?"

Devlin waved his hand, and Theo headed off to the guest rooms without looking back.

"Sar!" Lash called. "Phone!"

I got up, and headed to the kitchen. It was Stephen, and he gave me the name and number of a Mrs. Rosalyn Hyan. "She's good, especially with young women. Call her tomorrow, Sar, I'm sure she'll make time for Elle."

"Thanks," I replied, the weight of what had happened crashing back down on me. "I'll call her tomorrow."

I hung up, and turned around to see Lash watching me. But what was unusual was Terian was there in the doorway, and he was studying Lash as if he was looking for something. Lash put up with his scrutiny for about thirty seconds.

"You got a problem, demon?" Lash hissed, turning to Tears and baring his viper fangs. "Don't make me think too hard on you, or I'll remember I promised you a few bullets."

"Don't think too hard. You'll blow a gasket in that pea brain of yours," Terian said bitterly.

Lash bristled immediately, and put his hand on his whip. "I don't care who your father is," he hissed angrily. "I'm going to kick your ass!"

"Lash, please," I said, stepping between them. "Terian, how is Elle? I left her a note and tried to visit this morning and left another message with Cia, but it's late afternoon already and I've heard nothing. Is she still sleeping or is she with Jenny or one of the werefoxes right now?" *I was going to go see her right now anyway, but it was better to know what I was walking into.*

Tears looked at me sadly. Lash eased back against the wall, his arms folded across his chest, his eyes on Terian.

"She cried as soon as she woke up an hour ago," Terian said. "She said to tell you she'd call you tomorrow, that she needed to not see anyone today. She's asleep now. I gave her a potion at her request, so she could sleep most of today and tonight. She's really messed up, Sar."

"I'll call her tomorrow," I said, feeling terrible. "I'll make her an appointment today, right now."

"Good," Terian said. "Theo's messed up over it, too. He blames himself for not watching her better. And seeing you with Lash this morning didn't help."

"Demon, I'm done warning you," Lash hissed.

"But I'm glad you're together," Terian said in a pained whisper.

It was hard to tell who was more surprised, Lash or me. Both our mouths dropped open.

"Take good care of her," Terian said, fixing his eyes on Lash. "Or I'll be coming to kick *your* ass, Lash. And there won't be anything left of you when I'm done but smoke and ashes."

Lash blinked, then shut his mouth and nodded. "Fair enough."

"I'll go wait for Theo," Terian said, walking out. "He shouldn't take long. Good-bye Sar."

"'Bye," I mumbled, wondering at his change of heart.

Lash came over and hugged me. "Why did he say that? He's never liked me."

"I don't understand it, either," I said, shrugging.

"Are you coming back to finish the movie or not?" Devlin called from the other room.

We headed back to sit with Devlin. Venus had joined him on the couch, and she was sitting on his lap. She looked at Lash and me with a little curiosity, her golden eyes interested as she scented the air. I picked her up, and settled her down on my lap as I sat between them.

"Mom, Dad said you are going to live here for good," Venus said happily.

"That's right," I affirmed, glancing at Devlin, who resembled the cat who'd eaten the cream.

"I'm glad," she said, a huge smile breaking over her face. "I don't want you not to live here, like you used to. I'd miss you, if you went to live somewhere else again."

"So would I," Lash hissed softly, as he leaned over and gently kissed my neck.

"And I," Devlin murmured, his eyes hot. "I think—"

"Can we play a game, now the movie is over?" Venus said excitedly.

I almost burst out laughing, from the stymied look on Devlin's face. "A short one," I said with a smile. "Go grab one, and bring it into the kitchen."

"I'll go with you, and help you pick one, V," Lash said, picking her up from my lap, and setting her on her feet. He took her hand, and before long, they were back with the board game Peanut Butter and Jelly.

Devlin protested feebly, but he was a good sport. Venus won, of course, though Lash came close to beating her. Devlin lost the worst, but then his thoughts weren't on the game at all.

Before long, I tucked V in, and she gave me a good night kiss. At that moment, I realized something. *Lash and Dev are waiting for me, but they can wait a little longer.*

"Venus, repeat after me," I said seriously. "Please?" She looked at me oddly, but nodded. I recited, "Now I Lay Me Down to Sleep." She said the words after me, frowning a little in concentration.

"Am I going to die like Devon?" she said softly, when we'd finished. "Are you worried?"

She reminded me so much of Elle in that moment I had to clear my throat a few times, before I could speak.

"No," I assured her. "You'll live longer than most weres or humans, V. But it's way past time you knew about God, and I learned this prayer, when I was little. I'd like to say it with you from now on, at night, if you wouldn't mind."

"I don't want anyone to have my soul but me," Venus said defiantly. "It's mine."

"You'll have it all your life," I guaranteed her. "If you should die, your soul will leave your body, and go to Heaven. The same thing will happen to

Lash, or to your father, if they should ever die." *I'm not really lying here, I hope.*

"Or you?"

"Or me."

"But then who would take care of me?" she asked, and her voice broke a little. "If you were all gone?"

She was growing up so fast, faster than T had. It was time I was the mother I had always lamented I wasn't, and stopped relying on others for life lessons that were my place to teach my children.

"Your brother, T, or Titus, or Terian, or even Theo would, if something happened to the three of us," I said in my best reassuring voice. "But nothing is going to happen, V. Not to us, and not to you. We are going to live here together and be happy for a long, long time."

"Are you always going to smell like Lash, like you sometimes smell like Dad?"

"Yes," I answered, hugging her. "And if you need your Dad or me in the night, don't be surprised to find Lash in our bedroom, all right?"

"Okay," she said, somewhat annoyed. "But he has his own room. Is someone else in his room now? Why do I have to sleep in my own room if he doesn't? He's a man."

I couldn't help cracking a smile. "Sometimes he might be in his room. I—"

"I heard him this morning in your room, making the noises you and Dad usually make."

I swallowed some saliva and coughed a little. I'd forgotten her hearing was so acute. "You'll hear him and your father make those sounds probably most every night," I said, making myself say the words. "And you may hear me. Don't be afraid, or worried, because no one is being hurt, V. And if you need your father, or Lash, or me, for any reason, just knock on the door. It doesn't matter what sounds you hear, if you need me or your dad, come to us."

"All right," she said, nodding and settling herself down into bed.

"Now get some sleep," I said. "I love you."

"Love you too, Mom."

I turned off her light, and shut the door with relief, hoping I was doing the right thing. But Native Americans had done okay, living in one room and children hearing everything, and seeing it, too. It was probably still done in cultures today, just not with any of the people I knew. Besides, the only alternative would be soundproofing and that might be dangerous, if she called out in the night needing us and Devlin or Lash were unable to hear her.

I went into Devlin's bedroom, and found him and Lash lying in bed naked, leering smiles on their faces. Or maybe they were laughing because they had overheard my conversation with V.

Giving them both an aloof look, I went past them to the bathroom, shed my clothes, dressed in my robe, and got ready for bed. Emerging from the bathroom, I stepped to the edge of the bed. Lash undid my robe, and slipped it off my shoulders. Grabbing my waist with his hands, he pulled me into the middle of them. Devlin kissed me roughly, touching my hot skin with his cool hands. Lash's warm hands parted my thighs. His tongue caressed my labia gently, seeking entrance. I moaned loudly as I felt his tongue tweak my clit once, then slip inside me, and began stroking.

"Sarelle," Devlin whispered seductively, his eyes hot molten gold, almost glowing in the darkness. "I've long wanted to watch you in my arms, as he had you this way."

I was already beginning to jerk under Lash's skillful administrations, unable to restrain soft cries of arousal. Devlin kissed my neck gently, but he mostly watched me, his own excitement growing at my aroused cries and shuddering body, as I grew more frantic and anxious for release. As much as I wanted it to last, Lash was too good for me to be able to withstand him for long. I came screaming loudly, my hands in Lash's hair, his hands holding my hips tightly, not letting me get away until he had left me weak and shaking, covered with sweat.

Lash kissed his way up from my thatch to my throat, as he had done those many months ago. He pushed his hips tight to mine, driving into me with a possessive hiss. He lasted only a few seconds before he came, shouting my name. He slipped out of me, and then Devlin was rolling me onto him, panting hard, and he drove the full length of himself into me with a savage cry. Reeling from my first orgasm, I welcomed Dev eagerly, pushing his rhythm from slow and gentle to fast and hard, wanting the sheer pleasure of being filled over and over to last even as I clawed my way to a second release. Too soon he was coming, groaning as he jetted into me, and I climaxed again, pushing my hips down on his as I yelled exultantly over and over. I collapsed on him as our orgasms ebbed and he hugged me to him.

"I love you," he said softly, looking up at me affectionately.

"I love you, too," I said quietly, feeling very, very self-conscious.

But Lash didn't seem to mind that I hadn't said those three words to him. As I eased off Devlin, he pulled me to him, and hugged me hard. "I've wanted to do that with you again," he hissed tenderly, sucking gently on my neck. "I remembered how much you liked it, and I've only ever done it with other weres before you—"

"Shh," Devlin said in a very soft tone. "I'm sure Sar doesn't want to think about you and other women when we're in bed, just as you don't want to think about her and—"

"Don't say his name," Lash hissed in a low tone, his arms tightening around me. "She's done with him."

I kissed him, and he kissed me back, and then he drew back from me, as if considering something, his dark eyes a little hesitant. "Sorry, if I offended you. Just lie here with us, Sar. We'll sleep."

I snuggled between them, and for the first time in weeks, I needed no drugs to sleep.

* * * *

That next morning, as we had breakfast, Lash told me that he would be gone for the day. I knew by the way he said the words that a "demolition" was in order. In short, someone was going to die.

"Please be careful," I said nervously, hugging him.

"This is a distance job. But I always wear a vest anyway, if not my armor. I have that same Kevlar that looks like leather that Devlin has, besides the black armor that you have a set of yourself. Both will stop most anything, save that blue fire. Nothing can stop that, at least, not yet, though some companies are trying new methods—"

I hugged him tightly, cutting off his words. Lash hugged me back. "I'll be back tonight. Titus will teleport me, when it's done. Rip will be here with you and Dev and V, so you'll be safe."

I moved to kiss him, but he held me at arm's length. "What?"

"I'm afraid of you kissing me for good luck, like last time," Lash hissed quietly, and I could see he was only half joking. "I don't want to end up in jail again."

"Then I'll kiss you when you get home," I said, hugging his body to me, burying my face in his throat. "And if you ever get arrested again, I'm teleporting you out of prison, I'm not leaving you there, not ever again, no matter what anyone says."

"Ah, you're sweet to say you'd rescue me," Lash sighed, nuzzling me. "My Sweetness."

He embraced me once more briefly, then he was gone, the door closing softly behind him. Shaking off my worry for him, I got moving with my own stressful itinerary for the day.

First, I called Rosalyn, the therapist. I expected to leave a message, but got her secretary instead. When a last minute cancellation for today was offered an hour from then, I took it, surprised as today was Sunday. Grabbing my novel, I teleported to Danial's, where I ended up in the woods instead of inside the house.

*Fucking Theo*. Grimacing, I walked to the door, and knocked. A second later, Jenny opened the door.

"Hi," I said, mustering a smile. "I need to speak to Elle. I got her an appointment in one hour—"

"Please come in," she said quickly, stepping aside. "Theo told me."

I bit my lip. *It's normal he would tell her. Now say something!*

"He was very upset," she added quietly. "But T doesn't know, or anyone else, other than that someone tried to kidnap her and she got traumatized as a result." She paused. "Elle's in the shower, and has been for the past hour. But if you wait here, I'll tell her that you're here."

*Fuck that.* "I'll go right in, thanks," I said bluntly, and gently pushed past her. I strode to Elle's room and knocked on the door, shooting a sad glance quickly at Devon's now empty room. Elle opened it, fully dressed. She hugged me, then gestured for me to come in.

"I have an appointment for you in a half hour or so," I said, closing the door behind us. "A woman named Rosalyn. She's a therapist. But we need to leave now, because I can't teleport you the first time. Luckily she's not far from Stephen's office."

I expected her to cry out in protest, to say she didn't want to go, but she just nodded, and said, "I'm ready."

We walked out to the great room together, where Jenny was waiting for us apprehensively. I said good-bye to Jenny as politely as I could, trying my best to be nice to her. *She's trying, and I should try, too. It's not her fault Theo is an ass.* Then I saw her ring finger, saw the huge diamond sparkling on it, and thought only about making it to the door.

She shut the door behind Elle and me, and we walked to the garage, where Elle keyed in the password. It had also been changed. I got into one of the Expeditions, and grabbed the keys from underneath the visor. I put the key in the ignition but abruptly stopped before I started it. *When were these last checked for explosives, or other magical traps? This morning? Or a month ago?*

"What?" Elle said, looking worried. "Mom?"

*Sigh.* I called Theo, and it went to voice mail. I tried T next, and got the same thing. *Shit, I don't have time for this.* I called Titus, and he was there in the next second outside the truck, before the phone rang twice. I looked at him in shock, my phone still to my ear.

"Your tracking spell is on you," he said with a smile. "And caller ID. What's up?"

"Thanks," I said quickly. "Can you check the SUV, to see if it's safe? We need to get to an appointment at noon. It's at a witch therapist's office, her name is Rosalyn—"

"Ros," Titus said, nodding. "Come out of the truck, and I'll teleport you both there. I know where her office is. You won't have to waste time driving."

We got out, Titus held our hands, and immediately, we were there. "I've got to get back to Lash, to watch his back," Titus said, hugging me goodbye. "Then I'll be with T later on this afternoon. Call if there's a problem, and I'll be here directly."

I nodded, and he disappeared.

"He seems nice," Elle said thoughtfully. "Why does Dad...did Dad not like demons? Terian is a good guy, too. He's marrying Sundown, and she loves him. I could understand him not liking them after what happened to him, but he didn't like them before that..." she trailed off.

"I'm not sure," I said, thinking on it as we walked inside the office building. "But your father has never liked them, for some reason, and I think Theo got some of his prejudice from him. Probably something in his past, Honey."

"Don't ever call me 'Honey'," Elle growled, her blue eyes shifting to yellow.

I felt terrible, guessing why at once. "I'm sorry, Elle," I said, deliberately using her name. "Your father had a lot of bad memories. He never talked about most of them."

"Maybe he should come to therapy, too," Elle said darkly. "If he ever wakes up."

I didn't know what to say to that. Elle sat down in the waiting area, and I gave the secretary Elle's name, and address. She asked who I wanted billed, and gave her my name, and then began to give her Hayden's address. She stopped me when she heard the name.

"I know that address. Ros got a call from Stephen this morning. Please have a seat, and I'll call Elle, when it's time. The appointment will be at least an hour, but if Elle wants to go on, it will be longer, as long as she wants to talk. Rosalyn has all her first appointments that way."

I nodded, and sat down. Fifteen minutes later, they called in Elle.

Two and a half hours later, she came out. I'd gone to the bathroom twice, and finished my book, and been dozing for the last forty-five minutes. But I wasn't complaining. I was grateful, that she was here getting help. I would have been happy to sit here and be uncomfortable for as many hours as she wanted to talk, and then to come back tomorrow, too.

"She wants to talk to you for a minute," Elle said, her voice emotional as she flopped down in a chair next to me.

I got up and went in. Rosalyn stood up when I entered, revealing she was very short. "I'm half troll, half goblin," she said in explanation, then smiled.

I didn't know what to say. I smiled and nodded in return, figuring that was polite.

"I know, being human, you probably heard goblins and trolls are ugly," she chortled.

"Yes," I said honestly. "But you aren't."

That was an understatement. She was beautiful, more so than I, if truth be told.

"Next you'll think this is some kind of magic," she said, looking at me a little sadly. "Humans always say that next, but it's not. This is the real me."

"Good," I said with a shrug. "Being pretty is a lot easier in this world than being ugly."

Roz looked a little taken aback, but nodded. "That's sad, but true. But it says something about you, that you said it so casually." She wrote something down on her paper.

I felt very self-conscious. This had been some kind of test. Was my reply good or bad? "If you had used glamour, I wouldn't think it bad, either," I added quickly. "It's like make-up, or hair coloring, or plastic surgery. Why not use it, if it makes you feel better about yourself?"

Roz looked at me with surprise, and then wrote more down on her pad. A lot more. *Shit, maybe I'm making a bigger hole for myself.*

"Do you know why I wanted to talk to you?"

I wanted badly to echo Lash's words and tell her I hadn't a fucking clue, but stifled the urge to joke just to break the overwhelming tension I was feeling. This was serious, and I did have a clue, having had a fair amount of therapy in my life. "Because you think she has issues with me to address, or because you want my help with some background on her, to clarify something in her past?" I offered. "Or both?"

She nodded. "Both."

"Go ahead."

"Elle has a lot of issues," she said frankly. "I'm very worried about her. She needed therapy without the additional trauma of her rape."

I nodded. That wasn't a surprise. Most everyone I knew needed therapy, except maybe V. Once she fully understood exactly who her father was, she'd need therapy just for that.

"She said her father's Theopolis," Roz said, reading. "But her Dad is Danial, and he's in a coma?"

I explained as fast as I could Elle's background, how Danial had raised her and she'd grown fast, with Theo being gone for her younger years. How she'd lost her younger brother recently, but had both an older brother, and a younger sister. I stopped abruptly mid-explanation, and looked at her. "I need you to confirm you're powerful enough to keep these secrets," I said bluntly. "Elle's rape is a direct result of my previous therapist's weakness."

"I am," Roz assured me. "You know of Titus, I believe? He and his…um, wife, Alerian, they came to me for counseling a century or so ago, and more recently again, too."

Wow, she was old. "Titus said he knew you."

"I'm older than he is. I do this work because I had a bad experience, in my early years, and I want to help women and couples to work past some of their problems, so they can be happy. I think it's a worthwhile endeavor."

"I'm glad to know you help couples."

Roz nodded. "I know of Devlin Dalcon, and what he's done in his time as Ruler," she said. Dark anger passed over her face, before it abruptly cleared. "I have also heard of Theopolis O'Connor, and Danial Racklan, and certainly of the infamous Lash."

"I'm not sure what Elle has told you about me," I stated quickly. "But—"

"I smell snake scent on you, dear," Roz interrupted gently. "I know enough from Elle to know it's his. I know he works for Devlin, and rumor is he's young again. He must have given Titus half his fortune for that potion he took that saved him. But what's five hundred thousand, or even a million, or ten million to be young again? I've done it enough times, myself."

I had so many questions I didn't know what to ask first. Lash was that rich? But then he was old, and he made a lot of money killing people. Being rich naturally followed. But millions? And that's how much it would cost to save him magically, if he were dying? How rich was Devlin that he could afford that? What was I Oathing into? *Focus on what's important.* "The same potion can be used more than once, for a being? And there is more than the one?"

Roz nodded. "They only last so long, and there are unpleasant side effects, depending on what is used. My troll nature makes me resistant to those, dear. But yes, there are potions with side effects that aren't too bad, though they are expensive in the extreme. But I doubt that is a problem for Lash, especially with Dalcon for a friend. Have Titus call me, when it's time. I can point him to the right texts, so he can find a better potion for Lash to use next time around."

"Why would you help him?" I said suspiciously with narrowed eyes. "Or Devlin?"

"I've seen a lot of women, and men in my years, and it's easy to see that you care about him. I've heard you may live a long life. I would guess you'd want him with you as long as possible. Part of Elle getting better is seeing her mother in a good relationship with a man who doesn't abuse her."

That had to be a dig at Devlin. *Sigh.* What could I say that didn't sound defensive?

"Lash has done much evil in his life, but he has never harmed a woman to my knowledge, at least not one who didn't attack him first. I've heard what he did for Elle, and how he saved you from a similar situation—"

"He did."

"But are you happy with him? Do you love him, Sarelle? You began a physical relationship with him when you were married, committed to another man, and often, those matches don't result in healthy relationships. Or ones that last, as evidenced by what happened with Danial, Theo, and you..."

She trailed off, seeing my face, and how upset I was.

"I am going to him as a snake," I said in a breaking voice, my walls falling down in pieces, and my tears following almost immediately. "I love him, I have for months, but I was married, and I tried to do the right thing!"

"There, there," she said, handing me a tissue. "That's all you can do, to try your best."

"But I still feel guilty, for what I did! He's a killer, and he's hurt a lot of people."

"You did wrong, having an affair with him like you did," she said flatly. "But you know that, and you did your best to make it right. Let it go, and get on with your life. Lash's misdeeds are his own, not yours. Your daughter needs you, and so will your son, with their father gone."

I didn't think that was all completely true, but I swallowed it, hook, line and sinker, because it made me feel so much better, to let go of my guilt.

"And so will your other daughter, with the kind of father she has in Dalcon. He has no respect for women, none at all. He thinks of them as objects to pleasure himself with."

"I know," I whispered. "That's been hard to deal with. But I'm working on it, and having Venus has changed him. Seeing what happened to Elle has also affected him."

"Some men never change," Roz said in a low voice. "Don't think that he has, Sarelle."

"Should I make Elle come and live with me?" I asked, changing the subject. "Would that be best? I could watch her a lot easier."

"Not for now," Roz said. "She needs to be where she feels at home, and that is Danial's house. But visit her often, and come with her, to these appointments."

"I will."

"And if you need counseling yourself, call for an appointment," she said, getting to her feet. "I always have room in my schedule for a woman who needs me."

On impulse, I gave her a hug quickly, and she cackled a little, and hugged me back. I left, wondering if she was going to write anything else down on her pad about that.

Elle was waiting for me, and we went to a late lunch at the local Pizza Hut. Even though she didn't talk much, I could see she was a little bit more her old self. Time would do the rest. Time, and love.

* * * *

That week passed quickly.

I had done some online Christmas shopping, but not much. I got busy on Monday, and ordered the rest of the gifts. Devlin had handed me a Mastercard much as Danial had, years ago, but his was not black—it was pure white, almost silver. I used that for most of the presents, though I used my own card for a few select purchases. Most of the gifts were gift baskets: bath stuff for Elle, a honeymoon food basket for Terian and Sundown, a wine basket for T, a breakfast-in-bed basket for Titus and Alerian, and a coffee basket for my parents. I also got Elle some art supplies, and T a few books. Venus, I got probably more than I should, but she was growing so fast, I worried she would be an adult by next Christmas. So I got her about five more board games, some movies on DVD, some CDs of children's music, some sneakers, and a large stuffed dragon so big she could ride it. I had Keith hide the boxes in one of the guest rooms, and snuck in there every day to wrap things as they came in, glad I'd had the foresight to order a roll of wrapping paper, gift tags, and bows with the presents.

It felt weird not getting Theo anything, but I told myself he had someone else to get him things. He didn't need anything from me. And what would I get him? A gift basket for breakfast-in-bed for two? *Bleah.*

I was glad too that Solutions, Inc. was shut down this week and next. I needed the time to finish two handmade presents I was making for Elle, and I was behind on both.

I was saved the embarrassment of asking for my Christmas tree and decorations, which had been stored at Danial's, when T showed up with it, the boxes of ornaments, and Elle on that Wednesday. That afternoon, three of us decorated the tree. Last, Elle and I carefully put on the spiders she, Danial, and I had made, and then I made us some eggnog. We sat near the tree afterwards, sipping it, and talking of nothing serious as we watched the lights blink on and off.

Lash came into the living room near dusk, staring first at the tree, and then at us. It was obvious he was uneasy, likely due to the strong scent of blood that followed him from another job he'd done earlier that morning, though there was none visible.

I went to Lash and hugged him. "I'm very glad you're home safe," I said with relief, self-conscious of T and Elle watching us. "Go take a shower, then join us if you want to. I'll make you some eggnog if you like, when you come down."

"Thanks, Sweetness," he said politely, nodding to me. "I'll be a half hour or so. Hello to you also, T, and Elle."

He went upstairs, and I turned to see T and Elle getting up. Terian had appeared. I looked at them, and they looked at each other uneasily. Terian looked at the ceiling, obviously uncomfortable.

"We have to get back," T said with a forced smile as he hugged me. "Jenny has her own tradition of going out and getting a live tree. So we are going out on Dad's...my land, and cut one down, and then we are going to decorate it."

"I understand," I answered calmly, feeling let down. "Thank you for coming, to decorate a tree with me. I enjoyed spending time with you both."

"I'm sorry we can't stay," Elle said, as she hugged me. "But we'll see you at Christmas, at Grandma's."

"I love you both," I said, and they disappeared. I sat down on the couch, rubbing my temples.

"Did they leave because of me?" Lash asked quietly, startling me as he sat down next to me, his hair still wet from the shower. *He had hurried to come back as fast as he could.* I felt a stab of anger at Jenny, because I'd have liked to have Elle and T spend more time with Lash and me, and also Venus and Devlin.

"No," I answered, leaning on his shoulder. "They have to get back to set up a tree with Theo and Jenny. It had nothing to do with you."

Lash hugged me. "I'm sorry. This can't be easy for you."

"You being here makes it easier," I said, burrowing into him. "I—"

"You set up a tree?" Devlin exclaimed, entering the room with Venus. "Why didn't you tell me, come get me and V? We would have liked to help!"

Seeing V's upset expression, I promptly felt worse than before. Surprisingly, it was Lash who made the save. "You can still help," he said quickly. "For some reason, we are missing a vital part of the tree, unless there is a new fad I'm not aware of."

I looked up, then narrowed my eyes. Theo was not about to part with his memories, not a one of them. Our tree had no star.

The three of them looked at me.

*Time for Mom to save the day.* I went to my craft room, and came back with a spool of silver thread, a needle, heavy wire, some silver material, some pipe cleaners, silver glass beads, a Sharpie marker in black, and scissors.

"Cut out a star," I said, and handed Devlin the scissors and material. "Leave me room to sew the edges together, about an inch."

"Bend this into the shape of a star, depending on how big he makes it," I said, handing the wire to Lash. "And make a spring on the bottom, to fit onto the tree."

"What about me?" Venus said with desperation. "I want to help!"

"You will, when they finish," I said, hugging her. "You need to tell me where to put the beads on the star, so it shines like a real star does. And I'll need help sewing the edges closed."

"Okay," she said with gusto. "Hurry up, Dad!"

Devlin grimaced, but he was already nearly done, and he handed me the cloth. He'd done a good job. But then, he'd become skilled with scissors, with all the doll clothes he'd cut out for V.

Lash was having more trouble with the wire, not because it was so heavy a gauge, but because he was so strong, it bent more than he wanted it to. But he, too, was nearly finished.

Venus showed me where to put the beads, and I sewed them by hand on the silver cloth. And then we all went into the sewing room, and I helped her sew the edges of the star together on the machine, leaving a big enough gap to turn it the right side out.

I slid it over the wire, pushed in a little stuffing, and then whip-stitched it closed. We went back out to the tree, and I handed the marker around, and we all signed the bottom of it, Venus with a wobbly "V", then Devlin dated it. Then he lifted her up, and she put it on top, completing our perfect Christmas tree.

* * * *

Even though Ulysses didn't show himself in those last days before Christmas, the feeling of foreboding lingered in the air like the scent of burned flesh. Lash put in a few hours every day on the computer looking for Ulysses, and spent time with Titus teleporting to the places Ulysses had been seen, or where previous attacks had been made. But he still could find no trace of him. Devlin told me quietly that had never happened before and it was easy to see that frustrated Lash, as he came home in terrible moods and spent hours in the gym afterwards alone, "working out his anger" as he called it.

But the other problem was Lash himself.

# Chapter Seven

Lash now spent every night with Devlin and me. He appeared about ten or eleven, and climbed in bed beside me, usually settling down against my back. Devlin wasn't about to give up his favored spot of sleeping on my chest, which he expected to be empty for him when he wandered in about four or five a.m. But usually after one coupling each, Lash and Devlin acted content to just hold me, and sleep. They also both abided by my rule, which was if I was sleeping, they didn't wake me, and if they woke me, it was not just for sex.

During the days while Devlin slept, I was awake and busy. And Lash began to come to me for sex. When he showed up at nine a.m. Monday morning in my sewing room, and closed the door behind him, I knew at once by his grin what he had in mind. I didn't mind: I'd half expected it, that he would come to me in the days so we could be alone. I was as eager as he was, as we'd been unable to touch like that for so long. I put my sewing aside at once, and almost ran to him, throwing my arms around him as my mouth opened on his.

Lash kissed me passionately, immediately easing me down to the floor, as he unbuckled his belt. He had me there on the carpet quickly, amidst the piles of old velvet. Lash kissed me gently afterwards, as he was pulling on his pants, then helped me to my feet. "Will you be here, for the next few hours?" Lash said, his hand already on the doorknob.

"Yes," I said, confused. "I want to put in a few hours on this—"

"Then I'll be back soon, for a longer visit with you," Lash said with a leer. "I didn't get to hear my name, and I'll be looking forward to that later." He left with a last parting grin.

Why was he acting so oddly? Maybe he was trying to be funny? Guess I'd have to wait and see.

An hour later, he was back and had me again. And the next hour, and the next. We had lunch together at noon with V and Serena, some sandwiches I had made. The afternoon was the same, though by then I was in Devlin's office using the computer, and the floor there was a little harder, but I didn't mind. I liked Lash's enthusiasm, and enjoyed his caresses. I loved that he couldn't seem to get enough of me, and to hear that satisfied note in his voice after I'd come for him.

But by the middle of the second day, I was beginning to get sore from all his attention. It was also getting hard for me to orgasm, because I'd had so much sex. There was also the problem that I couldn't get much work done, as just as soon as I got back into whatever I was doing, Lash would show up again. In short, I needed a break. So, after the eleventh time, as he was pulling on his pants, I stopped him.

"Lash, I have to ask, is this, um, normal for you?"

He buttoned his jeans, then buckled his belt. "It's because I'm younger than I was," he said proudly. "Theo probably wasn't like this, I know."

Well, sometimes he had been, but I wasn't going to say anything. Next Lash would think this was some sort of competition.

"I just feel like I'm twenty again, Sar. And now that we can be together like this, I want you as much as you will let me have you." Lash looked down at me, suddenly concerned. "Are you sore? Did I hurt you?"

"I'm a little sore," I admitted. "I want you to be happy, but—"

"I am very happy, to be your lover again," Lash interrupted, kissing me. "But I don't have to take so long, if it's a problem. I'll be really quick from now on."

*Wait a minute. He is going to be quick? That's his solution?*

"Just tell me, when you want to come, when I have you," Lash said lustily. "And I'll make sure you do. Tell me, too, if you want me to go down on you, or...other things. I need to get back to my training. I'll see you shortly, Sar."

Abruptly, he was gone again, leaving me to sink back into my chair and ponder what he'd meant by "other things." It was surprising that he hadn't offered to give me a break, like he had back in the Everglades. Maybe with enough time, he'd relax, and some of his desire for me would lessen. As much as I wanted him to want me, this was too much.

Wednesday, Lash was gone on his job. But Thursday, Lash seemed to be insatiable. No matter how many times he had me, he still seemed to want me as much as he had the first time. But he had me fast now, climaxing in the space of a minute, where before he'd taken five or ten. Since I spent most of that day working on my sewing, trying hard to finish Venus's present, he knew right where to find me. Even then, I couldn't make myself refuse him; I loved pleasing him that way. I treasured his eager moans when he first pushed into me, and his loud cries as he came inside me. As always, I cherished the way he held me so tightly to him when he came, as if he could never put his body far enough inside mine. But part of me was sad, too, because for all the times he'd made love to me, he never said anything to me about his feelings for me. He never told me he loved me, or that he was in love with me. And being told I felt good just wasn't the same.

I told myself not to be surprised. He wasn't the type to bare his heart easily. But as the days went by, I began to wonder if he did love me.

* * * *

Things came to a head on Friday afternoon. I'd just finished sewing for the day, and been heading into the kitchen for a drink of water. I grabbed a glass, filled it at the sink, and drank it down greedily. It tasted so good, but I was thirsty. I'd been having sex all afternoon. Lash had come to me almost every half hour. *It's good I was almost done, or I never would have finished V's present...*

Then I felt Lash behind me, rubbing his body against mine. I didn't have to look to know he was erect again; I felt him against my rear as he moved his hips suggestively against me. I gave a mental sigh as I felt him reaching up from behind me to squeeze my breasts.

"Come upstairs with me," Lash hissed. "We have a few minutes."

I'd had enough of the "wham, bam, thank you, Sar" treatment. "Sorry, I'm busy," I said, not turning around to him. "Maybe later."

"I'll make it worth your while, my Sweetness," he said in my ear. Then he began kissing down my neck, his hooked fangs brushing me.

"Anything I want?" I said, keeping my back to him.

"Anything you want that won't take more than a half hour."

"No can do," I answered, smirking a bit. "I need more than that."

"Why does it always have to be what you want?" Lash hissed in my ear, real anger in his voice. "What about what I want? What I need?"

I turned my head to look at him, anger in my eyes. Why was he irritated? I'd given him what he wanted all fucking week! Almost every fucking hour! Today had been too much. What was I? A sex slave?

Then it hit me. *Lash needs to have sex as a snake.* He'd told me that human sex brought the desire to have sex in animal form. Well, maybe it was Theo who had told me that, I couldn't remember. How could I not have known that at once? Maybe Devlin had told him I was planning on coming to him as a snake, and he was just trying to hold off until I could, but he needed this in the meantime.

My anger left me in a rush, and my love for him welled up inside me. I turned around, and reached down for him, sliding my hand over the hardness of him. He hissed sharply, and kissed me hard, grinding himself against me.

"Come upstairs," he whispered, breaking the kiss.

"If you need me, I'm always here for you," I whispered, stroking him.

"I need you *now*," Lash hissed eagerly. "Come with me. Now!"

I put down the glass I was holding, and took his hand. He half led, half dragged me to Devlin's bedroom, and lay me back on the bed, pulling off my jeans, hissing loudly. He pulled off my underwear next, and pushed my legs apart, sliding into me immediately. He let out a loud hiss of pleasure, hammering himself into me as fast as he could, sliding his hands up under my top to cup my breasts. He squeezed them, massaging them as he thrust into me again and again. A second later, he shoved himself deeply into me, riding me to the bed as he came, reflexively clenching his muscles again and again as he let go inside me with a snarl of pleasure. It was then I realized the door to the bedroom was still wide open.

Thank God Devlin had taken Venus to Titus's house for the afternoon. He'd said they had some business matters to discuss, and I'd just nodded, not wanting to hear if it had anything to do with anymore fake construction work. At least there was no one here to walk in on us.

Lash pulled out of me almost immediately, and I felt suddenly used. He'd done that all week, as soon as he was sated, after I'd told him I was a little sore. Why didn't he want to cuddle with me like we used to? We did at night, but only when we slept, when Devlin was with us. Did he not care about me anymore, besides liking sex with me? Or was this all it had been all along, and I'd been too blind to see it?

I rolled over on the bed away from him, drawing my knees to my chest, trying not to give in to tears.

Lash went to reach for me, and I recoiled. He froze, and pulled his hand back at once. He sat on the bed, his arms close to me but not touching me. "I want to be with you again, if you'll let me. But I needed to come first, Sar. I wasn't going to last long enough to bring you this first time."

There was more going on here than that, and it was time I said something. "Never mind that. You said you'd do what I asked."

I felt him move closer, and run his hands over my arms. When I didn't flinch, or tell him to stop, he hugged me. "What do you want?" he said, kissing my neck. "Oral sex? To be in the shower? In the truck? On a table? To be on the piano keyboard? Just tell me what you want and I'll do it."

Where had he got that last one? *Whoa.* "No," I stammered, trying to focus. "I need to know something."

"Then ask," Lash replied. "You know I'll tell you the truth. Always."

"You said you cared for me. What does that mean, exactly?"

The silence stretched for a long minute.

"I care for you very much Sar," Lash said, hugging me.

"Do you love me, Lash?"

Lash was quiet for a long time. But he didn't let me go.

"Answer me."

"I care for you, Sar. More than I've ever cared for any woman in my whole life. I want you more than I've ever wanted any woman, too, were or human. You make me happy, being with you, making me food, talking and laughing together. It's so good, waking up with you in my arms—"

"I asked you a question," I said harshly. "Answer me. Yes or no?"

Lash looked at me and sighed. "No," he hissed very softly. "No."

I felt so crushed I couldn't speak. I couldn't say anything, keeping my tears in by force of will alone.

Lash held me close. "I smell your hurt, and I'm sorry. But you wanted the truth."

"I'm sorry, too," I said heavily. Then I took his arms from around me, and got up from the bed. Lash got up as well, and stopped me from leaving, putting his hand on my arm. I tried to pull away, but he pulled me into his arms, and held me close.

"Why isn't it enough that I care for you?" Lash hissed, upset. "I know you take pleasure in me, Sar. I meant what I said, that I'll do anything you need me to. I'll be faithful to you. I give you my word I haven't been with anyone else, and I won't be, if you—"

"It's not that, Lash. I never doubted your faithfulness. It's that you aren't in love with me. You don't feel for me like I feel for you."

There was dead silence that stretched. Then slowly Lash pulled back from me and held me at arms' length. He looked down at me, his eyes wide with disbelief. "You love me?" Lash rasped out. "*Me?*"

"I have for a while," I said, trailing my hand up to caress his cheek. "It was hard to be around you all these months, and not tell you, or even touch you, to keep telling you I couldn't be with you, when I wanted you so much."

"Sar, I want you to touch me very much," Lash said gently, trying to hug me "Please, come here—"

"No," I said, evading him. "I thought you loved me, thought that I heard it in your voice that day in the Everglades, when we were together. I thought I saw it in your eyes, that last time you kissed me. But you don't."

"Why are you so hurt?" Lash hissed angrily. "Because I won't say some words to you?"

"No. Because you don't feel them. And I thought you did. I fantasized about you so much, in my mind I made you the man I wanted you to be, not the man you are."

116

"What the fuck does that mean?" Lash said loudly. "I'm only ever been honest about what and who I am! You know the man I am! I never pretended to be anyone else!"

"I do know the man you are," I said sadly.

That seemed to enrage him. "I can't give you something that I can't give anyone," Lash hissed loudly. "I've never loved any woman I bedded! Never, Sar!"

As I turned from him, he pulled me back into his embrace. "But we don't need love to be lovers, Sar," he hissed. "I—"

"I do," I whispered.

Lash went totally still. "Why are you saying this now, when we can finally be together?" he uttered. "You know how long I waited to be with you, how hard it was, watching you with Theo, and Dev, and Danial? Being in jail, and not seeing you, and then having you here living with Dev, and seeing you every day and not being able kiss you or touch you at all! You're all I want! You're all I think about! And I know you want me."

"Desire isn't enough. I feel empty now after we've been together, Lash, almost used."

Lash bared his teeth at the word 'used.' His lip curled up, and his eyes went completely to snake. "I'm sorry that you're so emotionally driven, that you can't just take pleasure when it's offered to you," he hissed angrily. "I'll stay out of Dev's bed from now on. And if you need a warm body to fuck instead of a cold one, I'm sure Devlin can ask Nick to join you in bed. I've seen the way you look at him, Sar, thinking about how he'd feel inside you—"

*How dare you!* "How can you not love me, after all the innuendoes, the advances, the stolen kisses, and all your pining!"

I knew I sounded like I was whining, and I cringed, feeling pitiful. But I deserved to know how other men had loved me so quickly, yet Lash, who'd been my lover for the better part of a year, still didn't, especially when I cared for him so much.

Lash looked at me in confusion. "I don't know what to tell you, what you want from me. I want you, I like living with you, sleeping with you. I care for you. I wanted to be your lover from the first time you told me to fuck you. For fuck's sake, it was thoughts of you that got me through jail!"

"Lash, you wanted me to give up my marriage to be with you!" I shouted. "You as much as said so, never mind that you never came out and said the words! And for what? Just good sex? Is that all you were really offering me? Is that all you wanted me for?"

"And what was I to you?" he hissed bitterly "You say you love me. Since when do you care how I feel, or even ask me what I want or need? You sure as hell didn't that day in the hotel, or afterward, either! You were happy to tease me with your words and your body all fall, get me hard, and then leave me to fuck your cougar!"

"God damn you," I forced out. My tears started to fall, even though I tried like hell to hold them back.

Lash went on, his words a tirade. "I noticed that you didn't give up anyone to be with me. The opportunity just landed in your lap, and you took it! Danial's comatose, and Theo gave you up willingly, you didn't leave him for me. You wouldn't leave him for me! You told me you wouldn't!"

"He tried to change me, Lash. That's the real reason he left me, because I wouldn't let him," I said hollowly, easing myself down on the edge of the bed. "He attacked me as a cougar."

Lash was holding me in an instant, and his anger shifted immediately to Theo. "Did he hurt you?" he hissed angrily, baring his growing snake fangs. "You just tell me he hurt you in any way, and I'll kill him, Sar. Danial's not around to stop me anymore."

"He didn't hurt me."

"Good," Lash said, running his hands over my arms, as he nuzzled my neck. "He'd better not even look at you, or I'll slit him open and tie his intestines in a knot. You're with me now, and I protect what's mine."

"You know what pissed him off most?" I said with rancor. "That I'd told you to change me, when I was saving you. That I'd do that for you, but not for him."

"You should've told him that you didn't mean it," Lash hissed acrimoniously.

I looked up at him in fury and tried to push him away. But Lash's arms were like steel cables around me.

"Sar, you're going to sit here and admit it, that you didn't want to be weresnake! I thought you did when you asked me to change you, and it made me so happy, that you cared about me that much to want to be snake for me. But as soon as you knew you didn't have to be what I was, I saw the relief on your face! You never intended to go through with it. It had just been a ruse to get me to take your blood, so you could feel like such the martyr for saving me—"

*Asshole.* "I did mean it!" I shouted at him, happy that my loud volume made him wince. "Theo heard in my voice that I meant it, and right after I said it, he tried to force me to be werecougar. He did it to keep you and me apart, more than he really loved me or wanted me! I had to shoot him in the heart to stop him, so I could get away!"

"Maybe you did mean it that night you said it, even if you didn't feel the same the day after. If so, I'm sorry. And I didn't know he tried to change you," Lash hissed, stroking my hair as he held me. "Devlin will kill him for you, after I tell him, or send me to do it."

"Don't tell him," I said wearily. "I don't want Theo dead. He won't be trying it again."

"I won't let him hurt you, Sar," Lash hissed angrily. "I'm pissed off he tried that! I'm not letting him get away with it! He needs to be taught a lesson."

"Why do you care what he does to me?" I shouted. "If you don't love me, why do you care?"

"Because I do!" Lash hissed stubbornly. "But I wish I didn't! Devlin was right. You can be a real bitch when you feel like being one! And right now, you're a royal pain in my ass!"

"If I'm such a bitch, and a pain in your ass, then don't be my lover," I snarled. "Stay away from me, and find someone else to sate yourself with, who doesn't mind if you fuck her and leave right after without a tender word. Hell, I'm sure if you call up Lyssa, she'll be happy to coil with you."

Lash shoved me hard and I flew backward to land on the bed, all the breath going out of me. "You want it that way, you got it!" he hissed, so furious he could barely talk. "You and I are done, Sar! Do you hear me? We're done!"

"Good! Get out and leave me alone!" I yelled at him, and he slammed the door as he left.

I decided right then and there to go get drunk. It was past time, really.

I got up and walked downstairs, just in time to see Nick struggling to his feet, blood on his face. I went to him and helped him up. I knew Lash had hit him just because he'd been in the way, and Lash had done that because he had been pissed off from fighting with me.

A Hummer started up, and a look out the side window revealed Lash barreling down the driveway, going about seventy.

Nick got on his cell phone. "Jerry, open the gates now, and get out of the way!" he said quickly, wincing a little from his rapidly healing cut lip. "Lash is headed your way, and if the gates aren't open, he'll go through them, and you."

Dejected, I left Nick, and went to Devlin's wine cabinet in the kitchen. I sat at the dining room table, uncorked a new bottle of Groom Shiraz, and poured myself a huge glass. I drank it down. Then I poured another. I thought for a few minutes about what I'd given up, and what I'd gained. Had this been what I wanted from my life? That was a resounding no. I hadn't wanted to lose Theo, or lose my beloved Devon, or lose Danial…

*Danial. I'll go see him.*

I swallowed my wine, then grabbed the bottle and glass, and walked to Danial's room, the room that had been Titus's. He was lying as he had been, still handsome, still so pale and cold, but his heart was beating. I sat beside him, and settled my hand and put it on his. I also poured myself another large glass of wine.

"Why won't you wake up?" I said softly. "Everything's gone to shit since you were hurt, Danial. I miss you so much, and I loved you so much! Wake up! We need you! I need you!"

But Danial didn't stir. He lay there like a statue, completely beautiful, and utterly unreachable.

"Can you even hear me? Does it matter that I come to you every few days, and talk to you? Will you be like this forever?"

I downed another glass, and poured the rest of the bottle into my glass. I debated smashing the bottle, but decided not to. *Someone, probably Robin, will just have to pick it up...*

I felt tears on my face. Robin wouldn't be picking up anything anymore. Robin was dead. Another casualty of Ulysses. Everyone kind and good was dead. Suri, Lander, Flora, Brennan, Demetri, Robin. And my beloved Devon.

Devon was dead. My favorite baby, my boy, the child I'd wanted so long with Theo. I wouldn't ever be having another one with him. No more baby cougars for me. No more Theo for me. No more Danial for me.

And now, no more Lash for me. And I was going to have to promise myself to Devlin anyway, or break his heart by telling him without Lash as part of it, I didn't want to be with him. My tears flowed faster, as I began shaking.

I'd loved Theo so much, and thought he loved me. But everything Theo had said he felt for me had been a lie, because of a spell, like my induced love for Devlin when he'd saved me with his blood. Theo certainly hadn't wasted any time proposing to Jenny. In fact, that had most likely prompted him to search for the separation papers, so he could divorce me as soon as he could. How could I trust how I felt for anyone anymore, or what they felt for me, knowing that? And Lash, the one man who'd had no supernatural power over me to make me love him, the one that I trusted my feelings for the most, didn't love me. He had never loved me. *And now he's told me we're done. He is probably headed to see Lyssa right now.*

I let out a sob, and downed my last glass of wine. I was feeling the effects of it now, and I was grateful for that. Everything seemed surreal. I cried for a while on Danial's chest. Then I looked down at him. *He's as pale and still as the night I first saw him.*

Suddenly, everything seemed very clear. I got out my knife from my pocket, the one Lash had given me. He'd sharpened it for me again recently, telling me to be careful. He'd overdid it a little. Before I thought too much about it, I flipped out the blade, and with a quick slice, I opened my wrist. It bled a lot more than I expected, blood welling up and spilling over onto the floor. Maybe I'd pressed too hard. Or maybe the knife had been too sharp. *Lash said to think of it as a razor blade...*

I leaned over to press the bloody wound to Danial's lips, and an iron hand grabbed my wrist. But it wasn't Danial's.

"What the hell do you think you're doing, Sar?" Devlin shouted, pulling me away from Danial. He put my wrist to his mouth and healed me, licking my blood off my wrist.

He sighed with pleasure just at the small taste, then hugged me hard right after, as if he'd just found out I was pregnant with another one of his children. "Your blood is almost like it was, Sar," Devlin said, utterly joyous. "It's the beginning of summer. A few more months, maybe weeks, and it will be as it was. I'm so happy."

Good for you, I almost said, but I was having trouble forming words. The wine was in full force now, and it was hard to think coherently.

"Were you trying to kill yourself?" Devlin whispered in my ear, gripping me hard. "Danial would've drained you. And even after, he wouldn't have awakened, and been how he was."

"I need to save him," I said stubbornly. Then I was screaming, trying to shove him away from me, almost flailing. "I need to save him! I didn't save him! I can't save him!"

"You can't save him," Devlin said firmly, holding me close even as I fought his attempts to restrain me. "But I will, Sar. I promise you that, no matter how long it might take, I'll do it. Have faith in me."

"I do," I said softly, slurring my words a little and calming somewhat. "I do."

"You need to come with me now," Devlin said. "Teleport us to Davy's."

I knew why instantly. "No," I said, trying to walk away and getting nowhere. "I don't want to see him."

"I don't care what you want," Devlin said forcefully. "You are taking us there, and making up with him."

"Fuck you, I'm not!" I yelled.

Devlin shook me hard, making my teeth rattle. "Listen, you bitch!" he growled. "Ulysses challenged me for my territory an hour ago. I need to fight him in a week. And I need you and Lash focused, because you need to help me prepare."

I was quiet now, listening to his words and trying to process them.

"Teleport us there now," Devlin said stridently. "Then just tell him you love him—"

"He doesn't love me!" I screamed.

Devlin ignored me, and kept talking. "—and that you want him back."

"You're just like him, you know?" I said viciously. "Always trying to make me give another chance to someone who doesn't deserve one!"

Devlin stared at me, looking so hurt I trailed off into silence. "You came back to me because he asked you to?" he whispered. "Not because you wanted to?"

# Chapter Eight

I was too drunk to make a quick save. But I was good enough even drunk to pull a quick diversion. "Yes," I admitted. "But the truth is I'd have come back to you anyway, because I needed your protection, Dev. I found out I can have children again. The demon blood healed me."

Devlin went from being hurt and sad to looking hopeful and ecstatic in the space of two seconds. He pulled me close, and ran his hand over my stomach possessively. "This is wonderful," he purred, his molten gold eyes filled with joy, and more than a little excitement. "That means we can have another child someday, Sar. I'd love that."

"Dev, truthfully, I don't know if I'd want to," I said brokenly. "Devon..." I dissolved into tears.

"Shh, we don't have to right away," Devlin said softly, stroking my back with his hand. "Don't cry, Sar. It's enough that you can, that we have that choice again. And we have decades to think about it, now that I can begin giving you my blood to keep you young. I'm so excited, and Danial will be overjoyed, too, when he wakes up. If things go as I plan, he'll be waking up very soon, Love. Don't cry anymore. Shh."

I hugged him to me, and slowly gained control of myself, deep shame descending on me. I'd broken my promise to Lash, and I'd hurt the one man who'd stood by me this past month from hell, no matter that he was telling me now that it didn't matter. "I'm sorry," I said tearfully, when I could talk again. "I'm such a bitch! I didn't mean to hurt you."

"I always suspected it," Devlin said, kissing me gently. "It was too pat, how you showed up right after Theo had his fight with Robert, after months of not seeing me or wanting to be around me, and suddenly told me you'd let me back into your life. But I wanted you enough that I didn't care."

"I do love you, Dev," I said, slurring my words a little. "Tell me you know I mean it! That I feel it, really feel it? I don't want you to feel like you did in the spring, when I thought I loved you, and I didn't! This time it isn't the blood, it isn't—!"

"I know it," he said, hugging me. "And it's okay, because I want you any way I can get you. I don't care if you were coerced into coming to me. I only care that you came, and that you're here now with me willingly—"

"I'm here with you willingly," I exclaimed, passionate in my drunkenness. "I want you, and I love you!"

Devlin drew back to look at me, grinning at my enthusiasm. "I know it, but it's always good to hear you say the words, Love, even drunk as you are. And we are going to Davy's now, where you are going to tell Lash that, too. He needs to hear it as well."

"Devlin, he doesn't love me!"

"He's devoted to you, Sar. He's never cared for a woman like he does for you, not ever. Don't deny him your love because he can't bring himself to tell you he loves you."

"You're saying he does?" I said softly, sobering up a little just thinking of it.

"I'm saying he's done a lot for you, to be with you," Devlin said, grinning down at me. "It's a pretty good imitation of love he's been doing practically this whole year, if he doesn't. But he loves differently than Danial or I do. He's been hurt a lot in his life, because of how he used to look, what he was, and who he is. He's never had a serious girlfriend, Sar, not that I ever knew about. He's probably afraid to love you, afraid you'd do what you did today, and tell him to leave you alone."

"Dev, he's been coming to me all week, and fucking me, and then leaving me right after!" I said crossly. "I'm sore, I'm feeling used, and I don't like the feeling."

"He needs to have sex as a snake," Devlin said bluntly. "Are you going to do it for him or not, Sarelle? Because if not, tell me right now and I will make arrangements with Lyssa."

I couldn't stand the thought of Lash being with anyone else. I especially couldn't stand the thought of him and Lyssa; it felt like a dagger in my heart. I could feel the pain radiating inside me, as I imagined him making love to her, wrapping his body around hers. "Terian's making the potion," I said very loudly. "It's going to be ready tomorrow!"

"Did you tell Lash that?" Devlin said probingly, folding his arms over his chest.

"I thought you told him! I thought he was doing what he was doing because he was trying to wait for me."

"He told me that he'd gotten Titus to make one for you, Sar. It's ready, and has been for days, ever since you spent that first night with him. Lash was only waiting for you to tell him you'd do it, and he was going to go to Titus and bring it to you himself, so he could walk you through the change. I told him to tell you what he'd done, to ask you to do it, and he said you already knew he needed that, that he wasn't going to ask you for it. That I was to say nothing to you about it. That he'd hold off as long as he could to give you time to come around to the idea. And then he'd go to Lyssa, if you couldn't make yourself do it."

"I was going to do it! Terian said it would take a week to make it!"

"Why not tell Lash that?" Devlin said with narrowed eyes. "He'd have told you he couldn't wait any longer, and that you didn't have to wait, anyway."

I looked at him and licked my lips, and then I looked away, feeling like a coward. "I wanted it to be a surprise."

"It wasn't that you wanted to give yourself a way out, if you decided you couldn't do it?"

"Maybe," I shrugged. "I'm a little afraid. I remember how scary he looked, as snake. It's one thing to hold him in my arms as a human and another to imagine him—"

"There's no time for your fear! Tell me now you'll do it, or I'll call Lyssa tonight, and have her drive there to Davy's. I know she came here to see him after he got out of jail, and that she still wants to be his lover. Once he sees her in snake form, he won't even fight his urges. Though when that part is over, he'll probably be with her as a human, too."

I imagined Lash holding her as hard to his body as he'd always held me, stroking her with his hands gently, crying out her name as he came inside her. "I'll do it!" I shouted. "I'll tell him tonight! I'll do it!"

"Good. Teleport us there now," Devlin commanded.

I did, grabbing hold of him as the walls of Hayden melted away to be replaced by the parking lot at Davy's.

I'd initially wondered how Devlin knew where Lash was. But it was obvious that Gary most likely had called Dev. Lash's Hummer was crashed through the front door and partway inside the building, and inside, every single chair and table was broken, most of the whiskey bottles were smashed glass behind the bar. There were bullet holes in the clock, in the mirror behind the bar, and Lash had spelled out his name in them on the interior wall. There were unconscious bodies scattered here and there, amidst the debris. At least, I hoped they were unconscious.

"Don't worry, they're werebears, brown and black mostly," Devlin said with a sigh, looking around. "Lash wouldn't fight a human, because even in the mood he's in, he doesn't want to go back to jail. He just broke their necks. But I'll be needing to replace everything."

It looked like a hurricane had hit in here, one that I was betting was sitting in the back room drinking. The jukebox was playing Thoroughgood's "I Drink Alone."

"I wonder why he's listening to that?" Devlin said, surveying the damage. "It's appropo, but he usually prefers 'Bad to the Bone'."

I hazarded a guess, remembering our shared sexy dance to the latter song, but said nothing.

We walked into the back room, to see Lash was at the back table, smoking a cigarette, and drinking what looked like a mug of scotch. He ignored us, looking at the far wall. I saw at least two empty whiskey bottles lying broken by his feet. As we watched, he downed the entire mug of whiskey, and poured himself the rest of the bottle. Then he tossed the empty bottle upwards, and fired his silenced 9mm, shattering it while it was still in the air. Pieces rained down. *Glad it's not the explosive gun. Otherwise, I'd probably have glass in my hair even at this distance.*

Devlin started for Lash, and I reluctantly followed. The song on the jukebox ended, and then began again. *How many times did he put it on to play?*

"Lash, come home," Devlin said quietly. "We both need you, and Sar's sorry—"

"Fuck off, both of you," Lash hissed, not looking up, and taking another drag on his cigarette. "Leave me alone."

Devlin looked at me and made a motion with his head for me to say something. I gritted my teeth and spoke. "Lash, I'm sorry."

"Fuck you, you bitch!" Lash snarled. "All the times I could've fucked one of my own kind, and I said no for you!" Lash hissed in rage, bearing his fangs, and glaring at me. He got to his feet, and faced both of us.

*How could he even stand after drinking most of three bottles of scotch?*

"Watching you simpering after that fucking cat, after how bad he made you feel about yourself, after his fucking morals almost killed you last year, after he left you when you needed him most! All those months we could've been together, and you going on and on about how you didn't want to lose him—"

There was enough hate in Lash's voice to drown in.

"—going on and on about how you loved him!"

"Stop it, Lash," I sighed, "Theo and I are done. We—"

Lash's tone turned low and venomous. "I wouldn't be surprised if he guessed I'd gotten you pregnant, and he did something to you, Sar, something that made you lose our baby."

Devlin gasped, and I cringed. *Thank God I told Devlin about my fertility before we'd come here.*

"He didn't do anything," I said quickly. "Theo wouldn't have hurt me, not to get to you. At least, he wouldn't have back then."

"You were pregnant, from when you were together in the Everglades?" Devlin asked me. "From being with him? That's how you knew you were healed?"

"Yes. We didn't know I'd healed, so we didn't use—"

"I suspected it was possible," Lash hissed.

I looked at him in shock. So did Devlin. There was only the sound of the song playing for several seconds.

"How could you not tell me?" I whispered. "We could've—"

"I wasn't going to wear anything with you," Lash hissed arrogantly. "I wanted to enjoy myself, Sar. And it wasn't going to feel as good with you, wearing a condom."

I just looked at him, and did a slow burn. And I wasn't the only one. "You took a chance on getting her pregnant *knowingly*?" Devlin hissed, his eyes bleeding to red. "Just so you could get off and have it feel good? You asshole!"

Lash had the decency to look slightly mortified. "I never meant to hurt her, for her to be hurt by what I did," he hissed insistently. "I just wanted to be with her, to make love with her skin to skin like we always had before. I hadn't been with anyone since her, so I knew I was safe. I knew she was safe to be with, because I knew her, knew the woman she is, that she doesn't sleep around. And if she got pregnant, if she was having my baby, I knew that fucking cat would leave her, like he's left her every other time she needed him! It wasn't just sex to me, I had feelings for her. And I could see she had feelings for me."

"You tried to use a child to get me for yourself?" I screeched at him. "How could you, Lash? How could you be so fucking devious?"

"I wanted you," Lash said with a shrug. "I wanted to be with you, for us to be lovers, and if you went back to Theo and he forgave you, you were never going to be with me again. But I knew he'd never forgive you having my child." Lash looked at me, and all of a sudden he was killing mad angry again. His next words were shouted, though they were hard to understand because they were half hiss, half words. He was as close to changing as I'd ever seen him with him still having legs, scales erupting from his hands and his face, and disappearing again as he yelled at me. "I'm not stupid, Sarelle! I knew I didn't matter to you, not like Theo did! But if I was the father of your child, I would have to matter to you, at least more than I did! I didn't know for sure if I could even get you pregnant, if I was fertile again, or even if you could conceive if I was! I only knew you smelled a little different, that the vampire scent had faded from your body, especially after you asked me what you smelled like."

My eyes teared up as I listened to him.

"I told myself as I watched you sleep that night after we'd gotten back, and we'd made love again that I hadn't done anything wrong, that you cared about me, that you were a good mother, that if I'd gotten you pregnant you wouldn't hate the baby, even if it was mine—"

Lash's voice was vibrating with emotion and I could do nothing but listen, as the words poured out of him.

"—that you wouldn't kill it, even if it was weresnake, like me."

Devlin decked him hard, and Lash went down under the force of the blow. But then he was climbing to his feet, shaking his head. He had blood trickling from his mouth.

"It's been a while since you and I danced, Dev," Lash hissed, wiping the blood off his mouth as it healed. "But we'll go round once, just for old times' sake."

Lash went for Devlin, and then they were struggling, Devlin trying to keep Lash from biting him, and Lash trying hard to withstand the blows Devlin was landing on him. I was surprised to see Devlin holding his own. Lash was slightly drunk though. That had to be working in Dev's favor. But Devlin was a lover, not a fighter. And Lash was the best there was. So there was only one way this fight could end.

Lash sank his fangs into Devlin suddenly, and Devlin screeched. Lash kept biting him, and Devlin slid from his grip to the floor, jerking slightly. Then he collapsed and lay still.

Lash reached over and grabbed his whiskey. He downed the whole of the mug of scotch, and I was very, very still. If I was quiet, maybe he'd fall over. His brain had to be pickled from all that scotch in such a short time.

Devlin lay at Lash's feet and didn't move. In a sudden motion, Lash threw his empty mug against the far wall where it shattered into pieces with a crash. Then he whipped around, and began walking fast towards me.

*How the hell can he still be upright?*

"If you were pregnant, I wasn't going to abandon you, Sar! I meant what I said, that I would have brought you to Hayden to live! And I never wanted you to have a miscarriage! I felt so awful that night you called me, that you were hurt, and it was my fault."

Now his guilt made sense. It was his fault. But it was my fault, too. I was a big girl, and I could have insisted on a condom, just for Theo's sake. I felt a shiver then, as all the ramifications set in.

"It wasn't your fault, what happened," I said softly, aware that I was here alone with Lash, and Devlin might be unconscious for hours. "Even if you knew I could maybe get pregnant, you had nothing to do with the miscarriage, Lash. Don't blame yourself for what happened."

"Can you forgive me, for doing what I did?" Lash hissed. The alcohol was finally having some effect on him. He was still moving quickly, but his eyes were glazed, and glazing over even more as he walked to me. "For not wearing anything? For not wanting to? For wanting to be more to you than just a good fuck?"

"Yes," I said, holding out my arms to him. "I forgive you."

"I'm sorry," Lash said softly as he came into my arms, tears in his glazed eyes. "I wanted you for myself! It was wrong for every reason and I knew it, and I did it anyway! Please forgive me! Please!"

"Shh," I gasped, holding him as he squeezed the life out of me. "It wasn't…your fault…what happened…" Lash eased up a little, letting me take a deep breath to continue. "I might have said no anyway, even if you'd said something, about what you suspected. I still find it hard to believe. And if you had used condoms with me, I'd probably be having Theo's child by now, because he wouldn't have used anything with me later on, thinking me safe, and he'd probably still be with Jenny now anyway, it would've been awful—"

Lash wasn't listening, still trapped in his guilt. "I'm sorry!" he yelled stridently. "Please forgive me, Sar, please!"

I hugged him tightly. "I forgive you."

"I don't," Devlin rasped, as he grabbed Lash, pulling him the floor. Lash let go of me, and then he was trying to bite Devlin again, his fangs dripping venom.

"Don't bother," Devlin said, hitting him again and again with all his force. "I took some anti-venom before Sar teleported us. I knew you'd try to bite me sooner or later, you fuck! Your bite is painful, but that's the most it'll do to me."

"Fuck you!" Lash hissed. "Let me up, or I'll cut you, Dev! I've been nice till now, but don't push it!"

"Sar was fucking *mine*, you asshole, and you knew it! You tried to sire your child on *my* Oathed One! Forget Theo and Danial, you fucked *me* over!"

"She wasn't Oathed to you then, shit for brains!"

Devlin growled "That doesn't matter!" and punched him some more. Lash was a mass of blood before long, but his torn and bruised flesh healed almost as soon as Devlin drew back his hand to hit Lash again.

*How is this helping anything?* "Stop it, Dev!" I yelled. "It doesn't matter anyway!"

Lash drew his knife in a smooth sinuous motion, and stuck it into Devlin's chest, right through his heart.

Devlin went still, and looked down at Lash in utter rage. "Bast—" he grunted, and then he fell backward off Lash to collapse on the floor

"I deserved a beating at your hands, for what I did to you," Lash hissed down at Dev. "But that's enough, and I'm not taking any more."

Lash drew out the knife, got to his feet, and came toward me again. I backed away, and he stopped, looking at me with confusion. Then he saw my eyes on the knife in his hand, and he resheathed it, after cleaning it on Devlin's prone form.

"You'll take me back, Sar?" he hissed hopefully. "Be my lover and my friend? I love being with you."

*But you don't love me.*

Lash saw my face, and his expression went cold in an instant. "You know, there's a pool table right here beside us," he hissed, his eyes flat and cold. "And I feel like walking down my fucking memory lane tonight."

He swaggered toward me, his eyes locked on me. But a second later, he went down sprawling again on the floor. Devlin had been hurt badly, but he'd managed to heal the knife wound while Lash was talking to me, and he'd grabbed him around his legs.

Now that Lash was down, Dev was trying to crawl up him to punch him some more. But Devlin wasn't quick anymore, he'd lost too much blood. He clung to Lash, and while he succeeded in keeping him from getting to me, he couldn't do much more than that. And while Lash was intoxicated, he was also fully healed.

Lash kicked Devlin off him, and got to his feet. In a swift motion, he reached down and picked Devlin up by the throat, lifting him so Devlin was at his eye level. Lash held him there with one hand, and looked at him. Devlin hissed at him, baring his fangs, but he wasn't strong enough to get away from Lash, hurt as he was.

"This time I'm leaving the knife in," Lash hissed meaningfully, and he drew it out of its sheath, flipping it up and grabbing it out of the air to get ready to stab Devlin with it. "You won't die, but you'll stay out of action until I pull it out, Friend. Because I've got another tool of mine I want to sheathe in *your* Oathed One, and that business is going to take the rest of the night."

I had to stop this. Things had gotten way out of hand. And I had only one thing to use as distraction: myself.

I stripped my shirt over my head, and prayed that the song would keep playing. This was going to be hard enough to do with a beat to work with. There was no way I could do it without any music. Thank God, I still felt slightly tipsy, or I wouldn't be able to do this at all.

"I think I want an apology, Dev," Lash hissed meaningfully, his knife still in his hand. "Why don't you tell me how sorry you are that you've been such a prick all fall—"

I stripped off my jeans, and strolled up to Lash, shaking my body to the beat.

"—keeping me away when she visited, telling me I couldn't touch her—"

He wasn't paying any attention, he was focused on Devlin. But Devlin looked over, and his eyes went wide.

"—keeping us apart, you fucking vampire—"

Irritated that Devlin wasn't paying attention, Lash glanced in the direction Devlin was looking. His eyes went wide, too.

The song suddenly stopped.

*Fuck!*

But in a second, it started again. Relieved, I gyrated my hips, thinking this was not a sexy song, but maybe that was relative. Did men care about songs anyway, when they went to see strippers? Probably not, was my guess. I'd see shortly. I kept my hips going, and slid down my bra straps, then I unhooked my bra, and let it fall. Lash and Devlin were motionless, watching me, their mouths open.

I ran my hands over my breasts, and squeezed, letting my head fall back, as I rolled my head to finally look up at Lash through my fall of blonde hair. "Do you want to fight him, or have me?" I said, rolling my hips, running my hands over my mostly naked body, licking my lips suggestively and smiling a come-hither look at Lash. "I'll be over here, if you decide on me. But maybe you'd rather beat on him than make love to me on a pool table?"

Lash looked at Dev, then back at me. Then he slugged Dev hard, knocking him to the floor. He ran to me, wrapping his arms around me. Lash kissed me, reaching his long tongue so far down my throat I gagged a little. As he had that night in the Everglades, he tasted of hard alcohol, but this time he also tasted of cigarette smoke.

*Ugh.* I tried to pull back from him.

"It's okay," he said huskily, drawing back from me suddenly. "Any poison left in my mouth from biting Dev is long gone, Sar, I shifted enough to lose my fangs, after biting him, so it's okay."

Shit! I hadn't even thought about *that*.

Lash was kissing me hard, backing me towards the table, holding me tightly so I couldn't get away. "That night, you wanted me to take you like I did Cin," he hissed raggedly, as he kissed down my neck. "But I didn't treat you as I had treated her. I was never gentle like that with her, Sar. I never went down on her. But it's past time I gave you what I used to give her."

Lash swiped his arm over the table as he had that night months ago, knocking all the pool cues and balls in a crash to the floor. Lash flipped me around, and bent me over the table, holding me there by the back of my neck. I heard the metallic hiss as he unsheathed his knife, and with two deft cuts, what was left of my underwear fell to the floor. A second later, I heard him unzipping his pants, and felt him rubbing himself on me. In spite of everything, or maybe because of it, I was eager to feel him enter me, and I let out a little cry as I felt him push inside me.

"God, I love how you always want me," he hissed, his tone pure lust.

Lash rammed himself into me, bringing a cry from his lips, and a gasp from mine. He held me down spread-eagled over the table with force and pounded himself into me, putting himself in to the hilt every time.

"You wanted this from the moment you first saw me, for me to put it to you like this," Lash hissed in my ear. "You knew what I was, how many people I'd killed, and the more you heard, the more you were turned on! Admit it, Sar!"

"No!" I gasped. "I didn't!"

"You knew who I was, what I was, that night you met me! Theo's probably been filling your head with horror stories about me for years!"

"I didn't know anything, just your name, from Dev," I gasped. "I only knew you were snake, that you were cold, and I wanted you to be warm!"

Lash seemed to lose his rhythm momentarily, then he resumed with a hiss. "You wanted me to fuck you! That was all it ever was to you, all I ever was to you, just someone to fuck, to take your mind off your problems!"

"I wanted to be with you, because I'd fallen in love with you," I said, turning my head with a little pain to rub my cheek against his scratchy one. He looked down at me, and I kissed him almost chastely. Lash slowed his pace, groaning as he loosened his grip on me. "I wanted to come to you so many times in these past months," I whispered, turning my head and upper body slightly to kiss him on his neck, and his face, then down his throat. "To tell you I loved you, to tell you I wanted to be with you and not Theo, to let you take all of me that you wanted—"

Lash was shaking now, and he grabbed hold of my hips roughly and sped up again. "I am taking all of you, right here tonight! As many times as I want to! And no one is going to stop me, not Dev, not Theo, no one!"

This was just like my fantasy of Lash, the one I'd acted out with Danial. I was just as into it as I'd been months ago, a loud cry of arousal tearing out from between my parted lips.

Lash looked down at me knowingly with slitted eyes. "You thought about me like this with you, didn't you?" he groaned, pulling himself almost out of me, and then swiftly slamming himself back in. "You fantasized about it, about how good it would feel, to be with me again, to feel me in you! And it had nothing to do with love! Admit it!"

I felt him, heard his lust-filled voice, and I gave right in to my need for him. "I fantasized about you for months, just like this!" I gasped. "I wanted you, that day at my house! I wanted you to take me! I want you more than anything! Please, don't stop!"

"I'm not going to stop, even after I come," Lash hissed seductively. "We're going for a new record, Sar, right here tonight. And you're going to scream for me every time."

"Make me scream for you!" I cried out, loving the feeling of being taken so completely.

Lash thrust harder onto me, and I trembled under the force of his desire. But he was closer than I was, and in the next second he spasmed hard, jolting me as he came with a harsh cry. He sank down on me a little, groaning as his body gave up his seed to me in a rush of warmth. After, he lay there on me, and didn't move, though I felt his breathing. *Is he ready to pass out finally? In any case, I won't get a better chance.*

I tried to move out from under him, wanting to get across the table to check on Devlin, afraid Lash had hurt him badly. He'd said he needed to fight Ulysses in a week. But I'd forgotten this wasn't role playing, that Lash was not Danial. My weresnake grabbed me before I'd gotten free of him, and pushed me back on the table. I tried to get away, but he grabbed me by my legs, and pulled me to him, flipping me over on my back. He curled one hand around the base of my neck, and gripped me. I struggled, but couldn't move.

"Where do you think you're going?" Lash hissed, as he crawled onto the table after me, laying down on me again. "You heard what I said! I'm going to have you over and over, right here, and you're going to beg me for more, like you just did."

"Lash, I need to check on Dev—"

"He's fine, he's probably enjoying listening to me have you," Lash hissed, parting my legs with one knee so he could slide his body between them, as he shoved his pants all the way down with his free hand. "And you've got other things to concern yourself with, like this."

Lash rammed himself into me again, and I groaned. I'd been sore before, and now I was raw. Just having him in me was a little painful, even though Lash wasn't really being rough.

"Scream for me," Lash hissed, holding still above me with effort. "I want to hear you scream my name. And not my nickname, my real name."

The alcohol had finally taken effect. Lash's eyes were so glazed I was surprised he could manage to have sex. Actually, I was surprised he wasn't on the floor unconscious.

"No one's called me by my real name in more than sixty years, not like this," Lash said, plunging himself in and out of me. "I want to hear you say it for me, Sar, to know you want me, the real me, not the Lash facade I've worn like a mask for so many years."

I felt like he'd knifed me in the heart, hearing the longing in his words. Here was the man I'd known that day in the Everglades hotel, the one I hadn't seen at all since Lash had been in jail. He'd been hiding this from me for months.

"Make love to me, Tristan," I said softly, looking up at him tenderly, as I slid my hand up to caress his cheek with my hand.

He went still for a long moment, looking down at me. "All you ever had to do was ask," he hissed tenderly, and in a smooth motion, he rolled over on his back, thrusting all the way inside. He moved my hips fast on his, and I could feel the climax building almost immediately, despite that there was slight pain also.

"Please! Please!" I whimpered, running my hands over his chest scales. "Faster!"

Lash moved faster, and I climaxed for him hard, screaming my lungs out. "Yes! Please! God, yes! Tristan! Tristan! Oh God, I love you!"

Lash kissed me deeply as I collapsed on him, panting heavily. But it wasn't a rough kiss, it was a tender kiss, full of longing, gentleness, and dare I say it, love. "I loved that, that it was the real me you knew was loving you, that it was me you wanted." He sighed, his speech slightly slurred. "Tell me again you love me."

"I love you, Tristan," I said softly.

Lash hugged me to him with a tortured sigh. "I wish that you weren't on the pill, that we could maybe make another baby inside you tonight," he hissed with a sea of longing in his voice. "I wanted you to have my child, for you to get pregnant from our time together, to come to me and say you picked me, that you wanted me, and not that fucking cat. I knew that I was a fool to even hope for it, but I cared for you, Sar, and I wanted you to care for me, to see that same look in your eyes that you had that night you came to me, when you told me you didn't want me to die."

The words were pouring out of him in a flood, hitting me with all the force of an emotional tidal wave.

"You're such a good mother, Sar. And I could be a good father, with you as my mate. You said I wasn't the man you wanted me to be, and you were right, I'm not good, not nearly good enough for you. But I can be a better man for you, Sar, I know I can, if you'll help me."

"Lash—"

"I wish things had been different, that I'd been there for you when you needed me that night—"

Tempest of Vengeance

"You were there for me," I interrupted, kissing him. "And I'll come to you as snake, Lash. I was just waiting for the potion to be ready. I didn't know you had already gotten Titus to make one."

Lash went still as a statue, and tilted my chin up so he could look into my eyes. "Please Sar," he groaned. "Don't say it if it's not true. Just the thought of you like that…"

"I will," I said, hugging him tightly. "We'll finally coil together like you wanted us to."

Lash let out a long loud undulating cry full of longing and wanting and needing so deep, it made me shiver in his arms. He rolled back over on top of me, and began thrusting into me fast, his body straining with need. A few seconds later he came, shouting my name.

"Sar! Mmmph! Uh! Sar! Ah! Uh! Ah! Ah!"

Lash looked down at me, panting hard, and there was such emotion in his dark gaze I went still beneath him. His eyes were human and they held the same look they had that long ago day in the hotel: warmth, affection, tenderness, and passion. Love.

"Sar, I…I—"

Then he let out a shout, jerking on me. "Youch!"

I yelped, because he was still inside me.

Lash pulled away from me, his erection slipping out of my body as he went for his knife. Over his shoulder, Devlin stood, pulling a syringe needle out of Lash's bare ass cheek.

"You...fuck..." Lash said, drawing his knife partway from it's sheathe. Then he collapsed on me, unconscious.

"You couldn't have waited another second?" I said sarcastically. "He was maybe going to say it, finally."

"He can say it to you another night," Devlin growled. "We've got to get back before dawn."

Dev pulled Lash off me, and then pulled Lash's pants up, and fastened them. He hoisted Lash's limp body over his shoulders. Looking at him covered in blood and so weary, I understood his annoyance.

"Get your clothes," Devlin said, raising his eyebrows as he looked at my naked form. "Much as I like to look at you naked, it's late. We need to get him back to Hayden."

I put on my clothes, save my slashed up pieces of underwear, which I tossed in the nearest garbage, then took us back to Hayden. Devlin let us into Lash's room with a key. He lay Lash down on a low bed, leaving him dressed. Lash was breathing deeply, but he wasn't moving other than that. I couldn't see much of the room, it was too dark.

"Will he be okay?" I asked.

"He'll be his normal nasty self tomorrow, but he won't remember this. Nothing from Davy's probably." His voice turned hard as steel. "You'd better go to him as snake tomorrow, Sar. Tell me now you'll get the potion from Terian ASAP in the morning, before it's even light. Or I'll call Lyssa tonight, so she's here beside him when he wakes up."

"I *said* I'll do it," I cut him off irritably. "I'll do it, Dev."

"Good," Devlin said softly. "Good."

He pulled me outside the room, and locked it behind him. "Now tell me exactly what it was that Lash did for you, in return for you coming back to me."

## Chapter Nine

"Sar, tell me, and do it now." Devlin's patience had lasted all of thirty seconds.

"Lash killed the Satar and his men," I confessed. "They were setting up to ambush Theo. I asked Lash to go watch the fight, to make sure Theo would make it back."

"You wanted Lash to kill Robert?" Devlin said, astonished. "You surprise me, Sar. I'd thought you'd be too straight laced to send an assassin to kill Robert."

"Lash wasn't there to kill Robert," I said bluntly. "He was there to make sure Theo wasn't hurt by sneak attack, which is what Satar was planning."

"Satar bit Lash that night, giving him that wound that turned septic," Devlin finished.

I nodded.

"Lash got you to come back to me as payment for helping you."

"Yes."

"I'm going to give him a raise for being so thoughtful, in light of the fact that he obviously wanted you for himself," Devlin said, cracking a smile.

"Don't," I said heavily. "He made me promise never to tell you. I feel horrible I broke that promise to him."

"Then I won't say anything," Devlin assured me. "As I said, it doesn't matter to me anyway, why you came back, just that you did. I knew you were going to, Sar, even if you didn't recover your ability to have children. You needed my protection. It was as simple as that."

Without any more talking, Devlin and I both showered, getting most of the gunk off us. I had a fair amount of blood on me from both Devlin and Lash, and once I realized it, I couldn't get it off me fast enough. Afterwards, Devlin and I lay down in bed.

My hand reached out and clasped Devlin's. "Thank you, for trying to defend me."

Devlin brought my hand to his mouth and kissed the back of it. "I knew he

137

wouldn't hurt you. But I was and remain pissed that he did what he did, because getting you pregnant would have endangered you again with the other Rulers. I am not the fighter he is, so it wasn't much of a contest. I knew when I first struck him that I would lose."

"All the same," I said, touching his cheek gently. "Thank you. It had to hurt."

"Some donor blood tomorrow will fix it," Devlin shrugged. "But you heard his words, maybe even others I didn't hear, when I was out for a few moments. There's no doubt he loves you, Sar."

Yes, hearing what Lash had said had reassured me he had feelings for me, but I didn't want to talk about that now. "How did he drink so much tonight, and still function, Dev? Three bottles of scotch is a lot, and he's not a big man. I kept waiting for him to pass out."

"Lash has always liked alcohol since he was young. But he started drinking more this year, I'd guess because he found out he was dying. Not a lot more, but enough so I noticed. He's been drinking heavily since he was in jail, and even before that, this whole fall. Some of it I think was to give up the smoking, after being in jail, but I'd guess that most of it was because it dulled his desire for you. Some of it also is all the stress of Ulysses. Lash drank heavily in Rio, too, those months we were there, when he had to be on guard every second. But then at least he was getting sex every night."

The dark woman in the photo. She must have been weresnake. *How many women did Lash have through the years? And why had Lash been on guard all the time in Rio? Devlin had had his bears...*

"So his tolerance for alcohol is very, very high," Devlin finished, interrupting my thought. "But no matter how much he drinks, it doesn't impede his fighting ability, so I never say anything about it. Anyway, don't worry about him. My guess is that now you're going to give him what he needs, he'll be drinking a lot less. And I think the smoking will probably be easier to quit, too."

Devlin moved closer to me, and hugged my body to his. I felt him stir against me.

"I want you," he whispered, kissing me. "Tell me you want me, Sar."

"We shouldn't, if you need me to get up early, it's got to be midnight by now."

"Lash will sleep till tomorrow afternoon," Devlin assured me. "The alcohol will add to the sedative I gave him. But you should get the potion from Terian by noon, no later."

I nodded.

"Are you in the mood?" he said, brushing my neck with his fangs. "I'll be quick, if you aren't. But I can't not have you at least once, Sar, not after seeing you dance like that."

"So you liked my dancing?" I teased.

"Very much," Devlin purred, kissing up my throat seductively. "I want you to dance for me again, sometime soon. But for now, just lay back for me, and let me do all the moving."

*Damn you, you're too hard to resist.* "You'll need to heal me first. I'm embarrassed to say it, but I'm—"

"Shh, I apologize. I should have thought of that, Love. Hold still." Devlin kissed down my body, his sensuous kisses bringing soft cries unbidden from my lips. As before, he kissed me intimately, and the dull ache I had been feeling lessened until it disappeared. I sighed with relief.

"Don't be sighing yet," Devlin protested with a sexy fanged smile. "I want all the credit for every sigh that passes your lips, and I don't want to rush."

I laughed, and turned to him. "Then just take your time," I said with lowered sultry eyes, and pushed his head down once more.

* * * *

Getting the potion from Terian went smoothly. I simply showed up in his lab, handed him the money I'd withdrawn from the bank a few minutes ago, and he handed it to me in a glass vial, telling me not to be alone when I took it. "But I don't guess that will be a problem for you," he said with a smirk.

"Thank you, Tears," I said quietly, tucking it into my purse. "By the way, what do you want for a wedding present? I'm sorry I didn't ask before now, but usually the invitation or shower tells the name of the bridal registry."

"A gift card for a restaurant, or movies, or anything, I guess?" he said, blushing. "But you don't have to get us anything."

"Of course I do!" I exclaimed. "I'm happy for you both. Besides, I owe you a lot—"

"You don't owe me anything," Terian said with an odd look in his eyes. "Not anything."

*What does he mean by that?*

"But Sun would like that," Terian added quickly. "She loves gift cards of all kinds. I'm not sure why, but she does."

"Then I'll get one for you both," I said with a smile. "Take care."

I left his lab, and promptly ran into Jenny in the hallway. "Sorry!" I said, and she gave me a smile in return. I gave her one back, thinking while I still disliked her, it wasn't her fault Theo had left me for her. And this meeting was opportune, as I'd wanted to talk to her. "Walk with me?"

She gave me a nervous look, but came with me. When we were outside, I stopped, and leaned against the nearest tree. Jenny looked at me uneasily.

"Do you have your phone?" I asked.

She gave me an odd look. "Sure, but—"

"Get it out."

Jenny produced her phone, and I began speaking slowly, so she would have time to enter the information as I related it. "Theo's birthday is sometime in May. He won't tell you about it, but that's when it is. Please make him a cake of some kind, and throw a party."

"Why are you telling me this?" Jenny said abruptly. "You think I need your help to keep him happy? Or are you tired of your vampire, and want him back now?"

I glared at her. *If I tell you the truth, that you're only alive now because you were practice for me, you'll be singing a different tune about dear old Theo.*

*Be nice, Sar. It's not her fault, not any of it. And Theo's been hurt enough. Everyone has been hurt enough.* "I care that Theo has a party every year on his birthday, and a Christmas tree, and—"

"We have a tree," she interrupted snottily. "I'm sure your children told you?"

"They did," I replied, nodding. "I'm pleased you have one for him. Tell me also if you want any recipes that he likes, Cia knows most of them, but—"

"So now you want to be friends?" Her voice was half anger, half disbelieving.

"No," I said coldly, letting all of my anger flood my words. "I'm not your friend. But despite he's an ass, I want Theo to have what he didn't most of his life, especially when he's lost his best friend."

"Terian is his best friend."

"He is now," I said in clipped deliberate tones. "Once they were mortal enemies. Danial was his best friend for over a decade." *Until I came along, and ruined everything, anyway. Sigh.* "You're coming into this saga late, Jenny. I'm doing you a favor here. But you don't want it, that's fine." I turned to leave.

"Wait," she called. "You need to know something. Theo intends to go with Elle and T to your mother's house for Christmas, tonight. And he's asked me to go, too." She forced a smile. "I'm sure you don't want us to bump into each other."

*Understatement of the year.* "I'll be there tomorrow, then. At night, so Devlin can come. So it doesn't matter if you go with them tonight. Be prepared for a few comments from my mother though."

"Theo already warned me," Jenny said, nodding. "I'm intending to be very, very quiet."

"Good," I said curtly, and left.

I returned home to Hayden, and went directly to Titus, who was waiting for me in his basement lab. He looked over the potion Terian had made, and determined that it was fine to use. I asked him point blank why it had taken Terian so long to make his, and Titus so little time, when they were for the same thing.

"Because of his blood, and also that he can't do dark magic as easily now," Titus said patiently in his bass voice. "You come to me from now on, Sar, and I'll make these for you. Terian is most likely going to be moving away from doing almost all magic for the next few years, if not forever. It's good he has his job with Theo. His days of making most of the sought-after potions are over."

"I'm sorry," I said, feeling bad and not knowing why. It wasn't my fault.

Titus gave me a long odd look, as Terian had, then he hugged me gently. "Don't be," he said. "You've been a good friend to him. You did what he needed you to. Terian can let you go now, Sar."

I gave him an odd look. "Is there something going on here I should know about?"

"He can be happy with Sundown. He's finally realized you were never going to be with him, no matter what happened. And that's good, that he's moving on."

I nodded. "Yes."

"Go now," Titus said coolly. "Your evil snake is waiting for you. I'm sure he can't wait to feel you in his coils."

*Jerk.* I left him without hugging him good-bye.

* * * *

By the time I got upstairs, showered, and conditioned my hair, it was noon. I also took time to call my mother to reschedule, notifying her of the impending "other woman" coming tonight to her door. My mom said everything was fine, though she hadn't known Jenny was coming with Theo. The way she said it, I hoped she didn't say something nasty to Jenny if she happened to catch her alone. She was clearly annoyed that her daughter had to come another night because of another woman that her daughter's soon-to-be ex-husband was bringing on Christmas. I was just happy Jenny had said something, before we'd all shown up together tonight, and were forced to be nice to each other because of the kids.

Devlin had already taken Venus to Titus's house for the day, to give Lash and me some privacy for the "snake lovefest." But he said he would be back in the early evening hours, about six or seven. "That should be enough time."

I'd rolled my eyes at his smirk, and told him to get going. Then I went into our bedroom, took off my clothes, and downed the potion. It was a little bitter, and kind of smoky tasting. Slipping out Devlin's bedroom door, I shut it behind me and walked to Lash's door, and knocked once. My legs went weak the very next moment, and then I was down on the floor, feeling so strange that I couldn't move right because I suddenly had no arms and legs, much less hands or feet. By some desperate flailing, I managed to curl myself up in a haphazard pile, but going around over and over had made me a little dizzy. I hoped to God Lash was awake, and had heard me out here, or it was going to be a long three hours.

A naked Lash opened his door, and looked down at me, his face in shadow. I tried to speak, but my tongue just came out and I hissed a little. Lash reached down to me, and picked me up, putting some of me over his shoulder, and around his neck. He closed the door, locked it, and carried me to the bed, where he put me down gently. He stood there for a long moment, just looking at me.

*Could he tell it was me?* I tried to preen seductively, and leaned back on the bed. But I didn't have any arms to steady myself, or balance with, and I ended up flipping myself over on my back. I righted myself with a twist of my body, glad I couldn't blush in this form. I felt so annoyed with myself for making myself look like an idiot that I hid my head under my torso, feeling a little ashamed as well that I couldn't control my altered body, and I probably wasn't looking in the least attractive. At least he had to know who I was now. *Fucking Lyssa probably knew just what to do.*

I heard Lash dialing his phone, and speaking. His voice seemed very loud when he spoke, almost like a vibration inside my head. "Dev, did you know that Sar…"

I peeked out to look at him, relieved he could recognize me.

"I wanted you to know that once I'm with her this way, I will probably want her to do this again for me. And I imagine she may want to as well, after this time. This is another thing I will not give up, if she wants this from me, and I thought it right to let you know that."

*His words were laced with strong desire.* I stretched out my neck hesitantly, looking in Lash's direction hopefully. Apparently, he wasn't turned off by the fact I couldn't move worth a damn.

Lash hung up his phone with a sharp click, and put it aside. He came closer to me, drinking me in with his eyes. "You're so beautiful, Sar," he whispered, deep emotion in his voice. "So beautiful. Just like I knew you would be, if you were like this."

He shifted fast, and fell in coils to the floor. I saw him coming up the bed,

142

sliding on the sheets in his hurry to reach me. Then he was coiling his much-longer body around mine, hissing softly. Soon he was wrapped all along the length of me, holding my body with his. He rubbed his head on mine gently, hissing, and then he laid his head over mine.

I had expected something like this, but not to feel as I did. Frankly, I had volunteered to do this for him, because I knew he needed it, and I didn't want him to go to someone else for it. I didn't expect to particularly enjoy making love as a snake. But it seemed that I was utterly complete, that feeling him like this around me was the best thing ever. I moved slightly in his coils, and he hissed a little. I heard his excitement in his hiss, and moved my body more purposefully, rubbing on him. He began to contract his body around me, moving gently.

I had never been held this completely. I gloried in feeling him everywhere about me, his muscles so strong, and yet so gentle. Then I felt him inserting part of himself into me. It was both familiar and not. It felt right, and yet strange. *The feel of him gently moving, touching me everywhere…*

I shuddered in climax, feeling something so alien and yet so familiar in its power. This wasn't like any orgasm I'd ever felt before, and it went on and on, as he kept moving gently around me. I let out a loud hiss of pleasure, and he hissed back at me, his sound almost strangely like encouragement. I hissed again as the climax ebbed, and again, he hissed back to me, though this time there seemed to be pleasure and contentment in the sibilant sound.

In the next second, he was sliding the lower part of himself over mine fast, contracting in rhythm around me. His hissing was intense, his purpose single-minded in the urgent way he moved on me. He contracted hard around me suddenly, squeezing me tightly. I writhed frantically, scared he might crush me in his coils. In the next moment, he loosed his grip on me, and I relaxed in his embrace.

He didn't uncoil from me, or take himself out of me. He just rubbed his head on me as he did before. I felt him again contracting gently around me, and as before, the feeling felt wonderful and totally encompassing. With a passionate hiss, I gave myself up completely to ecstasy.

This went on for the next two hours. Lash brought me to climax, again and again. Unlike human sex, each orgasm was as intense as the last one had been. I had never before made love so intensely, over and over with no rest for so long a time, and finally, my body just gave out. I passed out asleep in his coils after the twenty-seventh time, utterly exhausted.

The metamorphosis back to human awakened me, spurring Lash to change form as well. Slowly our arms and legs materialized, as we became human once more, our bodies still embracing. Spent, I looked up into the dark eyes of a very human Lash, and smiled weakly. He eased me up on the pillows beside him, and put his arms around me, spooning me. I lay in his arms for a while, just resting. I felt like I'd run a marathon, and I hadn't done that much work. He must be exhausted, even being were.

"You were right," I sighed, stretching happily. "Coiling together did feel good. You felt so wonderful wrapped around me. God, you were so good, Lash. It felt so amazing—"

Lash didn't move, comment, or look at me. I froze, and looked away, filled by a terrible thought. *Had I felt bad? Moved wrong?* I cringed a little. I hadn't known how to slither at all. Maybe I was supposed to coil around him, too? "Did I not do it right?" I whispered. "I'm sorry. I wasn't sure how to move."

"You were perfect," Lash whispered, running his hand down my side, and hugging me close. "You felt wonderful. You did just what a female snake should, which is mostly just hold still, but then fight just a little, near the end."

It was in his voice how relaxed he was now. I hadn't ever heard him this relaxed in all the time we'd been together, in almost all the time I'd known him. He'd needed badly to get release as an animal. I opened my mouth to ask him why he hadn't just asked me to do this for him, and I realized he had, when he'd told me about Theo. It hadn't all been him being a good friend. He'd hoped someday for me to do this for him, even back then. That was what Devlin had meant by his comment, and I understood why. That he'd needed me to come to him like this, willingly without him asking, maybe to know that I'd meant what I said. That I really loved him.

Lash sighed heavily. "Why did you do this?" he said finally, sounding irritated. "I was going to stay away from you, not be your lover anymore like you asked me to."

"I knew how much you wanted it," I whispered. "I wanted to be with you that way, to see what it would feel like. You always talked about it with such desire."

"Was that the real reason?" Lash interrupted, stroking my face. "Wasn't it just that you couldn't have me? That I'd said we were done that made you come to me as a snake? You know me, Sar, know how much I wanted that. You knew I wouldn't be able to resist having you, when I saw you as a snake. That I needed it so bad I wouldn't be able to say no, even if I wanted to."

It was in his words that he didn't remember last night at Davy's at all. But I did, and that made his sarcastic words a little easier to take. "The real reason was I'm in love with you," I said. "And I wanted to be with you like that, to know what it felt like, why you liked it so much. And I ordered the potion after that first night we were together, because I knew you were going to need this from me."

"I did need it," Lash groaned, stretching, and caressing my hip, his fingers rubbing the bear tattoo that snarled there. "I hadn't been with another snake since Cin. It wasn't even an issue for me anymore back then, when I was so much older. But ever since we made love in September, I've been fighting the urge to have sex as a snake. The acupuncture held it at bay, like my desire for human sex. When we began to be lovers a week ago, the urge came back stronger than ever. Once I had you in my bed, I couldn't get to you fast enough, Sar. But I couldn't stop looking at you either. I'd waited so long to see you that way, wanted it so much, imagined it since that first time with you, dreamed about it for months."

He reached over and turned my face back to him so he could kiss me, and then he was molding my body to his, holding me. "I didn't think you'd be snake for me," he admitted softly. "Not when it came down to it. I thought you staged that fight so I'd stay away from you, because you knew I wanted you to do it, and it was easier than telling me you couldn't bring yourself to do it, that to let me have you in my other form was too much to ask."

"It was so good with you," I said, kissing him, then drawing back to look at him. "You felt amazing. It is true, I was a little afraid to let you coil with me. I didn't know if I could do it, but I had to do it. I didn't want to lose you over it. And I just couldn't stand the thought of you being with someone else, especially that fucking Lyssa."

"I sure as shit can tell how much like Devlin you are becoming, even without his blood," Lash said with a smile. "Living with him has changed you, that you would admit that to me." He stroked me softly. "Terian made it for you?"

"Yes."

"Will you come to me again like this? I'll pay for the potions, if you'll agree to be snake with me, let me coil with you. Titus has agreed to make them for me, for us. The money's nothing to me."

I looked at him, uneasy. What if Devlin got jealous, once he heard how much I liked it? He expected me to tell him later tonight, I knew. Worse, what if he asked to join us like this, to be a snake, too, with me?

"Devlin said he didn't mind," Lash said softly, both understanding and not understanding. "Titus can make them for us, Sar. No one else needs to know that we are lovers in this way. I won't tell anyone, if you want this to be a secret."

I kissed him softly. *Screw it, it doesn't matter. He matters.* "You can tell anyone you like, Lash. And I will do this for you again, if you'll agree to kiss me here and now," I said, my eyes warm with affection.

Lash grinned and kissed me. "I'd love you," he said.

My eyes went wide. His eyes went wide with shock a second later, when he realized what he'd said, and then he was speaking fast, trying to cover it. "I meant, I'd love to, Sar. I always like kissing you—"

"Lash, I know what you meant, and it wasn't that," I said.

Lash looked away from me, and said nothing.

"You can say it," I said softly. "It's okay, if you do. I—"

"I'm not going to say it!" Lash said loudly, his voice a hiss through his forming snake fangs. "Not now, not ever!"

I said nothing, too taken aback to utter a sound.

"You have enough men that love you," Lash snarled. "Devlin's in love with you. He's practically obsessed with you. I've seen how you treat him! I'm not going to be like him, hanging on your every word, hoping you'll let me touch you when you have a few spare hours, grateful for the crumbs you throw my way!"

I got up from the bed before he could finish. Grabbing an extra shirt of his from the floor, I put it around myself. *Bastard!* I'd done so much to be with him, to make him happy, and this was how he felt? I'd given him everything he'd needed and nothing had changed. I had been stupid to think that coming to him like this would change anything, that it would get him to love me, when everything else I'd done for him hadn't been able to win his heart. Hadn't I learned anything, from our fight yesterday? Who cared what had happened last night? If Lash had to be drunk to tell me how he really felt, whatever love he felt for me wasn't worth it. He wasn't worth it.

Lash looked up at me defiantly, his eyes flat, and his fangs bared.

"I love you, Lash," I said quietly as I buttoned the shirt, not looking at him. "I did this for you because of that, because I can't really be weresnake for you, and I knew how much you wanted it. But you are right. I should have respected your wishes and left well enough alone. I should have let Devlin call Lyssa, and you could have woken up with her, instead of me."

Lash said nothing.

"I won't bother you again, or touch you in any way beyond friendly," I said bitterly. "I'm sorry if I hurt you. When I Oath to Devlin tomorrow, I'll tell him that you and I aren't part of the Oath. That you don't want to be part of it, because you don't want to be with me."

I went to leave, before the strong charade I was trying so hard to maintain crumbled under the weight of my sadness. I got three steps and felt him spin me around to pull me into his arms to hold me tightly, almost squeezing the life out of me. "Don't leave. Stay with me, please," he hissed softly. "I care for you, Sar. I want to be with you, to be part of your Oath, if you want me to be. I'm sorry for what I said yesterday. I know I hurt you and I'm sorry."

I stayed silent.

"I'm very glad I woke up to you. I wouldn't have wanted to wake up to find I'd given in and been with someone else. Not Lyssa, not anyone else! I'm glad I finally got to share my animal side with you, that you enjoyed being with me. It was better than I imagined it would be, and that's saying something—"

"But you don't love me."

"You can't want me to lie to you. So what do you want me to say?"

"Tell me you could come to love me, in time."

"I don't know," Lash said finally. "The truth is, I don't know. I don't know much about love, Sar, even though I've lived so long." He paused. "I know it's not what you want to hear. I'm sorry for that, that I can't just tell you the words. I want you, and I need you. I like you. And I'll be faithful to you, Sar. I won't be with anyone else, ever, if you're willing to come to me like this. Can that be enough for you, at least for now? Can you give me time?"

I said nothing, just hugged him back. *Maybe*. I'd have to think about it.

"Will you come to me as a snake?" Lash said hesitantly. "And let me be with you again, like we were today?"

"How often?" I said, sliding my hands up into his hair.

"I'll ask Titus. There may be a limit of how often it is safe for you to become a snake. I don't want you to do anything risky. Say once a week?"

"Yes, I will," I replied, "If you'll agree to join us tomorrow, to witness the Oath, and to take a promise from me, when I give one to Devlin. I don't want to be without you ever again. I'm going to promise myself to you, like I'm doing for him, that we'll always be lovers. Both as snake and as human. If that is part of the Oath, he won't be able to separate us again, ever. If fact, he's agreed to do everything in his power to see we are never separated again."

"If you want me there, I'll be there," he said in surprise. "Are you sure you want to give me that promise? You know how I feel about promises, Sar. I'll hold you to it, and if you break it, we will be done, this time for good."

"Yes," I said emotionally, "If you still want me that way."

"You know me well enough not to need me to answer that," Lash hissed tenderly. "You know how I feel about you."

*Did I?* I thought I had. But I'd been wrong then. Maybe I was wrong now.

*No.* I would believe that he meant what he said. I'd give him time. What did I have to lose?

"I don't want you to be jealous, watching him with me. We'll have to consummate the Oath, after we give it. He'll have to drink my blood, and give me his."

"I'm not a jealous man, usually," Lash said in an offhand manner. "At least, I never have been in the past. And I'm not going to be jealous of Devlin.

We are too good of friends, Sar."

*That's a blessing. If it's true.*

"Come back to my bed," he said, kissing my neck. "I'd like to hold you, and sleep a little with you. I'm sorry we couldn't cuddle this week, Sar. But the more I was with you, the more I wanted you, and I had to leave you right after, or risk being with you over and over and hurting you in the process. My body was crying out for release in animal form, and the more I was with you, the worse it got. Dev had told me that you were considering it, and I wanted to wait for you, and not rush you, but I couldn't stay away from you for long, no matter how much I tried. Every minute felt like it was hours—"

The words were pouring out of him. I was beginning to think it happened usually right after he had sexual release. "It's okay," I said, kissing him gently, rubbing my cheek against his moustache and goatee. "I understand now, and I understood then, too. I was just feeling hurt—"

Lash kissed me gently, running his hands over me, finally pulling me close. "Come to bed, Sweetness," he hissed affectionately. "Let me hold you, so you know you are cherished."

I took his hand then, and let him lead me back to bed.

\* \* \* \*

In a few hours, there came the inevitable knock at the door. Lash got up and opened it, admitting a smiling Devlin, obviously happy that everything for our "first time" had gone okay.

"Sar, today is Christmas Eve," he said. "Your parents expect you, Elle, Venus and Theoron, don't they? Is it tonight or tomorrow?"

"Tomorrow night, yes, and I need to go," I answered. "Will you and Lash come with me?"

"You want us to go with you?" Devlin said, surprised but perceptibly pleased. "Are you sure?"

"Please," I said. "Theo is going to stop by with Jenny tonight, plus T and Elle. My mother admitted to me that she told him that even if he's leaving me, she still thought of him as a son, and to stop by. But we can avoid him and Jenny if we go tomorrow night."

"We'd be glad to come," Devlin replied. "Let me go arrange to have Titus and Rip here to man the fortress, while we're gone tomorrow."

Lash helped me up, and we both got dressed slowly. I was so exhausted that I'd have gone to bed then and there if it hadn't been a holiday. But it was, and nothing mattered more to me tonight than being with my youngest daughter on her first Christmas Eve.

\* \* \* \*

Christmas Eve at Hayden was simply beautiful. The decorated tree was sparkling with lights, the snow was swirling down outside, and I had some of my loved ones about me, if not all of them. It was nice also to have a semblance of privacy, as the bears had been instructed to stay in their own quarters on both Christmas Eve, and Christmas Day.

Lash was so relaxed that night he was almost a different person. He'd always been kind to Venus, but he was almost overboard that night, fawning over her, giving her all kinds of treats, like chocolate and ice cream, letting her ride on his back as he pretended to be a pony for her. I could see how happy he was, and it made me feel good, to know in a large part that was because we were back together now.

Venus was ecstatic, especially when I told her she could open one of her presents, as was my family's tradition on Christmas Eve. I gave it to her, and she tore the paper to shreds in 2.4 seconds. Then she was shrieking, and holding up the one present that had taken most of my waking hours to create in the past month.

I'd long since cut up all of Devlin's velvet clothes, and I'd had plenty of velvet, enough for three quilts really. So I'd stored the rest. But as I'd gone through the clothes, some had been exceptional in their beauty. Most of these had been handmade, going by the stitching, and initially had caught my eye as they had been made for a woman. I'd asked Devlin tentatively if he minded me saving a few I liked, to alter for Venus, or for myself. I guessed they might have been Annabelle's, though I was surprised velvet could last that long. I hadn't wanted him to be hurt, if he saw me wearing some clothes that had belonged to his long lost love.

Devlin had looked a little sad, but gave his consent. And out of that idea had grown our daughter's present: a miniature ball gown of silvery white velvet, with crystals sewn all over it, festooned with seed pearls, glass beads, and lace. It was almost a wedding dress, it was so replete with ornamentation. So I'd made her a veil to go with it, and Devlin had bought her a tiara of cut glass crystals that I had attached the veil to.

"It's so beautiful! Can I put it on now? Right now?" Venus asked excitedly.

"You can try it on," I said gently. "But only to make sure it fits—"

"I want to wear it now!"

I could tell whose daughter she was, if not by her arrogant expression, by the demanding tone in her lovely voice. "—but tomorrow you can wear it to see your grandmother and grandfather. All tomorrow night. Okay?"

"Okay!" Venus agreed, already leading me by the hand to the nearest bathroom, the one off the kitchen.

I helped her take off the red velvet dress she was wearing, and slipped the white gown over her head. I could see at once it was a little too long. But that wouldn't take too long to fix, I thought, as I buttoned up the back. It would have been easier to install a zipper, but the carved pearl buttons were beautiful, and likely had been made by hand. I fastened the last of the three, then tied the white sash at the back in a large flouncy bow, realizing at that moment why the dress was too long.

"How does it look?" Lash hissed from outside the door. "Come out, so we can see."

"I forgot the crinoline," I called out. "Can you get it? It's in my sewing room."

"What's a crinoline?" Lash asked. "What's it look like?"

"I'll get it," Devlin said, laughing, "Before your time, Lash."

Lash grumbled something good-naturedly.

Devlin was back in a moment, and handed the tulle and lace underskirt through the door. I had Venus raise the skirt of the dress, and I lay the crinoline down, so she could step into it. She did, and I raised it, tying it around her waist with a simple ribbon.

Venus looked at me expectantly. I knew that look well from Devlin, the look that said she was waiting to be admired. "You look beautiful," I praised her. "Go out and show your father, and Lash."

Venus almost knocked me over getting out the door. She pranced into the living room, beaming.

"You are beautiful, Venus," Lash said in a hushed voice. "You live up to your name."

Devlin looked a little stricken as he beheld his daughter. But after a moment, he nodded almost imperceptibly and began to smile, even as he blinked back tears. "You are beautiful, V," he said in an emotionally charged tone. "You are incomparable."

Venus basked happily for a few seconds. Then she looked down at her feet, and frowned. "I need shoes," she said sadly. "I don't have matching shoes."

"You have them," Lash said, and handed her a pair of silver flats that sparkled. "Merry Christmas from me."

Venus gave a cry of delight, and snatched them out of his hand. A second later, she had kicked off her shoes, and put them on. "They're perfect!" she said happily. "Thank you, Uncle Lash!"

Lash grinned happily at her, then at Devlin and me.

Venus hugged me, and whispered, "Thanks, Mom. I know it must have taken a long time to make. Longer than the star, and you didn't have all of us to help."

I had been thinking her too grabby and ungrateful. Her sudden about-turn floored me. This also was familiar, as Devlin was the same way. I knelt before her so I could look at her.

"I'm glad you like it, V," I said, hugging her. "I'm glad to be here with you."

I was suddenly hit hard by the fact that Devon had never got a Christmas present, nor seen a tree, nor tasted eggnog. He was never going to. Never. He was cold ashes, in the ground, with none of us there with him.

I hugged Venus so tightly, she let out a little gasp of surprise. Then she hugged me back just as hard. "I miss him, too," she whispered sadly. "I miss him, too, Mom."

I felt like I was going to lose it for a few seconds, and then got control of myself. I wiped away my tears, and hers, and kissed her on the cheek, taking my time to stand on my wobbly legs. "Come and take it off," I said, my voice clear. "Then it's to bed with you."

V nodded, and followed me upstairs, where I got her ready for bed. Soon, she was in her bed, saying her prayers with me as we did now every night. I kissed her, and left, turning off the light. Then I walked back downstairs.

Dev and Lash were sitting there by the tree sipping some wine, a filled glass for me waiting near them. I paused for a minute, studying them. They were so opposite, it was hard not to, when they were like this.

Lash was so much smaller and dark, his skin tanned-looking, his black hair unkempt as always, all in black, but still his usual cold-weather jeans, turtleneck, and heavy cotton shirt. His weapons were strapped to his belt, as always, though his gun wasn't visible. Dev was so much bigger: tall, broad shouldered, so fair, his shoulder length golden hair shining in the reflected light from the tree, carefully styled to look not styled at all. And as usual for any kind of occasion, he was dressed like the king he was, in a white silk suit that had to be designer over a red silk shirt, with some soft-looking shoes made of white leather.

How had such opposites become friends? How had the friendship lasted for so many years, with them being so different? Theo and Danial were similar in being different, but they at least had wanted the same things, more or less. Even so, I wondered that they hadn't been headed for a parting of the ways even without Danial's injury, now Theo had his own family. But knowing both Lash and Dev, I wondered that Devlin's cruel actions hadn't driven Lash from him over the years. Had the promise of being young and never dying been reason enough for his unshaking loyalty? That was a big lure, not dying. But something seemed to be missing, to not make sense about their relationship.

"Love, come in and sit with us," Devlin said, turning to me. "You can look at us closer that way, instead of from across the room."

I smiled and blushed a little as I went over to him. He handed me my glass of wine, and I sat between them.

Lash downed his wine in one swallow, and got up. I gave him an alarmed glance. "I need to go and check in with everyone," he said with an easy smile. "I've let it go too long as it is. Someone's probably asleep at their posts, and I'll have to kick their asses. But I'll be back in an hour or so."

He left. One of the Hummers started up, then lights shone briefly in the front window as he drove down to the front gate.

Devlin eased me down into his arms, and we sat there for a long time, saying nothing, watching the tree sparkling, and looking at the pile of presents beneath it. Devlin had put them there at my request earlier that evening, when I had been getting dressed with Lash, and Serena had been keeping Venus occupied.

"Dev, where is Serena? Why isn't she here? Is she with T, or Nick?"

"She went to church. Don't worry, two bears are with her, at my insistence. But she goes every Christmas Eve."

"I didn't know she was religious."

"She used to be Catholic," Devlin said musingly. "I don't think she is anymore. Maybe Protestant?"

"I wondered why she was never around when Titus, Terian, or Rip were around."

"She disapproves of them, though I think she knows that they are not like what her church teaches her. They are not evil, not inherently, despite that they were born in Hell."

"Who is?" I said, sipping my wine. "Everyone has flaws. Even me."

Devlin laughed richly, and hugged me. "You did a good job with the dress," he said softly in my ear. "You recreated it in miniature perfectly."

"Was it hers, Dev?"

"Yes. The one Anna gave me her Oath in, all those years ago. I had it made for her, because Anna knew she wouldn't be having a traditional wedding if she agreed to be with me, and she said she wanted to wear a white gown. It was very important to her to do that, for some reason she never was able to really define, and so it was important that it be the most beautiful one I could have made for her. She loved it so much—"

"You shouldn't have let me cut it up," I stammered, feeling awful. "I'm sorry—"

"No," Devlin said, hugging me, and sniffling a little. "She would have understood, and also been happy to know that a child of mine would one day wear it. And I know you took a good portion of the material not needed for Venus's dress for our quilt."

"Yes. I'm using what I could save, mostly the lower part of the plain white velvet skirt."

"It wasn't doing anyone any good in a box. It has made me sad to look at it, all these years. I couldn't let it go either, though, and so had a witch enchant it, and a few other of Anna's clothes for me, so the material would not crumble, or decay. I'd forgotten that." He paused a moment, and then continued. "I'm happy Venus will wear it, and when she outgrows it, I'll have it mounted, and framed. The spell still holds to the fabric, though the dress itself will be in other forms. Who knows? Perhaps a child of Venus's will one day wear it, or their child, or grandchild. That would have made Anna very happy, to know that her dress had become an heirloom of our family. And I will look at the squares on the quilt every night, and remember her."

Devlin sipped his wine, and I discreetly wiped my filling eyes again. "It makes me happy that you have brought my past into the present in a way I can remember it without being sad," he whispered. "I didn't know that was possible. It's good to finally be happy again." Devlin seemed to consider something, and tilted my chin up to look at him. "But are you happy, Sarelle? Here with us?"

"Yes," I said, sipping my wine. "But I do miss my other children, and my parents, and—"

"Speaking of which, we should go see Danial," Devlin said, his voice sorrowful. "He should not be un-visited tonight. Come, Love."

I got to my feet, and followed him upstairs, glad I'd not had to say his brother's name. Devlin was always saddened by any mention of Danial.

Danial was as he always was now: unmoving, cool, and darkly handsome. I hugged him, and gave him a gentle kiss, and Devlin embraced him as well. He gave no sign he knew we were there, or that he heard our words, though I told him about Venus, and about the gown, and Devlin added in his two cents. When we were done, Dev and I looked at each other. "Merry Christmas, brother," he said finally. "I love you. Come, Sar."

We left Danial as he was, and returned to our spot on the couch. Devlin got us each another glass of wine.

"I don't remember a Wintermas being so melancholy in all my history," Devlin said, hugging me. "And that is saying something. It's true, I have not celebrated one for years, but I wish it was happier, especially being your first with me, and Lash. V had a good time, but—"

"I am happy," I said in exhaustion, getting to my feet. "But I'm ready for bed, Dev."

"Come upstairs then, Love. Lash can join us when he comes in from checking on the guards. And tell me as we undress, how was it, to be animal with him?"

I followed him upstairs, with a last glance at the sparkling tree, then into the bedroom.

"Sar? Do you not want to tell me?"

I looked at him as I pulled off my sweater and jeans and gave him a wide but tired smile. "Very good. But I'm so exhausted, and he did all the work. It was nonstop, for hours."

"Hmm. Maybe I'll have to train beforehand," Dev mused. "I'll ask Lash, and also Titus."

I thought that very funny for some reason, and stifled a laugh. Dev took no notice; he was too busy thinking of the possibilities, by his expression.

"Come to bed," I said, swallowing the last of my wine. "And snuggle with me. I need that more than anything."

"Your wish is my command," Devlin purred, and crawled into his arms. I was asleep in a few moments.

* * * *

Christmas morning, I woke up to find Lash carefully placing a small velvet box on my upper chest, right above Devlin's sleeping form.

"Merry Christmas, Sar," he said softly, propping himself up on one arm to look at me.

# Chapter Ten

To say I was shocked was an understatement. Lash was not the type I'd have guessed to buy me jewelry. *And the big question: was a ring in there?* "You didn't have to," I said, not sure what to say. "I wasn't sure you celebrated Christmas."

"I usually don't, because Dev doesn't. But as it looked like we would be celebrating this year, I got you these."

I relaxed instantly, because there couldn't be a ring inside with him saying "these." I opened the box to see it contained small gold earrings. "What are these?" I said, peering at them. "They look like...flies? Gold flies?"

"Deer flies," Lash blurted, laughing hard.

"You gave me *deer fly* earrings?" I said, looking at him like he was crazy, because I thought he must be. "Why?"

"Because—" he began, then started laughing too hard to get it out.

"Say it, you whackjob," I said, trying not to grin. "Why?"

"Because you like things that bite you and drink your blood!" Lash managed, and then he was choking, he was laughing so hard.

"What are you laughing about?" Devlin said grumpily, waking up. "I'd better still have all my hair, Lash. None of my blood donors can come today."

"You're okay, Dev," Lash said, still laughing uproariously. "I promised you I'd never do that again to you, anyway."

I wanted to laugh myself, imagining what Lash must have done to Devlin, but I managed to stifle most of it. "You bring bad taste to whole new levels," I said, yet I couldn't help smiling.

Lash finally stopped laughing, his easy expression sliding into a wide grin. "I wanted the jeweler to make me some mosquitoes, instead, but he said he didn't have delicate enough tools."

I wondered when he said that if there wasn't another reason he'd given me these. Mosquitoes would remind me of the Everglades, and what Lash and I shared there.

155

"Do you like them?" Lash said, suddenly hesitant.

"If you get them out of the box for me, I'll put them on," I answered with a joyful smile.

Devlin wasn't moving or saying anything, just watching us. Lash unfastened the earrings from the case, then handed them to me one at a time. I thought them pretty, despite Lash's reasoning behind the gift. And the more I thought about his reason, the more hilarious I thought it was. "Thank you," I said, kissing him gently. "I like them very much."

Devlin looked up at us, his expression very guarded. "We should get up," he said, moving off me reluctantly. "Venus will be wanting to open her presents. I also have something for Sar myself."

I blushed, though I had expected this. "Dev, you shouldn't have. I—"

"You're here with us," Devlin interrupted. "And you are going to give me your Oath tomorrow night, Sar. I'll include Lash, as I said I would. That's enough for both of us." Lash said nothing, but he nodded in agreement.

It dawned on me that both he and Dev thought that I hadn't gotten them anything, and they were trying to reassure me. I was more than content to let them think that, for now.

* * * *

Christmas breakfast was delightful. Devlin had gotten a potion the night before from Titus, so he joined Lash, Venus, and I in eating some pancakes, eggs, toast, bacon, hash browns, ham and sausage. It was true he only had one helping, and Lash had two, but at the speed Lash ate, Devlin wasn't made to feel he rushed any, even though as usual he had only five minutes to finish eating. Serena was absent, visiting Theoron at his request to spend Christmas morning with him at his home. I wondered about Nick but said nothing, as it certainly wasn't my business. I was feeling odd enough not having T or Elle here for breakfast. But it made sense that Elle was with her father, and that I'd see her later on. As for T, he was almost a full adult now. He had his own life to lead, and one day, he'd have his own family.

I felt really old and unnecessary, thinking about all that. But then Devlin hugged me, and I looked over at Lash talking with Venus, and decided it was okay. I had people who loved me, and people to love, and that was what Christmas morning was truly about anyway.

Our breakfast was largely undisturbed, save by Terian, who came by to drop off a gift basket from both Titus and Leri, and some wine from he and Sundown. I offered him some breakfast, which he was glad to accept. Apparently, Serena was discussing her faith with Jenny and T this morning, and he was glad to be absent from that, though Sundown was there listening.

"It's hard enough just moving around today," Terian said with a groan.

"But Chr...my G...um, He wasn't even actually born on this day—" I began.

"Doesn't matter, it matters that so many believe he was born today," Terian said, scarfing down ham and bacon and sausage in large quantities, so much so Lash was eyeing him with an irritated look. "It's a huge outpouring of belief, and it makes me feel weak."

"Why is that, exactly?" Lash hissed, his tone interested. "I have heard that alluded to by Titus, that it is not the religion itself, but the faith behind it that causes you pain?"

"I'm not telling you anything," Terian said, giving him a dark appraising look. "You might use it against me someday."

Lash shot him a look of bared teeth, and then he got that Terian was joking with him. Lash seemed not to know what to do when he realized that, so he grinned. "I probably would," he said finally, and laughed. "Keep your secrets, Tears."

We all went quiet, hearing Lash use his nickname. Lash seemed ill at ease the moment all of us focused on him, and I quickly covered for him, asking Terian if he had gotten the basket we sent.

"Yes, and thanks," he said, eating the last of his pancakes. "It got devoured last night, when we were sitting, and talking..."

He trailed off, and now it was me ill at ease, thinking of the friends I'd made over the past few years all sitting there without me, and not missing me at all. But this time Dev covered for me.

"Titus got my present as well?" he purred.

Terian blushed, and nodded. "He said to thank you. He needed...them."

Devlin nodded, but that had put a pall on the conversation. Because I was guessing what Devlin had sent to Titus. *Dead bodies as presents? Eww.*

Terian hugged Venus and I good-bye, nodded to Dev and Lash, and a moment later, he was gone.

"Shall we open presents?" Devlin said with a grin, and Venus ran for the living room with a shout.

"I guess that's a 'yes,'" Lash said, chuckling.

I loaded the dishwasher, and put the pans in the sink to soak. Then I went in to join them.

The presents took an hour to finish, in spite of there being a pile of them. But Venus made short work of the wrapping, taking about .5 seconds to rip it off on average. Devlin took a lot of pictures with his phone, and it was true, most of the presents were for Venus. Books, movies, dolls, clothes, toys, and shoes. But she was polite, and thanks were given, after a while at least.

Devlin had gotten me several gifts: a silvery velvet robe, and also a new black velvet robe for lounging, and a huge basket of chocolate, and also a pair of bear head earrings not unlike the ones Danial had gotten me with his symbol. Like those, these bears had red eyes, not green.

I felt self-conscious, but I took out Lash's earrings he had given me, and put Devlin's on. He nodded in appreciation.

Lash had also gotten me a few other small gifts. A gift certificate for Amazon.com, a gift certificate for Penzy's spices, and a pair of well made, top-of-the-line work gloves. I was touched, that he knew me well enough to know I needed work gloves. I'd never gotten them as a gift before, not even from my parents. I had not a single pair to my name here at Hayden, as all the spare pairs that I'd stockpiled at my house were ashes.

I gave him a smile and said thanks, and tried hard not to make it seem as though this gift was nothing other than a small tool I was grateful for. But as I opened them, and looked up at Lash, he caught the look in my eyes, and I saw it reflected in his eyes, before he changed, his eyes going flat. I thanked him quickly, and moved onto the next present, putting the gloves aside.

*He's right to hide, and you'd better do the same.* I didn't want Dev getting jealous on this morning of all mornings. It was enough for both of us that his gift had touched me deeply. I'd have time to thank him privately later on in the evening.

I gave Devlin his own copy of *Sweeny Todd*, a six-month subscription to a flower bouquet of the month club, and his own handmade robe of silver lamé, with a silver-gray velvet collar and sash. He seemed to like it, telling me he would wear the robe for me later. I presented Lash with a bottle of Ardbeg 1974, which he almost salivated over. But according to the experts on the Internet, it was the best scotch to be had on the market today. It had taken a large chunk of my savings to procure it, but hell, what was money for, if not for things like this?

Soon, all the presents were opened, and Venus was happily coloring on the floor in a new book, with new crayons, dressed in a fairy costume I'd made for her. Lash, Devlin, and I were curled together on the couch watching *Sweeny Todd*, when we heard the phone ring. Lash answered it, but when he called to Devlin to pick up, I knew by his voice that something was very wrong.

I got to an extension in time to hear Samuel's panicked voice. "Devlin, Harriet seems to be succumbing to the vampire virus," he said brokenly. "Her body's turning colder every day, and she seems to be unable to eat solid food, or anything but blood!"

"How much of your blood did you give her?" Devlin said loudly. "Too much and she'll turn and lose the babies!"

"I gave her only a small amount, as you instructed, and when her teeth began to get sharp, I stopped. But she's had only a few drops in December! And I've taken none of her blood! What is wrong with her? She wouldn't wake up for me this morning, and when she did, she acted drugged!"

I felt the blood drain from my face. I was glad I couldn't see Devlin. Harriet was losing her resistance to the virus, and Samuel's blood was too potent now for her system to resist. But she'd gotten dependent on vampire blood to live, from what Titus had done to her with my blood, and she needed more of the virus in her body. It had to be that! She had my symptoms, the ones I'd had when I'd needed more of the virus!

"Your blood is too strong for her," Devlin said finally. "I'm half your age, Samuel. You are turning her! You need a vampire who is not as strong to give her their blood. Because like Sar, she needs vampire blood now to live. You don't give it to her soon and she'll die!"

"I thought of that first! Michael has given her a little of his blood this morning, as a favor to me," Samuel said angrily. "He is younger than you, but it didn't work! She reacted as if she'd had my blood, and her teeth began to get sharp at once!"

Harriet most likely needed more of my resistant blood, and another transformative spell from Titus. But how to get it to her? What if it killed her, in her condition? What if it killed her children?

I sank heavily into the nearest chair, because it was all a moot point. My blood was mortal now, not the way it had been when Titus had used it for the spell last time. I couldn't save her, even if I found a way to get my blood to her. She was going to die for sure.

"Let me talk to Titus," Devlin said quietly. "I assume you have consulted Cyrus?"

"Yes, and he said he had no experience with this, that there was nothing he could do that might not kill her! I fired him on the spot in my anger, and he's already left my estate!"

"I'll call you back," Devlin said quickly. "Five minutes. Keep her awake, Samuel! Even if you have to hurt her, do it! She loses consciousness now, she may never wake up."

"I'll do it," Samuel stated, and I heard a click, as he and Devlin hung up.

I walked into the kitchen. Lash hugged me gently, but didn't say anything. Two minutes later Devlin came down the stairs, dressed, Titus in tow.

"Devlin, it probably won't work," Titus was saying. "She's got to be five months pregnant by now, and any kind of transformative spell will hurt the babies."

"What about just some of Sar's blood, mixed with yours?" Devlin said, leaning on the table, and looking down pensively. "Wouldn't that help her resistance, at least a little?"

"She'll probably die anyway," Titus said irritably. "I told you this would come back to bite us in the ass."

"It served its purpose at the time," Devlin said with a growl. "Truthfully, I never expected your spell to work as well as it did, to change her enough so she could remain pregnant this long."

"I'm good at what I do," Titus said, pride in his deep bass voice. "You know I'm one of the best. That's why you hired me in the first place."

"Well, then figure out something to try!" Devlin said, slamming his hand on the table. "You have another three minutes!"

Lash cleared his throat, and we all looked at him. "We don't need to save her," he hissed softly, his eyes flat. "We need to save the babies. That is what Samuel truly cares about, not Harriet."

I felt a chill, and moved my eyes to the floor. Devlin and Titus didn't move.

"If Harriet dies and the babies with her, Sar's going to be in danger again. They'll want her. And it'll get out eventually that she can still have children—"

Titus gave me a look of shock, but Lash's eyes were on Dev, and he kept going.

"—but if we can save the children in Harriet, Samuel and Perseus will be busy enough with them to leave Sar alone. Zane isn't important enough to matter, not since Robert got killed."

Robert had worked for Zane? No wonder he'd seemed to have lost so much standing at the party. It would be like Danial losing Theo, or Devlin losing Lash.

"Samuel took some of his territory over, near Egypt, and Zane might even be deposed soon, if he doesn't hire another gunslinger. So that leaves only Michael as a problem, and I'll bet if we agreed to give him some of Sar's blood, enough to give him his own dhamphir with another female, and told him what to do, he'd leave her alone, too."

"But you are talking about killing women, Lash," I said in a strangled voice. "Using them, and then killing them. Their bodies won't be able to take it, as Harriet's can't! They'll turn!"

"To save you," Lash said, meeting my eyes, his tone unhappy. "I don't like it either, Sar. But I'd do it, to save you. And it would only be Harriet, and maybe one other woman. And turning is not the same as dying. Harriet would probably not be discarded, if she turned, if Samuel's baby lived."

"But what if that's not enough?" I broke in, furious suddenly. "What if Michael wants more than one? God knows, one doesn't seem to be enough for any man I've had a child for!"

Devlin narrowed his eyes, but Lash just looked at me and nodded. "Point taken," he said. "That's my only suggestion. And we are out of time."

"I've got nothing," Devlin muttered. "Titus?"

"I'll give you a potion to give her, like last time," Titus said, rubbing his hand on his eyes. "Give me a few minutes. And Sar, I'll need a little of your blood."

"It is back to being summer, almost," Devlin said. "It should work."

"I won't guarantee it will save either the woman or the child," Titus rumbled. "It may kill her instead, but I have no other ideas either. And she'll turn for sure if we do nothing, and then the children inside her will wither and die."

"Sar, get dressed," Devlin said quickly. "You'll need to watch Venus while we're gone, and Lash, you'll need to come with me, as soon as the potion's made."

"What? Where?" I said. "Where are you going?"

"England, of course," Devlin said with a roll of his eyes. "To Samuel's country estate."

* * * *

An hour later, Lash returned with Devlin and Titus. They slammed in through the front door, and the three of them went directly into the kitchen, and opened a dusty bottle, splitting it three ways into large pint mugs. It went without saying that if Titus was imbibing, it was blood, not wine. I knew when I saw that whatever had happened couldn't be good. I pulled up a chair at the table, and sat down, keeping an eye on Venus in the dining room who was still going to town with her new coloring books.

For a while, no one said anything—they just drank, and looked irritated.

"Did she die?" I asked finally.

"No," Lash hissed. "But she almost did."

Titus continued, "When the potion hit her system, she went into cardiac arrest, and she was dead for thirty seconds. She recovered, under the ministrations of Samuel's medical team, and she's stable now, but she hasn't regained consciousness. The babies are stable, and doing well. The good news is I think she will eventually regain consciousness, with what we did for her. We've bought her some time, at least. The bad news is that Samuel accused me of trying to kill her, and I got us out of there only by a hair's breadth."

"But the worst of it was I'd hoped to procure some of Samuel's blood for Danial, in return for saving her," Devlin said miserably. "I'd hoped he'd be grateful, if we helped her, and give it to me. It would go a long way to making

Danial like he was—"

"Dev, Danial is not going to be like he was, not ever," Titus growled, finishing his wine and standing up. "The sooner you realize that, the better off you'll be—"

"Fucking shut your mouth," Devlin hissed, his eyes red. "Leave, Titus. Now."

Titus snarled, showing his rows of fangs and promptly disappeared.

I went to Devlin and hugged him, but said nothing. There were no words of comfort I could give.

\* \* \* \*

That night went as well as could be expected. My parents had showered presents on the three children, and T, Elle, and Venus enjoyed themselves. My mother complimented me on Venus's dress, and was polite. But I could see she still didn't speak to Devlin, though he tried his best to be as polite as possible to her. She did go overboard being nice to Lash though, and I saw how ill at ease he was, wondering why she was doing it. Finally, he pulled me aside in the upstairs hallway before we had dinner, and asked me why she was fawning over him.

"I don't know. I think she favors weres over vampires. And she's never liked Devlin."

"I just want her to not pay so much attention to me. Dev's getting mad."

I rolled my eyes. "Devlin knew this was how it was going to be when he agreed to come."

"Can't you say something to her?"

*My mother? Yeah, right.* "I could tell her you are my lover, too, if you want. Then she'll either treat you like she's treating Devlin, or she'll outright scream at you for sleeping with me."

"So your plan makes me a leper, or a john. That's great, Sar."

"It's only for a little more, Lash," I said, giving him a hug. "Then we'll go home."

As I moved past him to go back to the party, Lash grabbed hold of me, and kissed me. I knew he was nervous and needed reassurance, so I kissed him back, then hugged him close, finally drawing back to gaze into his dark worried eyes. *This is our first Christmas together. I want him to relax, and enjoy himself.* "I'm glad you're here with me tonight, that you came with us. I love you very much."

"What the hell is this?" I turned to see my stepfather looking at us from the bottom of the stairs. It was obvious he'd heard me, from the expression on his face.

162

*Ah shit.* "I..." I trailed off, not sure what to say.

Lash slipped his arm around me possessively, took a deep breath, and gave my stepfather a forced smile. "I'm your daughter's lover, as well as Devlin now. She means a lot to me. She loves me, and I care for her. I'm not going to hurt her, like Danial did, or leave her, like Theo did. I care for her children as if they were mine. And I'll protect her with my life."

My stepfather was looking at Lash with his mouth open.

"Now that you know the truth, welcome me, or tell me to leave," Lash said quietly, not letting go of me. "I'll go right now, if you ask me to, and never darken your door again. But she and I will be together as long as I live, or until she dissolves us. And about that, you have no say."

My stepfather looked at us a long moment, and then he shifted his eyes to someone else. I looked over and flushed to see my mother standing there, looking at us appraisingly.

"Are you the reason Theo left Sarelle?" my mother asked flatly.

"Some of it," Lash said flatly back. "But mostly it was because he wanted Sar to become what he was, and she refused."

"Define 'some of it'."

"We were intimate one time, when we shouldn't have been. Theo forgave Sar that, but he couldn't forgive her caring about me, because he hated me. It drove a wedge between them."

"That's all of it?"

"Pretty much," Lash replied.

"About time someone told us the whole truth for a change," she said, her eyes flinty. "Theo gave us some bullshit about irreconcilable differences. I like that you were honest. Come back in, as it's time to eat. You are welcome here, Lash."

"Thank you, Ma'am," Lash drawled respectfully, smiling for real this time.

Dinner was a good affair. Devlin had brought a tiny bit of the potion with him, and he ate a little bit, shocking my mother, though I knew it pleased her, that he had gone to such trouble to be able to eat her cooking. When he complimented her in glowing terms on her roast, she began to soften a little towards him.

Venus opened a few presents afterward, but she was the only one who did that night. T and Elle had opened their presents the previous night, and of course, my parents had not been expecting Lash. My parents had not gotten me anything this year, it seemed. I didn't know why, though I suspected it was because my mother didn't want to get Devlin anything. But I was pleased to see they had already started sampling their coffee gift basket.

Terian arrived at nine to collect Elle and T, and with a last hug, they left. I was sad to see them go, but I suspected that they were worn out. Two sets of holidays couldn't be easy to manage, especially with not only a new stepmother, but also a new stepfather-to-be.

When they had left, and Venus was again coloring on the floor, my stepfather brought me and my mother another glass of wine, and some scotch for himself and the guys. And we sat for a while and watched the flames flicker in their wood stove. I felt a pang, seeing that. I missed my wood stove; it was nothing but rusting metal now, and utterly useless.

"Are things safe yet?" my mother asked bluntly. "Is that bad man dead?"

"No," Devlin said, rolling his glass in his hand. "But he will be by the end of this week. Next week I fight him, and I'll kill him."

"What if you lose?" my mother said with worry. "What about Sar, and V?"

"I don't intend to lose," Devlin said, fixing her with his eyes. "I've defended myself against up-and-comers for two hundred years, Tina. This is not my first fight. Don't concern yourself."

"Sar will be with me," Lash hissed in what I suspected was supposed to be a comforting voice. "She'll be safe, and so will V, while the fight is taking place."

"But are you any good?" my mother said frankly, and Lash burst out laughing. He finished his scotch, and then grinned at her.

"You know of Theo's reputation? What he truly does for Danial, that it is not security? That he is better known for his body count in Danial's service than for any other reason?"

My mother went a little pale, but my stepfather cut his eyes to Lash, and nodded.

"I saw that, on the Internet," Chris whispered. "Nothing proven, all conjecture, but there was a lot of it, a lot of killings that were attributed to him, and to Danial, though your brother, Devlin, he was only mentioned once in passing."

"Then you saw my name too, I'll bet," Lash hissed with an evil looking grin. "Though Devlin pays well to see there is no mention of him on the Internet that isn't favorable."

"Yes, I saw that," my stepfather said, swallowing hard. "I wondered about that—"

"Lash," Devlin hissed, his eyes tinted red. "Don't go into all this now."

"They should know this," Lash said with a snarl, turning to Devlin. "They may need to live with us someday, if there is danger. Better for them to find out now who we really are, and take it seriously. The time for being polite and fake is long over."

Devlin shrugged, and sipped his wine. Lash turned back to my parents.

"Anyway, as I was saying, I do what Theo does, but I'm better than he is at it. Your daughter and granddaughter will be safe with me."

"But what if Devlin loses?" my mother said a little frantically.

"I'll be there to make sure he doesn't," Lash said, a cruel grin again on his face. "So will Titus. Don't worry about it."

"But—"

"Drop this line of thought, Ma'am," Lash hissed. "Things may need to be done. Bad things. You don't really want to know this anyway. I hear that in your voice."

"You are right, I don't," my mother said, taking a long drink of wine. "I don't."

"We should go," I said, looking at my watch. "It's late."

"Before you do, your mother and I need to ask you something," my stepfather said uncomfortably. "We didn't get you any Christmas presents this year. We had planned, back when your house burned, to chip in some money to help you rebuild, instead of getting you and Theo presents this year, for your birthdays, or for Christmas. But now that you've separated, it looks like he's living at Danial's house with Theoron, and that you plan on living with Devlin and Lash?"

"Yes," Devlin said, reaching out to grip my hand. "Lash, V, and Sarelle will live with me."

"Will you sell the property?" my mother asked. "Your barn?"

"I don't know," I said, shrugging. "I have asked T about it, and he's considering maybe building something there again."

"You shouldn't sell it," Lash said firmly, and we all looked at him, a little shocked. He had never voiced any opinion on this at all.

"Elle always liked to ride, and so did T," he continued. "So do you and Dev. Maybe you could keep horses there. There's a barn for it, even if you've never used it for that purpose."

"I never thought of that," Devlin said slowly. "Danial always liked to ride so much—"

"Is he dead?" my mother said quietly.

"No, but he's still comatose," Devlin whispered. "His heart beats, but that is all."

"I'm sorry," my parents both said. Devlin nodded, but said nothing.

I decided it was time to go, before Devlin's mood turned from introspective sadness to melancholy to anger, which was the usual progression. I got to my feet, and so did everyone else.

"We'll wait then, until you decide," my parents said, hugging me, and then Venus. "You have most of the winter yet."

"Shh! I'm already thinking of spring," Lash said with a grin. "I'm looking forward to it!"

My mother hugged him, and though he seemed surprised, he hugged her back. Then she released him, and turned to Devlin. He looked at her hesitantly. She gave him a long-suffering look, and beckoned him to come hug her. He gave her a radiant smile, and picked her up off her feet as he hugged her.

"I still don't really like you," she said with a grin. "But I love my granddaughter very much."

"I love your daughter, Tina," Devlin said with a wide grin. "So consider the feeling mutual."

My mother burst out laughing, and relief washed over me. *Things aren't going to turn out so bad after all.*

After we got home, I put Venus to bed, then made my preparations.

\* \* \* \*

Devlin sat before me on his bed, waiting naked under the covers, just the upper half of him revealed, his golden chest hair shimmering in the candlelight. I stood before him in the same gown I had worn for him the first time I had given him my Oath. Lash was beside Dev, but he was leaning back on top of the bed in his black jeans, his arms under his head, watching me with his dark eyes. His chest was bare, his wiry muscles even at rest looking ready for action in an instant.

"Repeat after me," Devlin said commandingly. "I, Sarelle O'Connor McGarran, promise you, Devlin Dalcon, and your brother, Danial Racklan, that I shall be yours, and no other vampire's, under pain of death, until life should leave me, or both of you should perish."

I repeated what he had said.

"I shall share myself with no other man, unless they are men you give permission for—"

Lash eyes darted over to Devlin, but he remained silent.

"—or Tristan Valeras, also known as Lash, under pain of death."

Lash relaxed considerably, as I repeated the words.

"I give you my love, and authority over me, understanding that I am given in return your love, your protection, and your life's blood, that is now my life's blood."

I repeated that, too.

"I promise that I shall not enter into any separate bond with Lash, be neither married nor mated—"

"She can't promise you that," Lash hissed angrily.

Devlin and I stopped talking, looking over at him in confusion.

"She can and she will," Devlin said simply. "I'm not having another jealous husband in you, Lash."

"By were law, she's already my mate," Lash retorted flatly. "And I'm hers."

Confusion evaporated in Devlin's angry intake of breath. *Get away from him, he's going to lose it!*

Before I could bolt, Devlin's fist closed on my hair. "You traitorous bitch!" he snarled at me, his eyes bleeding to red. "You said nothing! When did you mate yourself to him? After I let you be together as snakes—?" Devlin let out a sudden pain-filled cry as he fell to his knees, the tip of Lash's knife poking out of his chest. I went with him to my own knees, as he didn't release me.

"Dev, let her go, right now," Lash hissed softly, twisting the knife a little. "This is not her fault. She couldn't tell you what she didn't know."

"I should kill you," Devlin uttered, releasing me. "Stabbing me in the back like this."

Lash pulled out his knife, and helped Devlin to his feet. Devlin promptly punched him in the face, and Lash fell sprawling to the floor, his mouth bloody. Devlin stood over him, his wound already healing, though blood glistened on his newly formed skin.

"Stop it, Devlin!" I yelled. "Lash, what are you talking about? We aren't mated."

"You fucking shit," Devlin said icily, staring down at Lash. "You're my best friend, and you do this, mate the woman I love to yourself, and you don't even tell me? On top of everything else you did in Florida!"

"I deserve that," Lash hissed shamefully as he got to his feet. "I'm sorry for it. I never intended to hurt you by doing it, or even to have either of you know."

I went silent, because I thought I understood finally. *This is the promise he was talking about, our first night back together.*

"How would I not know?" Devlin said incredulously. "What are you saying?"

"I was dying," Lash said softly, his eyes moving past Devlin to center on mine. "I knew I'd met a woman I could finally care for, in Sar. I sent her a knife, and carved on it a symbol that said 'mate'. With it, I asked her if she would be mine. I didn't expect her to say "yes," Dev, or to ever see her again even! But she came to me, wearing the knife, and let me have her—"

"And by doing that, she said 'yes'," Devlin finished, slowly nodding. "You're right. But she didn't know what she was doing."

"Her actions spoke louder than any words," Lash continued, looking at me with pride. "She risked her life for me, told me she'd let me change her, if that's what it took to save my life. That was enough for me. I've thought of her as my mate ever since."

"That's why you were faithful to her, taught T what you did."

Lash glanced at Devlin and nodded, then turned back at me, his eyes moist. "It almost killed me, being with you that night. But you'd come to me wearing the knife, and you didn't reject my advances. I had to try to consummate us, even if it hastened my death."

"Why didn't you tell me?" I cut him off, shocked. "I asked you what the symbol meant, Lash. You told me to leave it!"

"You were married then," Lash said, averting his gaze. "Your thoughts after I healed were only of your husband, and your son. I thought if you knew what we'd done, you might tell me that you couldn't be my mate, that you wanted it nullified. I didn't. I wanted to share that with you, at least while there was the chance that you would give Devlin your Oath, and ask him to include me. I wanted to mean something to you, Sar."

*Even if you can't tell me you love me?* I kept silent, not wanting to speak my thoughts.

"I understand your desire, Lash, but she can't be your mate," Devlin said with a trace of reluctance. "I want Sar to be immortal, not weresnake. Part of her Oath tonight is her word not to let you change her."

"It's enough she'll change for me magically," Lash supplied quickly. "She doesn't have to be weresnake for real. I don't want her to lose the chance to be immortal, either. We can still be mated, according to the literal were definition, so long as she comes to me regularly as both snake and human."

"That's why you always wanted this so much?" I asked, enjoying this romantic side of him I'd rarely seen. "Because you wanted that commitment from me?"

"Well, that, and it feels really good having sex with you that way." He grinned lecherously.

I rolled my eyes, unable to resist smiling back.

"I'll agree to this, so long as you don't interfere with her and me," Devlin said reluctantly. "Don't ever get between us again, Lash."

"I'll defend her with my life, if I think you're hurting her," Lash replied in a low cold tone. "Even if it means hurting you to get you to leave her alone. You didn't want Theo to harm her. That was part of the first Oath she gave you. I feel the same way about you hurting her. I know you like to hurt women sometimes. I've cleaned up the messes often enough over the years—"

"Shut your mouth," Devlin growled.

Lash went silent, but the damage was done. I'd been feeling romantic about tonight's Oath, if a little uneasy. Now I felt like I was making the biggest mistake of my life.

I backed away toward the door from the both of them. "I'm done with violence," I said, my tone mirroring Lash's in its coldness. "I know you both have dark sides, and I'm telling you right now, I want no part of that. So if you think you can't restrain yourselves, say so now, and we'll call this off."

Devlin sighed. "I'm not going to hurt you, Sar. I'm done with that, Lash. If I need to get off that way, I'll go to Hillary and Tiffany for that. They are masochists, as you well know."

Lash looked at him for a long moment. "So long as that's understood, I won't get in the way of you and her, no matter what you do together. And if she agrees to do something that causes her pain, I'm not going to get in the way, either. So long as she's willing, it's okay by me. But you're never going to force her again like the first time you had her, Dev. Not ever. And I won't stand for you making her cry like you did in the past, either."

"I promised her that I would try to be the man she needed me to be," Devlin said softly, his golden eyes on me. "I mean to keep that promise."

There was silence for a moment.

"Sarelle, do you want to be his mate, officially?" Devlin said finally. "Or do you want to break the bond between you?"

I looked at Lash, who was waiting nervously for my answer. "Can I be his mate, if I'm still married to Theo? It seems unlikely it's legal, to say nothing of being moral."

"You aren't married anymore, you're legally separated," Devlin corrected grumpily. "And it doesn't matter, anyway. The literal rules for weres are that you are mated if you both promise to be with each other and not another of your species. Usually, that is taken to mean monogamy, but that is not a requirement for all types of weres, as some were species allow several females to a male, or vice versa. I know you aren't going to be with another weresnake, Sar. The only requirement besides wanting to be mated is that you have to be together with your mate-to-be sexually in both animal and human form. You've already done that. Technically he's right, you are already his mate, though in the strictest terms you weren't really mated to him until you assumed snake form and let him be with you—"

"Stop with the technicalities, and let her answer you," Lash hissed, angry.

"Yes," I said tenderly, looking at Lash. "Yes, I want to be his mate."

Lash let out the breath he'd been holding in a rush, and grinned back at me, his dark eyes joyful.

"Fine, then repeat after me—" Devlin started.

"Don't we need a justice of the peace or something?" I interrupted.

"Someone to make it legal?"

"I'm Vampire Ruler of a continent," Devlin said imperiously. "My word is law. But even if I were only a State Ruler, by law, I have the authority to execute rogue vampires, discipline errant Oathed humans, kill any human I wish, and officiate, when necessary, over both Oathing and mating rituals between any and all supernatural creatures in my domain, along with other rights to—"

"Enough already!" Lash broke in. "I want to be mated, not talked to death."

"Repeat after me, Sar," Devlin said. "I promise that from this day forward, I shall be the mate of Lash and no other weresnake—"

I repeated it.

"—I promise that I shall come to live with you, my Oathed One and my mate, for the rest of my days, or until you both should perish. So I swear, this day of December 26, 2013."

As I said the final words aloud, he gave a happy sigh, then nodded once. "I, Devlin Dalcon, accept your Oath, Sarelle O'Connor McGarran, both on behalf of myself and on behalf of my brother, Danial Racklan." He said the words slowly with pleasure, carefully pronouncing each one. Then he turned to Lash. "Your turn, Tristan."

"I, Tristan Valeras, also known as Lash, promise you, Sarelle McGarran, to be your mate," Lash hissed sincerely, the tone of his emotionally charged words uneven. "I promise to protect you as best that I can, and to be faithful to you, until my life leaves me. Whatever you need, I will do my best to provide you."

Lash turned to Devlin. "Time for your promise, Darian," he hissed with a smirk.

"It's my middle name," Dev said grumpily, before I could comment. "My father loved the letter 'd'." He paused, and then began. "I, Devlin Dalcon, promise you, Sarelle O'Connor McGarran to give you my life's blood whenever you require it, and to be your lover until my life ends. I promise to confine my lovers to women you know of, and give permission for."

*He can't bring himself to say only Hillary and Tiffany. But they might die someday, so this is probably better to say. Maybe.*

"I promise to never be with another woman sexually on the grounds of our home, the land called Hayden, without your permission. I promise to let you be with your mate, Lash, as a snake, to be alone with him, to coil with him when the need arises. I promise to protect you, support you, and love you. So I swear, this day of December 26, 2013."

"I accept your promises," I said softly, feeling tears well up in my eyes.

"It is done," Devlin said, giving me a smile, though his eyes were troubled. "Come to us, Sar. We'll consummate it with you now. I will have my lawyer draw up the legal papers in the morning."

I came to them with a soft sigh. Lash and Devlin embraced me between them, trailing kisses down my neck. I lost myself in the sheer joy of their touch, and the relief that finally I had made a choice for myself that was my decision, for better or worse.

\* \* \* \*

I woke up the next morning feeling wasted. Lash and I had drunk almost a bottle of wine each, though Devlin had had a glass too in there somewhere. Devlin was lying on my chest, his arms around me, and Lash was against my back, his arms around my waist under Devlin's.

"Good morning, Mate," Lash hissed softly, as I looked up at him a little bleary eyed. "You look a little worse for wear. Do you feel okay?"

"I'm okay," I croaked out. "I just never drink that much…usually."

"It was a lot for you," Lash hissed, laughing. "I probably would be hurting too, but I had a lot more to eat than you did."

*That and your alcohol limit is probably measured in cases of wine.* I gave him a kiss, and he pulled me against him, his hard erection against the middle of my back. He moved his hips against mine suggestively, sliding his hand down from my breasts to caress me intimately.

"Again?" I asked, and kicked myself mentally for phrasing it like that. *Damn Theo.*

Lash scented the air. "What is it? You're upset."

*Oh, forget it, Sar. He's happy with Jenny, and you're happy here with them. It will take some getting used to for this to become your life, but it's better this way for everybody. This way, everyone gets a happy ending, including you.*

"Mate?"

I gave him a loving smile. "Yes, I'm your mate now. You have only to tell me you want me, Lash, and I'm yours."

"Then I want you now, Mate," Lash said eagerly. He kissed me, winding his tongue around mine and stroking me gently. I moved over slightly, letting go of Devlin and turning to Lash. He embraced me, quickly entering me with a sigh. "I love the feel of you," he hissed in my ear. "Part of me still can't believe this is real."

"Why, when you know how I feel about you?" I said between kisses.

"Because you aren't like any of my past lovers," Lash replied, without missing a stroke. "By the time I knew the difference between a 'good' woman and an 'easy' one, it was too late. No good woman wanted me near her, even weresnake women."

"I was once anyway," I quipped.

Lash gripped my face, making me look at him as he loved me. "Hush, Mate. You're a good woman. You tried to be a good wife to Theo, a good Oathed One to Danial and Devlin. You gave them children, when they told you they wanted them. You're a good mother. You went through a lot in the last years, but you never gave up trying to do what was right."

"You're being too generous." *And something of a chauvinist, not mentioning my chainsawing ability.*

"You tried to keep your promises to Danial and Theo, and kept most of them. Even when Theo was taken, and Devlin took you, you were faithful to Theo. You protected Devlin, keeping what he did to you secret to keep him safe. And when you knew he was, you told Theo the truth. And you told him the truth about you and I, too. He wouldn't have found out, otherwise, not from any of us."

I put my hands against his chest, stopping him. "How do you know all this?"

"I'm very intelligent," Lash said proudly. "And I got a lot of inside info from Brian."

I laughed, and Lash took the opportunity to thrust into me deeply, changing my laugh to a low moan. "I feel lucky you wanted me," he said, kissing me down my neck. "And I'm going to spend the rest of my life showing you how happy it makes me that I'm your mate."

"Then stop talking and show me now," I said lustily.

"Yes, shut up and stroke her," I heard a languorous voice say, then Devlin appeared behind Lash, his golden eyes full of desire.

"You're awake," I began, then Lash turned my head and kissed me, cutting off my words.

"Yes, I'm awake," Devlin said, moving closer to us. "Get ready for round two, Sar."

\* \* \* \*

It was late afternoon before I left the bed. Even then, it was only because Devlin had made reservations for the three of us for dinner and was not about to miss our first foray into the world as a triad.

"I can't move," I said with a long yawn, my entire body aching gently. "I don't think I can go."

"I'll carry you, then," Lash said, sliding his arms under me. "You need to eat something."

172

"We all do," Devlin said, yawning himself. "I'm ravenous."

"I could use a few steaks myself," Lash hissed, as he carried me into the bathroom. Then he helped me in the Jacuzzi, and climbed in himself. "Ahh!" he said as he slid into the water beside me.

Devlin slid into the water on the other side of me. "We've got about an hour," he said, yawning again. "Then we'll need to leave for the restaurant."

"Where are we going?" I asked playfully.

"The one by your old house," Devlin said, as if it were the only restaurant we could have possibly chosen. "That's your favorite, so Lash says. I've never been there."

"You'll like it," I said, reaching out to take hold of his hand in mine. "They have a good wine list."

"Are you sure, Sar?" Lash said, lifting me slightly and scooting himself under me, so I was sitting on his lap in the water. "You have friends that used to go there with you that knew you and Theo, and your parents sometimes go there, too. You and I ran into them that one time at brunch."

I kissed him on his scratchy cheek. "This is my life now. You're both part of my life. I'm happy to go there with you."

"Good," Lash replied. "I thought you might prefer not to have everyone know that you were with us…um, until your divorce is final."

"I'm not hiding what we are now, not from anyone. That would be pretty shitty behavior, if I did that," I said sharply, grimacing in distaste.

"Sar's not like other women you've known," Devlin said, squeezing my hand. "She wouldn't have agreed to be with you, Lash, if she was ashamed of you."

"I know that," Lash said, still holding me close. "But on some level, I'm still surprised."

I thought about reminding him I loved him. But then I'd have to hear his silence, because he couldn't say it back to me, so I remained silent.

# Chapter Eleven

We sat in the Jacuzzi for another half hour, just luxuriating in the water and bantering playfully. Even sated as we both were, we were too happy not to want to tease one another and share laughter.

"Come on you two! We've got to go!" Devlin called from the bedroom.

Reluctantly, Lash helped me out of the tub, and we both walked into the bedroom. Devlin was already dressing, and from the clothes strewn all over the room, it looked like he was having trouble deciding what to wear. "What do you think, Sar?" he said, holding up two shirts. "I'd like us to match. Do you want to wear red or blue?"

"Wear black, so we can all match," Lash said in irritation.

Devlin gave him an annoyed look.

I cut in, determined to nip this in the bud before it got any farther. "Stop," I said gently. "Both of you listen to me."

Both of them turned to me.

"I don't want any jealousy between the two of you," I said calmly, but with force behind my words. "I want to be with you both, and to not have the endless bickering that Theo and Danial have done since the moment Danial found out I'd let Theo move in with me."

"Fine, what should we wear—?" Devlin started.

"Let me finish!" I interrupted sharply. "It doesn't matter, if I wear certain clothes to please one of you, or spend more time with one of you on a particular day, or have more sex with one of you than the other—"

"Well, we all know which of us that would be—-"

"Shut up, Lash!" I rebuked him. "I gave you both my promise for a reason: there isn't any need to fight over me now. I want you both to be happy, and I'll do my best to make sure neither of you feels like you're less important to me than the other is. But you both need to help me make this work. I can't do it all on my own. Theo's jealousy ruined what he, Dev, Danial, and I could've had. I don't want that to be us in a few years. I want what we've made to last."

Devlin came over to me and hugged me. "As much as I wanted it to work

174

before, and as hard as Danial tried, you're right, Sar. It wasn't good for any of us trying to share you three ways, but none of us men wanted to be the one to walk away and lose you. Most nights, the three of us will sleep together here in my bed. But I'll let you be just with Lash sometimes, and sometimes I'll want him to leave us alone, too."

"I'm okay with that," Lash interjected, nodding once.

"—so we'll make it work," Devlin finished. "But tell us—both of us—if you're feeling pressured or overwhelmed like you were before. I don't share well, I never did. Lash is probably better at it than I am—"

"Dev," Lash hissed dangerously.

"What? You've been in similar situations," Devlin said, shrugging. "And I might need reminding."

"Then I'll remind you with my fist," Lash hissed meaningfully, though he was smiling. He came over and clasped my hand in his.

"So, please tell us if you're unhappy, and we'll try harder," Devlin said, brushing his fangs over my neck lightly in a teasing motion. "But now we have to get moving or we'll lose our reservation. So what color are we wearing?"

I looked over at Lash, and then back to Devlin, considering. "You wear white, I'll wear silver gray, and Lash can wear black?" I offered.

"Sounds good," Lash said, nodding. "I'll go get my clothes."

"You should move some of them in here, since you are going to be sleeping here," Devlin called after him as he left. "I'll make some room, or we'll get another wardrobe."

"Ok," Lash called back.

"Is he just going to walk over naked?" I asked.

"Sure," Devlin said, smiling widely. "He's proud of that young body he has now, Sar. Much of it is a were thing. They feel comfortable not wearing clothes."

Theo hadn't been like that, save in bed. I'd chalk it up to experience. But I did have a concern about tonight to voice to Devlin that had nothing to do with Lash. "Dev, if we go to this particular restaurant, you have to behave. I mean it. I'm not embarrassed, but—"

He nodded. "I'll act more as your friend, not your date. Nowhere else, Sar, but I understand it will take some time for you to let go of your human morals. So I'll do this for you and Lash. I will also wait to feed until tomorrow night."

"Thanks," I said softly.

Lash came back in a few minutes to find us dressed and waiting for him. Devlin had put on a pair of white jeans, and a white sport coat with a golden turtleneck that brought out his eyes. He'd also strapped a gun and shoulder holster on, for extra precaution. I'd put on a long denim skirt and the silver gray chenille sweater that was Devlin's favorite, over a black turtleneck. Lash was in his trademark black: polar fleece turtleneck, heavy wool sweater, and black jeans.

"We need to get you into some other colors," Devlin said mildly, as we three walked down the stairs. "That funeral attire is okay sometimes, but it's depressing day after day."

"Fuck off," Lash replied just as mildly. "I like black. I've always worn black."

"I think you'd look handsome in red, or blue, and maybe green," I said hesitantly. "And especially in white."

Lash was quiet, considering my words. *It's a start.*

"Get in the back with me, Sar," Devlin said, opening the back door for me. "Until Ulysses is caught, I want anyone who may be observing to assume that Lash is just your bodyguard, like he is mine." He grinned. "One that I allow certain liberties to, though, of course."

"He's right, Sar," Lash said, nodding. "Even after Ulysses is caught, I will want to keep our being mated under wraps. Otherwise someone may come after you to get to me."

The restaurant was a good hour from Hayden, but Lash made it in a little over forty minutes via some backroads shortcuts, and some fast driving. As soon as we walked in, a friend and favorite waitress, Lori, noticed us. She tried not to look too shocked as she led the three of us to our table.

"Good evening! Good to see you, Sar. Um…what can I get you to drink?"

Lash looked at me uneasily.

*It's obvious she remembers him. Devlin's so eye-catching, she won't be forgetting him either.* "Lori, this is Devlin, and you probably remember the man sitting next to him—"

"Tristan," Lash supplied softly, when he saw I wasn't sure what to call him in front of her. "It's good to see you again, Lori."

"Tristan. That's pretty," Lori replied, smiling. Lash tried not to grimace.

"A bottle of your best Shiraz, with three glasses," Devlin said winningly. "It's good to meet you, Lori. Sar has often said this is her favorite restaurant, and I have wanted to come here with her for years. But better late than never."

Lori gaped at him, clearly at a loss for words for what he had implied. *I need to excuse myself to explain a little. But what to say? That they were both my lovers?*

"Coming right up," Lori said, and dashed off to get the wine.

"I knew we shouldn't have come here," Lash grumbled.

"Hush," I said, getting up. "I'm going to the ladies room. I'll be right back."

Lash looked worried, like I might decide to slip out the back. It was sad but also comical.

"Women do this all the time, go to the ladies room when they've just arrived," Devlin said, perusing the menu. "Look at the menu, Lash, and don't worry about it."

Lash hissed at him, then turned his attention to his menu.

I visited the ladies room, and managed to grab Lori as she was walking past from the bar. "Hey. Wait a minute, Lori."

She looked at me, clearly unsure what to say.

*Wing it and try not to sound like a slut.* "I'm not sure how to say this, so I'll just say it. Theo left me for another woman. We're separated, truthfully, we've been separated a year. But we were working on getting back together this past fall, when you saw us."

"You guys looked worn out that day," she said sadly. "I'd heard about your home, being lost in a fire. I didn't get a chance to tell you that day, but I'm sorry."

"We're getting divorced in a few days," I continued. "Theo's getting remarried the very next day." At least, according to what my mother had told me, he was.

"I'm sorry," Lori reiterated, then smiled. "But it looks like you've moved on yourself."

"Yes," I said giddily, then blushed. "I'm really happy."

*Why the hell did I say that? Post-coital bliss, probably.*

"You should have fun with him, Sar, and not rush into anything. Divorce can be painful."

"It is," I agreed, biting my lip.

"I didn't want to say anything, but Theo has come here once already with that other woman, for lunch one day."

Stricken at her words, I got control of myself with effort. *It's a free country. He can bring her here, so long as he never shows up here with her on a Friday night, anyway. Or a Sunday morning, either. Tristan and I might want to come here for brunch again sometime.*

"He didn't say anything to me about who she was," Lori continued. "But I saw he wasn't wearing his wedding band, and that his woman had a diamond on. The waitress told me later that they were celebrating getting engaged, and I figured you two had split up, and that it had to do with another woman."

I couldn't bring myself to say anything, so I just nodded.

"I'm glad you have someone," Lori said pleasantly. "Have a good time tonight."

I nodded, and followed her back to our table, letting out a weary breath when I reached my seat. Lori poured the wine, and we all had a taste.

"Very good," Devlin said, smiling charmingly at Lori. "I already ate, but they are ready to order, I believe."

"What can I get you two?"

"I'll have the buffet," Lash said, handing her his menu. "Your brunch was excellent."

"I'll have the chicken Madeira," I said, handing her my menu. "And an order of stuffed mushrooms, crab. Will Dave be here later singing?"

Lori nodded, smiled, and left.

"What did you tell her?" Lash whispered urgently. "She's being friendly now. And who is Dave?"

Devlin leaned in close, curious, his wineglass in his hand.

"I told her Theo and I broke up, and I'm with you. He's already been here with Jenny, so it was easy. Dave is a singer who comes here on Fridays. I love to listen to him sing."

"He's not as good as I am," Devlin stated, half irritated, and half jealous.

"No human is as good as you are," I said, giving him a smile. "But you'll like him, Dev."

Lash finally got some words out. "You told her you're with me? Really?"

"Yes, really," I said, and then I grabbed his head and kissed him quickly.

Lash held perfectly still, until I drew back from him. "Breathe already!" Devlin said, and Lash let out his breathe in a whoosh.

"Go get some food," I said, smiling at him. "Make sure you eat some salad. You'll like the fish, I hope."

"Bring her a crab cake," Devlin said. "She likes them."

I looked over at Devlin, surprised he knew that.

"Danial gave me a complete list of your favorite foods, back in the Spring," Devlin said with pride. "I memorized it."

Lash rolled his eyes, and went to get some food. He was back in a little while with a ton of meat and fish, a crab cake for me, and a single piece of lettuce. I laughed, thinking at least it was a start. I had gotten a salad for myself from the salad bar, and Lash and I dug in. The food tasted wonderful, as always.

Dave arrived shortly, and set up his equipment. Devlin looked over and did a double take. "That's an Ovation," he said, his eyes wide. He got up, and went over to talk to Dave.

Lash rolled his eyes a little. "Devlin always had a thing for music."

Devlin spent the next half hour talking to the musician as he set up, casting glances our way every so often to make sure we weren't having too much fun without him.

Lash went back to the buffet four times by the time Lori brought out my dinner and our appetizer. "Sorry about bringing the mushrooms so late," she said apologetically, setting everything down. "We're busy tonight."

"Not a problem," I replied, giving her a smile. She smiled back, and left.

"Why are you being so nice?" Lash asked, eating a forkful of fish. "You're usually way more exacting."

"Because she's a friend of mine, and it's not a big deal," I said with a shrug. "Here, try one."

"I don't eat fungus," Lash said with the look of someone who expected to eat a piece of mushroom and find out it was poisoned.

"Try one," I said cajolingly. "You'll like the crab meat, if nothing else."

Lash watched me savor two before he tried one. He ate the filling, and then the mushroom. Then he ate the rest, one after the other. "You were right, those were good!" he said, grinning.

I rolled my eyes, and Lash looked immediately uneasy. "Shit!" he hissed. "I'm sorry. I probably wasn't supposed to eat them all myself."

I put his hand on mine, and felt him tense. "Why are you so nervous? Are you regretting coming here with me?"

Lash took a deep breath and let it out. "It is because I want to be here, that I wanted to be with you like this so much, and I'm worried about fucking it up," he whispered. "I've had women friends and acquaintances over the years, Sar, like Robin and Gina. I've been with a lot of women. But I've never been intimate with a woman I called my friend, and wanted more than to just be her friend and have sex with her. There were a very few women through the years who were both lover and friend, but even they were more 'friends with benefits' than girlfriends. But I never felt like I was missing out. I thought that was all there was, before you came along. It's complicated to explain, and I'm doing a bad job of it. Fuck!"

"I think you're doing fine. Go on."

"I'm not like Dev," Lash continued in a blunt yet hesitant tone. "When I told you in the spring that I wasn't good at the after part of sex, I meant the before part too, or any part that's not about physical love. I don't know any poetry, or pretty compliments to tell you. I'm not used to caring so much about every word I say."

"So don't," I offered, patting his hand. "Just be yourself with me. That's who I want to be here with anyway."

Lash gave me an uneasy look.

"Tell me something funny," I said, smiling widely. "I love your sense of humor."

"Well, I do have one joke I could tell."

I leaned closer, and Lash whispered a few phrases in my ear. I blushed soundly, and he laughed. "You are vile," I teased.

Lash laughed harder. "I'm funny-vile!" he corrected, smirking.

The rest of the evening passed quickly. Devlin seemed content to play the single friend to our loving couple. Lash relaxed after a while, and was his normal funny self. I only got a little annoyed when he began to talk longingly about a sixteen-year-old girl behind us that Dev had been eying appreciatively for the last half hour.

"I can almost see her breast, Dev, she doesn't have a bra on."

Devlin leaned over to get Lash's view, looking very interested and hopeful.

"I'm getting you a shirt that says 'Old Letch' on it," I threatened. "Stop staring!"

"You're right, she doesn't have a bra on," Devlin said lustily. "Very nice."

"You probably want to have sex with her," I said, rolling my eyes.

Devlin looked at me, and began to protest his faithfulness. "I said I wouldn't, Sar."

"Yes, I'd like to have sex with her," Lash said bluntly. "I'm admitting it right here. She's young, and hot, and it's natural, that as a male were, I'd like to have her. But—"

"But nothing," I interrupted. "I'd shut up, if I were you."

"I'm just saying—"

"You ever want to get laid again, Mate, you'll shut up right about now."

Lash shut up, and Devlin laughed. I cast a scathing glance his way, and he promptly shut up too.

After dinner, Lash and I had dessert, apple pie for him, and cheesecake for me.

"So now you're my mate, you kind of have to make me pie, right?"

"I don't have to do anything, Tristan," I said loftily. "But I'll make you some pie, if you're nice."

"I'm always nice."

"You two have got it bad," Devlin said, grinning. Lash gave him an uneasy look, and went quiet. I also went quiet, unwilling to bring attention to what Devlin was alluding to.

Soon after, Devlin paid the bill, and we got up. We'd walked almost to the door, when I realized we'd forgotten to tip Dave. He'd been on a break, and it had slipped my mind. I began rooting in my purse for some bills.

"What is it?" Devlin said, giving me a strange look. "I already paid for the meal, and left a tip."

"We need to tip Dave," I said, not looking up from my search. "I forgot."

"I can go back," Lash offered, digging in his pocket for his wallet. "I should have paid for something tonight, anyway."

"No, I'll go" Devlin said, reopening the inside door. "I feel embarrassed for not remembering to tip him, after talking to him for a good portion of the night. I did what he does, in my early years as vampire, and it's sometimes a hard time making a go of it. And I didn't need to pay for food."

I thought about mentioning that Dave got paid separately from tips. But I knew he'd appreciate a big tip, so I stayed silent and let Devlin go back in.

"Do you want to wait inside, or go outside?" Lash asked.

"Outside," I said. "I don't want to block the hallway."

As we walked out under the door canopy, I noticed it was sleeting. *Oiy. At least I'm not driving.*

"Come here," I said, pulling Lash close. "I need a little."

Lash gave me a gentle kiss, and then drew back. But I'd had a large glass of wine, and I wanted to feel him wanting me. "Kiss me like you mean it!" I said with a ribald smile.

"What do you mean, 'kiss you like I mean it'? I always mean it!" Lash hissed, and then he was kissing me over and over. The more he did, the more I giggled, and he chuckled, until we were laughing hard, too hard to really kiss at all, but neither of us cared.

Devlin came out, and gave us an annoyed look, once he saw we had been having fun without him. "Are you both ready to go home?" he said jealously.

Lash let me go, and walked ahead of us to the car, watching around us in case of attack. Devlin slipped his arm around me, and we strolled a few paces behind him. Lash got in when he reached the car, and I moved to do the same, but Devlin blocked me.

"Kiss me," he said jealously, his eyes hot. "And I want to feel that you mean it, Sar."

"Get in the car," Lash hissed from inside. "We don't have time for this. Sar's getting cold."

*There's a better way to handle this than yelling.* "Not out here," I said seductively. "Get in the car."

Devlin bared his fangs, and I put my finger to one of them, touching the razor sharp point carefully. "Get inside, if you know what's good for you."

Devlin studied me for a second, then got into the car, scooting over so I could slide in next to him. "Lash, don't start the car," I said. "I'm going to try to take us and the SUV to right outside Hayden's gates."

"Okay," he said.

With a concentrated effort, I teleported the three of us, and the vehicle to outside Hayden's gate. Lash buzzed us through, and began to drive us up to the house.

"Lash will you stop the car, and stand guard for us?" I asked throatily.

"Sure," Lash replied, surprised. "Let me park in a place that I can see in all directions, though we should be safe enough here on the grounds." He pulled over into a turn off to an access road, and shut off the Hummer. "We're good," he said.

I grabbed the front of Devlin's shirt, and pulled him to me, kissing him hard. In a second, his arms were wrapped around me, and he was pulling me onto his lap. I could feel him ready for me, and I rubbed him with my hips. Devlin growled a little, and began to slide my denim skirt up.

"No," I said. "Hold still."

I undid his pants, and freed his cock, stroking him with my hand. Devlin's eyes closed, his lips parting. I eased myself down on my knees, thinking to myself it was good Hummers had a big back seat. Devlin was breathing fast now, his golden eyes almost glowing. I kissed his prick and nibbled gently with my teeth, as I had that day months ago, when he'd first told me that he was so sensitive. He moaned, and his body jerked beneath my lips. I took the tip of him in my mouth, and he tried immediately to slide himself into me. I pulled back, and looked up at him. "You had better not move again, or I'll stop for good," I said, grinning.

"I could tie him down for you, so he can't," Lash hissed mirthfully.

"He'll behave," I said seductively. "Please hold my hair, Lash?"

I felt him gather it, and hold it gently out of the way.

"Say you're going to behave, Dev," I said seductively, running my tongue over him. "Say it!"

"I'll behave," Devlin moaned, twitching under my hands. "I'll behave!"

I began kissing him, over and over, stroking him with my hands and lips until his muscles were contracting anyway, despite his efforts to keep still.

"Please," Devlin groaned, reaching his arms out for me. "Please, Sar, I'm so close—"

I could tell he was—could taste it on his skin. "Then come for me," I purred. Taking a deep breath to fill my lungs with air, I took all of his cock into me. I immediately fought the urge to throw up. I shook slightly, fighting myself. Devlin grabbed my head, holding me still as he thrust up into me, once, twice, and then he was screaming, spasming in my throat as he orgasmed. "Ah!"

Devlin thrust into me, letting out cry after cry. I let him, until my air ran out. Then I gently pushed against him, and he released me, slipping out of me. *He's still hard; he's not done.*

Devlin pulled me up to straddle him. He pushed my moist underwear aside, and slid himself up inside me to the hilt. I was slippery with excitement from Devlin's sexual release, my channel accepting his large stiff penis eagerly. I let out a passionate cry and began moving my hips immediately, feeling my climax already beginning to build.

"You think you're the only one who can tease?" Devlin growled, laughter and lust mixed in the throaty sound. "Lash, hold her."

Lash grabbed my arms from behind, then drew my hands over my head, folding them just in back of my neck.

"Hold still for him," Lash whispered, kissing my ear lightly.

I trembled, but continued to move my hips. Devlin stopped me, forcing my hips to stay still. "I decide when you come," Devlin purred. "And I say you're going to wait, Sar."

I opened my mouth to protest, but Devlin pushed up my shirt, and pushed down the cloth of my underwire bra, baring my breasts. He leaned in, sucking my nipple, and my objection became a groan of desire. But he held my hips firm beneath him, not letting me move.

I began to jerk in his grasp, crying out. "Please, please!"

"No," Devlin taunted, releasing one breast, and turning his attentions to the other, tearing another gasp from my throat. "But I'll give you something to tide you over."

Devlin grasped my hips firmly in his hands, and gave one long thrust into me, pushing himself all the way in. He held himself motionless, then slowly, five seconds later, he pulled back out, and began again. I let out a long low moan, and tried to fight him, tried to move on him, but Lash held me still, and so did Devlin, making me wait, prolonging the agony. Desperate for release, I tried to bite Devlin, as he suckled me, and he drew back with a laugh. "Tell me you love me," he whispered. "Tell me you're mine."

"After I come," I snarled in my frustration. "And only if you rock my world!"

Lash let out a snicker, and Devlin's eyes went red. "Lash, move her when it's time," he growled. "You know what to do. Until I'm done with her, hold her fast in place."

I had a second to wonder what that was about, and then Devlin was thrusting into me, moving me on him, and two seconds later I was closing my eyes and screaming my release. Devlin bit down on my neck, still moving in me, just as Lash yanked my hair backwards. My head jerked back, and Lash grabbed hold of the back of my neck and pushed my face down into Devlin's throat, stifling my startled cry.

I tasted warm maple sugar with a faint coppery flavor, and my orgasm intensified to mind-blowing. I bit down hard, wanting more of Devlin's blood.

Lash released my arms, so I could twine them around Devlin. I sucked hard, drinking him down as he was drinking me, as he loved me. Dev convulsed, pushing his hips hard to mine as he spasmed, his fangs coming free of me as he screamed out over and over as I fed from him. His wound closed a few seconds later, as our orgasm ebbed. By that time, I was panting in his arms, as he kissed my neck wound lightly, healing it.

"Well?" he said, looking very pleased with himself.

"I love you, Dev," I said, snuggling into him. "I'm yours."

"And mine," Lash added softly, caressing my hair.

"Ours," Devlin supplied, inclining his head at Lash. "You're ours, Sar."

"Yes," I said, contentedly. "I am."

Lash started the SUV, and drove us the rest of the way up to the house. We parked inside, and got out. But before we got to the door, Lash backed me against the garage wall, and began to undo his pants.

"Can't wait to get upstairs?" Devlin said, laughing.

"No," Lash said brusquely, giving him a get-lost-look. "Why don't you go check on our guards for me?"

"Okay," Devlin replied with a chuckle. He went through the door to the kitchen, closing it behind him.

Lash turned back to me. "Is it okay?" he said seriously, even as he trembled beneath my hands. I pulled him into my arms and kissed him hard. Lash wasted no more time. He pulled off my underwear, and pushed down his jeans, baring his engorged penis. I reached down for him, wrapping my hands around the hot shaft. He let out an eager and excited hiss, then kissed me as if he would devour me before breaking off to speak. "That day, in here with you, I wanted so much for you to tell me that you wanted me one last time," he said, looking into my eyes. "To tell me that it didn't matter what anyone said, that you wanted me to take you again right here, that you were dying for it, to feel me in you."

"I am dying to feel you. I want you in me, Mate. Now take me!" I said coarsely.

Lash shuddered in my arms. He picked me up, his hands under my rear, and stepped closer to me. In one motion, he impaled me, letting out a loud hiss as he entered me. Then he was loving me, and I lost all sense of time and place. There was only him, and me, and my love for him. For the first time in a long time, we came together, shouting as we gripped each other, as I contracted around him, helping him to empty his seed in me.

Lash eased me down the wall, until I was standing again. I held him close to me, kissing him gently. I felt him softening slightly, and then he slipped out of me, easing himself back into his jeans with a contented sigh. He buttoned his pants, and helped me put on my underwear, holding it out for me so I could step into it. Lash kissed me again, and then he was lifting me, one of his arms under my legs, and the other under my back.

I gave him a funny look, as I grabbed on to his neck with my arms. "What are you doing? I can walk just fine."

"You're my mate," he hissed meaningfully. "The only woman I'll ever be mate to, the only one I've ever wanted like that. And I'm taking you to our bed, so I can show you the best way I know just how much you mean to me."

I reached out and brought his forehead to mine, then let out a deep contented breath. "You should never think that you have to watch your words, that you don't know just what to say to me," I said in a breaking, uneven voice. "Because I can tell you exactly when I first loved you. It was that moment you told me you wanted to die in my arms."

Lash looked at me in surprise. He walked in through the doorway, kicking the door shut behind us before he began to walk up the stairs. "I thought maybe it was after the pool table incident," he said with a laugh, his dark eyes flashing.

"That helped," I giggled, stroking his hair. "And saving me, and talking with me about things we both like. And always respecting me enough to ask my permission, to make sure that having sex was what I wanted, too. No one else has ever done that."

"I hadn't done that before with a woman, ever. Waiting each time for her to tell me it was okay, I mean. But I felt it was right to ask you," Lash said, his tone hesitant. He settled me on the bed.

Devlin came in a few seconds later, shutting the door behind him. "Nick wanted to talk to you," he said in a serious tone. "There's been some suspicious activity near our western field."

*That field is over near the back of Hayden's land, a good mile away or more. There's no close road.* I shifted in bed, suddenly uneasy.

"What kind of activity?" Lash asked, immediately all business.

"Looks like just some tents," Devlin finished. "But who camps in the middle of winter?"

"Could be poachers, after deer," Lash said, turning to me. "I'll be right back," he said tenderly, stroking my cheek with his callused hand. "Wait for me?"

I nodded.

Lash strode out and closed the door. Devlin grabbed me in his arms in two seconds, and suddenly he was singing to me, holding me in his arms. He reached up with my hands to place them around his neck, and put his hands at my waist. Then, we were dancing.

"The strands in your eyes that color them wonderful

185

Stop me and steal my breath.
They're emeralds from mountains, and frost of the sky
Never revealing their depth.
Tell me that we belong together
Dress it out with the trappings of love.
I'll be captivated, I'll hang from your lips,
Instead of the gallows of heartache that hang from above.
I'll be your crying shoulder,
I'll be a love suicide—"

I looked up at him lovingly and finished the song with him. "And I'll be better when I'm older. I'll be the greatest fan of your life." We both held the last note, and then let it fade into silence.

I looked up into his melting golden eyes.

"Will you?" he asked softly. "Will you love me forever?"

"I already do," I said, bringing his lips down on mine.

The kiss was gentle, and Devlin drew back to sing me the rest of the song. This time I joined him in singing it. When we were done, I noticed Lash leaning against the wall.

"I wanted to hear you both," he said, giving me a surprised look of pride. "Sar, I didn't know you could sing."

"I'm pretty good, but Dev's much better," I said, blushing at his praise.

"You were really good," Lash rectified. "Will you sing something else?"

"What?" I said, blushing hard now.

"Something that's happy. Nothing about lost love," Lash offered. "Despite Dev's extensive repertoire, I don't know many songs myself, if they aren't from the seventies and earlier. And I don't know any mushy…um, love songs."

I thought for a moment. "I do have a song I've been meaning to sing for Dev for a while."

Devlin looked afraid, but smiled bravely. "Please do, Oathed One."

"Be advised, I'm going to garble some of the words," I warned. "I haven't heard it in years."

"What's the artist, and title?" Devlin asked. "I can sing it with you, even if it's a woman; I'll just sing a lower octave."

"Pat Benetar," I said. "Can you guess the song?"

Lash didn't get my teasing dig, but Devlin did, by his mortified look. "Not 'Heartbreaker' I hope?" he whispered sadly.

"No, though I've wanted to sing you that on more than one occasion," I smirked, feeling only a small pang at his discomfort. "What did you just ask me to tell you? That 'We Belong', of course."

"Ah," Devlin said, relieved. "I can remember that one."

He and I took a breath and began.

"Many times I've tried to tell you, many times I've cried alone.

As always, I'm surprised how well you cut my feelings to the bone.

Don't want to leave you really, I've invested too much time

To give you up that easy, to the doubts that complicate your mind.

We belong to the light, we belong to the fire,

We belong to the sound of the words we've both fallen under,

Whatever we deny or embrace, for worse or for better,

We belong, we belong, we belong together."

We finished the song, and Devlin kissed me gently.

"I was wondering at first if that was a love song," Lash said thoughtfully. "It sounded bad to start with. But the end was nice."

"I'm glad it wasn't the other song," Devlin said with relief. "I've heard that one too many times as it is."

"You *are* the right kind of sinner to release my inner fantasy," I said in a lilting tone.

Devlin clapped his hand over my mouth, making a face. Lash laughed, garnering a look from Devlin that was part annoyance but also part pride.

"I'm ready for bed," I said, gently removing his hand. "Are you going to stay up, or not?"

"I need to make one last pass around, and then I'll be back," Lash replied. "Titus sent an owl to spy on the tents. Titus will watch through its eyes, and wake me, if it's anything of concern. T's coming for sparring in the morning."

"You must like him, to still be teaching him," Devlin commented casually.

"It's nice, having more than one friend," Lash hissed defensively. "T's a good kid, not to mention my mate's son. His safety always mattered to me because of Sar, and that he's your nephew, but it matters a lot more now, after what's happened." He left quickly, shutting the door behind him

I sank down on the edge of the bed, my memories hitting me like a pile of bricks. Devlin sat down beside me, putting his arm around me. "Do you want to talk about it? Would you rather go and talk to Rosalyn? Titus said she's very good."

"I'm okay," I said softly, pushing my agony over Devon's death and Elle's rape back under it's careful wrapping. "I'm not ready to talk about it, Dev, but I will be eventually. Time is the only thing that's going to heal that wound."

"Take all the time you need," Devlin consoled. "Lash and I are here for you."

"I need to clean up," I said, standing and stretching, "and put on my nightgown."

"Don't dress for bed. I'd prefer you slept naked, Sar. Lash would, too."

That was blunt. "All right."

Devlin laughed. "It feels good, to have your skin against mine," he said with longing. "You're always so warm, and it feels so good to me, because I'm so cool." He stopped abruptly. "Would you like it, if I made myself warmer?" he offered. "I can, if you like?"

"You're fine as you are. But thank you for being considerate."

Devlin took my hand and kissed it. "I'll try to be considerate always," he said lovingly. "But tell me if I'm not. Lash is right, that I sometimes enjoy being, um, hurtful. I don't want to hurt you. It's good that he is part of us, so that he can keep me in line. And being jealous is good for me, too. I appreciate you more."

I thought that odd, but let it slide. It was a very Devlin-like comment.

Devlin was curled up beside me in bed when Lash came in a few minutes later and began undressing. "Well?" Devlin said, annoyed. "Was it anything to worry about?"

"Titus is still watching them through the owl's eyes, but they are just sleeping," Lash said with a yawn. "He'll wake us, if they do anything. Rip will take over at dawn with a crow, but unless they make a move, there's nothing to see. And I'm tired out."

The three of us snuggled together, and fell asleep.

# Chapter Twelve

The next morning, when I awoke, I awoke alone. I was scared at once, as it was only eight or so, and shrugged on some clothes as fast as I could. I wanted to just put on my bathrobe, and go looking for Lash and Devlin, but if there was trouble, I wanted to make sure I was both armed, and dressed for running.

Once I had on my knife, and my new explosive bullets gun buckled on, I stepped into my sneakers, and threw open the door. Walking quickly downstairs, I went into the kitchen to see Serena and Nick having breakfast. I saw before she looked away that whatever feelings she had for T were not in evidence this morning: there was too much guilt on her face. Nick on the other hand was grinning ear to ear, a defiant look in his eye as he stared back at me. I hoped Serena had told T about how she felt before doing this. But even if she hadn't, I didn't have time to worry about that this morning. "Have you seen Lash, or Devlin or Venus?" I asked, worried.

"Devlin is in the ballroom with Venus, playing some music for her on the piano," Nick said easily. "Lash is with Titus, looking into those men who were camped in the field last night."

"Was there an attack?"

"No," Nick said with a shrug. "They packed up and left this morning. But Lash went to check it out anyway."

"It's nothing," Titus rumbled from behind me, his bass voice coarser than usual. "Some hunters poaching deer. We found a pile of guts, and some evidence of a salt lick, a piece of bloody rope, and a lot of blood, deer blood."

I breathed a sigh of relief. I felt even more relieved to see Lash come in behind Titus and shoot me a quick smile.

"He's right, it's deer blood," Lash said, sitting down in the nearest chair and pulling me down on his lap. "How about breakfast, Sweetness?"

"Sure," I said. "But I should go see if Venus wants any."

"She already ate," Devlin said, striding in behind a smiling Venus dressed breathtakingly in gold satin. "I'm glad to hear it was nothing."

Nick got up, and took Serena's hand, and without one word, he led her out of the kitchen, and up the stairs. A door shut a few seconds later upstairs.

"Well, I can tell spring is coming," Titus rumbled, his teeth like knives in his grinning face. We all burst out laughing. "I need to get moving. I've got to take my future daughter-in-law to a cake tasting, and later to pick out shoes," he said. "Call me, if you need me, but not unless its an emergency. Today is my day off."

"Agreed," Devlin said, nodding once. "Rip will be around, as T said he didn't have any meetings this next week, because of the holidays."

That reminded me, Elle was due for her next therapy session that day. I gave her a quick call, and arranged to bring her to see Ros about noon. Then, I fixed Lash a speedy breakfast, after which he excused himself, saying he would go later with me to the therapy to guard us. I told him it wasn't necessary, but both he and Devlin insisted. He left right after as he said he had some target practice to do, giving me a quick good-bye kiss. For a while, I sat with Devlin and V in the ballroom, and Dev played us both some music on the piano. It was nice, to hear the crystal notes so beautifully played, and know they were only for V and me. I knew I had work to do on the computer, but put it off. This was something like a honeymoon for me, and damn it, I was going to enjoy it.

Later, I made V and me a quick lunch, and as I was clearing the dishes, the doorbell rang. Devlin went and got it, which I thought was odd, and figured he must be expecting someone. When he came back, he handed me a bouquet of what had to be five dozen roses, fire and ice of course. But the bigger surprise was what was in the huge sheaf of papers he handed me.

"What's this?"

"Our Oath contract," he said with a faint smile. "Legal protection for me, and for you. Just like a prenup, save of course, we are already Oathed."

Shit, I'd never read through all this, not in a week. It was now or never in terms of trusting him. "Tell me what it says, so I can feel comfortable signing it."

Devlin gave me a soft look. "It says if I die, you and V get everything I have, save what is for my trusted employees, like Lash and Titus."

"But you said if you died, I and everything you own went to the vampire who kills you."

"Go to Michael, as I said. Take this, and V, and he will see you get what this refers to, as well as protecting you. There is a great deal of hidden money, Sar, and other assets. No smart being who has lived through centuries keeps even half his wealth under his own name. As it was, I am sure half of Ebediah's assets eluded me, even though Titus found a good deal of hidden caches in his castle. He was too old to have so little."

"What else does it say?"

"Basically, that I am to deny you nothing you ask me for, if you hold to the conditions of your Oath. And it says the same for you, and spells out what we swore to the night before last. We would have signed it yesterday, but your mating to Lash had to be added in, in terms of what he and you promised to each other, and to me."

"And if I break my Oath to you?"

"That I owe you nothing, and you must leave Hayden, if I ask you to, leaving Venus here with me." Devlin's voice had turned hard. I debated asking for more details, but I wasn't the one who'd most likely break the Oath, so it didn't matter that much. Which led me to say, "And if you break it?"

"That you can leave me, or stay here, and I still must deny you nothing, not money, not Venus, not even my blood, or my body, if you still wanted me as your lover." Devlin's voice was more than a little sad. "My lawyer was not happy, but I told him that it had to be that way, that I had told you it would be."

"And Lash?"

"In addition to his promise to you, he is named as something like executor, should something happen to me and if he survives me. He is also named as the guardian for you and for V, should he survive you as well. He can act as me, in the event of my death. I've given him the power to do everything I do, complete control. And if he should be dead, that power passes to you."

This was pre-nup, marriage contract, will, and also power of attorney. *Shit.*

I skipped to the last page, 562, and signed on the bottom. Devlin did as well.

Lash came in for a moment, and when Devlin explained to him, and answered his questions—almost the exact ones I had asked—he signed it as well. Devlin took the signed copy, and placed it in the prepaid FedEx Next Day Air pouch, and sealed it. "Drop it off when you are out?" he asked, handing it to Lash. Lash nodded.

Devlin kissed me good-bye, and I kissed him back, stunned, but also grateful that he had done this for me.

\* \* \* \*

Five minutes to 2 pm. found Lash and me waiting outside in Ros's office, Elle having just gone in. But this time I'd come prepared, and brought two books. Lash had as well. Today he was reading the collected works of Frank Miller's *Batman*. He seemed to be enjoying it. At least, he wasn't scowling.

Almost two hours later, Elle appeared, Ros behind her. She smiled at me, and then her eyes rested on Lash. She motioned to me to come in, indicating to bring him, too.

*Great.* I nudged him, and told him the therapist wanted to see us.

Lash shot me an alarmed look. "Not again! I don't have anything to say," he hissed. "I didn't come here for that."

"Then come in and just refuse to talk," I said, standing.

Lash sighed and got up. We went in and settled into the couch. It was comforting that this time, I could snuggle into him without feeling any guilt. He wrapped one arm around me, stroking my side gently. Ros looked at us for a few seconds and smiled. "You seem to have resolved your relationship," she said pleasantly. "You seem to be happy together."

"We are mated now," Lash hissed, and grinned. "And we are both very happy."

"Are you?" she said, her voice sliding into a probing tone. "What about Devlin?"

"What about him?" Lash answered abruptly, changing at once, his eyes going flat and his clipped words sliding into a hiss.

"I know him. I know that he would not have let Sarelle just be with you, excluding him. So my guess is you're sharing her."

"So what?" Lash hissed angrily. "Sar wanted that."

"Did she? Or did she do it just to be with you, because she loves you?"

Lash didn't look at me, but I took a breath anyway and spoke, because I was not going to stand for him being made to feel guilty for anything, not anymore. "I gave Dev an Oath of my own free will, Ros. Last time, Devlin demanded it. This time, I told him I had several conditions, and he agreed to all of them. He spoke them as part of the Oath—"

"It's true, I heard them," Lash interjected.

"—and I told him if he screwed up again, that was it, we were finished."

"Do you really believe he'll let you go, if he screws up?" Rosalyn said, looking at me like she was surprised I could be so naive. "Which, by the way, is a question of 'when,' not 'if'?"

I was beginning to get annoyed. It was one thing for me to think Devlin was a jerk. It was another to hear someone else say it, after how much he had been trying lately not to be one. "Yes, I just signed a paper not three hours ago—"

"No, I know he won't," Lash hissed, his eyes locked on Rosalyn's. "But if that happens, I'll ask Sar what she wants to do. If she wants to leave him, I'll help her do it."

"You're going to kill him for her?" Rosalyn said quietly. "Because you and I both know that's the only way he'll ever let her go. He's never relinquished anything he considered his."

"I'm not killing him, not ever!" Lash hissed, baring his fangs wide. He got to his feet, and stared at her. "And we are done here. I don't have casual conversations with creatures that ask me to kill my friends. And know that if you weren't helping Elle, I'd torch your office with you in it, just for saying that in front of me."

Lash strode to the door, and through it, slamming it hard behind him. Ros seemed unconcerned, and turned to me.

"Sarelle, I'm sorry, if my questions upset you—"

"They don't upset me," I said, getting to my feet. "I just think they are pointless. I need Dev's protection. I have a child with him. And part of me just flat loves him, despite what he is, and was—"

"And will be?" Ros added, looking up at me.

"That too," I said, and turned to leave.

"Sarelle—"

"Why did you ask us to come in and talk now? To upset my mate? What?"

"I want to make sure you are making choices for the right reasons."

"What are the right reasons, Ros? Because I want to, or because it makes the most sense? Because of emotions, or because of reason? You talk to people, and some say one and some say the other—"

"Which is yours, for Oathing to Devlin?"

"Both," I said, looking at her with my hand on the door. "Because down deep, it's what I want right now, to live with Lash and he at Hayden, to be with my daughter, and to be near Danial, even if he doesn't know me."

"Then you did it for the right reasons," Ros said, looking at me with a serious expression. "I truly hope it works out for you."

"Me, too," I said quietly, and then I left, shutting the door behind me.

* * * *

The day of the fight approached. Devlin and Lash spent a good deal of time sparring in the gym each morning. Every following afternoon, women came to feed Devlin, to replenish the blood and energy he lost at Lash's hands. The intensity of their training was impressive, especially as the fighting they were doing was hand to hand combat without any weapons, save fangs. Devlin had explained that his fight with Ulysses would be with no weapons, and no armor, giving me angst that Ulysses would find a way to bring in some hidden weapon, a concern I didn't voice. This wasn't my Oathed vampire's first Challenge. Like Theo before him, Dev needed my surety in his triumph. My belief in him, coupled with his relentless training worked. Each morning when he got up, Devlin seemed stronger and faster than ever. Yet by the end of the day, Devlin would be so exhausted he would fall asleep in my arms right after we kissed goodnight.

Lash took the opportunity while Devlin was feeding in the evenings to spend time with me. He would often tell me he wanted to thank me for lunch, and spirit me away for a few hours of gentle lovemaking and talking in his bedroom, or Devlin's.

One afternoon, as Lash was drawing a bath for us in his room, I was jerked out of my languor, seeing a familiar speck struggling in the water. I made a lunge, almost shoving Lash into the filling tub as I dove for the drowning spider. He went to one knee with a surprised hiss, but he caught himself with his fast reflexes, steadying himself. "Sar, what the hell are you doing?"

I didn't reply, frantically reaching for the little dot, but missed, the dying creature swirling through my fingers. I made another slower grab, but missed again, and let out a little cry of frustration. I bit my lip, and slowly cupped my hands underneath him, and brought him up out of the water, breathing a sigh of relief. I very carefully dripped the dot in some water on the edge of the tub, and watched hopefully for signs of life. But though the legs of the spider twitched a few times, he didn't scuttle away. I decided with sorrow that I'd been too late, and settled into the water with a dejected sigh.

Lash climbed in with me, but didn't speak. He and I watched the spider for a while, but it didn't move. I blew a little on the motionless creature, but only succeeded in blowing him off the edge of the tub into a dark shadowy spot between the tub and the wall. *At least I won't have to see the tiny corpse.*

"Is she dead?" Lash said quietly.

True, most spiders were female, though I'd always thought of them as male. "Yes, he's dead," I said, feeling tears start immediately. "I was too late, and I didn't notice in time."

"Sar, it's okay, it's just a spider, there are a lot more outside—"

I began to bawl in earnest, and Lash pulled me over close to him in the water so I was cradled against his chest, not saying anything. He held me for a long time, and rubbed my back, and eventually, I stopped crying.

"I would never have guessed you had such a soft spot for spiders," Lash whispered, kissing my forehead. "But maybe I should have, seeing how you feel about snakes."

I smiled a little at that and hugged him, but I didn't tell him what the spider had represented to me. What I'd shared with Danial had been between us, and that long ago spider that had surely perished when my house burned. I hadn't saved either of them, in the end. But when I'd had a choice to help, or not help, I'd done as much as I could. That had to count for something.

When Lash and I got out of the bathtub, I went to his sliding glass door, and out on his deck. It was a beautiful sunny day, almost sixty, very abnormal weather for this time of year. But tomorrow, the day of the fight, a snowstorm was coming in, and the temperatures would plunge back to freezing. Lash had taken the afternoon off, saying days like this came only once a decade in winter, and he wanted to enjoy it with me. I sat down looked out over Hayden, thinking about how beautiful it would all look in summer. It would be partly mine, too, something I still found unbelievably exciting.

"Sar, come quick!" Lash said from inside the house. "I think your spider is alive!"

I bolted to my feet, and ran inside. Lash was shining a flashlight into the dark corner where the spider had fallen when I'd blown on him. I looked, and sure enough, the spider was sitting there. I blew on it a little, and it scuttled quickly away into a crevice. An overwhelming sense of relief flooded me, that I hadn't been too late after all.

"Now I'm going to have to remember to look for Frank every time we do this," Lash commented with a rueful smile. "I don't want him to die now, after he's gotten a second chance at life."

"Frank?"

"Why not? If we're going to save his life, and you're going to cry over him, we might as well name him. And you know I like Miller."

I giggled. "That's as good a reason as any, I guess."

\* \* \* \*

The day of the fight dawned, with gusting snow and bitter cold. At high noon, Lash and I drove Devlin in one of the Hummers to the site of the battle, a towering graveyard mausoleum high on a hill that had recently been completed. The granite wasn't weathered, the carvings in the stone very easy to read.

Ulysses was already there, waiting in his car.

Everyone got out of the vehicles as soon as we'd parked. Like Devlin, Ulysses was completely clothed in armor, with a visored helmet. As agreed, he'd brought only one of his men with him, but though the man was not a demon, he was as big as Titus.

"Polar bear. And Alpha, I'm guessing," Lash said frostily. "I wonder what Ulysses promised him for his help."

"Money and revenge," the bear snarled loudly, hearing him. "I used to work for Ebediah, Lash. All of us polar bears did. You should pick a master who has less enemies."

"I'd rather pick one I can trust," Lash said easily. "Is your master ready?"

"Why's she here?" the bear growled. "One second only was agreed."

"I'm not fighting," I said, showing him my hands. "Pat me down if you want to. But I am part of the spoils going to the winner, as Devlin's Oathed One. I deserve to know if he's fallen, to be one of the first to know."

"Fine, but you are to stay back from the fighting, and I'll search you for weapons," the bear said. He proceeded to do so, and pronounced me clean.

We five went inside, and Devlin and Ulysses proceeded to take off their armor. I hadn't seen Ulysses since that night I was his prisoner, and seeing him as vampire left me unnerved. His green eyes were glowing bright as traffic lights, and his skin shone as Devlin's did. *He's been training hard for this, too.*

An involuntary shudder of doubt slid down my back, and I turned away, seeking a spot from where to watch at a safe distance. I found a rough box that had contained brass handles for the crypts, and turned it over near one cold granite wall, fashioning myself a rough bench. I sat down and waited, anxiously wrapping my long wool coat around myself. *It's freezing in here.*

Lash and the bear took up watchful positions by the door, as Devlin and Ulysses began circling. Surprisingly, this was done without any words, or posturing by either of them, something I found surprising, at least from what I knew of both of them.

Devlin struck first, and knocked Ulysses to the ground with a quick blow to the face. But Ulysses was up in an instant, and he bloodied Devlin with two kicks to the face. It was hard to see them move, as both of them were moving as fast as they could, much faster than a human could move. Before long, Devlin and Ulysses were both bloodied, but they healed almost as soon as the blows were struck. I'd never seen vampires heal that fast, the fight before me reminding me of some of the climactic battles in recent vampire movies I'd watched, lending it a surrealist quality that I tried to focus on to ease my quaking nerves. *He's defended his throne for two hundred years. Calm down. Wait for the signal.*

Maintaining their speed and the constant healing was exerting an enormous strain on them both. Both of the vampires began to falter slightly, their wounds ceasing to heal completely. Ulysses launched himself at Dev just a little too slowly, bloody fangs bared. Instead of sidestepping, Devlin crouched and came up under him, slamming him down onto his back with a crunch of breaking bone. "Now!" he shouted.

Everyone erupted into action. I bolted to my feet, and ran toward Devlin. Ulysses was struggling hard, his spine already healing, but Devlin was holding him down. The alpha bear charged the grappling vampires, but Lash's whip shot out, and sending the bear sprawling. I reached out for Devlin, diving for his outstretched hand. The instant I felt his fingers touch mine, I teleported us to Hayden's basement.

We landed in a heap, and Ulysses snarled at me, lunging with his teeth to try to bite me. I scuttled away from him, and into the arms of Titus, who shoved me behind him, baring his rows of teeth at Ulysses. Devlin grabbed hold of Ulysses, slamming him back to the concrete floor with another hard snap of bone.

"How did you do this, make her both demon and vampire, while still making her seem human?" Ulysses snarled. "She is no faerie! We met on holy ground to prevent any teleporting!"

"Bastard," I said, glaring at him as I stood. Then I disappeared, teleporting back to help Lash. I arrived to find the mausoleum empty, and ran to the door.

Outside, Lash was fighting hard in the gathering snow. Ulysses hadn't planned for teleporting, but he'd planned for Devlin's ultimate destruction should anyone but he and his bear come out of the mausoleum alive. There were ten dead bears on the ground, most half changed with claws and fangs, flakes still melting on their cooling bodies, and gaping holes where their hearts had been. Lash was fighting the last two on their feet, Ulysses' alpha bear with Lash's knife in his heart just to the left, feebly trying to crawl away. I watched him but didn't approach him, because even mortally wounded, he was probably more than a match for me.

Lash broke the neck of one bear with a hard snap, and the other, realizing he was the last one left, ran. Lash tripped him with the lash of his whip, and dragged him backwards, screaming.

With a sharp crack, Lash broke his neck, too.

He looked up at me, and I motioned to the alpha bear. Lash bared one fang in a grin, and strode over to him. The bear swiped at him with a hand grown into a claw, but Lash stepped aside, evading him almost effortlessly, and deftly pulled out his knife. The bear gasped in a single breath, but never had time to scream as Lash severed his head from his body.

I felt my stomach turn, but forced my bile down. There was still much to do. There was no time for getting sick. The snow was coming down faster and faster now.

Lash reached into a leather pouch on his belt, and pulled out a piece of paper and a vial. He read it, while pouring a tiny bit of the powdered mixture into his hand. A second later, a small ball of blue fire sprang into life in his hand. He threw it on the alpha bear's body. Seconds later, there were only ashes. He did that over and over, until the only evidence left were the two weremen with broken necks, and rapidly disappearing ashes on bloody snow. Lash tossed the two weremen in the back of the Hummer, and after checking it over for traps, we both got in. As agreed, I teleported it to Hayden's gate, and then did the same with Ulysses' car, a black Pathfinder. Something nagged at me, but I couldn't think what. I had too many other things to think about.

Leaving the two cars and prisoners in Nick and Keith's able hands, I teleported Lash and I back to the basement just in time to see Devlin sink his fangs into Ulysses' neck, and began swallowing him down. Ulysses screamed, and tried to fight him off, but Devlin held him almost effortlessly.

Devlin reared back, and turned to Lash and me, his face a mask of blood. "Bring Danial!" he said loudly, holding a struggling Ulysses in his grasp. Then he sank his fangs in again to the hilt, and Ulysses screamed once more, still fighting hard, though his efforts were weakening. I shivered, backing away, remembering being under those fangs myself, years ago.

Lash was up the cellar stairs in a moment. I just watched, telling myself this wasn't murder, it was justice, that Ulysses had hurt Danial, and he deserved to suffer for it, to die as he had planned that Danial would die. Devlin continued to drink from him, and Ulysses still tried to fight him, but soon, he was only struggling feebly in Devlin's grasp.

Lash came down the stairs, carrying Danial in his arms.

"Lay him down here," Devlin said, rearing back again to sink his fangs in a third time.

"No," Ulysses said weakly. "I'll not end like this. I can't! My sister, she—"

"Your sister got what she wanted," Devlin said, his voice hard, but without malice. His golden eyes burned. "If you knew her at all, you knew Heather was self-destructive. I knew when I turned her years ago that she wasn't going to be one of the ones that made it. Just as you aren't going to make it, either."

Devlin sank his fangs in one last time, and then snapped his head backward, ripping out Ulysses' throat. Ulysses' eyes bulged, and his hands went to his throat, but Devlin grabbed them, twisting them behind his back with one hand and grabbing Ulysses by his hair with the other. Then he lowered him over Danial's prone form, letting the blood drip onto Danial's face.

I didn't want to see this. Lash put his hand on my arm, and squeezed gently. I turned and buried my face in his chest, hugging him, glad the worst was over.

"Most new vampires don't last," Lash whispered to me. "They get drunk on the power, or forget what time of night it is, and they get destroyed. There are more than a few hunters who target new vampires exclusively, Sar, ones less than a year old."

I was going to ask him why no one had sent hunters after Devlin, since Ulysses had, but Lash saw my look, and answered before I had the time to ask it.

"They usually won't go after Rulers, not of any territories. Vampires don't work together, save for one thing, and that when they feel personally threatened. Rulers are untouchable, so far above regular vampires as to be almost Gods. You remembered what happened with Samuel and the others, when Danial was drained. Ulysses was declared persona non grata. He would have been killed on sight by any vampire anywhere who saw him. He only challenged Dev because he had to become a Ruler, to save himself. As a rule, Rulers don't kill each other, or even fight, though as you've seen with Devlin, sometimes it happens. And there are no rules for that, just survival of the fittest. Treachery is normal, even expected. I know Samuel and the rest will be relieved to hear Ulysses is dead, just as I know Dev's standing with them will increase, since he killed Ulysses when none of them could."

I didn't reply. Some of this I'd heard before, that day with Devlin and Steven back months ago. The rest I'd surmised.

There was sudden movement, and Ulysses let out a sharp cry of pain. I looked to see Danial holding him tightly, swallowing him down in great draughts. Devlin had released Ulysses, and was standing over Danial, watching in pleasure, blood still on his smiling lips. For a long time, there was no noise, save the sound of Danial's drinking, and Ulysses' soft cries. Finally, those died off, as Ulysses slipped into unconsciousness.

"No more," Danial said, his voice raspy from months of disuse. He pushed Ulysses off him, and lay back on the floor. I noticed that he looked like his old self again, no longer a statue. I wanted to run to him, but stopped myself. It was possible he was not the Danial I had loved, and Devlin had warned me to be careful of him, not to go to him until Devlin had made sure it was safe.

"Take it all," Devlin said, bending down beside him. "You need to be as strong as you were, even if you—"

"I don't want the power again to be Ruler," Danial said.

Devlin gaped at him in shock. "What are you talking about, Danial? You need to be Ruler again."

"No," Danial said, sitting up. "You are most likely Ruler of the States again now, Dev. And it's past time for me to admit I'm not the vampire you are."

"Danial—"

"No, Dev," Danial said firmly, wiping some of the blood off his face. "I was careless, and I almost lost my life because of it. I've had enough of playing in my brother's shoes. I only want to go back to my company, be with my son. I'm not cut out for this—"

Devlin grabbed Danial by his hair with a snarl, and shook him hard. Danial hissed, and his eyes went red.

"You are going to take his blood," Devlin growled deeply. "You are going to drain him, as he drained you, until his heart stops. We are going to rule North America together, Danial, because I need to know there is someone ready to protect Sar, should something ever happen to me!"

"You know I'm not your equal!" Danial shouted. "Everyone knows it,

Dev!"

"You are going to learn to be," Devlin hissed back. "Whether you like it or not, you are going to learn to be, Danial. As you said, it is far past time you did."

"No," Danial growled. "No, I'm not—argh!"

Devlin had pulled Danial to his feet by his hair. Danial staggered, having not stood for so many months, but the blood he'd taken from Ulysses was already working, already revitalizing his systems, and though he swayed, he didn't fall.

"Theoron has taken over your company," Devlin went on. "Theo and Terian are helping him. He's an adult now, Danial. They don't need your help, having had to go it alone so many months. But Elle is still recovering, from what she went through at Ulysses' hands. She needs you more than ever. Venus needs her uncle, she's hasn't seen you not 'asleep' in months, as we told her you were. And Sar needs you too."

Danial looked up then and saw me. "Who are you?" he said.

I swayed and almost fell over, but Lash caught me in his arms.

"You know who Sar is," Devlin said sharply. "She is our Oathed One, and the mother of your child."

"She does not look like I remember her," Danial said slowly, staring at me. "I remember Sar, remember her dying in my arms even as that demon who killed her laughed."

I shot a worried look at Devlin. He ignored me, gazing at Danial with puzzlement.

Danial noticed Lash beside me, and gave him a rueful smile. "But you I unfortunately know, Lash, though you look younger than I remember you being. Where is Theo? And if this is Sarelle as you say, why is she here with you, and not with her husband?"

Devlin came to stand beside Danial, and put his hand on his brother's shoulder. "Many things have changed, while you were apart from us," he said gently. "Sar, come to Danial, let him taste your blood. He will remember that, even if your form is unfamiliar to him."

I walked over to Danial and hugged him, not caring that I was getting blood all over my shirt. *It's enough that he's awake, and talking again.* Danial hugged me back, the familiar feeling of his arms around me comforting.

Danial separated from me, looking at me expectantly. I tilted my head to give him access to my neck vein. Without preamble, Danial bit down gently into my flesh. I winced in pain, but made no noise, holding him close, tears slipping out even as I tried to blink them back. He made soft noises of contentment as he fed from me, but gave no other response. As the seconds passed without anything more, I grew more worried. *Dear God, let him remember me. Let my blood be close enough to what it was to trigger his memory.*

Danial pulled back from me, giving my neck a gentle kiss to heal it. "Dev, this is not Sar. Her blood is not as it should be, like spring."

My stomach roiled, as I felt Lash come up behind me again, and take my hand. I squeezed his hard, trying to breathe quietly, wanting this moment to pass, for Devlin to fix it somehow, for the romantic reunion I'd dreamed of to magically replace this heartbreaking nightmare I hadn't anticipated.

"You know how much I loved Sar, as you did," Danial went on. "But I can taste this is not her, though this woman's blood is unusually close, almost like summer."

I turned to Lash with a sob, and he hugged me, stroking my hair. "Shh."

Danial noticed us, his attitude becoming spiteful. "Obviously, this is one of your...women you share with Lash. Sar loved Theo, she was his wife, she would never have touched Lash, not in a million years."

"I'm telling you this is Sarelle," Devlin said, his tone bitter. "It is you who are not remembering right, Danial. Sarelle fell in love with Lash this past summer."

Danial bared his fangs in a vicious snarl. "Why are you doing this, trying to pass off one of your whores as the love of my life?"

"Can you not see how much she cares for you?" Devlin said abruptly, his tone switching suddenly to umbrage. "You are tearing her heart out with your words, with your denial of her! Stop being such a thoughtless bastard!"

Danial turned to me, his face smoothing into the polite mask that he wore at his Hallow's parties for the clients he didn't care for but felt he could not be rude to. He came to me, took my hand, and kissed it. "You should go and change clothes," he said softly. "I've made you a mess, Lady. But I thank you, for your blood."

I nodded, and darted from the room, Lash coming after me. At the door, I turned for one last look. Ulysses was still moving weakly, trying to crawl away. Danial grabbed him roughly, and then sank his fangs to the hilt in Ulysses' neck once more. Ulysses let out a cry of pain, his desperate eyes locking on mine in an unspoken plea. Devlin shut the door softly, blocking my view.

"Come." Lash led me to Devlin's room, and helped me take off my clothes, and get in the shower. He locked the door, then braced it with a chair. Then he took off his clothes as well, and got in the shower with me, putting his gun within reach. For a long time we just stood under the spill of the water, holding each other silently.

"I'm sorry," Lash hissed sorrowfully.

I hugged him, saying nothing. What was there to say? I was sorry, too, that Danial didn't remember me, that he was confusing me with Anna, or some other woman. *It's something that he remembers a Sar who he did love once. For now, that'll have to be enough.*

\* \* \* \*

Devlin carefully broached the subject early the next morning, when he, Lash and I awoke before dawn.

"Danial still loves you, Sar," he said, caressing my back. "But his memories are not what they were. I don't know if it is temporary or if it is permanent damage, from him being without a heartbeat for so long. Titus said if his memories were altered, that it would be permanent. He does not have amnesia. This is not a daytime soap opera, unfortunately."

"What does he remember me looking like?" I murmured, my back to him. "Is he confusing me with Anna?"

Devlin eased closer to me, and wrapped his arms around my waist. "You need to brace yourself."

I tensed beneath his touch, waiting anxiously.

"Spit it out, Dev," Lash hissed, his fangs extended. "Tell her and stop dragging this out."

"There was a woman Danial loved a few years after Anna died," Devlin continued. "Her name was Gabriella. She was the first one I took from him, and her loss was probably the hardest to bear. She died tragically, at a demon's hands." He paused. "He remembers his Sar as looking as she did, and not as you do."

"What did she look like?" I said more harshly than I meant to, as I turned over in bed to face him.

His eyes held apprehension, the gold of them gleaming in the darkness. "You remember Angelica and Monica?" Dev said tentatively. "She looked like them. Black hair, and bright blue eyes, with maybe a little green in them." Devlin paused, as if gathering himself. "You remember the photos of Danial and me, when we were together with a woman, or women? They were all of a type, Sar. Danial has always favored dark hair and blue eyes exclusively. At least he did, until he met you."

I looked away, trying not to cry, as Devlin hugged me tightly.

*How did I never see it?* I'd looked for a pattern in the women that had been in the pictures I'd gone through of Devlin's, but I had really been looking for one with Devlin. And there had been no pattern, not with him. He liked women of all coloring, and sizes, too, though he seemed to prefer buxom women, with larger breasts and hips. But Danial had always been with a dark haired woman, if a woman was in the picture. For most, I couldn't see the color of their eyes, as the pictures had been in black and white. But there had been one small oil painting of Danial and a woman. She had been dressed in blue, with blue eyes and dark hair, Danial with his arms around her, and Devlin posing on the other side of her. *Monica and Angelica looked like sisters. That woman Erica, the one he'd tried to hurt me with when we'd first broken up, Danial had said she'd had black hair and blue eyes, too…*

"Sar," Devlin said, interrupting my thoughts, "Danial somehow thinks you should look like Gabriella did, and have Anna's blood. Please give him time. When he is around you enough, he will see you for who you are, I'm sure of it—"

"What if he doesn't? What if he never remembers me, or what we were to each other? He thinks I'm dead now anyway!"

"Shh," Lash hissed, stroking my hair. "He will love you again in time, Sar. He fell in love with you once, and you are still you."

I didn't reply. *He fell in love with me because I saved his life one night. But without that, he probably wouldn't have given me a second look. How can I be the woman he fell in love with when the woman he remembers isn't me?*

\* \* \* \*

The next day, when I went downstairs to make Lash and Venus breakfast, I found Danial in the kitchen. I braced myself for some comment, but he just looked at Lash and me, smiled slightly, and said good morning. I felt very odd seeing him so casually while knowing he didn't know who I really was. To calm myself, I ignored him and focused on making breakfast with Lash. Danial stayed just long enough to get a glass of water, then left.

Seeing my upset, Lash made no mention of Danial at all. Then Venus asked quietly, "Why doesn't Danial like me anymore?"

I hugged her, pushing aside my own sorrow. "He does, he's just been through a very bad time. Please understand, V, the way he acts right now has nothing to do with his feelings for you. He just needs some time, after that long sleep he had."

She nodded, but her huge golden eyes remained sad.

Devlin came downstairs, as we were finishing breakfast. Lash took him aside, and told him what had happened. He picked Venus up immediately, and went in search of Danial. I stayed with Lash, knowing it was best without anyone saying anything.

In a half hour, Devlin was back, sans Venus. "Danial is playing with her," he said, resting his hand on my shoulder. "He remembers her, and they are getting along fine. He was upset because he saw you and her together. The way

203

you might have felt if you'd witnessed Monica taking care of T, when he was little."

"Dev, I can't do this," I said, taking a deep breath, and trying to be calm. "I can't not be who I am, just because he doesn't remember me."

"I will talk to him again later," Devlin said in a soothing tone. "Don't concern yourself. You know Danial, Love. He is polite to a fault. I told him just now if he has anything to say about you at all, he was not to say it to you, but to me. That you were mistress here, and could do whatever you pleased, and he was not to say or do anything to offend you. He agreed to this."

Lash didn't comment, but his expression said he thought this solution of Dev's was sub-optimal.

I went for a long walk later, taking time alone to decide if I should try further to make Danial remember, or leave him alone for now. Darkness and Ghost ran ahead of me, happy the snow was only a few inches deep. Thankfully, Titus was doing a good job of keeping a trail open for my daily walks.

After a solid hour of weighing the pros—heartfelt reunion, everyone back to normal—to the cons—Danial voicing again that I was one of Devlin's whores, I decided to do it. No matter how much it hurt, I had to at least try, after all he had done for me over the years.

About five, I fluffed my hair as Tatiana had shown me long ago, and put on a deep red long sweater. I tried to put the fox head choker on myself, but it wouldn't fasten. *It's been too long since he's shared blood with me. Whatever was in my system's long gone.* I debated putting on the fox head earrings by themselves, but decided against it. *It may enrage him.* I debated removing the diamond ring he had given me and the swirled wedding band of many colors, but decided against it. *He saw that already yesterday.*

I went to one of the guest bedrooms—Danial's new bedroom, according to Dev. His few older books of poetry were there, and the carvings Theo had made for him in their cabinet. I noticed with a jolt that the Woman and the Cougar were there too, but didn't say anything. Because the biggest surprise was T there visiting with Danial.

My son glanced at me as I entered, his expression distressed. "I'm going to go now, Dad. If you want to come back to work—"

"No," Danial retorted flatly. My mouth dropped open, as I gaped at him comically. But more surprise followed as he continued. "I spent too many years working. I should have spent them with her. I should have spent every minute with her! And it's too late now. She's dead."

"Mom is not dead, I told you—"

"T, I loved your mother. Don't tell me lies to make me feel better, or because you think I'll forgive that bastard you are calling your partner."

"Terian had nothing to do with this!"

"He wasn't there, that night she was attacked! She died because of him! And I was hurt because his uncle wasn't doing his job! Demons can't be trusted! They'll let you down every time!"

"I love you, Dad," T said, his voice rough with emotion. "But I can't listen to this. Good-bye."

T strode out, and Danial reclined back on the edge of the bed. I hesitantly went in and sat next to him. He looked at me with hostility, then his expression softened.

"I'm sorry, for your loss," I said quietly.

"Thank you...um…?"

"Call me 'Lady'," I said, staring at him penetratingly, hoping to see a glimmer of memory surface.

Danial just nodded. "Thank you, Lady. My son doesn't seem to understand, but I hear compassion in your voice, something that piques my curiosity. Why should you empathize with me, since we do not know each other?"

Danial's words were hard, but also etched with deep sorrow. That only made his manner a trifle easier to bear. "Because I heard about what you have lost, and also about your family."

"That bastard Ulysses orchestrated the rape of my daughter," Danial said, his eyes glowing red. "Devlin refuses to kill him. He said he needs him alive for some reason."

*For Lash, in case he began to fail.* I stayed silent, knowing my explanation would not give him solace.

"I feel like I've lost everything that ever meant anything to me."

"You have your children, and your brother," I said, putting my hand hesitantly over his. "You are alive. That's something."

"You are right," Danial said, wiping his eyes. "She can live on in me." He let out a breath, then glanced at me. "You should go. I'm sure my brother is looking for you by now. His desires need sating on an hourly basis. But you probably know that well, Lady."

*It's obvious there's not even a glimmer.* I took a deep breath, and went to leave.

"Please Lady," Danial called softly from behind me. "I would ask that you never wear red again in my presence. Though you don't look like my Sar at all physically, there is something about you when you wear red that reminds me strongly of her. It makes me remember her, and I still feel the pain of her loss too deeply."

"I don't mind, Danial," I replied, keeping my back to him so he didn't see my sudden tears. "It's very touching that you loved her so much."

"I think about her every hour of every day. She was the love of my life, even when she was married to my best friend. When she finally agreed to be mine, to live with me, those were the happiest years of my life. Even when we were fighting, and her blue eyes would flash with fire—"

I brushed the tears out of my eyes, and tried to compose myself enough to listen.

"I never stopped loving her. She was so strong. She had so much heart, and hope. She was kind, too, especially to even the smallest of animals."

"I'm sure she loved you just as much," I blurted. Then I bolted, before I lost it completely.

\* \* \* \*

Later that evening, Devlin came upstairs and settled in bed with Lash and me. I had just finished relating to Lash the crashing and burning of my big plan.

"I'm sorry. I tried again as well," Devlin said with a sigh as he settled himself on my chest. "I also got nowhere."

"Isn't there some spell?" Lash mentioned casually. "I can't believe there isn't something that demon could do to make Danial remember the man he used to be."

"Titus said the memories themselves are altered. If Danial had forgotten, there are spells that could be used. But he said it is like a bone that was shattered, and grew back together. There are some small shards that ended up in the wrong place—"

"Can't Titus re-break them, then?" Lash interrupted. "It works for bones."

"But not for minds," Devlin replied with a grimace. "Titus said he was amazed Danial came back as much like himself as he did. He said it is usually much worse, and to count our blessings."

*Easy for Titus to say. He isn't the one who's been forgotten.*

\* \* \* \*

The next morning, Lash awakened early as he usually did, and got dressed to do his rounds, giving me a kiss to say he would be back later to shower with me. But in his eyes was an unspoken question. I nodded my answer. He nodded once, then left without a word.

After he left, I waited a good ten minutes, then disentangled myself from a still sleeping Devlin. Dressing quickly with purpose, I went downstairs and made myself some cereal and a bagel. My new routine was familiar and comforting, something I'd found a respite the last few months. Any other morning that would have been a good thing, but not today.

I slipped in a tape on my ancient Walkman as I sat down, glad it was one of the things I'd brought to Dev's home earlier on, when I'd first began doing work for him. I'd never listened to music at Danial's, but there was no phone here I had to answer. So far I'd resisted Devlin's offer of an iPod, though I admitted when my old machine went, I would likely take him up on his offer. Working in Devlin's study had its drawbacks, being so close to the dungeon. I didn't want to hear anyone screaming. Or any other noises coming from in there, for that matter.

I ate breakfast listening to some Concrete Blonde's *Jesus, Please Forgive Me*, trying to put myself in the mindset for murder. I'd never killed in cold blood before, never killed anything except in self-defense. But this morning, I was going to.

## Chapter Thirteen

Gathering my courage, I put my dishes in the sink, and went downstairs to the basement, and then on to the dungeon.

Ulysses was there, sleeping. He sensed me as I entered, opening his eyes and baring his sunken face in a rictus smile. "So Danial doesn't remember you," he said with malice. "Poor, pathetic girl. It must hurt to have lost the love of a great man like him."

"Save your insults," I replied scathingly. "I'm here to give you some blood, if you have the strength to get to me and take it. I want your help, if you're strong enough."

His face went blank in an instant. "Why would you help me?"

"Because I was a victim of Devlin just as you were. Just like Diana was. If he'd left me with Danial, or with Theo, I wouldn't have all the pain I have now. I wouldn't be hunted, I wouldn't have been in hell the past year. I want it to end."

"What do you want from me?" he asked, suspicious.

"Take enough of my blood, and go to his room. It's at the top of the stairs, to the left. No one is about, and he has no guards. Stake him as he sleeps. He's a heavy sleeper; he won't even hear the door open—"

Ulysses looked eager now, but also crafty. "What do you want for your help in freeing me, Sarelle? You know I'd kill him given any chance, so you must want something besides that."

"Two things," I said quickly. "I'll need your blood the rest of my life. I want your word you'll give it to me, for as long as you live. I can't live without regular doses, or I'll die, from what Danial and Devlin did to me. And Danial will have nothing to do with me now. I don't want to die."

"I swear it," Ulysses said, nodding. "And the other?"

I looked at Ulysses. "Give me your word you won't hurt anyone else in the house if I free you, including me. I love my daughter, she is innocent, and I don't want anyone here harmed, or any continuation of this vendetta of yours. My son T is not to be harmed, or Elle, or anyone else besides Devlin. I'm sick of blood and death and loss. I'm sick of this whole Vampire world, of always being in the darkness, of always being fed on! I want out of it, to just live somewhere quietly until I die. You can come to me, and give me the blood on a regular basis, but otherwise I want no more of any of it. Venus will come with me, and she and I can disappear. I have some money hidden away." The sincere bitterness and hate in my words were almost thick enough to choke me, but I got the words out with effort.

Ulysses narrowed his eyes. "I wouldn't have thought you'd have it in you, to kill your lover. You Oathed to him again willingly, or so I heard."

"He took it by force." I paused, then pushed the last of my speech out. "I'm in love with his best friend, and he's in love with me. Devlin forbade me being with him, unless I gave him the Oath. We want to be free of Devlin, so we can just be together, the two of us. But he can't bring himself to do it. They have too much history together. I'm not strong enough, not to mention Dev could probably stop me with just his mind." *You're rambling, wrap it up.* "Once it's done, Lash will protect me, and Venus. It might not be a great life, but it will be a good enough one. I want this fucking choker off my neck. I'm tired of being owned."

Ulysses gazed at me, considering. "I saw the way Lash looked at you, how he touched you. It's fact that you'll never get that choker off any other way except by Devlin dying. But why should I trust you, Sarelle McGarran?"

I took a deep breath, my feeling of betrayal as I spoke the words making me nauseous. "Because I understand you wanting revenge for your sister, for what he did to her, and later Diana. Dev's hurt a lot of people thoughtlessly. You risked your life, even became vampire, to try to even the score. You sacrificed yourself for her, in a way. I respect that, even if I'm horrified by the means you used, and the lengths you went to." In a softer tone I added, "Your sister is alive, and unturned. Once you kill Devlin, she will awaken, and be free of him. He told me this himself, so it must be true. She's in a room by herself, under a spell, as she has been for over a month."

When I mentioned that Diana was alive, his eyes went wild with hope. Then fear smashed down. "Why did he not kill her?"

"He planned to. V stopped him. It's only because of my daughter that your sister lives."

Ulysses nodded. His words when he spoke were emotional. "I give you my word, Sarelle, the same word I gave Diana, that I would avenge Heather," he said, his green eyes locked on mine. "I will only harm Devlin." He paused. "Lash, Venus, and you should leave Hayden today and disappear, at least for a few years. The Rulers will know you and he played a part in Dalcon's death. I'll give you my protection, but I know enough not to trust Samuel." He paused again. "There is a werebear living here by the name of Jerry. He's been feeding me information this whole time. When you feel that you need more of the blood, call Hayden and ask for him, only him. Say that you are Heather and that you need a visit soon from me. He'll contact me immediately. Just call, whenever you need the blood. Within a day I can come to you, or you can teleport to me here, or some neutral ground, whatever works best."

I nodded. "Agreed."

"Set me free," he whispered seductively through the bars. "And I will set you free."

"Come to me," I said nervously, swallowing hard. "And please be gentle when you feed from me. I've been bitten so often for so long that now it always brings me pain, not pleasure. Devlin also took a lot from me last night, so please don't take too much, or I'll lose consciousness."

Ulysses got up with ease, walking across the cell towards me. *Danial didn't come close to draining him, though he's clearly much weaker. Did Devlin give him some human blood, to keep him healthy?* Afraid but determined, I opened the door with the key Lash had left for me this morning, and set Ulysses free. He stepped outside the cell, then stood before me, staring at me.

I trembled under his steady gaze, but didn't run.

"I'll feed from you after I kill him," he said finally. "And then only if I need to. I'll need your help with Devlin, and if you're too weak, you won't be able to give me assistance. He is far stronger than I am now."

This wasn't part of my plan. "What do you want me to do?"

"Distract him," Ulysses instructed. "Go into the bedroom first, ahead of me. If he's awake, pretend you want him, whatever it takes so you have his full attention. Otherwise, he may sense me. Yell 'now' at the opportune moment. I'll come in, and kill him."

"Okay," I said, offering him a sharpened stake that Lash had left for me near the base of the dungeon wall.

He took the stake, then to my surprise, he kissed my hand. "I'm sorry, for what I did to you. Understand that this was never about you. I had to get revenge for my sister."

"I understand," I said coolly. "Please follow me."

I went ahead of him, creeping up the stairs. Ulysses waited outside the door I indicated, motioning for me to act.

I entered the room, walking quickly to the bed. I caressed the shoulder of the sleeping form. "Devlin, are you sleeping? I need you—"

Ulysses burst through the door with an evil smile, stake in hand.

The door slammed shut behind him. Ulysses whirled to throw the stake, as

Lash hit him with enough force to knock him across the room into the sliding glass doors. The stunned vampire grabbed the curtains as he fell. As planned, they came down with the sound of tearing cloth, letting sunlight flood into the room. Devlin, hidden under two heavy blankets on Lash's bed, was protected. Ulysses was not.

He shrieked, his skin already smoking, trying to get out of the light. Lash picked up the vampire's smoking form with his gloved hands as I opened the glass doors. He tossed Ulysses out through opening onto the large deck into the snow, pulling off the thick black curtains Ulysses was desperately trying to cover himself with in the process. Ulysses screamed louder, over and over, as his skin began quickly to flake off, then to burn and crisp. The burning vampire tried to get past us to safety, but Lash with a snap of his wrist curled his whip around him, then dragged him back into the sun, holding him beneath its light as more and more smoke poured off him, his skin blazing alight as if he'd been dipped in gasoline.

"Scream for me!" Lash hissed loudly, with brutal satisfaction, holding Ulysses with his whip. "You're so fond of burning people, have a taste of it yourself!"

"Why?" Ulysses shrieked, his lips peeling, melting. "Why, Sarelle?"

"Because you hurt my daughter, and the people I love," I shouted at him. "I don't need a reason better than that."

"Dalcon deserved it, he deserved—"

"Elle was *innocent*!" I screamed at him. "I would have killed you just for that, you bastard! Just for even trying to hurt her like that, for thinking it! You sealed your fate when you hurt her!"

"No! It can't end like this! I can't fail my sister, I can't! Argh! Argh!"

Ulysses screamed for a long time, his vengeful cries becoming desperate shrieks, his skin blackening and burning, melted fat sizzling and bubbling on the deck. Finally, he collapsed, first to his knees, and then completely to the deck floor. He kept burning, kept smoking, the stench sickening. An hour later, all that remained of him was a large black scorched mark on the deck floor, and a diminishing pile of ashes, blowing away in the gentle wind.

Lash coiled up his whip, looking sadly at the burned parts of it. The braided leather had charred from the heat and broken in places. "I'll have to get a new one," he said with a sigh, looking sorrowful. "This one's had it. Vampires burn too hot, even for the heavy duty protective spells Titus put on this."

I hugged him, and kissed him. "I'll buy you one, Lash," I murmured gratefully, holding him. "Thank you for helping me kill him."

"I told you if you ever needed my help, it was yours," he hissed tenderly, kissing my cheek. "Though I wish you had just let me kill him in the cellar, and not risked yourself. A full clip or two of the explosive bullets would have done it, weak as he was."

"I wanted to see him burn. He had it coming, Lash. I remember Devlin's screams. I hear them sometimes again, in my nightmares. And I remember how we found Elle..."

Lash looked down at me, his expression searching. "I was worried for a minute, Sar," he hissed. "You sounded like you were really going to do it, let him kill Dev, and run off with me. I heard some truth in your words."

"I had to sound believable," I said, averting my gaze. "I needed him to come willingly. We'd never have gotten him up here where we could get him into the sun unless he thought I was going to help him." I paused. "And there was some truth to my words. Some of the bitterness I feel in my situation is real. I did admire Ulysses a little, for going after his sister's killer, despite him being human and Devlin being a Ruler, and so powerful. But I could never have been anything but an enemy of someone who'd done what he did to Elle. There was no other way for this to end. A bullet was way, way too quick and painless for him."

Lash hugged me, his tenseness leaving his shoulders. "I'm glad he didn't feed on you," he whispered. "I was never comfortable with that part of the plan. Even being under that cloaking spell, and being close enough to hear everything, I was worried. If he had wanted to hurt you—"

"I'm fine," I assured. "And Devlin's also fine. He'll be asleep for hours. Titus said that injection I gave him would ensure he stayed out."

"You know he's going to be pissed," Lash interrupted, grinning slightly. "He wanted to hold Ulysses for a while, to torture him."

"I wasn't risking it," I said with a shrug. "You kill your enemies, not keep them captive."

"I agree," Lash said, pulling me tight against him. "I feel much better knowing he's ashes."

"You aren't even a little regretful?" I said, caressing his cheek. "You know part of the reason Devlin was keeping him alive was going to be to provide blood for you, if you needed it."

"Shh, don't talk about that," Lash hissed, hugging me close. "It wasn't worth it. As you said, you kill your enemies. Because of what you and I did, we know who the weak link was that cost Robin her life." His tone turned low and scary. "Jerry will be getting a visit from me this afternoon. Keith, Seth, and the other bears have already grabbed him, on my orders, and should be on their way to the cells with him about now. And when I'm done, Titus will have his monthly meal ready for him when he gets to work tonight."

*Eww. Don't think about it, Sar. Don't grimace too much, either, or you'll make Lash feel bad, for what he'd had to do in the past.* "Come on," I said, breaking away from him. "We'd better get Dev back in his own bed. I'm worried about him here in your room, so vulnerable, and so close to the sun."

Lash nodded. He picked Devlin up wrapped in the blankets, and carried him back into his own bed, where I lay him beneath the sheets, and gave him a gentle kiss. We walked out, locking the door after us, and back into Lash's room, where I helped him rehang the curtains over the sliding glass door, plunging the room again into darkness.

Lash came to me, wrapping his arms around me. "Can I interest you in some celebratory sex?"

I giggled, then turned to him. "You didn't find me just by scent, did you? You can see in the dark, can't you?"

"Of course, though it's not the same as regular sight," Lash said, his tone both amused, and also surprised. "Most weres can. But I can scent you too, Sar. My sense of smell is better than my eyes, in the dark." He paused. "Sar?"

"Mmmhmm?"

"I want to know something, about you...and Theo."

"Ask."

"Well, two things, actually."

*Must be important, to swing his thoughts off sex.* "Ask already, then."

"If I'd died back in September, and you were still with Theo...would you have taken Ulysses' deal, to be free of Devlin?"

"No. He hurt my daughter. Even if he hadn't, Devlin I know well enough to manage. In spite of his actions sometimes, I do believe he loves me. Ulysses would have just been another master who would have used my dependence on him against me. I don't want another man having control over me. I don't want another man in my life who *wants* control over me."

"You know I don't want that, right? I mean, I want you to let me know where you are, and sometimes to promise not to go places or do some things, but that's so I can protect you."

"I get it," I kissed him tenderly. "So what's the other question?"

"Come to bed, and I'll ask it."

We took off our clothes, and got in his bed, lying together, our bodies entwined. "Spill it," I said finally, when he hadn't made any move to speak.

"What did you talk about, with him?" Lash's voice in the darkness was very hesitant, yet also driven.

"What did I talk about with who?"

"Theo."

"When?"

"When you were together."

I gave him a look to let him know I thought his question was very odd, then turned on the light near the bed before turning to face him. "Why do you want to know this?"

"You seem to not know a lot about weres and yet you were married to one for over a year. Hell, you dated, well, lived with one for longer than that. You did things with me as friends that you didn't do with Theo, like discussing books, getting sushi, or lying in the sun. He was your mate, and you acted as though you loved him. So in all that time you were together, what did you talk about, that you don't know so many things about weres? Did he not talk to you?"

"We didn't talk a lot, like you and I do," I said, blushing. "We watched a lot of movies, and we bantered a lot, made a lot of jokes, and we had a lot of sex. I had work to do, and so did he. We had children to raise. A good part of the marriage we were working on our problems, like the women he'd been with before and after me, my attraction for Danial, my health, the people trying to kill us. Later, it was Devlin and Danial, all that sharing me that no one really liked. That was what killed it, I think. We stopped talking sometime during the marriage, and he started dictating things to me. And…" I trailed off.

"Go on, Sar."

"I had Titus break the bond between Theo and me, after I got back from the Everglades."

"Why?" Lash was incredulous. "It's rare what you shared with him."

"Because I loved him enough to let him go, because he wasn't going to be happy sharing me," I forced out. "I think now a lot of what kept us together was the bond. Yes, the sex was good, even great. But although I liked him, cared for him, what did we have in common? Almost nothing. Once we hit problems, we fell apart. Without that bond to keep us together, Theo would probably have left me when I began to want Danial. And that's even if he ever admitted he liked me in the first place. Without that spell that night, he wouldn't have kissed me the first time, or dreamed with me. There would have been nothing to start, so there would have been nothing to end."

Lash was silent, his expression thoughtful and introspective.

"Why did you want to know all that?" I asked him again.

"I want not to lose you like he did," Lash hissed, clearly agitated. "I want to not make the same mistakes he did with you. But my temper's a bad one, Sar. Sometimes I'm as bad as Devlin, worse really, though I know you haven't seen me like that too often, mostly with Theo."

That went without saying. I still remembered his confession at Davy's. *He's got no memory of that night. There's no point bringing it up now.*

"I want you to tell me, if I'm doing something wrong," Lash hissed, holding me against him, his cheek pressed into my hair, my face in the crook of his neck. "Tell me, so I can fix it, before you decide it's easier not to try anymore to make it work. I don't ever want to fight with you again the way we did a few weeks ago."

"It's a deal, if you'll do the same for me," I said, and kissed him. He pulled back, and gave me a tilted-head look, like he didn't know what I meant.

"Lash, you should have told me very bluntly that you needed me as a snake," I said gently. "You should've told me that you had gotten a potion for me, for us—"

"The first I already did," Lash said a little testily. "And I was worried you'd refuse."

"I told you I loved you," I replied, trying to keep my irritation in check. "I need you to be honest with me."

"Talk about honest! You should have told me immediately when you realized you were in love with me. That very moment, you should have been calling me," Lash hissed forcefully. "I would have been on the road in the next minute, coming to get you so we could be together, no matter who stood in my way, Danial, Dev, or Theo. I knew you cared for me a little, but—"

"Should I have said 'I care deeply for you'?" I mocked.

"Don't be sarcastic about this, or I'll spank you," Lash hissed sharply, "You've been in love before, Sar. You knew what you were feeling. I hadn't been before—"

Lash went silent, realizing what he'd just admitted. We didn't speak for a minute, just holding one another.

"I wanted to say what I felt a lot of times," I whispered in his ear. "But I was afraid to."

"Tell me again."

"I love you, Lash."

Lash didn't reply. He just hugged me close to him, as if he would never let me go.

\* \* \* \*

That Devlin was not happy when he came to was an understatement. He was livid I'd dosed him with a sleeping potion, and incensed to find Ulysses dead. But when Lash told him about Jerry's betrayal, and also the information that Jerry had given up before Lash killed him, Devlin thanked Lash and I for killing him instead.

Lash had discovered from Jordan, Elle's attacker, that Ulysses was watching Danial's home, to see who came and went. We'd always assumed the watch point was from some location on or near the road that led to Danial's hidden driveway, but we'd been wrong.

It came to light through Jerry that Ulysses had sold Robin's werewolf pelt for a massive cloaking spell. It hid the two large RV's that he'd parked on Danial's land off the road that he'd bought with money from the first stolen werebear pelt. He'd been lurking and plotting there all along, with no one the wiser. But the most chilling thing was that Bill Winger, Elle's tutor, had been helping Ulysses, feeding him information on patrols and guard routes, so that none of the guards, not even Theo or Tears, had noticed any comings and goings from Ulysses' camp. That was how he'd known where to find Danial that night he and T were attacked. How he'd known where to find Sundown, that day she was attacked. Bill had mistaken her for me, when he saw her driving past. Ulysses had even been using Danial's vehicles; the van Elle had been attacked in had been one that had belonged to Lander that had been sitting in storage for the last few years. The Pathfinder Ulysses had driven to his challenge fight with Devlin had been the one Danial had purchased for T, when he had first learned to drive.

That very afternoon, after killing Jerry, Lash and Titus went to Danial's home and together with Theo, Terian, and T, they destroyed the rest of Ulysses' camp. Lash wouldn't talk about it after, except to say vengeance had been done and there was nothing left but ashes. But Devlin told me later that there had been evidence that Jerry was going to act to let Ulysses free inside Hayden, and also arrange to have the gate open, in order for an all-out attack to take place, one involving more than fifty werebears, all polar bears that had once been employees of Ebediah. Devlin said nothing about what had happened to those bears, or the two from the day of his battle with Ulysses, but he advised me to wear my headset in the basement for the next month when I worked down there on e-mail for T. I agreed, and asked nothing more.

Bill was brought to Hayden by Lash the day after Ulysses died, shaking and shivering, but untouched. But when he saw Devlin baring his fangs evilly, he wet his pants in sheer terror.

Devlin, denied of his own revenge against Ulysses, took out all of his anger on Bill, setting him free outside at dusk, telling if he made it over the wall of Hayden, he would be allowed to live. My vengeful vampire lord spent the night playing with the former tutor, and came back before dawn licking his lips. I knew by Dev's pure satiated look that he'd let Bill get to the wall, and almost over it before killing him. But I didn't shed a single tear for that bastard.

The most unsettling thing was the unexpected discovery of a werefox pelt in Ulysses' camp. It had not come from one of Danial's foxes, but some creature had lost its life. We reasoned that this was how Terian had found out about Lash and I, that one of Ulysses men, perhaps the sorcerer killed by Terian, had been spying on us that night we'd returned from the Everglades. That they had overheard what had happened, and seen that Terian was the weak link, and the key to infiltrating Danial's home. Because it was clear from Jerry's confession that Ulysses hadn't been able to set up camp at Danial's until Terian had been out of the way.

After hearing that, I felt responsible in a way for what had happened. Devlin hugged me, and assured me that Terian did, too, asking me to let it go. "Ulysses would have found some other way to infiltrate Danial's, if not that one," he said soothingly. "Don't blame yourself." But secretly, I wondered if that were true.

* * * *

Lash and I were lying in bed one afternoon. Devlin was feeding in Titus's old room, and I knew he would be a while, as he'd said not to expect him to be joining us until after nine or so. Lash had used the opportunity to make love with me, as he often did, and then we had slept a while, our bodies entwined. I'd cried when I awoke from a dream of Devon, and my weresnake mate had held me, saying nothing.

"I never got to know what he looked like," I wailed. "I won't recognize him, when I die, if I go to where he is."

"He'll recognize you," Lash whispered gently. "And he'll come bounding up to see you, probably knocking you over. You'll hear him purr again, Sar. You'll see his human form then, too. He'll probably look just like Theo."

"It's funny," I whispered, smiling bitterly. "But humans have wreaked the greatest hurt on me. It wasn't a vampire, a were, or even a demon. It was humans."

"What do you mean?" Lash hissed softly, pushing my hair back from my eyes. "Ulysses was human, but all vampires start out as human."

"Not that. All this started because Theo was taken from me by a human, who wanted to sell him for profit, and because another human wanted to use Danial and he for target practice. You know the story?"

Lash nodded that he did.

"Danial and I were over, Lash," I sighted, looking into space. "But when Theo disappeared, I went back to him. I couldn't give up on Theo, though, so I promised myself I wouldn't Oath to him, or marry him. I told himself it was the mortality difference, but it wasn't, not then—"

"Sar, this is water long over the dam, and down the river."

"—but I knew he wanted a child, and I thought to myself, I could give him that instead. I had wanted one anyway, after being Elle's mother. But I had no idea all this would happen."

"You mean Devlin wanting you, and the Rulers wanting you, and all that?"

"I never thought about it. But Theo brought it up, right when we first went to see Carol. He was right, Lash. Everything that happened later built on my having Theoron with Danial. And if Theo hadn't been taken, I wouldn't have gone back to Danial. I'd have stayed working at the metal fabrication plant. Theo would've married me, and would've quit working for Danial—"

"He was going to quit?" Lash said, rolling his eyes. "Sar, there's no quitting this line of work. You do it until you get killed. That's it for a retirement plan."

"He said as much later. But even so, I'd have let Danial go, probably only seen him a few times a year in passing. Elle wouldn't have known him well, either. I would've had more children with Theo. Devlin would never have been interested in me."

"That's untrue," Lash hissed softly. "He was angry, very angry for what happened to him at Terian's hands, Sar. So was I. He blamed you for it, more so than Terian, or Theo. You know Devlin well now. You know he would not have been out of power for long, no matter what he had to do to get it again. I would've done what I did for him with Ebediah probably, and he would have become a Ruler again. As soon as he was a Ruler again, I would've come for you, to bring you to him, no matter where you were, or who you were with."

I shivered, because it was there in Lash's tone that he was telling the truth.

"But why are you thinking of this now?" Lash hissed. "In the world you speak of, most everyone's lost in misery. Danial never knows the joy of being a father, or loving you, and he's alone. Devlin's powerful again, but despite him probably laying everyone in sight, he's not happy as he is now; he's emotionally empty, and still angry at the world for losing Annabelle. Danial and he are still estranged. You are a prisoner of Devlin's, having had at least one child for him by now. Theo's dead by my hand. And I'd be dead for sure."

I hugged Lash against me tighter. "I'm very, very glad you aren't dead."

"Me, too," he agreed, laughing a little. "So why are you thinking of this?"

"Because so much would've been different. I'm not saying it would be better—"

"You are thinking of Furface, because he made you feel as if you're to blame for the way things turned out," Lash hissed, annoyed. "He wouldn't be happy, either, Sar. If a challenger like Robert hadn't killed him, I would've killed him when I came for you. Devlin only came himself that night to take you because he thought you were alone, with maybe a human boyfriend, if that, and there was no real risk to him. If he'd known Theo was living with you, he'd have sent me to get you, and bring you to him. In that world, I was never your lover, never knew you like I do, Sar. And as much as I might have felt sorry taking you from your family, I would have done it, probably killing Theo in the process. I don't want to admit it, but the truth is you had caused the events that led to Danial getting Devlin deposed. I would've wanted revenge myself on you for that, as you were the one who sealed my fate, doomed me."

I wondered what he would have done to me for revenge, and decided I wasn't going to ask. I still remembered Devlin's confession more than a year ago; I didn't want another one to keep me awake nights. "Titus might have told Dev what was needed to save you. He'd have no reason not to then, with us not being together."

"Save he hates me, and always has," Lash hissed angrily. "But you're right. Devlin could've drank Ebediah's blood, and let me have Sola's. I possibly could've lived, if Titus had given me that potion he had talked about." Lash tilted my head, so I looked at his eyes. "But Devlin would've tried sooner or later to have a child with you, no matter what else happened. He would've tried until he succeeded, Sar. The other Rulers would've wanted you then. He also would have shared you with Danial, eventually, and you'd have had a child with him, too, in time, probably called Theoron. You would've ended up Oathed to them both in that world, too, most likely living here as you do now. But—there's no way to say this nicely—you'd have been fucked up in the process. Devlin has hurt women in the past, Sar, and enjoyed it. I don't like to tell you bad things about him, but it's fact that he would've broken you, when he bent you to his will. You'd have fought him, and he'd have liked you fighting him, liked showing you that no matter what you did, he was going to have anything he wanted of you. He'd have been sorry after you had his child, when he would've cared for you, maybe even loved you, but by then it would've been too late."

"Stop," I said, sickened. "You're right, this is pointless to discuss."

"Listen," Lash hissed, "Know this, Sar. The only thing truly different in that world is that Theo's dead and I killed him. And that you and I would never have been together, because you'd never have forgiven me taking his life." He paused. "I never want to hear you utter another word about what might have been, because the thought of not knowing you, not being like this with you is so awful I don't want to ever think about it, or have you think about it, either. There is no world but this one, where we sleep together every night, and you're my mate."

I clasped him to me and hugged him. "I'm sorry. I didn't mean to make you feel bad."

"The point is I feel good," Lash hissed contentedly, rubbing his scratchy cheek against mine. "I've been alone my whole life, even when I had a woman

I called my own. But I have you now, and Venus and Dev, too. I'm happy." He paused, his tone becoming tender. "Even though you're still hurting, when enough time passes, you'll be happy again, too, Sar. I'm looking forward to that time, when I see you truly smile again." He paused, stroking my back with his hand. "Mind you, I'm not rushing you to heal your hurt. Tell me, if you need me to hold you, or give you space, or whatever. I'm here for you, and Dev is, too, even if he gets moody about not getting his way."

"Thank you," I said gratefully, burrowing into him.

He sighed, and held me close. For some time after, we didn't speak. Then abruptly, I realized I had a question for him. "Titus knew what you meant with that knife you gave me, didn't he?"

Lash nodded. "He can read most languages, Sar. He saw the symbol, and knew what I was asking you, even if you didn't. That's why he was so permissive about the sex, after he found out we had been together. He knew you were my mate then. He knew you'd come to me willingly. But even though he knew I was loyal to Devlin, he could tell I wanted you for myself. That's why he recharged the tracking spell on you, and made sure that Devlin found us together. He didn't trust me not to grab you and take off."

I ran my hands over his chest, stroking gently. "But you wouldn't have done that."

Lash looked at me and laughed, but it was a mocking laugh. "Don't be so sure," he cautioned, kissing my cheek. "When I was lying with you that last hour, making out, and we were waiting for Titus to come to get you, I was thinking hard about it, about asking you to come with me and just take off, to be with me. But I couldn't do it, not just because of Dev, and the damned tracking spell, but because I thought you might still need the vampire blood to live. I didn't want you to die, or for me to have to turn you into snake."

"I almost tried to get you to bite me, that day back in the spring. To turn me."

Lash lifted my chin, so he could see my face clearly. "When was this?"

"That day Dev forced me to wear his collar," I said, blushing at the memory. "But it was for selfish reasons. I thought if I was weresnake, you'd help me escape him, want me for yourself—"

"I did want you for myself, even then," Lash admitted, kissing my shoulders. "I wanted you to wear my snake colors, so I could think of you in snake form."

"But I was pregnant then," I finished. "I thought my children would die, if you bit me, and I couldn't risk it."

Lash drew back. "I remember now," he said softly, his eyes dark and serious. "I saw you reach out to me, and I wondered if you wanted me, the real me. But when you took your hand back, I decided you'd just been going to ask me something, and reconsidered. I never slept Sar, not when we were out in the open, and vulnerable, though you did. We were together, and that was enough." Lash kissed me again. "I wouldn't have bitten you, even if you'd asked me to. It would've killed your children, changing for the first time, and I could never harm a child. Not ever." There was something in his tone, some old pain, that made me hug him tighter. But Lash did not elaborate.

"But if Titus was so permissive, why was he against us spending time after we came back? He went on and on about staying away from you, every time he talked to me."

"Because he didn't want you with me, just like he hates that we are together now," Lash said acrimoniously. "He doesn't like to think of me anywhere near you, much less in you, you who he considers his daughter. He refused initially to make the potion for me to give you to become snake. Devlin finally had to force him to do it. But he seems to have calmed down some. Is he still giving you any shit about me?" Lash's tone had turned angry by the end.

"He's not happy," I admitted finally. "But he can see that we care about each other, and he knows that we're officially mated, and that being yours is part of my Oath."

"How does he know?" Lash said quickly. "I never said anything."

"I told him," I confessed. "I wanted him to leave you alone, and I'd heard enough badmouthing of you. So I told him, and he relented. He just reminded me again that he felt like a father to me, and he hoped that I was happy."

"Good," Lash said, grinning. "Maybe I'll call him 'Dad' next time I see him, just for kicks."

I hit him lightly and he laughed, smirking at me. "You have anything else to confess?"

The moment he said the words, it hit me that I did. I turned to Lash with tears in my eyes.

He went still immediately. "What is it?"

"I'm so sorry, Lash. I broke a promise to you. I told Devlin why I came back to him—that it was because of you helping me."

Lash's eyes went flat instantly, the rage emanating from him so hot it was making him twitch. I stayed motionless, a little afraid, watching him get it under control.

"Why?" he got out finally.

"I was drunk, and angry," I admitted, crying a little, and feeling stupid. "You and I had fought, then you'd gone to Davy's. I'd cut myself deeply on the knife you'd given me, and was trying to bring Danial back—"

Lash's anger disappeared, and he clutched me to him tightly. "Dev stopped you? Healed you?"

I nodded.

"And?"

"Devlin told me to go and make up with you. I was angry, and it slipped out."

"How did he take it?" Lash asked warily.

"He said he'd suspected, but he was upset, until I told him I could have children again, and then he said he didn't care."

"You told him that, too?" Lash said, letting out a breath. "Well, that's—"

"He knows about our baby, about my miscarriage."

"Sar, I'm guessing Dev didn't take more than an hour to show up at Davy's, and find me passed out. How the hell did you have so much time to discuss all this?"

"Lash, you told him about the baby. You were drunk, really drunk, but you were awake, when we both found you. You don't remember, but I came to Davy's with Dev. You fought—"

"No, I went to Davy's and trashed the place, and then drank myself into a stupor. Dev came and got me, and brought me home, I guess. You woke me up the next afternoon."

"No, I went with him, and we found you drinking, and you called me a bitch."

He gave me a look that said he didn't believe me, but was unwilling to call me a liar. "Why do I not remember this? I always remember what I've done, drunk or not! What the hell happened, Sar?"

"Dev stuck you with something while you were, um, distracted, and it knocked you out. He said you wouldn't remember."

Lash looked at me with flat eyes, but this time it was because he was very, very nervous.

"What else did I say?"

*It's obvious he's afraid to know.* "You said some things, Dev said some things. You fought with him, and stabbed him and bit him. Then you had me on the pool table again."

"Shit, I want to remember that! Was it as good as last time?" He grinned widely.

I gave him a look that said it had not been the same. "Not really, no."

He hugged me. "I didn't hurt you, did I?" he said hesitantly. "Please tell me I didn't hurt you."

"You were rough, and angry," I said honestly. "But when I told you how much I loved you, you calmed down. You were very tender, near the end."

Lash actually blushed. His voice when he spoke was more worried than

222

ever. "What did I say? What did I do! Tell me everything, word for word!"

I looked at him warily, debating what to edit out and what to tell him.

He saw the look in my eyes. "Please tell me I didn't cry," Lash hissed with repugnance. "Anything but that."

"You didn't cry," I said honestly.

"Tell me what I said to you, all of it," Lash said staunchly. "I need to know what I said, especially if I made you any promises."

So I told him all of it, though I minimized what he had said about thinking I had healed and not telling me, because it would only make him feel guilty, and it didn't matter anyway. After, Lash and I lay together unmoving, just holding each other.

"We don't have to talk about it further," I ventured finally. "I—"

"I'd rather not talk about it," Lash said in relief. "Except to tell you that everything I said to you was true, Sar. None of it was a lie."

"I never thought it was," I assured, hugging him close.

"I heard you that day, you know," Lash said, changing the subject. "That day you were talking in the kitchen with Serena. She'd asked you if you were afraid of me, if I'd been bad in bed."

"She said there was no one listening," I said, blushing furiously.

"No, she said she heard no one nearby," Lash corrected, smiling faintly. "I was there, holding completely still, because I wanted to know what you would tell her. I was angry about having to give up being with Cin, and I thought if I told Devlin that you abhorred me, that maybe he would assign a bear to guard you instead. I was sure you were going to say how much I repulsed you, that it had been awful with me, how much you detested what we'd done. But when you told her I was good, I was shocked. I knew it was a lie, and that intrigued me, that you would lie out of kindness for me when you didn't even like me, when there was no one who would even know of the lie except her." Lash gripped my body to his, squeezing me in his arms. "It didn't take me long to start falling for you. And when you came and told me you couldn't bear to let me die, that was it. I was lost."

I kissed him tenderly, and then drew back from him. "When is your birthday?"

"In the summer, in June," Lash said, looking at me in confusion. "Why?"

"I wanted to know if I'd missed it," I said, hugging him. "I'm glad it's coming up soon."

"Does that mean I can't have a present now," he teased, kissing his way down my shoulders.

"No," I responded throatily, reaching for him. "Come here."

* * * *

New Year's Eve was a pleasant affair. We all overindulged, and had a great time in the process at a loud party in the ballroom. Most everyone was there, save Theo and Jenny, of course, and Sundown, who was feeling nauseous and stayed home. But Terian came for a brief while, and T, Rip, Titus, Leri, Serena, the bears and their mates and girlfriends, and even Elle and Danial. It was time for a big celebration, now that Ulysses was finally dead, and Danial was awake, even if he was still not his old self. Devlin had a good time playing both his piano and host, and I enjoyed my first time playing hostess at his side. Lash did security for the party, but he told me ahead of time that he would celebrate with me the next day, if I felt up to it. I assured him that I would. As the New Year began, I gave Devlin a kiss, hugged Venus in my arms, and thought that life was good indeed.

* * * *

The next day, Titus and Devlin gathered with me in the Silver room, and Devlin gave Diana a kiss. Before she stirred, and fully awoke, Titus teleported her and I to Africa, where a waiting Nineva was there to take custody of her.

"What do I tell her?" he said quietly, looking with unease at Titus, who pointedly ignored him, his attention on Diana in his arms.

"Tell her that she had cholera, that she has been sick for a long time," I said, gazing at Diana as she began blinking her eyes. "Tell her that she graduated." I handed him a folder. "Here are the papers to prove it. Tell her that she's a nurse, and arrange for her to get to this Peace Corps camp. They are expecting her."

"Why are you doing this?" Nineva said in a low rumbling tone that was too close to Theo's for my liking. "She's the sister of the man who caused you terrible suffering."

"Because she never wanted any of that," I replied, stepping back from him. "She only wanted to help people. She has a good life in front of her, if she can only forget the past."

"Something happened to Elle, didn't it?" Nineva asked.

I shot him a look, but didn't answer.

"It's in your voice, Sar. Tell me."

"Yes," I said in a brittle tone. "I have to go now. Please see she gets there?"

"You know that Zane may come after her anyway," Nineva said, looking at me out of the corner of his eye as he took her from Titus. "He'll not draw the distinction you did, that she's innocent."

"She has a chance to live, where she wouldn't have before," I said with finality. "This was the life she wanted. That's all I can give her."

Nineva just looked at me sadly. I knew he was going to say something, and I didn't want to hear it, especially if it was about how a woman's duty was to become were if her husband asked her to. And I didn't want to hear about his harem, either. "Thanks for your help. Take care."

"You're welcome," Nineva said, his tone suddenly aloof.

*He's been talking to Theo.* Or maybe he'd seen my ring finger was bare. Either way, it didn't matter. I nodded to him, then Titus and I teleported home.

# Chapter Fourteen

Lash and I were sitting at the kitchen table one Saturday morning in silence, later that same week.

I'd been having dreams of Devon the last few nights, which was causing me to lose sleep. As much as I liked waking up with Lash and Dev, dreams of my lost son kept leading me to the expectation of waking up in my old bed, Theo in my arms, and Devon beside us in his little bed.

*God, what I'd give to wake up just once and see little Devon curled up twitching in his sleep...Leave it, Sar. There's no use remembering what's ashes and dust.* I rubbed my eyes, then felt Lash's hand on my arm.

I looked over at him, my expression haggard. "Do you want to talk about it with me?" he hissed softly. "I see your eyes when you first wake, and I can guess what you've been dreaming these last few nights. I can feel how much you miss what you've lost."

"Not really," I replied tiredly, trying to manage a smile and failing. "It's not that I don't want to share it with you, it's just—"

"I understand," Lash hissed, his tone low and rough. "It was the same for me, when I lost my loved ones. I didn't talk about it for years."

"I'm sorry," I said, putting my hand over his.

"It was a long time ago," Lash said heavily, glancing away from me. "But it still hurts bad, when I remember how much I loved them."

I wanted to know then what had happened to Lash's family, a story he had never told me. But I didn't feel comfortable asking him about it, when I wasn't willing to talk about my own pain. "You're right that I'll feel better, as time goes by," I said hollowly. "I know that on some level. Right now it just feels raw."

"I know you lost your first mate, too, Sar. Your first husband," Lash added quietly.

I nodded, waiting for him to elaborate.

"I want you to know, you aren't going to lose me like you lost him," Lash hissed staunchly, pulling me gently into his arms. "I gave you my word, Sar. I won't ever break it. And even if I began to fail like before, I won't die without a fight like I almost did last time. I'll do whatever I have to, even if it's as horrible as before, so I can stay here with you, and protect you."

"I know you will," I assured, embracing him. "And you aren't going to lose me, either."

"Are you going back to bed, after breakfast? Devlin said you might stay up today."

"Probably not," I answered, yawning. "I want to spend some time with Venus, until her lessons in the afternoon. And I'm caught up on the e-mail work for T, finally."

"Would you want to go out for lunch with me later, then?" Lash offered. "I have a busy morning, but my afternoon in free."

"Sounds good to me," I said, finally locating a smile, and giving it to him. "Say meet back here about noon?"

"That's doable," Lash affirmed, nodding. "Maybe we can catch an early movie, or something."

"Okay," I agreed, nodding. "It's a plan."

Lash gave me a quick kiss, and then he was out the door, putting his dishes in the sink on his way out. I loaded the dishwasher, and went back upstairs. Devlin was sleeping soundly, so I left him there, and went and showered. When I got out, I kissed him awake. He finally opened his golden eyes on the fourth one, lifting his head to kiss me back gently.

"Where are you off to?" he said, looking at my clothes. I was wearing the outfit Lash preferred, the tan leather duster and the dark brown top, with my tight jeans. "Must be somewhere with Lash, with the colors you're wearing."

"I'm spending the morning with Venus, and then going out to lunch with Lash. He mentioned a possible movie afterwards."

I wondered if Devlin would be jealous, but he just gave me a soft look, and a gentle hug.

"Have a good time with him," he said, looking searchingly into my eyes. "I'll see you a little after dusk. I have conference calls for later in the evening, but we can have dinner with V before that."

"I've been meaning to ask," I ventured sexily, leaning in and kissing his throat lightly. "When can we do again what we did that night the three of us went out to celebrate our Oathing? It felt incredible, that time with you in the car."

Devlin groaned, when I bit him lightly, then pushed me back gently. "Stop it, Love," he said lustily, "or you won't be leaving at all." He regarded me thoughtfully for a moment, before he answered. "I'd say we could do it once a month or so," he said finally. "Typically, I'd do it only once with a woman, to complete the turn from human to vampire, the first and last blood I'd give her."

"I thought it might be something like that. You enjoyed it a lot, I noticed."

"Very much," Devlin grinned, his eyes melting hot gold just thinking of it. "Clinically, it's the virus in my blood, wanting to replicate itself. It's like sex, that there is that same orgasmic rush, both when I bite down fully into flesh and taste blood, and when I'm bitten lightly by a human, and feel their teeth get sharper and sharper as they began to bite harder and harder..." Devlin shuddered deliciously, and then stretched languidly. "But with you being resistant, we could do it once a month, if I didn't take much from you at other times, or give you any blood outside of that. But we'd have to be careful, Sar. Truthfully, I'd not have risked it with you, if I had drunk like I usually do from you at all in the last few months."

"Wouldn't it be safe?" I persisted. "I didn't get sharp teeth this time."

"You did, just very briefly," Devlin remarked with an uneasy smile. "I felt them, as you bit me, and it felt so good I had to scream. A few seconds later when you kissed me, they were normal again. But still, it will be at least a month, Love."

"All right," I agreed. "I'll look forward to it."

"As will I," Devlin proclaimed with longing. "Now kiss me, My Love, before you go."

I nodded, and with a last kiss for him, I went to go find Venus. She was playing with Serena in the ballroom. She seemed to love that room best, for some reason. When she saw me coming toward her, she ran to me. "Mommy!" she said in her high yet perfect voice. "Have you come to play with me?"

"Yes," I said, smiling down at her. "What are you playing, V?"

"Vampire Barbie," Serena said, trying hard to keep a straight face. "We're having a Hallows party. I'm sure you're dying to come."

"Will you make me some more doll clothes, Mom?" Venus said charmingly. "I need some more ball gowns."

"Sure," I said, taking her hand, and walking with her back to Serena. "Come with me later to my sewing room, and tell me what colors and material."

"Silver and gold," Venus said, as if that was the only choice there could be.

I couldn't help smiling down at her. She was so much like Devlin, so sure of herself. "Silver and gold it is," I said.

For the next few hours, Serena and I helped Princess Venus hold court at the party she had thrown. She had all of Devlin's arrogance, and she was exacting, as she made her guests toe the line. But I was glad to see she wasn't treating her underling dolls that Serena and I were giving voice to like they were only servants, she was treating them as friends, too. It was a start, anyway. I'd take what I could get.

The morning passed swiftly, and soon it was time for Venus to go to her tutor. Unlike Bill, who'd been human, this was a supernatural tutor, some faerie relative of Leri's. She seemed nice enough, though I'd told Devlin I wanted to see her credentials, at some point, even if they were in some language I couldn't read.

"Have a good rest of the day," I said, giving my little daughter a kiss and hug goodbye. "I'll see you tonight, to have dinner and read you a story."

"I love you, Mom," she said softly, looking at me with her beautiful golden eyes.

"I love you too, V," I said. I watched her go, deciding then and there to try my best to let go of what I'd lost. Thinking of Devon all the time wasn't going to bring him back to me. I had a child right here who needed me, who wouldn't be a child for much longer. *A few years, if I'm lucky.* Cursing Theo wasn't going to make things better with him, or make him be more permissive with Elle spending time with me. Everything was better this way, anyway. He had someone that was his, and only his. He could spend every night with her, in her arms. And Elle and I were finding time to get together now, even if it wasn't as often as I'd have liked.

*If only Danial was as easy to let go.*

I still could not seem to get past the loss of Danial, because the wound from him wasn't just sore, it remained freshly raw, no matter how much time passed. He could not move on from his own loss, and to see him grieving me constantly, day after day, and not be able to ease his pain was agony. He always treated me with respect, but a little more of me died each time I looked into his eyes and saw he no longer loved me, or knew me as anything but "Lady," Devlin's Oathed One. Danial also knew that I was Lash's lover, as did everyone else by now, though we had kept the mating part of the Oath we'd done secret from everyone, as Lash had requested. But just knowing Devlin had a "new" Oathed One was too much for Danial to deal with. Danial hated that I had taken his "Sar's" place so quickly in Devlin's affections. I'd heard him arguing enough nights with Devlin, accusing Devlin of "disgracing Sarelle's memory with your current whore." So I tried to avoid him as much as I could, but I still ran into him sometimes. Happily, this afternoon, I managed to avoid him.

I checked my watch. *I have a half hour to kill.* Too little time to sew, or do really anything. But I could peruse a little poetry. Devlin liked that I'd sometimes quote some to him. Maybe I could find something a little off the beaten path. I wasn't naive enough to think I could find something he didn't know, but maybe something he'd only read once or twice might be possible, especially if it had been written in the last thirty years or so.

I ducked into my "study" as Devlin called it. The purple guest room held some books of Danial's that Theoron had been getting rid of, and books that Devlin had bought me to replace the ones I'd lost when my house burned. Devlin had even talked about knocking down the wall, to connect my sewing room and the study, until I'd told him I'd had enough excitement, at least until late spring.

I paged through one of my newer poetry collections. Here was one: Diane Wakoski, circa 1970. The poem's title was "A Poet Recognizing the Echo of the Voice." I read it for a few lines, then decided it wasn't fitting. It didn't seem to be about love. But I saw the third part, captioned "Beauty" and underneath, a quote by Yeats. I recognized it, as Dev had quoted it to me once, months ago, as he was watching me brush my long hair:

"—only God, my Dear, could love you for yourself alone, and not for your yellow hair."

The poet, Wakoski, had seemed to address that poem in the third part of her poem:

"And if I cut off my long hair,
If I stopped speaking...
If I stopped crying...
And never let them see how accurate my pistol shooting is, who would I be?
We are all the textures we wear.
We frighten men with our steel,
We fascinate them with our silk
We seduce them with our cinnamon—"

*Pies?* I thought, then resumed reading.

"We rule them with our sensuous voices,
We confuse them with our submissions
Is there anywhere a man who will not punish us for our beauty?
He is the one we all search for,
He is the one we all anticipate.
Beauty looks for its match, confuses the issue with a mystery that does not

exist."

I felt with shock that this poem was fitting. Just not for Dev. As if by some design, my eyes fell on the poem below it, titled "When You are Old."

"How many loved your moments of glad grace,
And loved your beauty with love false or true;
But one man loved the pilgrim soul in you,
And loved the sorrows of your changing face."

Then I looked at my watch, and put the book aside. I had to hurry, or I was going to be late meeting Lash. And it was suddenly very important to me not to let him wait for me, as I had so often this week.

I made it to the kitchen at noon, to find Lash waiting for me anyway. He was dressed in his "good" black clothes, and I gave him an appreciative look.

"Are you ready, Sar?"

I nodded.

We went out and got into his truck, and he started the engine. "Where to?" he said, turning to me. "What do you feel like eating?"

"Take me to the restaurant that you took me to, back last spring. We'll get some sushi, to celebrate the New Year."

"You sure?" Lash hissed. "We may run into some of Theoron's people there." I knew what he was saying: that there was a remote possibility of seeing Theo there. And while he might be with Terian or T, he could also be there with Jenny.

"It doesn't matter if he's there. I'm with you, Lash."

"Okay," Lash said with a nod, and he drove us there in silence.

When we arrived, Lash and I got a table, and I excused myself to visit the ladies' room.

"Order for me, please?" I said, as I got up. "I might be a minute or two."

"Are you okay?" Lash said, giving me a sudden worried look. "We could go somewhere else if you want?"

"I'm fine. I want to take my hair down, and fix it a little. It might take a minute, or five."

"Okay," Lash said with a shrug. "I'll be here."

I returned to him ten minutes later. "Everything okay? Did you order?"

"I ordered for us. I also got you some wine. I thought you could use it."

I knew he had just wanted some sake, but I didn't say anything. Besides, I did want some wine.

"Your hair looks nice down," Lash added quickly, giving me a smile.

"I'm glad you like it," I said back, giving him a smile back.

We talked about Venus a little over lunch. I also brought up Serena's infatuation for Nick—and vice versa—that was still going strong. Even after all this time, I hesitated to call it love, at least in front of Lash. I didn't want him telling T, because I didn't know if T loved her or not, and I knew he and Lash still sparred most every other day in the early mornings. "So you've noticed them?" I asked innocently.

Lash nodded.

"Do you know if he likes her the way she likes him?"

Lash shrugged. "Hard to say. Nick's a good guy, but he knows how good-looking he is. He probably enjoys his time with Serena, but that's as far as it goes, even with everything that she did for him. And I know from Titus she did a lot for him, Sar."

I wondered what he meant by that, but let it slide. From Serena's comment to me more than a month previous, Serena had done something for Nick after he'd gotten hurt—a.k.a. skinned—that had cost her the ability to change into a coyote. If her loss was what I imagined, I didn't want to hear Lash describe the process. "That's sad," I said, to close the subject. "She really likes him. I'd hoped they'd end up together."

"She should tell him how she feels, if she loves him," Lash said, his eyes meeting mine meaningfully. "He might be the last to know, if she hides it from him."

Lash was reminding me, as he often did, that he wished I'd told him I loved him when I first felt it, and not waited months. "I'll tell her that," I assured amicably. "Maybe she will."

We finished our meal, and Lash paid the bill. I could tell he was surprised that I didn't offer to pay, but I didn't make an explanation. He'd insist on paying no matter what. Lash might be my mate, but he was still a male chauvinist when it came to some things.

"Want to come for a quick walk with me?" I asked, as we neared his truck. "I still owe you one."

"Sure," Lash agreed. "Let me grab my extra gun from the truck first."

Lash stashed it in his pocket, locked the truck, and we headed out, blinking hard in the bright sunlight. I reached out and took his hand, clasping it in mine, and he gave me a smile. We walked down the street, and over by the bridge near the creek the town was named for. I let go of Lash's hand, and he slipped his arm around me instead, as we looked over the bridge edge, watching the water flowing under it fast. The creek was almost a river today, rushing from the heavy storms earlier in the week. A lot of the snow had melted in the rain, and there was sure to be flooding in the lower ground. *But Hayden's on high ground. We'll be okay.*

I took Lash's hand, and led him down the pathway at the end of the bridge into the nearby park. There was an old teeter-totter near the entrance, and I walked over to it with him. "Sit down."

He gave me a look that said no way.

"Sit down, if you know what's good for you," I said harshly. Lash gave me a funny look, but he sat down, straddling the seat. I sat down facing him. The metal seat was small, and there was just enough room to wedge my hips close to his.

"What are you doing—?" Lash started to ask, and then he stopped as he felt my hands reaching up under his vest and his shirt to run over his chest.

"What's it feel like I'm doing?" I said, and kissed him hard, opening my mouth on his. Lash's arms went around me in an instant, reaching under my buttocks to pull my body hard against his. I felt his penis against the front of my jeans, hardening quickly as I kissed him. I reached down between us and cupped him with my hand through his pants, making him groan into my mouth.

"For me?" I said huskily.

He nodded, then kissed me again. I got up then, moving away from him and earning an incredulous look in the process. I reached into my pocket, and took out a key, showing it to him in explanation.

Lash's eyes had been dark with lust before, but when he saw the key they turned black as pitch. "You weren't at the bathroom."

"No," I purred, licking my lips suggestively. "I got us a room in the hotel down the street."

"Why?" he managed, clearly stunned. "I don't understand."

"Come with me now, my Mate," I said softly, reaching out my hand to him. "I have something to give you that's long overdue."

Lash froze, then quickly got up and took my hand without saying anything and followed after me out of the park and down the street to the hotel lobby in a kind of shock. I led him to the hotel room, and opened the door, locking it behind us. Then I turned to him. "Sit on the bed."

Lash sat down on the edge. I took off our shoes, then faced him, and began to take off my clothes. Lash reached for me, but I pushed him back to the bed gently. "No. Stay there for now."

That same surprise was in his eyes again, only stronger. "Why?"

"Shh," I said, putting my finger to his lips. "Take off your weapons."

He placed his weapons on the end table near the bed, and then was silent, watching me as I finished undressing. When I was naked before him, I pushed him back to the bed, laying my naked body on his clothed one. "You have made love to me many times in the past weeks, and before that, too. But I have never really made love to you. And I want to now, Lash. Just lie there for now, and let me touch you."

Lash nodded, his breathing already fast and excited.

I kissed him tenderly, and slowly began unbuttoning his shirt. I removed it, then did the same with his vest and turtleneck. When he was down to his T-shirt, I helped him take that off over his head. Straddling him, I ran my hands over his upper body, kissing him everywhere on his arms, his chest, and his neck as he groaned, and thrust up with his hips, grinding against me. I kissed him lower, and began to unbutton his jeans. I slid them off, with a little help from him, then his socks. Lastly, I slid off his underwear, and placed that in the pile with the rest of his clothes. I kissed his lower body, running my hands over his legs and thighs.

Lash was impatient now, wouldn't lie still for me. I turned my attention to his engorged member, and took him in my hands. He gasped, and went still.

"That's better," I murmured, then gently licked him, and bit him softly. His hands reached down to caress my face as he jerked beneath my administrations. I slid my mouth over him, sucking him, enticing a sharp cry of arousal from his parted lips. I cupped his testicles in my hand, gently rubbing them.

Lash was moving all over now, surreptitiously trying to get into a position to enter me. I obliged him, taking him into my throat, and stroking him. Lash began panting, and jerking slightly, even as he tried to hold still for me. *He's close to orgasm.*

When he tried to pull me up to straddle him, I pushed him back, taking my mouth off him. "Come for me," I commanded in a sultry voice, my green eyes dark as a forest at midnight.

"No, Sar, I can't do that to you."

I'd expected this. Lash had refused to do this that day in the Everglades, too, his excuse that he didn't want me to have that memory of him. I wasn't sure if it was because of something someone had said to him before in his long life, or just that he personally thought it was too disrespectful to do with me for some reason. I'd relented that day. Today, I was not relenting. "Yes," I said firmly. "I want you to, Lash. It's okay."

"No," he said, trying to draw himself out of my grasp. "I'm not going to use you like that."

"I want to do this for you," I said forcefully. "It's my choice, to do this with you. You are not using me. Now relax, and let me love you."

"You're sure?" Lash said, uneasy. "I don't want you to be hurt by me, or feel like—"

"I know you would never hurt me," I said, and then I swallowed him again, and began to stroke him.

"Ah, Ah!" Lash cried, thrusting and shaking as I moved on him. I could feel how close he was, from what I'd done to him with my hands and kisses. I squeezed his balls in my hand gently, and sucked him harder, tightening my lips around him.

"Ah! Ah, God!" Lash cried as he thrust up into me, almost choking me as he spasmed inside me. I swallowed him down, still moving on him as his body gave up his seed, his muscles contracting and releasing again and again. He collapsed back on the bed with a final groan, panting hard. I slid his still erect penis out of me with a last kiss, and then I began to kiss my way up his body again.

"Fuck me, that was wonderful," Lash moaned. "You felt so warm and wet."

"I wanted you to feel me around you, caressing you," I whispered. "I want you to know you are loved, that you aren't alone anymore."

"Sar," he hissed softly, his dark eyes full of emotion, "I never doubt it, when I'm with you. I feel your love for me, how strong it is. It warms me more than the sun ever could."

I hugged him, and he rolled over on me, sliding himself into me with a grunt of passion. "I love to feel you beneath me, my Mate," he hissed softly, as he moved on me, kissing down my neck. "To feel us joined together."

"We are joined, body and soul," I pledged lovingly, arching my back to push my body closer to his. "I'm yours."

"As I'm yours," Lash hissed tenderly. "Now hush, and let me love you. It's your turn to cry out for me."

"Drink from me, like you did before," I said quickly.

Lash stopped completely, in shock. He looked down at me for a long moment before speaking, his expression serious. "It might hurt, if I do. You've got to have bad memories of the pain you felt when you saved me, Sar. I've hurt you enough, in the time you've known me. I never want to hurt you again."

"You never took very much. Take it, as you love me. Just a little. I want you to."

Lash kissed me, and then his serious expression evaporated, becoming a huge grin of mirth he couldn't contain. "You're so twisted!" he chuckled, his dark eyes shining. "I love it, that you think the way you do."

"No one has ever gotten me the way you have," I said, smiling up at him happily. "I think I care about you most of all for that, that you understand who I am, and like it, and don't think I'm strange, for the way I think and the things I say."

"Oh, I think you're strange," Lash hissed, as he began to move on me. "But it's a good strange, like me. We're the same, Sar. We care about the same things, like the same things. And I like the things you say. I like that you're like me, that you say things out of the blue, and sometimes they are so funny I can't

235

stop laughing. No woman's ever made me laugh before, not like you do."

Lash kissed down my neck, and with gentle pressure, he slid his hooked fangs into me. They were so small they didn't hurt much, and he was very careful, as he always had been before, not to tear my skin. He gently drank from me as he loved me, and I caressed him, loving the feel of him inside me completely.

A minute later, Lash gently withdrew his fangs, pausing his lovemaking. "I love the taste of you, the smell of you, the feel of your body," he hissed, kissing my face, my neck, and my lips in tandem. "I love your strength, and your softness, your passion and your tenderness. I love everything about you, Sarelle McGarran."

Lash paused in speaking, then continued. "I love that you said 'yes,' that you wanted to be my mate, that you saw the man inside me, that you loved me even when everyone told you there was nothing good in me," he hissed, his voice choked with emotion. "I love that you believed in me, Sar. No other woman ever has. You believed in me enough to risk your life for me. I care about you most for that, for believing I could be more than everyone thought I was, including me."

I kissed him deeply in reply and he stroked me gently with his tongue. Lash pulled back, and looked down at me, as he began moving his body rhythmically on mine once more. "Cry out for me, my Mate," he hissed affectionately. "Tell me you love me."

I crested the wave, and Lash felt me begin to come. He thrust into me hard and deliberately, turning my soft moans into loud screams as he deepened my orgasm. And this time, I said to him what I knew he most wanted to hear, what he'd been hoping to hear from a woman for years. "Oh, Tristan!" I screeched in pleasure. "I love you, Tristan! Yes! Yes! Yes!"

Lash faltered when he heard me call him by his real name, and then he was shaking over me as he thrust rapidly into me, sucking my neck gently as he began to jerk, climaxing in my arms. He shouted my name as he came, clutching my body to his so hard he bruised my skin. As our orgasm ebbed, he sank down on me, breathing hard, our skin covered with beads of sweat.

Lash was trembling in my arms. I held him close, stroking his hair, feeling his fangs brushing my neck. *What I'd said to him moved him so much he partly changed to snake.* "Shh, it's okay."

"I...I love you, Sar," he hissed softly, his face buried in my neck, still timorous. "I feel what you feel, all of it. God help me, I love you so much I'm drowning in it. And if I was dying, I'd want to die just like this, here with you."

"Shh," I said tearfully, overcome myself. For a few minutes we didn't speak. Part of that was my shock—that Lash had finally said the words I'd waited for so long.

"I never told a woman that before," he said finally, clearly uneasy. "I feel like I'm lying at your feet helpless, and offering you my underbelly, waiting for you to crush my head with your foot. It was part of the reason I held off for so long, telling you the words, because I knew I was going to feel this afraid."

"I'm not going to hurt you," I said emotionally. "I love you. I'm glad, that you love me, too."

"It's like a fire in my veins, what I feel for you," he murmured. "It's with me all the time, every time I think of you, see you, or smell the scent of you. I always thought Dev was a hopeless romantic, to waste so much time writing poetry, or composing songs. I never understood why he bothered, or what the point was. But I get it now. He was trying to give the feelings form, to share what he felt in a way the person he cared for could understand."

I held him to me, his breathing slowly quieted, and he rested his head on my shoulder. We didn't speak, but it was like the other times we'd spent together like this, where it was okay we weren't talking, because it was enough to just be together, holding each other.

"I was always on the outside looking in," he whispered. "I've never felt like this, that I was part of something."

"You're part of me. I'm only sorry I didn't tell you how much you meant to me months ago, Tristan. That night in the hotel room, when you first changed for me—"

"I saw it, in your eyes," he interrupted. "And no matter what I told you, no matter how much I denied it, I know you saw it in mine. I hadn't had human eyes for so long, Sar, I'd forgotten I needed to hide my emotions, how easy it was to see what I was feeling in my eyes. I didn't mean for you to see what I felt, I didn't want to complicate your life any. I meant what I said later, that you had enough men that loved you."

I remembered what he'd admitted to me and Devlin in Davy's, and knew that was a white lie. He had meant to complicate my life, he'd wanted to get me pregnant, so he could be with me instead of Theo. But I left it alone, because it was past, and it didn't matter. And the absolute truth was I had briefly considered asking him to use protection that day. But when he had told me that he'd not been with anyone but me, I'd decided not to. Because, like him, I really hadn't wanted to use any, either. I'd wanted to feel his skin on mine, in mine. And I deserved my share of the blame for that. "You were the one I wanted to love me," I murmured. "Because the moment I knew you were dying, all I could think of was getting to you, to save you."

"Hold me in your arms," he asked softly. "I want to be in your arms, Sar."

I held him to me, and hugged him, running my fingers through his hair as I kissed him.

"Tell me again you love me," he whispered, clutching me.

"I love you, Tristan," I said tenderly. "I love your fierceness, your wacky sense of humor, your air of danger you always seem to carry around you, your tenderness, your strength and speed. I love your silence, that sometimes it's enough for you to be with me and not talk—that words between us aren't always necessary."

Tristan, my Tristan, looked into my green eyes with his dark ones, and then he kissed me very, very gently. He gave me a soft tender smile, and caressed my cheek with his hand. Then he nestled himself in my arms, and soon after, he drifted into sleep. I held him as he slept, stroking his hair, thinking that maybe we were both a little crazy. But I realized something, too, holding him there in my arms.

I was happy. Not content, not satisfied, not okay. I was happy, groundbreakingly happy, earth-shatteringly happy, as I hadn't been since that long ago spring with Theo, before he'd been taken and everything in my world had changed. And I was holding the reason for that happiness sleeping in my arms.

"This is what I wanted from my life," I said softly, looking down at him. "This is all I ever wanted, just to be this happy, to love someone, and to have someone who loved me, the real me. And you've given that to me, Tristan."

Maybe I hadn't been the best person I could've been. I'd made mistakes, but screw it, so did everyone else. And I was going to let it go, all the things I'd done wrong, because ruminating about it for the rest of my life wasn't going to change anything.

I had Tristan. We had each other. It was enough that he was with me, that I had him here in my arms, and despite all I'd lost, I hadn't lost him.

# About the Author

Tara Fox Hall's writing credits include nonfiction, horror, suspense, action-adventure, erotica, and contemporary and historical paranormal romance. She is the author of the paranormal action-adventure *Lash* series and the vampire romantic suspense *Promise Me* series. Tara divides her free time unequally between writing novels and short stories, chainsawing firewood, caring for stray animals, sewing cat and dog beds for donation to animal shelters, and target practice.

## Other works by the author with Melange Books, LLC

*Return To Me*
*Surrender to Me*
*The Origin of Fear in* Spellbound 2011 Anthology
*Night Music* in Midnight Thirsts II Anthology
*Partners* in Midnight Thirsts II Anthology
*Kink* in Wicked Christmas Wishes Anthology
*The Oath* in Wicked Christmas Wishes Anthology
*Bedtime Shadows Anthology*
*Make Me Behave Anthology*
*Latham's Landing, An Anthology*
*The Oath*
*Her Frozen Heart, in* Frozen Anthology
*Night Music*, a Novella

## The Promise Me Series
*Promise Me, Book 1*
*Broken Promise, Book 2*
*Taken in the Night, Book 3*
*Taken for his Own, Book 4*
*Promise Me Anthology, Book 4.5*
*Immortal Confessions, Book 5*
*Her Secret, Book 6*
*Point of No Return, Book 7*
*Lost Paradise, Book 8*
*Dark Solace, Book 9*
*Eye of the Storm, Book 10*

## Coming Soon
*Sundown-Serena—Promise Me Series, Book 12*
*The Perfect Moment,* in Propose To Me Anthology